M. J. Cumming.
Clair Cottage
11 Smith's Lane.

THE MORNING WILL COME

No race could have suffered more bitterly during the past half century than the Jews, especially those unfortunate enough to have been born in Central Europe. This poignant novel tells the story of Isaac Noller, a Jew born in Poland in 1867, and taken, as a child, to Berlin; of his romance with an English girl, Rose Clavering, and of the different destinies of their five children, one of whom turns Nazi, bringing added tragedy into the lives of his already suffering family. It is a grim story, with moments of bitterness, but the author, writing with unusual sympathy and insight, captures the joys as well as the sorrows of her characters. She gives a human study of family life lived under abnormal and often terrible conditions, showing the ultimate triumph of love and mutual endeavour. This is one of Miss Jacob's most deeply absorbing novels.

NAOMI JACOB *has also written*

POWER
JACOB USSHER
ROCK AND SAND
YOUNG EMMANUEL
THE BELOVED PHYSICIAN
THE MAN WHO FOUND HIMSELF
" SEEN UNKNOWN . . ."
THAT WILD LIE
THE PLOUGH
ROOTS
PROPS
POOR STRAWS
GROPING
THE LOADED STICK
FOUR GENERATIONS
" HONOUR COME BACK——"
THE FOUNDER OF THE HOUSE
BARREN METAL
TIMEPIECE

FADE OUT
THE LENIENT GOD
NO EASY WAY
STRAWS IN AMBER
THIS PORCELAIN CLAY
THEY LEFT THE LAND
SALLY SCARTH
UNDER NEW MANAGEMENT
THE CAP OF YOUTH
LEOPARDS AND SPOTS
PRIVATE GOLLANTZ
WHITE WOOL
HONOUR'S A MISTRESS
A PASSAGE PERILOUS
GOLLANTZ
MARY OF DELIGHT
EVERY OTHER GIFT
THE HEART OF THE HOUSE
A LATE LARK SINGING

One-Act Plays
THE DAWN
MARY OF DELIGHT

Autobiography and Biography
ME: A CHRONICLE ABOUT OTHER PEOPLE
" OUR MARIE " (MARIE LLOYD)
ME AGAIN
MORE ABOUT ME
ME IN WARTIME

ME IN THE MEDITERRANEAN
ME OVER THERE
ME AND MINE
ME LOOKING BACK
ROBERT, NANA—AND ME

General
ME IN THE KITCHEN

THE MORNING WILL COME

By
NAOMI JACOB

THE BOOK CLUB
121 CHARING CROSS ROAD
LONDON, W.C.2

MADE AND PRINTED IN GREAT BRITAIN BY
MORRISON AND GIBB LIMITED, LONDON AND EDINBURGH

ONE

Isaac Noller sat with a light rug over his knees, for in spite of the morning sunshine he felt a chill in the air. His blood was running thin, he remembered. He was no longer the young man who had scorned to wear the woollen scarves which his aunt knitted for him and who boasted that he never felt the cold.

He sipped his sherry thoughtfully, savouring its taste with satisfaction. A good sherry, a drink for people of taste, unlike those terrible cocktails ! They were the ruination of decent palates. The young people of today had no palates, he chuckled.

" No palates," he said softly, " for food, drink or—music." His grand-daughter, Gweneth, had once boasted laughingly to him that the most important thing in her kitchen was a contrivance for opening tins ! Gweneth was a fine girl, handsome—though not as handsome as his lovely daughter, Miriam—and in many ways clever, but he doubted if she would have known how to prepare the delicious roast goose which had been his wife's speciality. Ah, those roast geese, complete with many small " side dishes " all designed to enhance the flavour of the succulent bird. Even Alice, and he loved her dearly, remained ignorant of many things which her grandmother had studied as a matter of course.

" Life moves so quickly, Papa," she said. " I haven't time to do all the things that Grandmama Rose did. It's far easier to buy furniture polish ready made in a tin, to buy jam and marmalade ready made—always provided you buy a good make. I'd never buy cheap jams, and as for marmalade, Max will only eat one kind ! I have a woman in to do the sewing; she does it far better and much quicker than I could. Anyway, she's thankful for the money, poor soul."

" Yes, yes, no doubt you are right, my dear."

" Of course I'm right, Papa. I've no doubt that some ancestress of yours wove her own linen, spun her own thread and even ground corn to flour between two stones ! I've heard my father talk exactly as you do. His mother came from Spain. Where did your family come from, Papa ? "

Where had they come from ? He realized that he had not the faintest idea. Uncle Stanislaus had lived in Berlin, but Isaac Noller did not know if that was his birthplace.

He had been born in Poland, he didn't even know where. Uncle Stanislaus had told him, but he had forgotten. He had forgotten so many things—and remembered so many too. He could recall his mother dimly, as though he saw her like a picture that has faded a little. She was tall, with a rosy face and bright eyes. His father was thin—he himself had always been thin too. . . . Their home was warm and comfortable, but he could not remember that it was luxurious. There was always plenty to eat, and the beds were warm and soft. In winter they slept on the top of the big stove with the heat rising and wrapping you round, making your eyes heavy and inducing you to let yourself drift away to wonderful places. Not real places, but those which belonged to dreams—where white horses pranced, and music was played and people sang and children threw brightly coloured balls into the air and caught them again, laughing, as they did so. His father was a *schneider*, he made clothes for people, and was very proud. He would say, " Today comes one who wishes for a new suit. Why does he come to me, to Ezra bar Noller ? Because he is told that I am the best of all *schneider* ! So," and he would laugh at mama and add, " This is how we shall grow rich, no ? "

She would reply, " Good workmen cannot be hidden. Truth will be known."

He had been very happy, he remembered, although Uncle Stanislaus told him that he had been only six years old. He had been born in 1867. There was laughter in the warm, comfortable house, and dishes which smelt wonderful, and people came and went and drank tea, and only sometimes grew serious. They would crowd round the table, their elbows upon it, their faces near to each other, and talk in low voices. Then it was as if a cloud came down over the house, and mama would look at the group round the table, and make a noise which sounded like " Tch, tch—you will serve no good thing with this talk. People have long ears ! "

Yes, he remembered all that, and other things too. He did not think that his parents were very religious people—though instinctively he knew that they were good people. There was a difference, he sensed even then. They both said their night prayers ; there were certain foods never eaten in the house, but they were not like the family who lived nearby—their name was Zanovitch. They were always saying prayers, but the beggars did not go rapping on the door of their house as they did on the door of the house of Ezra bar Noller. Mama would give them a piece of bread and a bit of fish, and sometimes a few small coins. She spoke to them in what Isaac remembered as a " nice voice ", and when they went away they always said something which made him feel pleasant inside.

" *Shalom*," they would say, and mama would repeat the word

and smile. Uncle Stanislaus came to visit them. He was rich and resplendent, his coat had a fur collar and his linen was very white and crackled when he moved. He had a beard and bright dark eyes; Uncle Stanislaus smelt good, like a beanfield.

The day was a Sabbath, it must have been a special feast day, for everyone was very merry, mama laughed a great deal and papa smiled and sang a very beautiful song. Isaac was allowed to drink a small glass of wine in a tiny glass like mama's thimble.

" Now," said papa, " you are a man among men ! "

There was a noise outside—the recollection almost drove Isaac to the wireless—but he sat still. It was all so long ago, even the sounds were less distinct. It was not the same noise as the one which chilled his blood now; this was the sound of horses' hooves. Men shouting. Someone knocked on the door, papa flung it open, and a voice shouted, " They are here ! Riding down the street. They have killed Marcovitch and his wife. Run, hide ! " Then the door shut and he heard the sound of feet running down the street.

Papa cried, " Stanislaus, take the boy ! Miriam, go with them —make haste ! "

Mama flung her arms round papa's neck, wailing, " I remain— with you. Life is nothing without you. Stanislaus—quick, with the child ! God, they are here ! Ezra—the papers ! Find them, burn them ! "

She embraced Isaac ; he remembered that her tears had been wet on his cheeks. His uncle was shaking, his face not white but grey. Isaac's hand had been seized and together with Uncle Stanislaus he had rushed out of the back door, his small legs moving like over-driven machines, his breath coming so quickly that it almost choked him.

He screamed, " Mama . . . Papa ! " but Uncle Stanislaus had caught him in his arms and held his face against his coat—made of such fine cloth—and had run like a hare. Where—for how long, he did not know. From time to time he saw other people running, heard them cry, " The Cossacks ! They are here ! " or " The Russians are upon us ! "

He did not really remember those words for many years, at the time they were only sounds; later they came drifting back into his mind, when he was older and went to school, when he heard of Russians and even of people called Cossacks. Then he heard his own voice saying them, those words; repeating them like a parrot, in a thin, child's voice, " The Cossacks are here ! " and " The Russians are upon us ! "

The rest of the journey was like a film, those films which he had seen which broke, and in the middle of an exciting scene went blank and after a time continued. There was a train, and Uncle Stanislaus buying food from someone who stood on a station platform. Isaac slept, and waking, cried because he was suddenly frightened for mama and papa.

"I want papa—mama ! Where are they ? " That terrible fear which grips little children and makes them feel lost and abandoned.

" They will join us shortly," Uncle Stanislaus said. " Remember that it is necessary to pack up the home, furniture, books and so forth. You must be patient. Dear little boy, be patient."

He must have slept a great deal, a sleep which was disturbed by dreams of frightened faces, and filled with the dreadful noise of horses' hooves galloping. Sometimes he woke, crying, " Cossacks!" and only when he felt Uncle Stanislaus' firm, kind hand on his arm did he drop back into sleep again.

He was being carried, people were crowding about them, hurrying past, carrying bags and parcels; then a horse and carriage which moved over the smooth surface of streets, and he nestled close to Uncle Stanislaus, asking when papa and mama would come. The answer was always the same, " Dear little boy, be patient—soon, soon they will come."

They stopped and a door was opened to them, a great wave of light rushed out and spread round them, and a woman stood waiting. A tall, thin woman, who cried, " Stanislaus ! What is it ? The little boy——? "

" The son of my brother," Uncle Stanislaus said, then laid his fingers against his lips for a second. He leaned forward and kissed the woman on both cheeks. She continued to stare at him, at Isaac, as if fascinated.

" Dear God ! " she murmured. " Ah, dear God ! "

He was bathed—the first time, it seemed, for many days, with soap which smelt of roses. There had sometimes been a few roses in their garden at home, they smelt so—that was how he recognized the scent. To this day the scent of roses took him back to the small garden, with a railing made of wood, and a little gate which was difficult to unfasten. He was almost asleep when he was put into a bed with a mattress which felt like the softest feathers. The thin woman leaned over him, and said that he must sleep, that angels would stand round his bed and bring him beautiful dreams.

He said, sleepily, " I've not said my night prayers . . ."

" For once God will forgive them. Say them in your heart as you fall asleep."

Days slid past, they became weeks, and then months. Papa and mama did not come, and he grew weary of always receiving the same answer and being told to be patient. Uncle Stanislaus and Aunt Anna were very kind to him; she gave him new clothes, new boots, and made small sweet cakes for him. Each day brought something new, even exciting. The house was warm and comfortable, the furniture seemed to Isaac to be very rich and splendid. There were many large pictures, and the carpets felt like moss under your feet. Uncle Stanislaus went out early in the morning. Isaac thought that he looked very fine, with his clothes made of fine black cloth, and his linen shining and white. His hat was made of silk; it also shone and looked like a stovepipe that has been newly polished. He wore gloves on his hands and held a newspaper under his arm. In the house all day, Aunt Anna and a fat woman called Truda were busy. Polishing, polishing—always polishing. When they had polished everything they went shopping and took Isaac with them. They bought a great many things, and Truda carried the baskets.

They returned home and cooking began. The kitchen was filled with rich scents, and smells which made you feel hungry. Aunt Anna kept glancing at the clock, saying, " I have another hour in which to prepare ! " That was how Isaac began to learn to tell the time. Aunt Anna pointed to the face of the clock with her finger and said, " When the hands reach there—that will be the middle of the day—twelve o'clock. When they reach *there*—it will be one o'clock, and your uncle will return to eat his dinner." He grew to learn too that when the hands reached fifteen minutes to one the excitement in the kitchen grew tremendous. Both Truda and Aunt Anna became hot, their faces shone and they ran about as he had seen hens do in the farmyards when someone came to feed them.

At five minutes to one Aunt Anna always cried, " There ! Now I must run upstairs to put on another dress, to smooth my hair. You also, Truda ! Dear, dear—it grows so late. What will happen if Herr Noller comes and his dinner is not ready ? "

One day Uncle Stanislaus did come to find dinner not ready. True, it was delayed only for a few moments, but Isaac held his breath and wondered what terrible thing might happen—to Aunt Anna, to Truda and even to him.

Aunt Anna said, " Only be patient, my dear, for five minutes, and your dinner will be served. Oh, to think that it should be late ! This is a catastrophe ! "

Uncle Stanislaus only smiled, and said, " Why do you get so excited ? Am I a starving man ? Five minutes ! Poof ! They are nothing ! At sea they have storms, tempests, shipwrecks—shall we bother over five minutes, then ? I shall take a glass of wine—for my health's sake."

When the dinner came it was even better than usual, with good soup and a splendid goose which exuded richness, and later, apple strudel. Uncle Stanislaus laughed and said, " I would wait not five minutes but five years for such food. Anna, you are the best cook in Europe ! "

The months grew into a year, Isaac was growing taller, Uncle Stanislaus talked every day of sending him to school.

Isaac was afraid, and said, his voice shaking, " Not away— for ever ? "

" For ever ! How could Aunt Anna and I do without our dear little boy ? No, for ever—certainly not. Just every morning, every afternoon, and then you return home to eat and sleep."

Isaac thought often of his father and mother, longed to ask questions regarding them, but he was afraid that his uncle and aunt might think that he did not wish to stay with them, that he did not really love them; so it was not until he had been with them for nearly four years, and was ten years old, that he broached the subject.

" My father and mother never came from Poland, did they ? " he said. Aunt Anna made a noise which sounded like " Oi, oi ! " but Uncle Stanislaus cleared his throat gently and began to talk to him. He spoke very softly, holding out his hand and drawing Isaac to him.

" We—your dear aunt and I—never wish you to know bad things or unhappy things. In this house we wish only to have good and happiness. There are people—in the world—who think and do bad things, who make other people unhappy. These people came one day to your father's house—to your mother's house—on him, on her, be peace. Your father, good man, begged me to take you away, to run out of the danger, to save you, to love you like my own son. You were their greatest treasure, and they thought only of you. I don't think you remember that terrible time ? "

Isaac nodded. " Not all," he said, " little bits I remember."

" Ah, I am glad that you remember only a little. Your father, your mother—it is sad, terrible. We shall not see them here, Isaac. But one day, if you are good, you will meet them again; yes, indeed, in a beautiful place where only good people are found, and where love is everywhere. Always pray for your brave father and mother, who thought only of you in the time of great danger."

" Then—they're dead . . . ? "

Uncle Stanislaus said, " They are with God, my little one. That is enough for us. They are safe, happy, watching you."

" Yes," Isaac said, " I see."—But he knew that he didn't " see " at all. " What about the bad people—who came with horses ? "

Aunt Anna, wiping her eyes, cried, " How he remembers ! "

He thought a great deal about this being dead. Once he asked
Aunt Anna why those men with horses had killed his father and
mother. She stared at him, her kind grey eyes wide, and burst out
with a violence which was strange to Isaac, " They killed them
because they were Jews ! They had no other faults ! They were
born Jews—that was all ! "

" Is it wrong to be born a Jew ? "

" These people wish to rule the earth, so they attack Jews because
they have land, cities, and the Jews have no land, no cities of
their own. One day they will have—ah, one day ! Until then
the Jews will suffer—yes, each time some tyrant wishes to show
his power, wish to——"

It was at that moment that Uncle Stanislaus came in and stood
for a moment looking from one to the other, watching Isaac's
small, white face, and his wife's, which was distorted with passion
and streaked with tears.

He said, " *Nu, nu!* Anna, my dear one, calm yourself. It is
of no use to speak to the child of these things. It does no good,
and only hurts you. I do not wish him to grow up with hate
in his heart, for hate is bad, hate limits—love widens and
enriches."

She cried, " Love ! You speak of love in the same moment as
those devils ! "

He went over to her and took her hands in his. " Yes," he said,
" I always want to speak of love. . . . Let me tell you—no, sit
down, you are shaking—the Catholics, yes, their pastor, rabbi, priest,
whatever he is, his name is Muldoon, talks a great deal about love.
In the past love has made lions tame, made wolves gentle, even
made stinging insects harmless. Maybe it is true, maybe it is just
stories; but deep down, there is a great truth in it all. We have
talked so much about ' justice ', and we have not got very far.
Now it will be good to talk about—love, eh ? "

Aunt Anna said, " Stanislaus, what have you to do with a rabbi
of the Catholics ? How do you come to know him ? "

Uncle Stanislaus chuckled—a pleasant, comfortable sound.
Isaac felt that the storm was over, even Aunt Anna seemed to
have forgotten.

" How do I know him ? He has been a missionary in India.
He likes to eat curry, with Bombay duck, fried coconut and many
other things. Myer told him that I had in my warehouse the
best curry powder, Bombay duck, coconut, raisins and so forth
in all Berlin. So Father—that is what they call him, Father—
Muldoon comes to me.

" He is small, stout, and laughs a great deal. He likes good food, and why not ? He likes my oil from Lucca, says, ' Ah, oil to make us a joyful countenance ! ' I replied, ' And, please, what of wine ? ' He laughed; when he laughs he shows all his teeth. ' To make glad the heart of man,' he said, Now he comes often, and we talk of many things."

She said, " Ah, trying to make a convert of you to his church ! "

" Oh, foolish ! " he said. " You're *meshuggah*, his church has plenty without trying to get Stanislaus Noller ! But he told me of these lions—well, we know about the Prophet Daniel—and these other beasts. I tell you he is a good man, and a funny man, always with a joke, a laugh, and smiling." He pulled a wry face. " Different from that Rab who comes to dinner here—Mendal. Oh, his long face makes me unable to digest my good food. *Nu*, we talk no more of these things. I shall take you tonight to the "—he paused and beamed at them both—" opera. Ah, now you feel differently ! Yes, Mozart. *The Marriage of Figaro*. Smile ! This is a great treat. Dear Mozart ! One day, Isaac, I shall tell you of this man —half man, half god. Small, little, laughing, crying, gay and sad. Come tonight, Herr Isaac Noller, to make the acquaintance of my good friend Herr Mozart."

That night was like living in another world. Maybe this was the world to which papa and mama had gone; if so, Isaac envied them and wished that they might have taken him with them. It was so splendid. The beautiful Opera House, the music, the people all listening, all come to hear this friend of Uncle Stanislaus— Herr Mozart. Uncle Stanislaus, magnificent in smooth black cloth, with a wide white shirtfront; Aunt Anna splendid in purple with lace and a necklace; himself wearing his best suit and a white linen tie.

The opera ended, people applauded and shouted, the singers came back and bowed, and with them a thin man dressed in black and white like Uncle Stanislaus. Isaac said, " Ah, is that Herr Mozart, uncle ? "

" My dear little boy, that is the man who has conducted the music. Herr Mozart is dead for many years."

Isaac was growing, not very tall—he would never be that— but his shoulders were wider and his arms began to show bunches of muscle. He did well at school, and when he was fifteen had passed all the required examinations. Uncle Stanislaus and Aunt Anna were pleased with him, and praised his application and industry.

" Soon," Uncle Stanislaus said, " it will be time to make decisions.

We shall have to discuss what you are to do with your life—what work most attracts you. Shall it be a learned profession or a trade ? —you must put on your thinking-cap and decide, my boy."

Aunt Anna said, " Oh, dear, please choose something *clean*, not something which means dirty nails and greasy shirts and trousers, Isaac."

Isaac smiled. He had a particularly pleasant smile, gentle and very kind. " I have decided," he told them; " I decided a long time ago. I want to be a merchant like you, Uncle."

The delight on his uncle's face was evident; he was pleased—more, he was flattered. He had long ago come to regard his business as a slightly humdrum affair. Not that it had ever been so to him, but apparently it was to other people. He was " just a merchant ". He loved his warehouse, loved the scents which filled it, liked the exotic names of spices; but to other people coffee—well, it was just coffee, as pepper was—pepper. Now to discover that his nephew, this clever boy, was drawn to the business gave him the greatest possible satisfaction.

The very ordinary, comfortable room, with its heavy well-polished furniture, and the faint smell of beeswax and turpentine which hung about it, seemed to exude happiness. Stanislaus smiled, Anna smiled and young Isaac looked from one to the other, his lips curved and his eyes bright. So Isaac went into the business of Stanislaus Noller, and was promised that on the day when he celebrated his twenty-first birthday he should be made a partner. The little household continued as it had always done. Wars left them unmoved, except that both Stanislaus and Anna gave generously to the funds for the wounded, mutilated, for the wives and children, for the poor children, orphaned by this dreadful —and to them inexplicable—thing, war.

None of them took any interest in politics. Stanislaus said, " My political convictions are that all men have a right to live in peace; they must not offend each other. I like coffee. Hans round the corner prefers tea. Then leave me my coffee, and give Hans his tea ! I pay my taxes—that is right and just. I use the streets, the postal service, the gaslight—I have a right to pay. These things do not mean that I support this or that political party ! Men must worship as they please—I think that I have chosen right, but so do the Catholics, the Lutherans, the people of the Greek Church, Moslems. Then, for them—it is right to worship in this or that fashion. There is no cause to grow bitter, to fight and contend, even—to kill. How often must God say, ' Tut, tut—why do they make so much fuss and grow so angry ? If I grew really angry I could destroy all people who did not think—*my* way. I

don't grow angry ! I am too wise, too old—before the world
was—I was ! ' ''

He was not very orthodox, Stanislaus Noller; he did not always
go to *shule*, he forgot many small forms and ceremonies; but he
extended that charity—which has come to be called " Christian
charity "—and might just as well have been called Moslem,
Lutheran, Catholic or Jewish charity—to all men with whom he
came in contact.

To Isaac life was one long round of excitement. The warehouse
was the most fascinating place in the world, and he loved to wander
there and speculate as to the places from which goods and merchandise had come. He loved the sharp smell of the peppers,
ginger, cayenne and cinnamon. The softer scents of vanilla,
coriander, cloves and dried figs. Then there was the stimulating
odour of coffee, the milder scent of tea—Indian tea, which was
faintly sharp, the exquisite teas from China which brought with
them not only the smell of the leaf itself but of orange blossoms,
delicate herbs and a fragrance which was sheer delight. Great
boxes of raisins, currants, dates; the cheaper dates in great com-
pressed slabs, the more aristocratic kind in long narrow boxes with
brightly coloured pictures of camels, date palms and Arabs on
their lids. Sugar which was white, which was brown, which was
a kind of dusky white and felt like sand when you allowed it to
run through your fingers, and sugar in lumps, with a hole in the
middle of every piece through which ran a piece of string. Even
that string was exciting ! Where had it come from ? What hands
—white, brown or yellow—had threaded it ? Rice, sago, tapioca;
pickled fruits, savoury pickles—sweet and sour, bitingly hot and
luscious with spices cunningly blended. Fruits in tins and jars,
lychee in their thin brittle shells, or floating in syrup which had
a hint of opalescence; peaches in syrup, in brandy—for the
very rich this luxury; pears, dried apples, apricots; huge tins of
pineapples; and as many fish in tins as there were in the sea—
sardines, herring, tunny, salmon, pilchards, mackerel. The place
was like an endless story of adventure, Isaac thought, dreaming
of the hazardous voyages which had been made to bring this
merchandise to Uncle Stanislaus, and which Uncle Stanislaus
would in his turn sell to the people of Berlin. Perhaps this consignment had come on board a ship which had fought its way
through terrible storms, when the sailors had felt that each minute
might be their last; perhaps the ship with its precious cargo had
lain becalmed, while the captain peered anxiously at the sky for
the faintest promise of a breeze. A captain visiting the warehouse
for supplies to take on board for a coming voyage had told him

that while coffee might smell pleasant to him—" You only smell it now and again "—to the crew who brought back a cargo of coffee the smell grew to be hateful. " Half of them get trouble with their livers before we've got the stuff unloaded." Rice, they told him, was a hateful cargo, dangerous, too, if the ship rolled badly. " I tell you, young man," said Captain Bloch of the *Rhine Maiden*, " if housewives knew where that rice had been, who handled it, they'd wash it a whole lot more than even the cleanest of them do. I could tell you things, my young fellow, that would make your hair stand on end and never lie down again ! "

Isaac didn't care. To him the warehouse remained a place of mystery, of excitement and of romance. The days sped past, and with each week he congratulated himself that he had learned a little more, added some item to his store of knowledge. Uncle Stanislaus beamed at him and told him that he did well, " Because," he insisted, " so long as you love your work it will never weary you, but always hold new interest for you."

TWO

ISAAC thought that Berlin was a beautiful city; the lime trees smelt so sweetly, there were flowers in the parks, new buildings were being erected, the streets were wide and the shops filled with fine things for sale. People looked happy and prosperous. True, sometimes news came which was disturbing—a disaster, a great earthquake, even a volcano erupting; but these things were far away, they didn't touch the Nollers. Once they heard that a king had been killed, killed in the street as he was driving home.

Aunt Anna said angrily, " He was a bad king ! A tyrannical monster ! "

Isaac hazarded that it might not be a bad thing to get rid of such people, but Uncle Stanislaus shook his head.

" No man has the right to take it into his hands to take the life of another—no man."

" He took the life of hundreds—it may be thousands," Aunt Anna objected.

" Because he did wrong, that does not make the work of an assassin right."

" Then if someone—important, powerful—killed me, killed Isaac, you would offer them your hand in friendship, eh ? "

Stanislaus smiled. " I didn't say that. But you cannot change systems by killing a king. The change of a system must come by the will of the people and the wisdom of the people's rulers. It must not come by murders, assassinations, beatings and injustices."

But that Spring Isaac was too happy to think a great deal of rumours and political assassinations. He was happy, he loved his work, he was well paid, although his uncle insisted that he must give a certain sum to his aunt each week to pay for his food, his laundry and the light which he burnt in his bedroom. Isaac did not believe in his heart that he really paid sufficient, but when he mentioned his doubt to Aunt Anna she was indignant and said that they neither kept a boarding-house nor were they usurers.

On this sunny afternoon Isaac had been to call on the managers of two very large, exclusive and elegant restaurants. A new consignment of *pâté* had arrived, and also some particularly excellent and highly expensive caviar. There was, in addition, a special brand of curry powder, which apparently contained all the spices of the Orient, and a new kind of jam—preserve they called it, *Fraise du Bois*. He had tasted some, eaten it with a delicate fresh

cream cheese, and it was delicious. True, they also had admirable
cherry jam sent from Switzerland, but that was no special novelty;
most of the goods from Switzerland were good. The managers
had been polite, interested and eager to buy his goods. He had
taken two very large orders, and walked along swinging his
despatch-case, feeling content and satisfied. His mind was filled
with plans, he wanted Uncle Stanislaus to send him travelling—
to England to buy some of their cheese, their famed Stilton. He
wished to go to Italy, to Spain and lastly to America. There he
felt convinced that he would find new delicacies, new ideas—
America was a young country, full of young people; more, they
were cosmopolitan young people—they would have adopted or
adapted the special foods of many European nations. No, he
longed to go to America! What an adventure! He had heard
of a kind of cake called " waffles " and a particular kind of treacle
which was eaten with them; of sweet corn—it sounded delicious;
of peach-fed hams. He wondered if he could persuade his uncle
to sell hams. He had heard a joke—not that Isaac was very good
at jokes—in which someone had said to an American, " What do
you do with all your fruit ? " The American replied, " We eat
what we can, and we can what we can't." It had taken him quite
a long time to see the point of that joke, but he realized that
America must make a special point of good and efficient " canning ".
He walked on, his head full of plans, ambitions, hopes. He was
walking in the best part of the town, and felt that—without conceit
—he cut as good a figure as any of the people he saw. His clothes
were excellent, his linen white as snow, his boots shone and his
hat was scrupulously brushed. He was not very tall, his figure was
thin but well made, and his expression both intelligent and essentially
kindly.

He pulled out his beautiful gold watch that Uncle and Aunt
Noller had given him for his eighteenth birthday. A splendid
watch which, when you pressed a tiny spring, chimed the hour.
It was delightful, that sweet, small sound. It was nearly five o'clock.
He decided to go into a café and drink coffee, and possibly eat one
of the delicious cakes which abounded in Berlin. He never grew
fat, and so he could risk such small indulgences.

The café appeared to be full, and he stared round him looking
for a seat. At one table there was only one person, a young woman,
quietly dressed, who did not raise her eyes but appeared to concentrate on her cup and two biscuits which lay on her plate. Isaac
went to the table, and bowing respectfully, said, " Please, do you
permit ? It appears that the café is very crowded today."

She raised her face for a moment, nodded, and he saw tha

her eyes were filled with tears. More, he saw that other tears had overflowed and were trickling down her cheeks. She was a very attractive young woman, with large eyes set in an oval face. Her mouth might be tremulous, but it was soft and well shaped, her nose was small and finely cut. She wiped her eyes with the back of her hand—it was obvious that she had forgotten her handkerchief.

Isaac seated himself, and extracted the meticulously folded fine linen white handkerchief from his breast pocket. He spoke very softly.

" Please allow me. Nothing is more tiresome than to find one-self without a handkerchief."

He slid it along under the table, felt her fingers close on it, and then watched her wipe her eyes. Her hands, he saw, were small and exquisite.

She said very softly, " That was kind of you—thank you."

She spoke good German, but he realized that she was not German born.

" If I do not intrude, fräulein, will you not confide in me ? I am very discreet. I shall not presume; only, to speak of troubles sometimes eases them."

He remembered as he spoke that he had experienced no trouble in his life, except the death of his father and mother—and that was so long ago. He had been shielded, protected, loved and cared for all the years he had lived.

She stared at him, then said impulsively, " I wish that I could. You see, I'm so lonely ! "

He nodded. " Now the best thing is to send away that tea and those biscuits. Let us have some hot coffee, really hot, with whipped cream. And cakes—delicious cakes. I am tired, you are lonely. I shall sit and listen with attention; you will no longer be lonely because you have a friend with whom to talk. Yes, please, I insist."

He ordered coffee in big cups with whipped cream floating on the top, cakes which were piled high on the plate and shielded from possible dust by a glass cover. She did not speak, but shot a glance at him from time to time; Isaac thought that she was surprised at her own boldness in accepting his offer, but apparently she did not resent his suggestions.

" There," he said, " drink that while it is hot. And when you are ready, talk to me. Let me tell you first, while you drink your coffee, I am one Isaac Noller. I am a merchant in spices, tea, coffee—oh, so many things with beautiful and exciting names and wonderful scents. One day perhaps you will let me show you the warehouse, and you will be transported to the gorgeous East, to places where splendid flowers grow and where the birds look like jewels flashing through the air." He laughed. " I allow myself to become carried away when I talk of my work. You must forgive me, please."

For the first time he saw her smile, faintly, almost unwillingly, but it was definitely a smile. He saw, too, that she was sipping her coffee and nibbling a cake. He felt satisfied and content. He must not allow her to go for a long time. He wanted to watch her, to hear her voice—discover its various tones and inflections. He longed for her to remain until he had laid the foundation—at least—of a friendship.

She said, " There is nothing to forgive. It is nice to talk—to listen to conversation when people are really alive. Where I live, I think that they are all dead, or nearly so."

Isaac said eagerly, " Please tell me——"

" I must begin at the beginning." Again she smiled, and he thought that this time the smile came more easily and remained a little longer. " My name is Rose Clavering. My father was in the army, and when he retired he married again, and my stepmother —well, she didn't like me very much."

Isaac thought, " This stepmother ! The woman must be a cretin ! How could she prevent herself—not only liking, but *loving* this beautiful girl ! "

" My father had given me a good education. I speak German——"

" And speak it remarkably well," Isaac interposed.

—" French, and of course English. My stepmother said that I ought to earn my own living. My father decided to go to Canada —he is very clever, and is going to grow corn. He is not very young, but he is energetic and likes work. Then there is my step-brother—the son of my stepmother's first husband—Gerald Midgley. He has gone with them.

" I wrote to my old schoolmistress, Fräulein Meister, in Hanover. She found me a situation as companion to Baroness von Mannerheim. She is old, old, old. She lives in the great house where her family have lived for years. . . ."

He nodded. " I know it very well, it is large and gloomy. The curtains at the windows look very heavy."

" Everything is heavy—heavy and dark. The windows, except in my own bedroom, are never opened. The servants are old, they despise me because they know that I earn my living as they do, and yet they must treat me with respect, and I can give them orders. They have to wait on me, and they resent it, because in

reality I am only a paid servant like themselves. I read to the
Baroness, in English, in German and in French. She corrects
my pronunciation of the French language . . ." She laughed, a
low, very attractive sound. " Her own accent is terrible ! I drive
out with her behind two fat horses, an even fatter coachman and
a very thin footman. She does embroidery and knitting and
tatting. Every thread, every piece of wool, gets into a hopeless
tangle. I have to unravel it and hand it back ready for her to
tangle again. I sometimes have to go shopping—to buy fresh
wool and silks. She insists that I get the wrong colours, or that I
pay too much or that I am away too long.

" Sometimes she wishes me to play chess—I play so badly too !
Still, she always wins and that pleases her. She plays halma also,
using long ivory sticks to push the pieces about. I used to like
halma—now I hate it ! There are no cats in the house, no dogs to
be companions ! Oh, I am well fed, my bed is comfortable, my
bedroom spacious; the house is warm—too warm—but it is the
loneliness of it that I cannot bear any longer ! Every afternoon
while the Baroness sleeps I can go out, for three hours if I wish.
But where am I to go ? I have visited all the galleries, the churches,
the museums ! I walk about the streets, looking at shop windows,
even then officers stare—and often do more than stare.

" I asked once if any of the Baroness' friends had companions—
like me. I thought that I might make friends with some of them.
She said that she knew of none and that even if she did she did not
wish me to be rushing about Berlin with strange young women !

" There are dinner parties sometimes, very grand and with a great
many dishes and many different kinds of wine. The guests are all
old—very old; they stare at me as if I had no right to still be young !
I *ought* to be content, very often I am, but there are times when I feel
that I cannot bear the loneliness for another twenty-four hours !
There, Herr Noller, I have talked a great deal and you will think it a
poor return for your kindness to have inflicted boredom upon you."

He said, " First, you have not talked too much; secondly, I have
not been bored; and, thirdly, the loneliness can be over from today,
if you wish."

"How, Herr Noller ? "

" I should like to be your friend. I have an uncle and aunt, the
two kindest people in the world. We haven't an army of servants,
but we have one who is the salt of the earth, and my aunt is a
superb cook——"

Rose Clavering interrupted gently. " I can cook very well, I
learnt at school."

" A bond already between you and my Aunt Anna ! "

" But, Herr Noller," she protested, " you don't know me. I can find out about you, if I wish to; people will tell me about your business and where you live. You know nothing about me—I might be an adventuress for all you can tell ! You're asking me to come to your house to meet your relations ! It's fantastic ! "

He laughed. " But we're fantastic people, we Jews. You don't look like an adventuress—because you aren't one. I don't propose to drag you to visit my dear relations tomorrow afternoon ! What I do humbly suggest is that I shall meet you, wherever you wish, in order that you can return my handkerchief, which I so kindly loaned to you ! Now, where will you meet me, or rather where shall I meet you ? "

Rose looked at him intently. He was a good-looking young man; it was obvious that he was sufficiently well endowed with this world's goods, and he had behaved kindly and in a completely charming way. She had suffered unendurably from intense loneliness, and the thought that she might have found a friend, might later visit his home, was attractive as a warm fire is to someone who has suffered agonies of cold.

" I shall be here," she said, " at this table."

He glanced round the restaurant, with its gilt and red plush, its great glass candelabra and its small orchestra playing on a platform at the farther end. They played sentimental music, waltzes, reveries, arrangements of popular songs and the more simple works of the great musicians. Isaac liked cafés, he liked to watch people, and he enjoyed the little orchestra as a kind of background for his thoughts. He realized that this afternoon he had not consciously heard the music—the wailing violin, the heavier notes of the piano or the deep throbbing of the 'cello. He had not noticed the people who were seated at the other tables, he had forgotten everything and everyone except this girl with the oval face.

He said, " I too shall be here. Now, may I walk home with you ? "

" Part of the way—not right to the house itself. The Baroness might be watching. She would be angry—curious and angry."

" Just as far as you wish, and not a step farther."

That was the first of their meetings, the first of many. Each time Isaac found her more and more entrancing. As their acquaintance ripened she laughed more readily, seemed to forget her loneliness, and to be eager for their next meeting. Isaac forgot that he had wished to travel, to go to India, Ceylon, Africa and most of all to America; he wished to stay in Berlin—within reach of Rose Clavering.

He had never felt strongly attracted to girls, had never passed through a time of mental confusion when life seemed difficult and his emotions overstrong, or his physical side inexplicable and rather dreadful. He had realized that he was no longer a boy, that he had a man's mentality, a man's body and even certain desires which belonged to maturity and were a sign that adolescence was passed. He had looked at pictures and felt a stir in his mind at their beauty; he had even thought of the day when he might stand under the *choopah* at his marriage ceremony, and had speculated as to what the girl who stood with him might be like. He had never experienced sexual intercourse with a woman; the thought of lying in a slightly frowsty bed with a woman who was virtually unknown to him made him shudder. He was fastidious, he was rarely intimate with anyone and made friends slowly. One or two of his friends had lent to him erotic and even pornographic books, hinting that they were of the greatest possible interest.

" And—whew ! " said Marcus Bauer, " they are exciting ! Don't leave them about for your aunt to read—no one knows what might happen ! "

Isaac took the books home and read parts of them. He was not a prig, he was not ignorant of facts, but these books appeared to him to be so limited. They told of only one aspect of love—if indeed it was love of which they spoke ! He wrapped them up carefully and returned them to his friend.

Marcus rolled his eyes. " Never read anything like that before, did you ? "

" No, I don't think that I did."

" It makes you feel—well, you know what I mean, don't you ? It's exciting, it's marvellous to know that one day you or I might have glorious times with lovely women."

Isaac said, " But these books—they're so dull. It's all the same thing over and over again ! And they are so badly written, these books ! "

Marcus grumbled. " How does it matter *how* they are written ! They tell you things ! "

Isaac smiled. " All right, have it your own way. I don't want to learn how to make love from—text-books ! "

" Then how the devil can you learn ? We can't afford to go to swell prostitutes ! "

" Oh, I shall learn—somehow," Isaac said, smiling his pleasant smile which completely prevented Marcus Bauer from regarding him as a prig.

Now, during the days when he realized that he was falling in love with Rose Clavering, he often lay awake thinking of her. Her smooth skin, the slim, narrow wrists and the long, delicate fingers of her hands. He knew that her ankles were fine, her legs straight and well-formed; he delighted in her beauty and her charm, but he never found his mind wandering back to the things which those books of Marcus' might have taught him, or longing to beg for favours from Rose.

" I am nineteen, she is four months younger. . . . If she loves me, even half as well as I love her, then we have the rest of our lives together. In the old days, Uncle Stanislaus always said, ' Dear little boy, be patient,' and so that is what I must be."

He spoke to Uncle Stanislaus of her, told him and Aunt Anna how they had met. His uncle laughed delightedly and said, " Who dares to say that the age of romance is past ! Here is romance at our very door ! "

Aunt Anna listened more gravely, and asked if Rosa belonged to the *goyim*.

" Upon my word, I don't know," Isaac said. " Religion has never entered into our talks. She knows that I am a Jew, for I told her when we first met."

" You have in your mind, in your heart, the hope to marry this young lady ? " Uncle Stanislaus asked.

" Unless I am terribly mistaken—in myself—unless I can marry Rose, I cannot imagine having the wish to marry anyone at all," Isaac told him.

Aunt Anna said tolerantly, " Ah, you are nineteen, my dear boy."

Stanislaus amended, " Remember, Anna, that at nineteen we feel all things very deeply, strongly. Ideas possess us ! *Nu*, may our good boy ask this young lady to come to visit us ? "

Several times Aunt Anna assured Isaac that she was making no special preparations for Rose's visit on the following Sunday. She protested that it was not necessary, begged to be informed why on earth she should weary herself, to say nothing of Truda—who worked so hard—and there again was the expense ! No, there would be a simple meal, and if this young lady expected elaborate dishes, then she must go somewhere else, for they would not be provided at the house of Noller.

Isaac agreed, repeating again and again, " How right you are, Aunt. Please make no preparations. Bread-and-butter, tea or coffee—this is quite sufficient."

" Oh the other hand," his aunt continued to pursue the subject, " I cannot have her return to her Baroness and say that I am not a good *baal*——"

" But all Berlin knows you to be a splendid housewife, Aunt Anna."

" Not the *goyim* ! I cannot have this young lady imagine that you are starved, that Stanislaus Noller cannot afford to keep a good table, or that I am unable to prepare food which is better than most to be found in Berlin. I shall do my poor best. . . ."

On the Sunday Isaac met Rose at a safe distance from the great gloomy house of the Baroness. The day was one of those exquisite days in early spring, when Nature seems to wish to assure the world that although they may have to face sunless days, chill winds and storms of rain, yet the worst is over, and from now spring will—actually—have the upper hand.

Isaac knew that his heart was singing; for the first time Rose was to visit his home, to see where and how he lived, to meet those two people to whom he owed everything—his uncle and aunt.

She came towards him, smiling, her head held high, looking, he thought, not only the essence of smartness but of complete charm. She wore a very plain coat and skirt of dark blue, the coat was short with large puffed sleeves, and the revers were of white cloth. The skirt reached to the ground and was very full. She carried a tightly rolled umbrella, her hat was plain straw with a navy blue ribbon round the crown. Into the opening of her coat she had tucked a bunch of violets.

Isaac said, " How charming you look ! "

She laughed. " Once, when I had no friends, I had no need to buy new clothes, now I have friends I must try to do them credit. I am glad that you like this."

He had almost hoped that she might comment on his own appearance, for he was wearing a new suit, beautifully cut by Meyer Brusch, and a tie which he had been assured was the latest thing from London.

They entered his uncle's house; Isaac had been given a latch-key when he was nineteen. The familiar, faint smell of furniture polish reached them, and Rose exclaimed, " Ah, that lovely smell ! That is how well-kept houses smell in England ! "

Aunt Anna and Uncle Stanislaus came out into the hall to meet them. Both were resplendent; Aunt Anna in stiff brown silk trimmed with brown satin ribbons, the silk so good, as she had explained to Truda, that it " would stand alone ". Her hair was elaborately dressed, and her cap was of ecru lace with twists of pale blue velvet of a deliciously pale and soft shade. Uncle Stanislaus wore a frock coat with rich silk facings, a stiff shirt which creaked a little when he moved, an elaborately tied cravat with a handsome pin in its folds, and across his chest a massive gold watch-chain from which swung a medal bearing a Masonic sign.

They were charming to Rose, and led her into the best sitting-room, a room which Isaac had never cared for. The chairs were stiff, and too tightly stuffed, their legs were too frail; the carpet was a mass of flowers—it seemed that whoever designed it could not restrain their imagination. Roses, lilies, forget-me-nots, poppies, pansies and dog daisies all bloomed there in glorious confusion. The curtains were of heavy, very rich golden velvet, brought by some merchant for Uncle Stanislaus from Genoa. Along one side of the room ran a large china-cabinet, filled with choice Dresden and Meissen china figures. Aunt Anna always stated that these were " without price ". The pictures—and there were many—were in heavy, very bright gilt frames. There was a portrait of Uncle Stanislaus looking completely wooden, and slightly epileptic, and another of Aunt Anna with an expression which boded no good to anyone. The rest were slightly anaemic water-colours of cows returning in the evening, or ewes gathering their lambs together for the night—simple, ingenuous things, highly prized by their owners.

There was also a piano, with two gilt candlesticks, and a front of highly carved fretwork with complicated convolutions, backed by a ruched panel of rich wine-coloured silk.

Rose said, " Forgive me, but what a beautiful room."

Aunt Anna smiled and replied that it was nothing ! No doubt Miss Clavering had seen *really* fine rooms in England.

" Nothing nicer than this, believe me."

They sat down, Stanislaus and Isaac both hitching up their trousers to prevent them bagging at the knees. Aunt Anna asked after the health of Queen Victoria, and being reassured upon this, asked if the Prince and Princess of Wales were in good health also. Aunt Anna expressed her satisfaction that the Prince was fully recovered from his illness.

Isaac said, " Aunt Anna, that was in 1872 ! This is 1886 ! "

She replied with dignity that serious illnesses often " leave their mark ". She wished to know if the Princess was actually as beautiful as she was reputed to be. Rose replied that she had only seen her once, and that her beauty " took away your breath ". Aunt Anna then turned the conversation to the German royal house. The wife of the Crown Prince was reputed to be good but not particularly popular, though devoted to her handsome husband. Did Miss Clavering not think that he might have been cast for the rôle of Lohengrin ? So handsome—but delicate ! Their son, well—he was said to be brilliant, mercurial, impetuous. Yes, handsome, certainly. Devoted, it was said, to his grandmother, Queen Victoria, but detesting his uncle, the Prince of Wales.

" Like most families," she said, " they have their differences, eh ? His arm—ah, it was a pity about his arm."

" Doubly so," her husband said, " for twisted and deformed bodies often indicate twisted and deformed minds, I think."

Then Truda announced that tea was served, and Aunt Anna began to make excuses for the poverty of the preparations which she had been able to make. She had been so busy, she had been making pickles and sauces, she had been " going through the linen cupboards ", for it was abhorrent to her to know that linen was not kept properly, and so Miss Clavering would forgive their modest repast.

Isaac's eyes twinkled when he saw the dining-table, covered with its splendid white damask cloth, the huge table napkins folded into the shape of fans, and the beautiful flowers in the silver epergne which stood in the centre of the table. On the sideboard stood two large dishes, one holding cold fried fish, cooked to that delicate brown of which Aunt Anna was so proud; on the second dish were two cold chickens shimmering with aspic. The table itself carried hot rolls in a folded linen cloth, every kind of cake imaginable, stewed fruit and a silver jug of cream; in glass dishes was a varied selection of his aunt's famous jams and marmalades. He glanced at Rose, and she smiled back at him.

The coffee was hot and fragrant; its delicious fragrance seemed to pervade the whole room, like a benediction. Uncle Stanislaus busied himself with the carving, Aunt Anna served the coffee, Isaac stared at Rose.

The visit was a success. Later, Rose, at Isaac's request, played the piano and charmed them all with her music. Not great music, not the music which sent Stanislaus and Isaac back from the Opera House as if they walked on air, but sweet, melodious tunes that spoke of quiet rooms and dim evenings before the lights were lit. When at last Rose protested that she must go Isaac accompanied her. It was wonderful to feel that she had been to his home, that both his aunt and uncle obviously liked her. She had been so charming to them both, never assertive, and yet never foolishly embarrassed and over-shy. She had praised the fried fish, the hot rolls and the cakes without growing fulsome or nauseating. Now, as they walked home in the twilight, her fingers resting on his arm, Isaac felt curiously and completely at peace. This was the girl he loved, whom he would love for the rest of his life. She was all that he had wished for and dreamed of, and in her his wishes and dreams had become realities. He did not speak, because he was not certain that his voice would prove sufficiently steady; he felt his eyes mist suddenly with tears. This was happiness, this was what men and women sought for all their lives, and which he—Isaac Noller—had found in a Berlin café.

Rose said, " Such kind, dear people. I have enjoyed myself so much. Tomorrow I will send a note to your aunt thanking her for her goodness. People like them—like you—have banished my loneliness ! Berlin seems a different place, because it contains my dear friends the Nollers."

He left her not far from the great gloomy house, watching in the shadow to see the big door open and close again behind her; then he hurried home. He longed to hear what his uncle and aunt would say about Rose Clavering.

They were seated in the parlour. It was obvious that they had been talking earnestly, for as Isaac entered there was a sudden silence.

He asked impulsively, " Tell me—did you like her ? "

Aunt Anna nodded, pontifically. " A very sweet girl. Intelligent also."

Her husband smiled at his nephew. " Indeed, one of the prettiest girls I have seen for a very long time—perhaps since the day when I met your aunt."

" Tch, tch ! I was never a beauty ! "

" An opinion never shared by your husband," he replied gallantly.

Isaac sat down and drew a deep breath. " I am glad that you like her, for she is the woman I love, and I am determined to marry her—if she will have me. She means everything to me. I know that I am young, so is Rose, but youth is a wonderful time, and we ought to spend it together. We ought to gain our experiences together, to learn about life together, to——"

Her voice was sharp. " Would she change her religion ? " Aunt Anna asked.

" I don't know," Isaac said slowly, " that I should be justified in even asking her to do so. If we were blessed with children, I should wish them to be brought up as Jews, but if, when they grew older, they wished to embrace some other religion—that would be something for them to decide."

" You would marry a *goyete*—a woman of another faith ? Where would you be married ? Not in one of her Christian churches surely ? Isaac, think well, seriously. You are a Jew, nothing can alter that; you have your own customs, beliefs, faith. Oil and water will not mix; they never have done, they never will. Isaac, think well, think very long and seriously."

Her thin face was white, her lips, when she ceased speaking, folded tightly. He saw that her hands were clenched, saw, too, that little drops of sweat had gathered on her forehead.

He turned to his uncle. Stanislaus looked grave, thoughtful, but he was composed. He turned to his nephew, smiling.

2

" In many ways your dear aunt is right, my boy. Fundamentally, she is completely right. It is not good to marry someone of another faith. It leads—very often—to discussions, arguments and the like. On the other hand, are we such pious Jews, are we so *froom*, do we observe all the forms and ceremonies which are part and parcel of the Jewish faith ? Yes, the great fasts, the great feasts—you have been *Bar-Mitzvah*, and we made great rejoicings for that event. For the rest ! You assure us that you love this *goyete*——"

" With my whole heart ! "

" I have seen her only once—today—but I feel that she is a good girl, a fine girl. I can tell you, Isaac, that the *shadchan* has spoken to me of good marriages for you—this girl with money, another who will have land, houses when her parents die—oh, there are sufficient girls who would look kindly at Isaac Noller, let me tell you ! If I can find a girl—rich, handsome, clever, with a fine family and a beautiful home, a girl of the Jewish faith,—what will you say ? "

Isaac looked from his aunt's white, tense face to his uncle's anxious one. For a few moments he did not reply, and it seemed that the gilt clock on the marble mantelpiece ticked more loudly, as if it urged him to announce his decision.

" I should say," he said at last, " with all respect to you both, that if I do not marry Rose I shall never marry at all. I want my life to be filled with happiness and usefulness. Without her I cannot visualize it containing either. I love you both very, very dearly; you have been father and mother to me—and what good, kind parents too ! But . . ." again he paused and drew a deep breath, " if you both forbade me to marry Rose—if she will marry me— then I must leave this house and find some work so that I can support her. To do such a dreadful thing would almost break my heart, but then . . ." for the first time since the conversation began he smiled, " my heart is no longer in my own keeping. I have given it to Rose.

" I think that hearts are strange things, you may give your heart away, as I have done, and yet—like a miracle—you find that you have more heart left than you had before. You have more to give away, not in the same manner that I have given mine to Rose, but to give ' love ' to people. I love you both more than I have ever done before, more than I believed possible. Your goodness and kindness are more evident to me, I see you both more clearly, and," again he smiled, " I love everything that I see and know in you both."

Stanislaus cleared his throat, and Aunt Anna wiped her eyes.

Noller said, huskily, " Ah, you are a good boy, a good son to us."

His wife, still dabbing her eyes, nodded. " Indeed, but—this marriage disturbs me. We may not be *froom*, many indeed would

call us *link*, but we live good lives, and we keep the Laws of the Faith
—to the best of our ability. For Isaac to marry a Christian girl—to
me it is terrible. Have we forgotten that the Christian persecuted
our race in the past ? "

Stanislaus glanced at her and said in the half-teasing voice which
Isaac knew so well, " Dear Anna—can you not remember *one*
occasion when perhaps Jews persecuted—*one* Christian at least ? "

" *Ach*, you wish now to give me ancient history, eh ? "

" A piece of history," he said, gently, " which is still remembered,
pondered over—a piece of history—listen, please—which perhaps
made the greatest revolution the world has ever seen. Yes, indeed,
I mean that. Father Muldoon may see it in one light, maybe I see
it in another, but that fact, and fact it is, remains. Please be a little
patient and let me try to tell you what I feel about this proposed
marriage. First, my dear Anna, shall we have some good coffee ? "

She replied with a certain good-tempered asperity, " All coffee
served in my house is—good coffee."

But the coldness had gone from her voice, and as she passed Isaac
on her way to make the coffee she laid her hand on his shoulder
lightly but very kindly.

The two men did not speak when the door closed behind her.
Stanislaus got up and walked over to the piano; he opened it and
began to play. He was not a particularly accomplished musician,
but he played with a fine touch and with great sensitivity. Now he
played the " Entr'acte of Rosamunde ", the lovely, melting music
of Schubert.

The notes which he touched so gently and tenderly filled the room
with melody which seemed to bring a solution to all their difficulties.
It came like soft fingers to smooth away arguments; like cool
hands laid on foreheads which had throbbed and drummed with
the antagonisms of ages. Isaac thought that Schubert spoke to them,
tried to make his meaning so clear that after his music had died
away the room would still be filled with memories of what he had
attempted to say.

" Listen, for I speak very gently," he seemed to say. " There is
one road we all tread—the road of life. Some march bravely, with
their heads up, stepping forward with courage; some falter, hesitate,
stumble, even fall. But there is the road, and it must be taken.
Strong or weak, what does it matter ? Some have weak bodies and
hearts of lions, others may be as giants with hearts which are feeble
and uncertain. Some are black, some yellow, some white, some are
Jews, Christians, Buddhists, Moslems, some have strange religions
which belong to countries of which we have little knowledge. Some
worship the God of the Jews, some the Christ of the Christians, some

their ancestors, some a great prophet. What remains ? This—
there are certain qualities which belong to all men, all people,
qualities which they can cultivate or leave to be overrun by the
weeds of avarice, cruelty and love of power. Essential goodness,
purity of heart, charity to those in want, honesty and truth—these
belong to everyone in the world. Cultivated, those things bring
peace, happiness, laughter and friendship. Neglected, they die,
wither and "—here Isaac thought that he heard Schubert laugh
softly—" only spoil the look of a garden which might have been so
lovely. I think sometimes that I wanted too many flowers in my
garden ! I was always gardening, that was how I came to burn
myself out ! There, I have finished—remember, *good* people are
good people, whether they stand or kneel to pray, whether they say
their prayers in Latin or in Hebrew. Sometimes I think that good
people are good in *spite* of their religion—I must not grow cynical.
Good night—good people. . . ."

The music ceased and Stanislaus rose and came back to Isaac.
He put his hand on the young man's shoulder, and said, " Ah, dear
Schubert, so gentle and so reasonable. He never storms and shouts,
as does that terrible man Wagner ! Sometimes," he spoke very
softly, as if he spoke his thoughts aloud but only for himself to hear,
" I am afraid of this Wagner. I feel that one day his outlook, his
music—music, dear God !—his violence, may be adopted by the
German people as a kind of creed. Tut ! I talk nonsense. Here
comes your good aunt with the coffee."

As they drank their coffee Stanislaus talked to them. Isaac felt
that he, too, must have listened to Schubert speaking, for he followed
the same lines. He spoke of essentials, essential good which
belonged, if they wish, to all men. He insisted that in each religion
there was fundamental truth, but that religions must be lived and
not smothered under forms and ceremonies. Order, respect, beauty
in liturgy, fine churches, temples, synagogues were good, but they
were not—all. He beamed on them both as he ended his homily,
saying, " All religious difficulties have been made by men. God
never propounded them, never invented them. Isaac, be happy,
and then, if you are not good, you will have yourself to blame ! "

THREE

ISAAC asked Rose Clavering to marry him, and she assured him
that she loved him deeply, completely. It was not only, she
impressed upon him, that she wished to get away from the gloomy,
heavily luxurious house of the Baroness. She would live with
him, happily, if they were poor as church mice. Tentatively he
spoke of his religion; she listened gravely, her brows puckered a
little with intense thought.

"I could not change my own religion," she said, "not even
for you, not even when I love you as I do. It would seem to me
to be—to be unworthy. I am not very religious, I think, but in
my heart my faith means something important to me, something
I could not possibly deny. You must keep your faith, Isaac,
attend your services. I will do my best—only you will have to
instruct me—not to make mistakes about cooking, which seems
to be so important. We will never argue about this—we love each
other, that is sufficient."

He held her hand tightly, and murmured something she could
not catch.

"What did you say?" she asked.

He answered, "I said, 'Enough for us . . .' I said it in the
Hebrew words. And if we should be blessed with children, will
you let them be brought up in the Jewish faith?"

She considered for a time, then said, "Yes, why not? Only if,
when they grow older, and if they wish to adopt some other
religion, they must be at liberty to do so—there must be no hard
words, no angry scenes. Will that content you, my dear?"

Content! He had never known such content, such happiness.
His uncle and aunt overwhelmed him with kindnesses. Possibly
Aunt Anna disliked the idea of her nephew marrying a Gentile,
but she liked the idea of him marrying Rose Clavering. Rose had
talked to her of cooking, of a certain recipe which she had for
furniture polish—"it was my grandmother's and she gave it to
me"—which seemed admirable. It was obvious that she liked
good cooking, good furniture, and it appeared that she would
make as good a housewife as Aunt Anna herself—"given time and
if she is spared to learn."

Uncle Stanislaus beamed upon Rose consistently. He realized
that this marriage would probably result in the loss of several
highly orthodox Jewish customers. He shrugged his shoulders,

33

and said, " They will be the losers, for nowhere in Berlin is there
a store to equal mine ! Suppose that my tailor has left his wife,
or she has left him—and small wonder if she has, for his temper is
abominable. I disapprove of partings between husbands and
wives, but," he chuckled, " I approve of his coats and the trousers
he makes for me ! "

They were married, a quiet wedding, for Rose had no relations
to be asked and Noller did not wish to risk his friends' refusals.
It was arranged that the young people were to live with Noller
and his wife; the house was large, they could have their own
rooms, and Aunt Anna would be company for Rose while Isaac
was at the business. The rooms which they were to have for their
own particular use were refurnished, and Noller saw to it that
everything was of the very best. Admirable, well-made furniture,
rich curtains, thick carpets and the latest thing in mattresses—
soft and yet completely hygienic. That was a novelty—the word
" hygienic ". It was applied to everything from beds to bathrooms.

They went to Italy for their honeymoon; life in Berlin had
seemed crowded with romance, but there in Italy it seemed to
overflow. The quiet moonlit evenings, the great stars like lamps
in a sky of velvet; the markets with their new and strange fruits
—fruits of bright colours and unexpected shapes. Every hotel
seemed more interesting than the last, people appeared to smile
more easily with each new day. Rose and Isaac laughed like
children, their eyes grew large as they gazed at the beauties which
Italy had to offer, and they were frankly greedy over the unusual
foods which were offered to them.

Even then Isaac found time to visit merchants, to arrange for
fresh consignments of fine oil, to give orders for the many and
various kinds of *pasta* which he predicted would have a ready
sale in Germany.

" If only," he sighed, " it were possible to transport their
delicious *funghi*, but they would never travel ! "

Rose said, " But surely it must be possible to *dry* them ! One
can dry coco-nut, apples, other fruits. Let us find out if they dry
these strange mushrooms."

They found them—dried *funghi*—and Isaac was convinced for
the tenth time since his marriage that he had found a wife who
was wonderful in every way imaginable. Olives he ordered, and
many kinds of nuts; rice too was good, if slightly smaller than the
varieties he had known. He longed to import silks, the brightly
coloured blankets which they found made from the residue of
the silk which was woven into materials for sale by the yard.
Scarves, pottery, ornaments—all these things made him long to

extend his activities. Rose shook her head. One could have too many " lines "; he was known as a merchant, a member of a fine firm; he must stick to the merchandise by which he was known.

" But agencies ! " she said. " That is different. Have samples, prices, and show them apart from the warehouse. Perhaps take a showroom—only for the trade, not to sell retail. You cannot be bothered with selling one teapot, one plate and so on. Quantity is what you must aim for."

He stroked her hand. " How clever you are, dear wife of mine. How glad I am that you were not born a man. Had you been you would have outstripped me in the business—and what a wife I should have lost ! "

Again and again he threw back his head and laughed, saying, " Oh, what *fun* it all is ! Business has always been interesting, but with you it is a wonderful game. *Fun!* "

Back in Berlin they were just as happy. Rose spent her days learning from Aunt Anna and, very diplomatically, teaching Aunt Anna in return. She taught her to make beefsteak and kidney pie, raised veal pies, steak-and-kidney pudding. When Christmas came round, Rose made Christmas puddings, mince pies and a magnificently rich cake, which she decorated, as Aunt Anna said, " like a professional confectioner ".

Isaac had achieved one of his ambitions, and had imported some of the famous English Stilton cheeses. Rose showed him how they were " treated " in England, how to scoop out a small piece and fill the hole by pouring in good port wine, then closing it again with the tiny plug of cheese.

" I have it on the best authority," said Stanislaus to his customers, " that this is treated in exactly the same way the Stiltons are treated for Her Majesty Queen Victoria and His Royal Highness the Prince of Wales. Eat this and you eat the facsimile of what is eaten at Windsor Castle, Buck-ing-ham Palace, and at the country house of the family called Sand-ring-ham."

Their first child was born in 1887 and was named Max. Isaac regarded his birth as something of a miracle, and the fact that Rose survived it a great and splendid blessing. Aunt Anna might assure him that Rose was young and strong, that she was capable of bearing many children, but Isaac knew differently ! He cared nothing for the fact that women bore children all over the world and emerged from the ordeal safe and well; Rose was different. She was his wife, his beloved, his whole world.

When the child was placed in his arms he felt his eyes fill with tears. This scrap of humanity, so small, so completely helpless, made his heart contract. How did he know what the future would hold in store for this—his son? Vaguely he wondered if to be responsible for bringing a child into the world were not too great a thing for any man to undertake.

Stanislaus smiled and said, " Now you have a son to say *Kadish* for you ! You are as fortunate as I am, for I have had a son for many years, a good son—his name is Isaac."

Isaac smiled a little uncertainly, and said, " Take your grandson, best of fathers."

The Times was filled with great doings. The Crown Prince had been to England to ride in the great procession which marked the long reign of his mother-in-law, Queen Victoria of England. The old Emperor died and the handsome yellow-bearded Prince took his place, only to fall a victim to a hopeless malady. The English Queen sent her own physician; he failed to effect a cure. People shrugged their shoulders—better to have left the case in the hands of German doctors. The young Emperor died, and his son became Emperor. He was young, handsome, training his moustache—which was to become the joy of caricaturists—in a manner that was copied by his officers in the army. He wrote music—people reminded each other that his grandfather, Prince Albert of Saxe-Coburg-Gotha had also composed hymns and dignified if not highly distinguished pieces of music. He quarrelled with his mother; it was whispered that he was definitely unkind to her. He was to dispense in a short time with the services of Prince Bismarck, and the English paper *Punch* to produce a cartoon illustrating the event.

Isaac was not interested in political matters; his home, his wife, his wonderful son and his business kept him fully occupied. Business was flourishing. At home everything ran smoothly, Rose was the soul of discretion. She never resented Anna and Stanislaus keeping feasts, she offered assistance when there were fasts to be observed. Her behaviour at the circumcision of her son had been admirable. She had given him into the care of Aunt Anna—and to whom Aunt Anna handed him she never enquired.

Life went on smoothly, safely, prosperously. Isaac assured himself that he was the luckiest man in the world. His second son was born in 1890, and was named Daniel. Stanislaus had refused to allow the child to be given his name, saying, " Daniel is a good name; maybe it will protect him from the lions, no ? "

" Lions, Uncle ? " Rose said. " Where are these lions ? "

" If I knew," he said, " I should tell you immediately, my dear."

" But you suspect that they exist ? " she asked, smiling.

" But lions have always existed," he told her, " only let us hope that our Daniel can drive them from his path, eh ? "

Two years later Aunt Anna died; she had been ailing for some months, and had consistently made light of her illness. She had sipped hot water, which she hated, instead of her beloved coffee, she had nibbled special biscuits which she assured Rose were completely tasteless. " It is my firm belief," she said, " that they are made of sawdust ! " She had never been a stout woman, but now she looked as if every ounce of flesh had been stripped from her. Stanislaus was distracted; he insisted upon doctors visiting her, the finest doctors and surgeons in Berlin.

Anna Noller smiled indulgently, and said, " If it pleases you, my dear. They know—really—no more than we do. But let them come, since you wish to be extravagant."

They came, they held lengthy consultations, they wrote prescriptions, and Anna listened and said nothing, except to reply directly to their questions. Sometimes she almost laughed in their faces, the elaborate farce which they played amused her. They all pretended, they all tried to reassure her, to reassure her poor gullible Stanislaus.

" Now," he would say, his face beaming with happiness, " with this new treatment we shall soon have you better ! This Professor Gutlich is the finest man, they say, in Europe for this complaint."

" And what is the—complaint ? " she asked.

" The complaint ? Can you ask ? It is a nervous disorder of the stomach. You are highly nervous, and this reacts on the stomach nerves, causing pain and distress."

" And loss of weight ? "

" Assuredly, for you eat so little."

She told Rose when they were alone, for Anna clung to her more and more, " I could laugh, if it were not so tragic for my dear Stanislaus. He is so childlike. They come and smooth their long beards, they pull long faces and frown, they clear their throats, and say, ' Hum-m-er,' and ' Aha ! ' They give me the same medicines with different names—and Stanislaus is happy they have—discovered something new."

At last, with her hand in Rose's, she slipped away, smiling at her husband and whispering that she would be better in the morning. Stanislaus was heartbroken; he appeared to have lost interest in his business, and left more and more responsibility to Isaac, even going to the length of remaining at home to play with the two little boys, whom he loved dearly.

Rose took over the household management, and so far as the

comfort of Stanislaus and Isaac went, nothing changed. Rose had watched and listened to Aunt Anna; she was quick and perceptive and content to shoulder responsibility.

Their third son, named Jacob, was born in 1898. Isaac had longed for a daughter, but Stanislaus was delighted. As for Rose, she said, " Boy or girl, what does it matter ? They bring their love with them."

People were talking about war; Dr. Starr Jameson had organized a raid in South Africa, and the young Emperor had ranged himself—by telegram at least—on the side of the old President, Paul Kruger. The raid had been a disaster, and William of Germany had sent his congratulations to the old Dutchman. People said that Queen Victoria was furious with her grandson. The clouds gathered and war was an accomplished fact. Rose asked Stanislaus if the Emperor would send troops to assist Kruger. He raised his eyebrows and spread his hands as Jews do when disclaiming any precise knowledge. " Who knows ? He is crazy enough to do anything, this young man."

Isaac said, " They say that the army in Germany is the finest in the world." There were times when Isaac felt that the young Emperor was a very dashing figure.

Stanislaus nodded. " It may well be; but remember two things, my boy. Armies have to be paid for—they are costly things— and also that after a time they must justify their existence."

" I think that Germany is proud of her army," Isaac objected.

" I am proud of my business, but I do not wish the warehouse kept locked up, only to show to visitors ! It must—work. It's a bad thing when armies have to work."

The old Queen died in January 1901, and even in Germany it was felt that her death marked the end of a era. It was said that she had exercised great influence over her grandson, William, and that now that influence no longer existed—well, it was regrettable. The Dowager Empress of Germany, who had been Princess Royal of England, died eight months after her mother. She had not, perhaps, been greatly loved, but she had been greatly pitied, and her death seemed to break the last link which bound Germany and England. It was said that the Emperor had referred to his uncle, Edward the Seventh, as " the old peacock ", that once when the imperial nose had bled the Kaiser had exclaimed, " There goes my last drop of English blood ! "

Rose's fourth son was born in 1902, when the streets of Berlin were deep in snow, and people hurried along trying to escape the cutting wind charged with snowflakes. He was called Stanislaus. The old man was showing his age, he seldom left the house, and listened with less and less interest to Isaac's meticulous accounts of all that went on at the warehouse. From time to time Isaac would look up from his notes to find that his uncle's eyes were closed and realize that he was asleep.

He talked very often of Anna. " I never knew what saints were until I looked back on my memories of her. I understand that she was one," he said. At times he even spoke of his dead brother and his wife, staring at Isaac and saying, " Ah, God was good, we two got away, but . . ." he would pause and raise his hand, " but it was by the express wish of your good father and mother that I left them. They were concerned not for my safety, but for yours."

" How blessed you are," he said to Isaac one evening. " A wonderful wife, and four fine sons—Max, Daniel, Jacob and now little Stanislaus. Never has the fact that dear Rose is not of our faith caused the least friction, the smallest embarrassment. That is how religion ought to be, how the differences of race ought to be. My old friend, Father Muldoon—he grows very old, that good man—spoke with me some days ago. We talked of faith: he said, ' Faith is the substance of things hoped for, the evidence of things not seen.' That, Isaac, is very clever. They are words spoken by a saint of the Catholic Church called—Paul. I have read some of his writings; he was a man who could argue closely, who could make fine distinctions. A man with—with a cold brain, a well-balanced mind, this Paul. At one time he was known by the Jewish name of Saul."

Stanislaus Noller died very peacefully, happy to have his family with him, and leaving no enemies. His business was left entirely to Isaac with the expressed wish that at least one of his sons should continue to run it when Isaac retired.

Both Rose and Isaac mourned their uncle deeply and sincerely; he had always shown his love for them, done everything to make their lives happy and secure. Rose urged Isaac to leave nothing undone which might prove to Stanislaus and everyone who knew him the love and respect which they bore him. She took no part in the Jewish ceremonies, and which she would not have understood had she done so; she effaced herself so tactfully during the days of mourning that all feeling of strain which might have existed, the result of the difference in religion, was removed.

Times were prosperous, trade flourished; but there were signs that Germany—at least, Germany as represented by her political leaders and her headstrong young Emperor—was conscious of growing ambitions.

The Emperor's speeches were not calculated to remove this impression. He swaggered, he rattled the sword in its sheath, he invited foreign monarchs and statesmen to attend his elaborate manœuvres, and openly boasted that his was the finest and greatest army in the world. There were incidents recounted when his attitude towards foreign visitors had been openly resented; one statesman said, after an official banquet of great magnificence, when the Kaiser had offered his guests his favourite " pink champagne ", " He is like his champagne, too sweet to be wholesome; on other occasions he is neither sweet nor wholesome."

In 1911, when Max was twenty-four, Isaac opened a branch in London and sent his eldest son over to take charge of it. Max was clever; he was energetic and loved the business as his great-uncle had done, and as his father had never ceased to do.

In 1912 he returned to Berlin to talk to his father concerning his marriage. He was looked upon kindly by the eldest daughter of Julius Berman, a man of considerable wealth, who had met with success in his business in the City. Alice Berman would come to her husband well endowed, she was attractive—Max showed the photograph which he carried in his pocket with every evidence of pride.

Isaac listened and nodded. " Why not? You approve, Rose, my dear ? "

Rose said, " She looks charming. It is easy to see that Max is very much in love. I'm right, Max, tell me ? "

Max, a good-looking young man, blushed and admitted that he found Alice his ideal woman.

" Puff ! " Isaac said. " What rubbish ! I introduced the ideal woman into the family, Max, over twenty years ago ! "

There was one other point. The Bermans were English Jews; more, they wished their daughter to marry an Englishman. Julius Berman insisted that if Max wished to marry Alice he must take out naturalization papers.

" Would you mind doing that ? " his father asked.

Max shook his head. " I don't mind; if I am anything I am a Pole, I suppose. My work is in England, English money supports me, I like the English, and they have been kind and very friendly to me. The English way of life suits me, and with an English wife —well, it might be better in every way."

Isaac said, his voice sharpening suddenly, " How might it be better in every way, eh ? "

Max's eyes met his father's steadily. " I think that you can answer that question, Father, as well as I can."

" Possibly, possibly."

Rose laughed. " How you two croak, like two old men ! "

So Max took out papers for British nationality, and married his Alice. Isaac and Rose went over for the ceremony, taking with them the youngest boy, Stanislaus, and the daughter—the baby of the family, Miriam.

They were both beautiful children, and the little girl was the light of their eyes. They loved all their children, admired them for their intelligence, their active brains, their ability to learn and their good straight limbs and strong bodies; but Miriam remained their abiding joy. She was beautiful and at six years old people turned to watch her in the streets. She and her brother Stanislaus were inseparable, they were seldom apart, and together evolved elaborate games which no one fully understood except themselves.

Stanislaus said, " There's father and mother—there's Max and Daniel, then there's me and you. Pairs, do you see ? That's why Jacob is—odd."

Miriam shook her curls on which her mother spent so much time every day.

" Don't 'ike Jacob!   Don't 'ike."

" Oh, you must like him because he's your brother. You've *got* to. God made him your brother so's you *could* like him," Stanislaus said severely.

Obstinately Miriam repeated, " Don't 'ike Jacob."

" If I did right, I'd tell mother and father—they'd whip you."

" Muzzer an' fadder never v'ip Miriam, never. Miriam is dere plecious lamb."

Stanislaus giggled. " One day you'll see the precious lamb get a good smacking ! "

" T'en I won't be plecious lamb ! I'll be somesing *not* plecious lamb."

In 1913 Daniel decided to go to America. For many years Isaac had bought American goods; he had been right when he decided that the Americans were pastmasters in the art of " canning ". Daniel, a level-headed fellow, old for his twenty-two years, pointed out that his father still had Jacob and Stanislaus to go into the Berlin business, and that he longed to strike out for himself. Isaac had no fear for him. Dan was made of good stuff, he spoke English fluently, there were plenty of Germans in the States, his business acumen was considerable. . . . Isaac gave his consent. Dan sailed for the States, wrote with confidence and hope. He had obtained a good position with a Marcus Henniker in New York. The work was that to which he was accustomed, he was to become a salesman for a time and travel to obtain fresh orders. Henniker was ambitious, and encouraged Daniel to find not only fresh markets but new types of goods.

Daniel announced that he intended to become a citizen of the United States.

It's a new country, a young country, Father. They've got energy, and they " go after " things. America has only room for " go-getters " and she treats them well when they get what they set out to find. This is the country for the fellow who intends to make good! I want to be one of them.

"Already," Isaac said to Rose, "he writes differently. He doesn't waste words. Well, I don't mind having a son who is an American citizen, do you ? "

"As long as it makes him happy, gives him better chances, of course not."

"They say that America is a young man's country," Isaac mused.

Rose asked Jacob if he intended to desert them and go and live in some foreign country. He frowned and said that no matter what his brothers wanted to pretend they were, he was a German, and a German he intended to remain.

"How," he demanded, "can you change a man's nationality by signing a few names on sheets of paper ? I call it unpatriotic to change your nationality. I don't want to be anything but a German, a son of the Fatherland." He made his statement almost defiantly, and Rose watched his pale face flush as he spoke. She understood him the least of all her children. Max was clever but uncomplicated; so was Daniel, though he was more forceful than his elder brother. Daniel " got there " by sheer effort and intense concentration. Max gained his success through sound knowledge backed by a charming personality. Stanislaus and Miriam—to be sure they were still young, but they were light-hearted, their impulses were kindly and friendly, they were clever and inventive. Jacob was—well, different. He was unlike the others in looks, being taller, thinner, and his face was long and narrow. His eyes were deep set and he appeared to care nothing for amusement. Where the others loved music and regarded visits to the opera as the greatest treats that could be bestowed upon them, Jacob scorned what he called trivial music, and only tolerated that of Richard Wagner.

"Your tinkling Mozart, your sentimental Schubert and your pompous Haydn ! People who had very little to say and took a very long time to say it."

He puzzled her, as she knew that he puzzled her husband; neither of them ever admitted it to the other, both felt that to have done so would have implied a certain disloyalty to Jacob. Stanislaus teased him for this serious outlook and what he called " Jacob's pronouncements ". Miriam frankly disliked him. Not, Rose felt, that Jacob was affected by what anyone thought. He was curiously self-contained and self-sufficient. He worked hard at school, his teachers reported that he was brilliantly clever and painstaking. A satisfactory boy so far as his work was concerned, but a boy who puzzled her and made her vaguely unhappy.

With 1914, Isaac knew that his sense of impending trouble became stronger, and when finally war was declared he sat in his armchair, his hands hanging loosely on his knees while tears rolled down his cheeks.

He was forty-seven, he had no fear that he might be called on to fight, and, had he been younger, Isaac Noller was no coward; it was the thought of war, the realization of all that it might mean, of the disasters which might follow in its train. His mind went back to Uncle Stanislaus, with his insistence that love was the greatest factor in the world, that love must be fostered and encouraged, and with love—tolerance, wisdom and understanding.

He visualized Europe, perhaps the whole of the world, bruised and bleeding, young lives lost; hunger, famine perhaps, stalking the earth. Disaster following disaster and, what was most terrible, that spirit of hate and greed, ruthlessness and cruelty running riot.

Stanislaus asked, " Is there to be a war, Father ? What is it for ? I mean, what has the death of the Archduke to do with us, or to do with England ? What is it we want to do to Belgium ?—it's all so muddled ! "

Isaac tried to explain, but always Stanislaus returned to the same question, " Is it right for the Germans to do that, Father ?" or, " Have the English a right to do that ? "

Jacob listened, his eyes cold and angry. " Of course German is right. Are we to abandon everything, then, because this man Grey takes it upon himself to give orders ? Orders to whom ? To the German nation ! Now we shall show this England something. They have swaggered and strutted too long, they have shouted about their Empire on which the sun never sets—let them see how much will be left to them once this war is over ! "

Rose sighed. " Oh, Jacob, if you knew how I hate to hear you talk in that way ! Remember that I was born English, it's still my country."

" Then, as a woman who has married a good German, you

ought to know that his country is yours, and to remember that with pride, Mother. I shall not remind anyone that my mother was born English, believe me."

" And remember, too," Isaac said, " that your brother Max is an English citizen, your brother Daniel an American one."

" I never wish to see either of them again ! "

He flung out, and Miriam stared after him, saying, " I don't like Jacob. He shouts ! Will he go and be a soldier, Mother ? "

Max wrote that he was joining the Army, he was waiting for no commission, he would enlist in the ranks; Dan wrote from America that while there seemed no reason why America should enter the war, if she should in the future, " I'll be there ! "

Stanislaus wished that he were older. " Not," he explained, " that I want to kill people, but—well, it would be exciting."

Jacob lied about his age and was accepted by the German Army.

" I am privileged to join the victorious army of the Father-land," he announced.

In those days the German Army was the victorious army, everything fell before its onslaught; only the Contemptible Little Army—" the lad sent to do a man's job "—stood against it. Retreating, grumbling all the time—" Watcher know abart it ? Wot the 'ell are we b——y well retreatin' for ? We've pasted 'ell outer the b——rs, ain't we ? " Horrible stories filtered through concerning Belgium. Rose listened in horror, her tears falling. Isaac muttered, " A mad world—aye, and a bad world ! War may produce heroes, but it produces blackguards and cut-throats as well, and, I believe, in a greater proportion."

Alice Berman managed to get letters through to them from time to time ; short letters which said practically nothing but that Max was well. Then in 1916 came word that he was wounded, and was in hospital in England. " Safe, thank God," wrote his wife. Jacob sent postcards; he was well, he was doing his duty to the best of his ability. Dan thought that:

After all, maybe America will be there! If America is there, your fine son will be pushing his way forward, shoving the Germans back over the Rhine.

For the first time for many days Isaac smiled. " Dan is an American ! "

The pendulum swung backwards and forwards, rumours were born and died. The Allies were in full fight, the Allies had rallied —but only temporarily. The Kaiser thundered, and announced that Almighty God—with the help of William of Germany—

would show the world the power of the Fatherland. Men had come from all the corners of the earth to defend England and the Empire—Canadians, Australians, New Zealanders, South Africans. Little " nippy " men from India, bearded giants from the same country, black, white, yellow, united in a common cause.

Food was growing short, the Nollers had a sufficiency and might have had more, but both Rose and Isaac insisted upon living sparingly.

Isaac looked old and haggard; true, he might have sold his stock for ten times its value, but he refused. " I might have come out of this war a rich man," he told Rose, " but—Uncle Stanislaus would have been angry ! " He stroked her hand. " He bred a tradition in me."

" I think God did that," Rose told him.

In March 1918 Stanislaus asked, " Don't you think that it looks as if we are winning, Father ? "

Isaac answered, " It looks, indeed, as if the German Army might be victorious, my son."

Rose laughed, and Isaac saw that her eyes—so often in these dreadful years dull and heavy with the tears she had shed—were shining.

" Children, both of you ! " she cried. " Have you never heard that the British lose every battle—except the last ? You will see ! "

Again the pendulum swung, and—when the days were growing dark, and the air cold, when even houses could not be kept warm as they had once been because of the scarcity of coal, the war ended. Max had been discharged from hospital, Jacob would return home to work again with his father, and, with the Americans in Germany, it was possible that they might see Daniel before he sailed again for the States. The Kaiser had gone, had fled to Doorn, to end his life cutting down trees.

Jacob returned; he had broadened and grown, his uniform was shabby and his hands ingrained with dirt, chapped and blistered. He sat with his legs stretched out before him, his thumbs in the top of his army trousers, and boasted.

He said to Stanislaus, " Next time you'll be able to fight ! This isn't the end, it's the beginning ! The Army was never beaten, the Army never can be beaten. Next time—wait, then you will see a victory such as the world has never seen."

Stanislaus said, " It's a pretty good imitation of a defeat, isn't it ? Why not admit it ? There's no disgrace in being defeated in a fair fight."

" I tell you, idiot, that we weren't defeated. We asked—we demanded—an armistice."

" What for, if you weren't beaten ? "

" Dear God, what a fool I have for a brother ! "

Jacob did not seem to like any of them very much—he expected his mother and Truda to wait on him, he argued with his father about business matters, and he tried to bully Stanislaus and Miriam. Then one evening Daniel walked in.

" Say, folks," he shouted, " the big boy's back ! Got leave for three days. Gosh, Stanny, how you've grown; and Miriam—why, you're a beauty ! I'll have to take you back to Noo Yark just to show 'em what a pretty girl can look like. Mum, Pop—how's things ? You're both looking fine. Mum, you're lovelier than ever. And—say—what'cher know, if it's not brother Jacob ! "

Jacob nodded. " How are you, Daniel ? "

" Fine and dandy, fine and dandy."

" Blown out with pride, eh ? "

" Oh, I'd not say blown out; maybe just a bit—puffed up."

" Might I ask why ? "

Dan's brown face hardened. Rose saw the compression of his lips. " If I thought you didn't know, soldier, I might tell you. See, the war's stale, let's leave it. Leave it to politicians who'll argue it out among themselves."

Jacob persisted. " The war may be over—for the time, but it is not finished. Next time the ending will be very different."

Dan yawned openly and rather rudely. " Aw, lay off ! Now, my little Mary Pickford, what about taking a peep in my grip and seeing what your big brother's got for you, eh ? "

He seemed to have plenty of money, his uniform was made of fine material, and his boots were such as the Nollers had not seen since the beginning of the war. He was well fed, his skin was clear, and his brain—as his father found when he came down to the warehouse—very acute.

" Pop, given a bit of time, you'll work this place up all right again. The stuff's just got to come in, you'll sell it. Now, I might as well tell you, I got a girl way back in Noo Yark. She's the daughter of my boss, Marcus Henniker. Now, the old man's all right, and I promise you that Lena's as nice a girl as you'd find in a month of Sundays. Regular girl, Lena's her name—really it's Angelina. A good looker too. Yes, they're a Jewish family. I'd like to have your blessing and mother's, and one day, maybe, we'll be over with a little Lena and a little Dan to show you.

" As soon as it's possible I'll mail you our list and when you begin to get stuff together again mail me yours. Look mighty nice on your letter-paper—Isaac Noller, head office Berlin, other branches London and New York. Eh, Pop ? Looks like times may be a bit rough—for a time—but they'll smooth out, and if I can help to smooth 'em for you—well, it's done ! Money short, Pop ? I can let you have some if it is—the United States pays her boys pretty good. Say, that's a grand country ! A country full of opportunities, just waiting to be taken. Wish you could come over and take a look."

While Dan was at home they scarcely saw Jacob. It was obvious that the brothers disliked each other, and Rose thought that it was scarcely to be wondered at. That was what war did, bred hate and bitterness. She had to admit that Jacob was aggressive, that he was always anxious to begin an argument, and that no amount of good temper on Dan's part could avert them. Alone with his mother and father, Dan was the most sweet-tempered fellow imaginable. He talked of his plans, his hopes, the girl he was going to marry, with a kindly, half-humorous expression. He had been in tight places, he told them, admitted that the Germans had fought well. " Only towards the end the poor devils lost heart. Food wasn't sufficient, they were stuffed with lies, bullied and blackguarded. I wonder how many German officers were shot—and by their own fellows ! But they were beaten to it, and it's just plumb silly to pretend anything else."

" Maybe you ought to have marched right into Berlin," Isaac said.

" Pop, you're wrong ! That would have meant more fellows being killed, and nothing is worth, really worth, losing another life for. I just forget who said that no war was a just war, and no peace was a bad peace. It's right too," He grinned suddenly. " Always, of course, provided that the best side—the chaps who make the peace—have won ! "

FOUR

Max Noller knew that he liked England. For that matter Max generally liked the places where he found himself, because really people meant more to him than places, and he was a friendly and gregarious young man. He had liked Berlin, but he liked London better; in Berlin everyone and everything appeared to be subservient to the Army. Officers shouldered their way along the pavements, pushing mere civilians into the gutter—if it pleased them—amusing themselves by pinching the buttocks of pretty girls as they passed and roaring with laughter if the girls showed either alarm or indignation.

He sensed that the Germans did not, as a nation, like Jews. True, they were willing to trade with them, even willing to borrow money from them, but—although the Nollers were tradesmen and so not admitted into high society—Jews were not " accepted ". He had heard that the King of England—the uncle of the Kaiser, who now had abdicated after making a general mess of everything—liked Jews, actually encouraged them to his court, went racing with them.

He had once asked his mother why the King of England liked Jews.

She smiled. " I suppose because he finds them likeable people, dear."

Max had always felt that he would like to have seen Edward VII, but he died before Max got to England.

Isaac's small warehouse in London was in Finsbury; it was in charge of an old man called Levitoff, whom the clerks and packers called " Leave-it-off ", to his great annoyance. He ran the place sufficiently well, but he was growing old and wished to retire. He had saved sufficient money to live on, his tastes were simple and he told Max that he was tired.

"I have grown sick of the smell of spices, of coffee, of pepper ! I have a small house, I want to grow roses—I shall forget other smells in their scent."

So Levitoff retired, and was duly presented with a marble clock, on which was a silver plate bearing an inscription. Isaac had sent a handsome contribution from Berlin.

Max wished him *Mazeltov* and he offered Max the same wish, then he departed and Max was left in sole charge. He liked it, he enjoyed responsibility, acting on his own initiative. He set the place in order as he wished it. Everything must be meticulous, scrupulously kept and spotlessly clean.

" Stock," said young Max, with the air of a Solomon, " well kept is half sold already."

He spoke English fluently, as did all Rose Noller's children, though with a slight accent, which was absent in the speech of his young brother Stanislaus and his sister Miriam. He was a pleasant-looking young man, with very bright eyes and an unusually high colour for a Jew. He looked, as indeed he was, exquisitely clean and immaculately turned out. Not that Max was ever over-dressed, but he disliked looking untidy, and hated to feel that at any moment of the day he could not meet a customer without having to rush away to wash his hands or to brush his hair.

The London branch of Noller and Sons did well, and under Max's direction the sales increased considerably. He had both energy and courage. He went down to the East End, to Commercial Road and Pennyfields Street to search for new Chinese " lines ". He went down to Shadwell to the shops where Russian food was sold, and made investigations there; he was not content with visiting only Soho, but he went to Saffron Hill to look for new Italian goods. He employed a traveller, Mark Mallett, to introduce his novelties to the big stores.

Isaac in Berlin rubbed his hands and said, " Max is a smart fellow ! " Max rubbed his hands in London and felt exactly the same. He had the Jewish characteristic of being able to assess his own worth correctly, and without conceit, but with conviction.

He lived in exceedingly comfortable rooms in Gower Street, for he always contended that " any fool can be uncomfortable ", and met Alice Berman at a dance given by her father to celebrate her twenty-first birthday. Max had met Berman in business several times, for Isaac had already opened his agency for Italian goods—lace, pottery, scarves and the like—and Max had set aside part of the warehouse for their display. Berman dealt, with enormous success, in " fancy goods ". Max, who had been through his salerooms, stigmatized most of the things as " rubbish ", and hinted that he could supply better.

Berman came down to Finsbury to investigate. He was a very tall, stout man who always wore a frock coat with silk lapels, and imagined that he bore a striking resemblance to the late King Edward. He brought with him a very small man, dressed exceedingly shabbily, as his clerk.

It was said that Julius Berman always took this man, Elias Solomon, with him, and insisted upon his dressing as shabbily as possible to mark and call attention to the extreme elegance of his employer.

" You think that this Italian stuff would sell in England ? " Berman asked.

" I think that stuff which is good, novel and the right price will sell anywhere—properly handled and presented," Max replied.

" So ! Have you had great success with it in England ? "

" I have been busy, sir, reorganizing the other side of the business; I wished to concentrate upon that. Now, having done that, I can turn my attention to the Italian goods."

" Ah ! " Berman was in the habit of prefacing his remarks with long-drawn-out exclamations. " I can, provided that the prices are right, give you sufficient orders to keep you busy. My business is the largest of its kind in London, in England—possibly in the world. Now, let us talk *tachlis*; as they say in England, ' cut the cackle and come to the horses '." He laughed, a deep, rich laugh. " You, the agent—I, the exclusive customer."

Max considered, then shook his head. " That would be very difficult, sir. I will give you the exclusive buying rights of certain lines; but it is obviously impossible to make sweeping promises concerning these things. For example, there might be new lines —lines of which I have at present no knowledge—silks by the metre, not in scarves, other things—fine glass from Venice, fine pottery, not this attractive peasant stuff. How can I promise you exclusive buying rights ? "

The great man nodded, looking like some immense idol in his heavy dignity. " Aha ! You have ideas, young man, I see this. Let us make a bargain; you will give me the buying rights of such lines as you have to show me now, eh ? That is, the lines which appeal to me. New lines—these ideas you have—must be shown to me first, when they arrive, eh ? If I take them, well and good; if not, you are at liberty to sell to other merchants. How does this satisfy you ? "

Max hesitated. Berman was rich, famous and powerful. He had plenty of capital, he could afford to " back his fancy ". He thought hard, took out his silver pencil and made a couple of notes—which meant nothing at all and were merely to gain time —before he spoke.

" Naturally I must submit this to my father, sir. He is the head of the firm. If he agrees, then I must make one stipulation, that when I advise you of the arrival of new lines, you or some accredited representative of yours must come to inspect them within forty-eight hours. Otherwise—I am at liberty to sell where I wish."

Berman considered, nodded and produced his cigar-case. " So ! May I offer you a cigar ? They are imported specially for me. You don't mind smoking in your place ? "

Max smiled, a particularly pleasant smile. " In this room, no— but in my warehouse I never allow it. My stock is too—delicate, too easily affected by strong scents, smoke and the like. Allow me to give you a light. I shall write to my father this evening. I hope that we may be able to do a great deal of profitable business together, sir."

In his private office Max offered old brandy, and served it in exquisite glasses. Berman twisted the stem of the big glass in his fingers and asked where they came from.

" These are from Murano, sir. I hope one day to import glasses of this quality and even finer. You know Venice ? "

" No, do you ? " The question came very swiftly.

Max smiled inwardly, the old fellow was afraid that he was " showing off ".

" To visit Venice is another of my hopes, sir."

Three days later he received an invitation to attend a dance given by Berman in honour of his daughter's twenty-first birth-day. Max smiled. He dressed with more than usual care, confident that his appearance was as impeccably correct as any young man's could be. He paid good prices for his clothes and insisted that they must fit perfectly.

Berman's house was large and luxurious, over-furnished and over-decorated. Max thought that one day when he had a home it would be very different from this. He preferred the rather heavy plainness of his father's house in Berlin, or the air of comfortable austerity coupled with good taste which characterized his own rooms.

Alice Berman was charming to him, she was an exceedingly attractive girl, incredibly smart, with that type of smartness which is the outcome of money spent lavishly with the best dressmakers. He danced with her several times, and asked her during their last dance if she would make one of a theatre party which he planned to give. He suggested *Milestones* at the Royalty, where Denis Eadie was making such a hit and where Haidee Wright was charming the whole town.

" It sounds delightful, Mr. Noller. I will ask mama if she will allow me to come."

He bowed. " I will—if I may—write and suggest a date."

" That will be charming."

The more Max saw of Alice Berman, the better he liked her, the more certain he felt that she would make an ideal wife for him.

He had no intention of standing still, he was going to climb the ladder of success and get as near as possible to the top. The theatre party had been a great success and Haidee Wright's line stuck in Max's head: " You've the one thing in the world worth living for—youth."

Youth, he was young, Alice was young, why waste their youth waiting ? He called on Julius Berman. Berman was cordial, he had made enquiries about young Noller and what he had heard satisfied him. On one point he was adamant—Max was a German, he wanted no Germans in his family; what was more, he refused to have them !

" I doubt if I am a German, sir, except, as it were, legally. My father was born a Pole, my mother an Englishwoman."

" Aha ! So much the better. Change your nationality, and I give you my permission to—er—talk to Alice. She's a lovely girl——"

Max interpolated warmly, " She is indeed."

" Mind, she's been used to the best and only the best."

" That I appreciate. I shall go to Berlin and speak to my father."

Isaac gave his permission, and Max became betrothed to Alice Berman. The wedding was lavish in the extreme; Bermans appeared to come from all parts of the British Isles. Max was represented only by his father, mother and young brother and sister. His brother Jacob had refused to come on the grounds that he disapproved of Max changing his nationality.

Max laughed and said, " He disapproves ! That's amusing. Anyway, I'm not more German than I am British, less so now that I am—legally at least—British. Jacob's a self-opinionated young idiot."

Berman was generous, and Max and his wife were installed in a house in Kensington. A house which was a little too large for them, but old Berman winked and hinted that there was plenty of time to fill all the rooms. Max and Alice agreed about furniture —they had not the same taste as Julius Berman and his handsome, stout wife. Their house was furnished carefully, with Sheraton, delicate pieces of Chippendale, and some Hepplewhite which Max had found. In the dining-room, the elegant sideboard with its little brass rail and fine handles stood bare of silver.

Berman grumbled, " No silver set out ! You've got plenty of silver, and most of it is very good. That empty sideboard looks— well, poverty-stricken to me ! Look at ours at home—takes Sulick a whole day to clean it. Everyone remarks about it."

He pulled down the corners of his mouth at their taste in

pictures, his own house was filled with immense stretches of canvas in wide gilt frames, pictures which he had bought at the Royal Academy, and for which he had paid fabulous prices. Max's etchings, fine water-colours and restrained engravings meant nothing to him.

" Why not have had at least one good picture in each room ? " he expostulated. " They give an air to the place. These insigni-ficant-looking things, wishy-washy water-colours, don't *look* anything. I'd not give you a tenner for the lot."

" One day, sir," Max assured him, " I shall be offered a good deal more than that for one ! "

" Ah, there are always fools in the world, I don't doubt. Well, if this is what you and Alice like—have it your own way."

Max was never passionately in love with Alice; he loved her in a temperate fashion—as he believed she loved him. He admired her wholeheartedly, and there was no doubt that she knew all that there was to know about running a house. She knew how to manage her servants, and with a cook, a housemaid and parlour-maid the house in Kensington was kept immaculate. She liked to entertain, and was an admirable hostess. She was extravagant over her clothes, but she had her own income and not only did she like to wear the latest fashions, but she knew that Max liked to see her well dressed.

He was kind, affectionate and hard-working—more, he bid fair to be highly successful. He liked enjoyment, was always pleased to take her to a theatre or even to a music-hall. His temper was good and sunny, and Alice Noller counted herself a particularly happy woman.

It was a surprise to her when the war broke out, and Max became restless and obviously unhappy. She watched him, noticed the almost feverish way in which he read the papers, and noted too the effect which their contents had on him. Finally, less than a week after war had been declared, he announced his intention of joining the Army.

" Oh, Max, must you ? "

He nodded, his pleasant face set into grim lines. " I think so. I'd hate to be ' fetched '."

Alice laughed. " That won't come for a long time; you have a business, you're comparatively newly married—there's plenty of time. You can begin to see about getting a commission, perhaps."

" I shall go in the ranks," and she saw the obstinate set of his chin.

" Max ! In the ranks ! It will be dreadful ! "

" Most of it will be that."

" The business . . . ? "

" There won't be a great deal doing in expensive luxury goods, or in imports from Italy if I know anything. I can dig out old Levitoff and he can run it with young Simons. They won't take Simons, he's got a game leg. They'll manage."

She showed her irritation—to have a husband who could escort her to smart restaurants, wearing a smart uniform, was one thing, to have a husband who wore one of those dreadful uniforms allocated to the " Tommies " was quite another.

" You take it all very lightly ! " she said.

Max stared at her. " Do I ? Do you really think that ? "

" You seem to do so ! "

" Ah, that's a different thing, believe me."

Berman applauded Max's wish to join the Army, but considered that to join in the ranks was " overdone patriotism ", and assured him that he'd not like the war or the life.

" I'm not altogether expecting to," Max said.

He joined a foot regiment, returned home wearing boots which Alice felt spelt disaster to her polished floors and a tunic which neither " fitted nor touched ". His hands looked roughened and rather dirty, and there was a faint tang which hung about his uniform, a mixture of inferior cloth, sweat and the odour of cooking. Max explained that the last was due to the steamy cookhouses.

" It's very unpleasant——"

" So is most of what emerges from the cookhouses," he said, and grinned.

It was a blow to Alice to realize that he could not escort her to smart restaurants, could not dance with her because such places were barred to " the ranks ". Once or twice she persuaded him to change into civilian clothes and take her out; he protested that he would get into trouble if he were caught, but allowed her to overrule him. She told him how delightful it was to see him looking civilized again, and he said, " That's one of the reasons we've got to fight. To make tails and white ties safe for democracy."

The night before he left to rejoin his regiment and sail for Flanders she watched him during dinner, realized what an effort he was making to be gay and self-confident, and felt a sudden rush of deep affection for him. Her eyes filled with tears, and she longed to rush to where he sat and put her arms round him. Already she had read casualty lists, seen the names of one or two men she had known, and for the first time she realized that one day, in the not-too-far-distant future, she might see the name of Max Noller among those " killed and missing ". Their eye met and he saw that hers were suffused with tears. He sent a smile flashing towards her, a smile which was charged with gaiety and affection.

He raised his glass, saying, " Bless you, it's going to be all right."

That night, when they went to their bedroom, with its twin beds of which old Berman disapproved so strongly, she said to Max, " Come and put your arms round me—dear Max."

He held her closely, his mind rushing ahead to what lay before him. He did not mind the discomfort, he was not unduly afraid of the danger, but he feared—in the depths of his soul—to come back maimed, or even worse, blind. The months ahead —who knew?—already stories had filtered through of barbed wire, bombs and hand grenades, and whispers concerning gas. He held Alice close; she sensed his apprehension and found herself whispering comfortable words to him, soothing him and trying to reassure him. That night Max and his wife were closer than they had been since their marriage, and when she woke she found him still beside her, sleeping soundly, his face calm and undisturbed.

He sailed, and letters and field postcards began to come through to her. His letters always contained some instructions regarding the business, but in addition he contrived to write of humorous incidents, and the letters were always cheerful. She had begun to believe that this state of things would continue for the duration when word came that Max was seriously wounded. For a month he remained in a base hospital in France, then he was sent home to England. He wrote to Alice saying that he had asked to be sent to a hospital in or near London, but that he fully expected to be sent to Newcastle or Glasgow. He added that " this is apparently the way they work things ! "

He was sent to a hospital near Chelmsford, and Alice closed the house in Kensington and went down to be near him. The first time she visited him in hospital she was conscious of a fear which almost overmastered her. She pictured him maimed, disfigured and looking completely unlike the man she had married. She found him looking incredibly thin, with great hollows in his cheeks and his eyes sunken deep in his head. His forehead seemed to be higher, as if the hair had receded, and the hands which he held out to her in greeting were white—like plants, she thought, that had been grown in the dark. She stooped to kiss him, murmuring that it was wonderful to have him back again.

" Yes, and all in one piece," he assured her. " The only trouble is that Jerry was so generous that one piece of shrapnel wasn't sufficient, he had to give me a whole packet of them ! "

" Poor Max, has it been very awful, darling ? "

" No, only like having a perpetual stomach-ache ! "

He enjoyed her visits, she took tremendous pains always to look her best, and Max liked to listen to the comments of the other men in the ward when she left. She always smiled at them as she passed, and gradually came to stop and speak to them, to bring them sweets and papers, even cigarettes.

The Cockney in the next bed to Max said, " Tell yer what, china, thet bit o' trouble an' strife o' yours is a bit of orlrite, strike me pink if she ain't ! " ; while the man in the West Yorks on the other side gave it as his opinion, " Clear what made yer dodge the b—— Jerries, lad. Got summat ter cum home fur Yon's a gradely lass, is yon."

A gaunt Scotsman, able to creep about the ward, trying to get used to being a leg short, and managing to propel himself along on crutches, said, " Ay, you're the lucky lad, Noller. Ye ken w'a' Burns said, d'ye no' ? ' Gi'e me the gurl wha has acres o' chairms . . . .' " he chuckled. He went on, " ' An' gie me the gurl wi' the weel-stockit farms ! ' Bi the luke o' things, ye've din well fer yersel, Maxie lad, eh ? "

Max grinned. " Not so badly, but I work too, you know, Sandy."

" Nae doot, nae doot, but the extra bit siller disna' come amiss, my laddie."

At last he was sent to a convalescent home, which he hated ; he missed the friends he had made—Bert, Ike, William and Sandy. It was like being moved from a preparatory school to a public school where he knew no one. Then weeks of boredom, and as his strength grew so did his impatience to be back at work. He gathered that while the business had not coined money, yet under old Levitoff it had paid its way. Max knew that his stocks had been ample, and congratulated himself. The Italian trade was at an end for the time being, but that could be revived he had no doubt.

After Flanders, the hospital and the convalescent home, the house in Kensington seemed almost unbelievably luxurious. To have his own bathroom instead of using a communal one, to sit down at a table laid with damask and silver, to see flowers in the rooms and to feel linen sheets again against his skin, seemed things to which he would never be able to accustom himself. The nurses had looked trim and attractive ; but it was a joy to see Alice, well dressed, faintly smelling of " Hubigant " and with carefully manicured nails.

He said to her, " Colour's what you miss, I think. In Flanders everything was mud-coloured, the men's faces as well; in the hospital there was a deadly sameness, even the red blankets seemed to lose their colour and became meaningless. The convalescent place was the same—though you could get out and see the green trees and the grass. Here it's the colour that is such a joy—your clothes, flowers, even the food we eat seems to have colour to it."

She said, " I always feel that colour in food is important."

Max stared at her and relapsed into silence.

When the Armistice was declared he drove out to see the crowds, drove to Buckingham Palace and felt a thrill when he heard the crowd yelling for the King. This was his country, and he was thankful—yes, thankful—that he had been able to fight for her. A small matter, and he'd been lucky; but, as the Yorkshire man used to say in hospital, " Ay, lad, theer's nowt like showing willing." Well, he—Max Noller—had " shown willing " and he was glad and proud that he'd been able to do so.

He left his car and walked slowly towards the Palace, staring up in common with the rest of the crowd at the balcony. They were yelling for the King, and presently he came with the Queen at his side. Max compared him with the swashbuckling figure with the upturned moustache and the magnificent uniforms. This man, with his wife, stood for all the men and their wives in the British Isles. A man with a short clipped beard and his hair parted in what was called a " militiaman's quiff ".

Someone said, " Yus, an' blimey, 'e went through the perishin' 'oop when that 'orse fell on 'im ! Might 'a put paid ter 'is bill thet night."

Max heard a woman say, " I've been told that she won't have any waste. Nothing but the simplest meals all through the war. I heard as they often have baked rice pudding ! May be off of gold plates, but it's rice pudding just the same ! Bless 'em both."

Then a slim young man came out on the balcony and stood smiling. Someone shouted, " Betcher glad ter be back, chum ! " and his smile widened. A man said, " I tell yer, bet 'e said, ' Not 'arf I'm not ! ' ondly we couldn't 'ear 'im. 'E's all rite, the whole perishin' R'yal Fam'ly's all rite. Same as you an' me—Gawd save the King ! "

" An' ter 'ell wi' the Kayser ! "

" Garn, we're goin' ter 'eng that flamin' bastard ! On Tower 'ill, it's all settled."

" Serve 'im bloody well rite, the ole so-an'-so ! "

Max walked back to his car. Of course they wouldn't hang the Kaiser, he didn't suppose they would hang anyone. The

British were like that, they didn't nurse grievances. Virtually they would say to William the Second, " Now, you see where this kind of impertinence leads you ! For the future, just behave yourself ! " They appeared to be incapable of nursing hatreds. He remembered a few nights ago when he had been to the Tivoli and watched Bransby Williams giving an impression of Fagin. They—the audience—hated Fagin, but they didn't hate Jews. He had given an impersonation of the Kaiser—they hated the Kaiser, but they didn't really hate Germans. They might have been hating the Austrians, but when Kreisler played his violin in the trenches Max had heard men in hospital say, " Proper luvely it was, made yer feel good. 'Course, Kreisler's not a German, the Austrians is diff'rent somehow." He wondered as he drove slowly home if any nation was capable of sustained hatred—except Germany. Possibly the French, but in the world today, or the world of tomorrow, a commercial world, there was not much room for nursing hatred. Provided that a country had land, natural products, minerals and the like, the commercial world could not encourage boycotts or hatred. His mind halted suddenly.

" What of the nation that had no land, no coalmines, no minerals ? A nation who had only their ability to make money, only the power to use their brains, their mentality ? " Hatred against them might be easy, because their power was either potential or something apart from what the land could produce.

He drove back to his father-in-law's house to join Alice. Old Berman was in great form, the war was over, and he was ready to predict a period of prosperity for everyone.

" Always a period of prosperity after a war, my boy. It's an economic rule."

Max said, " But is it a sound prosperity or a false one, a kind of inflated rise of buying and selling ? "

Julius shrugged his well-padded shoulders. " That's not the point. Wise men make hay when the sun shines——"

" And lay in a stock of umbrellas," Max added.

It seemed that he was right, that stout, slightly overdressed Jew merchant, for trade boomed everywhere. True, the ex-Service men did not find life too rosy. They found too that it was difficult to get back the jobs which they had left to go and fight to make the land " fit for heroes to live in ". As Julius explained, they were in the minority, and the majority were doing well enough. He said that he had never known business so brisk, never known people so ready to spend, and, as he said with irrefutable logic, " If there wasn't the money about—well, they couldn't spend it ! "

The war, in the opinion of Julius Berman, had been very much worth while. Max, going from his elegant house in Kensington to Finsbury, knew that he could so easily have been in agreement with Julius; he would have liked to have believed Julius was right, to join in the chorus that all was right with the world. Everywhere he saw apparent evidence of prosperity, well-dressed people, people who were determined to have a " good time ". On the other hand, again and again he passed men turning the handles of street organs which bore notices announcing their war records. Records which might have given any man a thrill of pride, which—you might have imagined—would have secured them work, and instead they stood in the gutter grinding out some popular ballad.

He tried to talk to Alice, who listened politely but with a certain boredom, and who said finally, " Darling, ever since you came out of the Army you've been an awful misery. One man playing a street organ—and you come home convinced that no discharged soldiers have managed to get work ! As papa says, you ought to take a wider view."

He thought, " So she has discussed this with her father ! "

" He says," Alice continued, " that what matters is the prosperity of the nation, not merely the individual."

Max stared at her, his eyes sombre. " *Aich mir a chiddush*," he said.

She made a gesture of impatience. " I wish you wouldn't speak that language—I've heard you do it so often lately; people will imagine that we come from the ghetto. I don't even know what it means ! "

" It means, my dear—' that's something new ' ! Men like your father have been saying that for years, it's stale—and, like a number of stale things, it—stinks ! Can't you see that the prosperity of individuals—of all classes, not only of people who live in good houses and can afford to run a car—*is* the proof of the prosperity of the nation ? "

She was offended and hurt, and showed it. She drew herself up, and her eyes met his coldly. He stared back at her dispassionately, but appraisingly. She was a handsome woman, she always looked smart and was immaculate as regards details—her shoes, her gloves, handkerchiefs and neck frills were always impeccable. She spent hours on her toilet, on running her home, playing bridge with her friends and arranging smart and amusing dinner-parties. There was scarcely an evening when the Nollers did not entertain or were entertained. She was not *froom*—the household of Julius Berman had never been that; she observed

the great days of her religion, but the synagogue which she attended
was the smartest in the West End of London.

Max, watching his wife, silent and depressed, thought, " She's
more successful in her own way than I shall ever be. She likes
success more than I do. I don't want to be a failure—a *shlemiel*—
a *shnorror*—God forbid, but I do want people to look facts in the
face. Particularly people of my own family ! "

Alice was tapping her foot in its beautiful shoe impatiently
on the thick carpet. " Oh, Max—don't be like this ! We're young,
let's enjoy life and have a good time. Papa says that you're clever,
that you can make a really big success in business—then be happy !
Don't gloom about because you see a few unemployed marching
through the streets making nuisances of themselves, or a discharged soldier playing a barrel organ. If he hadn't *some* money,
he couldn't hire the organ every day ! May Cohen told me that
some of those men make as much as seven or eight pounds
every day ! Anyway, what can *you* do ? It's not your business, it's
something for the Government to settle. Now, Max dear, be
reasonable."

He nodded. " I expect that I'm a great bore. I'll try to be more
satisfactory. Forgive me, Alice."

She smiled—she had a charming smile which disclosed
beautifully kept teeth. " Dear Max, wanting to take the whole
of the troubles of the world on your shoulders ! Even if you
could—you don't suppose that anyone would thank you, do you ? "

" I don't suppose so. . . ."

He tried, tried very hard, to appreciate to the full his pleasant
house, the fine furniture, the delightful little *objets d'art* which
Alice, who had a flair for such things, picked up from time to
time. He took himself to task, told himself that he *ought* to be
happy, that he was ungrateful and ungracious. Alice told him
that she was going to have a child, and he thought, " Now everything will be different ! " without trying to analyze how the birth
of his child could affect England as a whole.

" I live on clichés," he thought, " feed on inane, worn-out
shibboleths."

The child was born in 1920, a boy who appeared to be perfectly
strong and obviously possessed magnificent lungs. Max liked
the baby, liked to look at it, give it his finger to hold and watch
it being bathed by a kindly, capable woman who ruled its life.
Then, as he watched, the old mental nagging would begin, and
he would find himself wondering what kind of a world the child
had entered, what destiny awaited him, what problems would
be presented to him as the years passed.

He was named Julius Max, and Alice gloried in his splendid
health and his good looks. She fluttered round him, with her
friends, declaring that he was " too sweet " and " adorable ", that
his eyes—he had large eyes—would make havoc among the girls
when he was older. No child could have had better care or finer
attention; Alice superintended everything, and knew to the
hundredth part of an ounce what food he was given every day.
She studied diets for young children, bought the finest and most
hygienic clothing, and never entered his nursery without glancing
at the thermometer which hung on the wall to see if the room
was kept at the correct temperature.

Julius was eighteen months old when Alice told Max that she
thought she was going to have another child.

" I may be wrong," she said, " I hope so—another so soon
would be a dreadful bore ! I'm only twenty-seven, I want to
enjoy myself."

Her second child, a girl, was born in 1922, and she was very
ill indeed. Max was terribly anxious and worried to death; he
felt that he had never loved her sufficiently, and that if she died it
would be a punishment for his lack of affection. He remembered
the number of times he had grumbled at having to go out to dine,
to dance at smart restaurants or to play bridge until the early
hours of the morning. He reproached himself, lashing himself
into a kind of false—almost hysterical—state of repentance.

A few days after the birth of the child he was in his wife's room,
moving very quietly in order not to disturb her.

She said, " Max, I'm not dying now ! There's no need to creep
about like some large mouse."

He came over to the bed and stood looking down at her. " I'm
so thankful that you're better," he said. " It was a dreadful
time for you, poor darling."

She smiled. " Well, it's the last time I shall go through it; the
doctor says that I shan't be able to have another—that's something
to be thankful for, isn't it ? "

Her tone possibly more than her statement shocked him. He
didn't really want more children; he was proud of them—the
boy was straight-limbed and well made, the little girl looked
like a dark-haired doll. " Something to be thankful for . . ." He
remembered his mother had always regarded the birth of another
child as " something to be thankful for ".

He said, " You're pleased ? "

" Relieved, shall we say. Two—a boy and a girl—are enough
in these days. Everything costs so much—look what it is going to
cost to keep them in clothes, to educate them, to start them

3

properly in life ! We really can't afford more than two children, my dear—so everything is for the best in the best of all possible worlds ! "

" I expect that you're right," Max said.

Alice grew strong again; she continued to run her children as she ran her house, efficiently, expensively and admirably. To Max, except that two upper rooms were handed over to the babies for a day and night nursery, except that he paid the wages of a nurse and a nursery maid to assist her, the house and its routine appeared unaltered. Alice entertained, went out a great deal, played bridge and saw all the latest plays. Max didn't actually mind, he was doing well and could afford it all. He liked his business, enjoyed being in the warehouse or going about town with samples of his newest and most exotic goods. Some markets were still closed or unreliable, but new ones had opened, and it seemed that with the war Italy had evolved new and more attractive goods to export. He was selective, he wanted nothing that could be found in half a dozen other warehouses— for Max Noller everything must be exclusive. His father wrote praising him, and longing to know when he would take a holiday and go to Berlin to visit them.

Perhaps too (Isaac wrote) *your beautiful wife will come with you and bring the two dear children—our first grandchildren. According to their photographs they are like angels.*

Max read the letter to Alice, who shook her head. " Oh, we can't take two young children. That means taking Nurse and Ellen as well—Nurse won't like to have both of them on her hands, she'll grumble, and I can't afford to lose her, she's valuable. I don't know that I want to go. You'll be immersed in business all day. I suppose you all talk German, and—well, I speak a little, but not a great deal. Maxie, you'd better go alone and enjoy yourself ! I'll take the children down to Frinton or Broadstairs."

" Mama and papa would have liked to see the children——" Max said.

" Then they must come over here," she answered briskly. " I should make them very welcome, and so would my papa and mama. Write and tell them that, my dear. My guest-room is simply lovely since I had it repapered."

He said, " I'll write tonight."

Rose replied that while they thanked Alice for her kind invitation it was difficult for them to leave home. Stanislaus was only twenty-two, and while he was clever and attentive, yet papa thought him too young to leave in sole charge. Jacob had given up the business and was working as an assistant editor on some rather obscure newspaper.

He is completely immersed in his work, and grows more and more silent. Living is difficult, and I am afraid there is a great deal of poverty. Dear Max, how glad we should be to see you, and how delighted you will be with both Miriam and Stanislaus.

Max read her letter carefully, in fact he read it several times; he longed to see his parents, his brothers and sister—though Jacob did not sound a particularly amusing companion—and his home. That night he told Alice that he was going to take a business trip to Germany in the near future.

FIVE

MAX was excited at the prospect of going to Germany; he bustled about his warehouse—which he had recently enlarged considerably—sorted papers, made extensive notes for the guidance of young Simons and declared that he would return with new lines which should be calculated to make London " sit up and take notice ".

Simons said to Mallett, " The boss is like a schoolboy going off for the holidays ! He's been a bit gloomy lately, but since he decided to go to visit his people he's like his old self again."

Mallett nodded. " That's so. I only hope that he gets some good new stuff. This boom won't last—I give it another four years at the most. Probably not that ! "

Simons laughed. " Who's an old gloomer now ? What's the good of meeting trouble half-way ? Anyway, food and stuff connected with food always sells."

" People can't live on spices and peppercorns," Mallett insisted.

Max sat in his office whistling softly as he worked; old Levitoff had been in the day before and had brought some roses from his garden. He had talked about them as if he had made them personally.

" Keep them in the office," Levitoff said, " in one of those old Chinese ginger-jars, look lovely. Scent the whole office. I'll do it, strip the stalks up a bit, look—like this. Makes them last better. There ! Aren't they beautiful ? How are the children, Mr. Noller ? That's nice to hear," as Max assured him that they were both well. " Children are like roses—like flowers—give them plenty of light and plenty of love and they do very well."

Max drew the old blue-and-white jar towards him and smelt the roses luxuriously, touching the petals very gently with the tip of his finger. Levitoff was right, they were perfect; he smiled at the thought of a city merchant wasting his time smelling roses and admiring them.

Simons came in to ask if he would see a traveller. " It's a young lady," he said. " I don't know who she's representing. She's not got an appointment. There's her card." He laid it down on the desk, and Max picked it up.

" ' Miss Elfa de Lucca'," he read, " it's not a business card, nothing on it but her address. Twenty-seven Wellington Road. All right, Simons, I'll see her."

Simons said, " Quite young, nice-looking. Change from old
Clutterson we had in this morning. Time he bought himself a
new top coat ! " A moment later he returned, saying, " Miss de
Lucca, sir."

Max rose to greet her, and realized that he was staring, staring
intently and in astonishment. He thought that he had never seen
such a beautiful woman in his life. She was tall, a little taller than
himself, her face was a perfect oval and her eyes dark and large.
She was dressed very plainly, but her clothes were good if not,
perhaps, in the latest fashion.

Max said, " How do you do, Miss de Lucca—won't you sit
down ? "

She bowed. " T'ank you, I em a little tired. I have walk' a
long way."

He laughed. " I'm glad that I was here, I shan't be in a few
days' time."

" You giff up the busi-ness, yes ? "

" Rather not ! Give up the business ! What an idea ! No, I'm
going to see my father and mother in Germany." He thought,
" What on earth makes me tell her that ? Why should it matter
to her ? "

" 'Ow nice," she said. " It is good to see one's parents. I
have only my mother, my father is dead. It was when he died that
we came to t'is country. Now I try to maka leetle monie. Some
one tell me you sell t'ings from Italia, so I come to you, Mr.
Nollaire."

He watched her, as if he tried to make a mental picture of her
face ; he liked her accent and the inflections which she used. He
liked the way she sat quite still while she spoke, he hated people
who fidgeted about.

" How sad to lose your father," he said. " I'm glad that you
still have your mother. Mothers are a great comfort." He smiled,
remembering that he would see and talk with his own mother in
so short a time. " Now tell me, how do you intend to make money ?
I shall be interested."

Signorina de Lucca drew a deep breath. " I am artist," she
said, " not great artist, but "—she smiled, Max thought, enchant-
ingly, " not very bad. I would like—no, I would have liked, yes ? "

He nodded. " Would have liked—that's correct."

" To have been famous artist, but this is not possible. I would
not ever have been so good as to be famous. Now I make pictures,
small pictures of Italia. I have books, photographs, and from
them—and my mind—I make pictures. I make them quick, and
they don't cost very much. May I show them to you please ? "

" I'd like to see them. Did you leave them outside ? No
don't move, I'll ring for someone to fetch them. And—I say—
don't you think that a cup of tea would be pleasant ? It's hal
past three, I always have one at this time."

" You are too kind, Mr. Nollaire."

Max told the office boy—who liked to be referred to as a
" junior clerk "—to bring in Miss de Lucca's parcels, and added
" Let me have tea, Jepson. And not that cracked cup they sen
in yesterday ! " He turned to the girl. " I hate cracked cups
don't you ? "

" They are bad," she agreed, " not very 'ealthy, I t'ink."

Jepson returned with two parcels, and she thanked him. Jepson
blushed deeply and said, " 'Snothing, I'm shore."

She began to unfasten the larger of the two parcels, then
removed her gloves and handed the pictures to him one by one.
They were small, about the size of a postcard, though some were
slightly larger. Max examined them carefully, and decided that
they were charming. Provided her prices were not too high, he
could sell them easily.

She told him the names of the places depicted in the pictures.
" There is San Marco in Venice—all peoples, I t'ink, go to Venice
—an' here the Bridge of Sighs, this—the Rialto Bridge. This is
the House of Romeo and Giuietta—only, of course, it was not her
house, because the poor girl only lived in the mind of your great
Shakespeare. So she never could have a house, or a tomb either.
That is what they call the Tomb of Juliet. Here is Saint Peter's
in Roma, and here some of mountains—in the Dolomites. That
rose colour is only found in the Dolomites. I have many more at
my house. Tell me, please—be very honest, are they—possible ? "

" Quite honestly, they are charming. I could sell dozens—
and here is the less pleasant part—if the price were right."

" Right ? " she repeated. " How do you mean—right ? "

" Well, not too expensive—so that people could afford to buy
them. That's what we call—the price being right."

" I see, thank you. Not too much and not too small, eh ? Just
—that is it, I think—a just price. But I make them so quick, I
don't want a great deal, only something that will help us a little.
May I show you some things in my other parcel, Mr. Nollaire ? "

" More pictures ? Ah, here is the tea. Jepson, put the tray in
front of Miss de Lucca, perhaps she will pour out for us both.
Thanks."

She moved her hands easily. Max found them fascinating. She
was—he sought for a word—deft ! She didn't fumble. He asked
if she liked English tea.

" Engleesh tea I like. But your Engleesh coffee—oh, it is terrible ! Always my mother and I was maka our own coffee in a Neopolitana machina."

" I know, I was brought up on German coffee—my home was in Germany."

" But you are not German man, no ? You speak like Engleesh, look like Engleesh also." He explained, and she smiled and nodded. " I am glad," she said, " for me, please excuse, you may have many Tedeschi friends, they have not very much good taste —what do you say ?—a little vulgaire, no ? "

" That and a good many other epithets I could apply to them. Well, Miss de Lucca, to get back to these very pretty pictures of yours. I have to leave for Germany in three or four days' time. I may be away for two or three weeks—I've not seen my father and mother for a long time. I should like to take these paintings to a friend of mine—now, at once. I ought to be able to give you his opinion—because he'll place a large order if he likes them— tomorrow. Will you leave your telephone number, please ? "

He watched the colour rise in her cheeks. She looked excited and pleased and the change of expression made her look younger. Max wondered how old she was—then asked himself what the devil it mattered to him !

She said, " I am afraid to presume, Mr. Nollaire, but in this other parcel is work which my mother and I do in the evenings. We enjoy doing it, we find that it makes the nerves soothed, tranquillized. Might I show you ? "

" Do—yes, do. What industrious people you are ! "

" It has always been what you call—playtime work for my mother; now—well, if we can sell these things it is better for us." She lifted out a fine blouse of exquisite lawn. Max thought that the embroidery was the best he had ever seen. Tiny bunches of flowers, wreaths of little roses, green leaves which might have been painted by an artist—each piece of work which she showed him seemed better than the last.

" But these are miracles ! " he said. " Of course, selling this type of thing isn't in my line exactly, but—oh, they're wonderful ! These must take months to embroider, surely ? "

" Months ! " she laughed. " Oh, please, no ! A week, a little more if it is very elaborate. The material is dear—costs a lot of monie, and so is the silk for embroidering—costs much. It is not possible to sell these for less than—it seems a great deal to ask—three pounds it would be."

Max shook his head. " I doubt if it can possibly pay you at that—these are exclusive things, not machine made. You must

work out carefully—look, I'll write it down for you. . . ." He
pulled a sheet of paper towards him and began to work out a very
simple cost-sheet. He gave it to her and she examined it carefully.

"But, please, this thirty-three and one-third, what does it
mean?"

He laughed. "It means thirty-three and a third per cent, only
that's just a bit of the trade mumbo-jumbo—it really means one
third of the whole, that's all. We use the other to mystify amateurs!
Now will you trust me with these precious things? I shall telephone to my friend now and go to see him immediately. Tomorrow I shall telephone to you—without fail." He walked to
the door, opened it and shouted to Jepson, "Just come and tie
up these parcels, will you, for Miss de Lucca?"

Jepson tied up the two parcels with an air which was almost
religious. Max watched him, smiling. He felt ready to smile at
most things, he thought, that afternoon.

"Thanks, Jepson. Car there? Put the parcels in, will you?
Now, Miss de Lucca, can I drop you, take you anywhere?"

"That is very kind, but I take the—a difficult word—*Chube*."

"Then until tomorrow, and thank you for coming to see me.
I know that we are going to do some first-rate business together.
Good-bye."

"Good-bye and good afternoon. Thank you very much."

He watched her walk away down the rather dingy street, and
continued to watch her until she was out of sight. She walked
well, with a good straight back, and held her head well. He
wondered as he drove to Julius Berman what her story was.
He fancied that he sensed tragedy somewhere, the death of the
father, the arrival of the two women in England, obviously not
too well endowed with this world's goods, anxious to make
extra money.

He took the lift and mounted to Julius Berman's office—all
heavy shining mahogany, red leather and a huge marble clock
flanked by two bronze horses. There was a cigar-cabinet against
one wall and an elaborate cupboard where Berman kept refresh-
ment for such customers as merited it. Julius leaned back in his
swivel chair and waved a hand in greeting.

"Ah, unexpected but delightful. What have you found? I think
you are pleased with yourself, eh? How is Alice? And the dear
children?—they grow more beautiful every day. What is the
time? After five. Not too early, I think, for a little refresh-
ment, no?"

"I'd like a drink, thanks. Now," when the drinks were forthcoming, "I want you to look at these."

Julius picked the painting up in thick, well-kept fingers, and Max found himself repeating Miss de Lucca's words, " San Marco, the Bridge of Sighs, the Rialto Bridge, the House of Juliet—only, of course, as the poor girl never lived she never had a house—or a tomb. This is Juliet's Tomb."

" Who says that she never lived ? " Julius asked.

" She only existed in Shakespeare's imagination."

" Ah, I don't know ! " He turned back to the pictures. " Max, they're good, you got something here, something—first rate. Now what about price ? "

Max lit a cigarette, Julius a cigar, and together they discussed and argued prices. Julius drove a hard bargain, but he was almost sternly just.

" So ! You want ten per cent, eh ? I've got to make a profit— I've got ideas about these things, they're unusual. Fifteen shillings a dozen, and twenty shillings for the larger size. If she's prepared to take on special orders, she can do so—provided they are a size and subject I don't stock. How's that ? "

Max said, " The girl won't get fat on that ! "

" I've got to make a profit, haven't I ? "

" You make that all right ! Well, provisionally—for the first gross. After that we'll discuss it again. Remember, she's got to buy the cards, buy paints—she'll not make a lot."

Julius nodded. " That's my offer, and it's a fair one. I'll take a gross—sample order—fifteen shillings a dozen small size ; larger size another gross at twenty shillings a dozen. I'm going to clear out a small stock-room, cover the walls with rough canvas, and show the samples pinned up there. I'll have a nice notice done saying she'll take private orders. What's her name ? What ? Elfa de Lucca—that's it."

He rang, and when a tall, red-haired man with sharp blue eyes answered the summons, he rattled off his orders.

" *Listen*, Murdoch, the small stock-room number seven. Clear it. Get the walls covered with rough canvas—what colour— what colour ? Oh, make it a nice palish fawn, see ? Fawn. Put something on the floor—carpet—to tone. Yes, tone, I said ! I want it to look like a little art gallery, same as those you see in Bond Street, King Street and those places. That's it, Murdoch, get it started. I want it ready for tomorrow afternoon."

" Tomorrow afternoon, sir . . ." Murdoch's expression held doubt.

" That's what I said ! "

The door closed, and Max picked up the parcel which held the blouses.

" Nothing that would interest you, sir."

" How d'you know ? You don't know what does interest me !
All kinds of things—pictures, old silver—everything," he chuckled,
" except bamboo furniture ! Now, let's see."

Slowly, almost unwillingly, Max opened the box and very
delicately lifted out the first blouse, holding it by the shoulders.
Julius leaned back in his chair, his lips pursed as if he were going
to whistle, but no sound came. At last, when Max laid down the
last of the garments, Julius spoke.

" Lovely stuff, ah ! West End stuff. Might do a great deal with
that. I've an idea——"

Max said shortly, " They're not cheap."

" I didn't suggest that they were," Julius said, surprisingly
mildly for him. " I said they were—lovely stuff. Remember old
Pearson who had that little old-fashioned shop in Bury Street.
Had it on a ninety-nine-year lease. Customer of mine. His orders
latterly were worth about tuppence. He'd got twelve years to
run. Wanted to retire. I bought the lease. Clear the place, have it
done up—elaborately, expensively. Reopen selling this stuff!"
The hand with its thick fingers and broad palm made a gesture
towards the froth of lawn and exquisite stitching which lay in the
box. " An idea, eh ? Proposition, no ? "

" Two women can't stock a shop, even if they work all
hours."

" We can get others—these foreigners always know dozens of
their own country people. Go to Italy while you're on this trip,
bring back this material—what is it ?—lawn, eh ? Bring back
anything they need. Go and see this woman, get her require-
ments. Let's get cracking. Time's money ! "

Max folded the blouses and laid them away—there was something unwilling in his movements. He was thinking that he didn't
want to go and see Elfa de Lucca, didn't want to discuss business
with her, didn't want to have a finger in this new pie of Julius
Berman's. He'd seen her, admitted that her stuff was saleable,
that was sufficient. That—he told himself—had *got* to be sufficient !
Yet he hesitated, and as he tied the last knot of the string which
went round the box he nodded. " All right, I'll see what I can do."

Julius beamed at him. " Good boy, Maxie ! Give my love
to Alice."

As Max left he heard Julius calling on the house telephone
that Murdoch was to come to him immediately. Max frowned.
Damn it, Julius went at things like a bull in a china shop. They'd
discussed nothing as yet.

At home he flung off his irritation; he ran upstairs to see the two children, and beamed delightedly when young Julius actually said several words which were intelligible. The little girl was a beauty, she got prettier every day.

" Knows me, eh ? " he said to the nurse.

" Of course she knows you, sir. This little sweetheart knows everyone, don't you, my poppet."

Julius clung to his father's leg. " Me—know—evers-li-un."

The nurse beamed at them impartially. " Bless them, they're as clever as paint."

Max laughed. " Is paint particularly clever, Nurse ? "

" Just a saying, sir, that's all."

Drinking his cocktail before dinner, Max complimented Alice on her dress.

" Darling, it's an old rag ! I've had it for ages."

" Just the same, it's charming and very becoming. Oh, your father sent you his love. He was in great form."

" You've been to see him ? Had you found something—world-shaking ? "

" Something which I think will be a success, and so does he." He found himself not unwilling to talk about Elfa de Lucca's paintings, and found that Alice was interested. Again he repeated his " set piece ", even including the bit about Juliet's house and tomb.

Alice listened with attention. " Didn't they really exist ? I never thought of that. You're bright, aren't you, Maxie ? Tell me about this painter. Is she young ? "

" Moderately—I honestly couldn't say."

" Pretty ? Some Italian women are lovely."

" Yes, good-looking, I suppose. Speaks with an accent, rather amusing. Lives with her mother in St. John's Wood—I've got the address—no, the telephone number somewhere. Obviously an educated woman. Father's dead, and I take it that they haven't much money. She and her mother make embroidered blouses. Wonderful work ! I'd not be surprised if your father and I start them in business. He's got one of his—ideas about it."

" You seem to have got to know quite a lot about her. I wish that you'd brought back some of the work to show me, Maxie."

He had brought back some of the work and locked it in his car. For some reason which he could not have explained, he knew that he didn't want to go and bring it, show it to Alice and listen to her comments. He said, " I will—some time. You're not generally very interested in my stuff."

" Darling, you can't expect me to be wildly thrilled over some new brand of paprika or a new line in curry powder. This is different."

After dinner, George Hawley and his wife came in and played bridge. Max was tired, he found it difficult to concentrate, and more than once Alice told him that he was playing disgracefully. George Hawley guffawed and said, " These City men ! Y'know, their lunches and their business talks are not—shall we say— conducive to clear heads. Eh, Maxie ? "

Max said, " I couldn't say." He hated being called " Maxie ", and recently not only Alice but half her friends had begun using the diminutive. He thought, " One day I'll ask George Hawley who the devil he thinks he's speaking to ! Damned familiar, guffawing brute ! "

He felt better the next morning, and chose a tie which he liked particularly and which looked very well with his dark brown suit. He was not a conceited man, but when he took his last look in the glass he thought, " Damn it, I don't look too bad ! I like these shirts. I must go and see ' George Washington ' and get him to make me some more."

In the office there was not a great deal doing; orders to be handed over for despatch, a couple of travellers—one a Chinese man with beautiful manners and an accent which might have come straight from Oxford.

Jepson said, " Wonderful how they do it, sir, isn't it ? "

" Marvellous. Go to night school, Jepson ? "

" I do, sir. Tikin' French and commercial Spanish."

" Good."

He went back to his office and lifted the receiver. He gave the number which Elfa de Lucca had given him the previous day, and waited.

She answered, " 'Ello, 'oo is it, please ? "

" Noller," he said, " Max Noller "—adding as an afterthought, or rather as an attempt to keep the whole thing on a strictly business footing, " of Noller and Sons. You called here yester- day——"

" Oh, how do you do, Mistaire Nollaire ? I have hop'et that you might telephone to me——"

" I saw my customer last night, and I think that everything is going to be all right. I also opened the matter of the blouses, and there, too, I think that there is every chance . . ."

He heard her laugh. " Mistaire Nollaire, I am stupid. I cannot understand all you say to me. I am sorree—please . . ."

He said, " Look, that's all right." Then speaking very slowly, " It will be better if we can talk—not over the telephone, eh ? "

" Yes—oh yes, bettaire."

" Then," he drew a deep breath, " can you meet me for luncheon at one o'clock ? Do you know Dean—D-e-a-n—Street, in Soho ? Then meet me, please, at the Papagallo—yes, that's right. There's a sign of a parrot hanging outside. One o'clock. Yes. Good-bye."

" Oh yes—I will be there. Good-bye."

Max leaned back in his chair, frowning. What on earth had made him do that ? Surely the girl could have come to the office, it was business, and it was to her interest to try to understand it all ? Confound it, he had promised to have luncheon with Carter ! He telephoned Carter.

" Look, old boy, terribly sorry, but I've got to see a man about some new stuff. Strange fellow, Chinese ! Yes, no doubt wants to sell me bird's-nest soup and oyster's eyes. I'll telephone you when I'm back from Germany."

He continued to frown. " What the devil do I want to lie for— what business is it of Bob Carter's, anyway ? "

He didn't take the car, but picked up a taxi. He was outside the restaurant about five minutes to one, and at one precisely Elfa came along Dean Street. He said unnecessarily, " Ah, here you are!"

" I am not late ? "

" No, no, beautifully prompt. Now come and try this place. It's not too bad."

" It means—those birds who can talk—this *papagallo*. Ah, there, as you said, is the picture of one. Once I had one, my father said that he was over one hundred years old."

" I believe they live to be a tremendous age. Now—what will you have ? " He ordered wine and watched her eat spaghetti very cleverly and neatly; she praised it, and he asked her to tell the proprietor. She spoke to him in Italian, very quickly, and it all sounded, Max thought, very friendly and amusing. When the meal was ended he said, " And now we can talk business. I hope that you'll be pleased."

He repeated, speaking slowly and carefully, his conversation with Berman the previous day. She listened intently, from time to time asking a brief question, and nodding that she understood when Max gave explanations. He said, " Now I am not going to say that you will make a fortune, Miss de Lucca, but it is definitely a—start. A beginning. The embroidery will, I believe, be the better-paying proposition of the two once we can get it started."

She said, " Please, what is—proposition ? "

She was intelligent, and assured him that they had friends who could also embroider; she was prepared to work very hard, and above all she was grateful because the scheme would give her mother so much interest and encouragement.

" She has been very unhappy, my poor mother. The world which she knew, and where she was happy and contented—is gone. There are great changes in my country. My father was a man of strong ideas, of great courage, and he was unable to—how do you say?—adapt himself to the changes round him. He thought them wrong and opposed them with fierceness. He died —it was all very terrible, and it was wiser that my mother and I should leave Italy.

" There was a little money, but not very much, for my father was a man of great generosity and gave with both his hands. We have not a house, you understand, we have a portion of a house. The people are very kind, and my mother speaks a little English to them. We can live—I mean we don't have to be hungry, but a little more is welcome to us. That is why I am so grateful to you, Mistaire Nollaire, for your interest and great, great kindness."

He met her eyes and saw that they were filled with tears.

" Oh, I've done nothing; nothing I'd not do in the ordinary way of business, Miss de Lucca."

" I don't think so ! I think that you are really kind, that your heart is kind." She flicked away the tears and smiled. " You will see, my mother and I shall work very well for you, only the best work will be good enough for Mistaire Nollaire."

Max said, " That's very nice," and signalled to the waiter for the bill. " I shall let you have a contract—only for the pictures, we must wait for the other things—which you must sign. I will also give you full instructions regarding delivery. Or—better still, if you can deliver the pictures to my office, young Jepson can take them round to my customer, eh ? "

" Jepson ? The boy with the round face who grows red when you speak to him ? I remember. I like this Jepson ! "

" One moment, before I go—in three days' time, can you let me know what you require for making and embroidering the blouses, please ? Good. Then—good-bye and thank you for coming to luncheon with me."

Max saw her again before he left for Germany, she brought him the list for which he had asked, and also delivered part of Berman's order. Max thought that he ought to tell her where to go to see her work displayed, but he put the idea from him. He did not want Julius Berman's heavy-handed jokes regarding " Maxie's pretty Italian ", neither did he want countless questions from Alice. In some strange way he wanted to keep Elfa de Lucca to himself.

At their last meeting she sat opposite to him in his office while he checked her list and made certain that he understood clearly what she needed. He finished and said briskly. " There, that's all right, then. Is there anything—personal—that you want that I can bring back for you ? "

She replied, " For me ? No, nothing, thank you, *caro*."

" *Caro !* " That meant " dear ", Max remembered. Had it slipped out inadvertently, or was it usual in Italy to call men " dear " ? It was obvious that Elfa was unconscious that she had said anything unexpected for she continued to speak of ordinary matters quite calmly.

When she rose to go she held out her hand, saying, " *Bon voyage*, and a safe return. I shall be glad to see you again, and I shall astonish you with all the work I shall have done."

With slightly overdone heartiness, Max replied, " Thank you, and we shall want all the work you can turn out. My customer is clamouring for more. If you are in any doubt, telephone to Simons. He'll be in charge while I am away. Good-bye and good luck."

The following evening he was in Berlin. How good it was to enter his father's house again, to feel his mother's arms round his neck and her kisses on his cheeks ! His father was deeply moved, and Max heard the shakiness of his voice when he cried, " Our dear son Max—our first-born ! "

Young Stanislaus was a handsome fellow, taller than Max, with well-formed features and an expression of great intelligence and complete candour. The little sister—" Little sister indeed," Stanislaus cried, " she is tremendous ! She never stops growing ! " —was beautiful. There was a graciousness coupled with great good humour about her, her smile came readily and her eyes danced and sparkled. She was faintly shy of the brother she had seen so seldom, but it was a pleasing shyness which held nothing *gauche* and foolish. Truda, too, was still there, a Truda who, despite the food difficulties during the war, had grown tremendously stout and the possessor of at least four chins.

" And Jacob ? " Max asked.

Stanislaus said, " Ah, our brother Jacob is a very busy and important man. He edits a newspaper ; whether anyone ever reads it I cannot tell you. He comes home very late and leaves very early. For this relief, much thanks ! "

His mother cried, " No, no, my dear, that is not kind ! Jacob works very hard and he tells me that the circulation of his paper increases every day. He has to go about a great deal, he must meet his journalist friends and have discussions with them."

"Have you seen his friends, Mama?" Miriam asked, her eyes wide. "They are queer-looking people, they seem always to be slinking along close to the wall. I met Jacob with one the other day—ugh!" she shivered. "His name was Streicher—Jacob called him 'Doctor'."

"There is nothing wrong, dear child," Isaac said, "in having a name like Streicher. Names are nothing, that is a good German name—even it may be a Jewish name."

"And 'Doctor' means nothing either!" cried Stanislaus. "Anyone can get degrees in these days—if they can pay for them!"

When Max was alone with his father they sat on either side of the fire, talking long into the night. Isaac seemed to have aged far more than his wife, who was still charming to look at, with a laugh which was gay and spontaneous.

Max settled himself in the arm-chair and said, "Ah, this is good! Now, Father, tell me—how goes everything?"

Business, it appeared, was reasonably good. There had been a time when practically nothing could be sold and very few goods obtained, but slowly the world appeared to be creeping—"creeping very slowly"—back to normal. There was still poverty, Isaac admitted, there was still too much unemployment; but he believed that, provided the whole economic situation was properly handled, Germany would be really on her feet again before very long.

"What disturbs me is not the economic state of the country, it is the mental attitude towards everything. There is hatred for England, which perhaps is not so strange, but in addition there is a *sense* of hatred, a mental attitude of hatred. One day this hatred, like some terrible boil, will burst—and, phew! the stench it will make throughout the world!"

Max watched his father's intent face, he seemed to see a painful struggle against a definite fear going on in his mind. He felt that Isaac sensed the weight of a threatening and overpowering disaster menacing the country. "But, my dear father, a whole country can't hate—at will, as it were. Can't hate without cause? People must have some direction for their hatred, surely?"

Isaac nodded. "One would think so, believe so, even hope so —but great masses of people can be swayed easily, my son; particularly if they are led cleverly, inflamed, provided they have someone who can 'ruffle up their spirits'"—he smiled—"so that the very stones of Berlin will rise and mutiny."

"But," Max objected, "against what body of people, against what object is this storm to be directed? It cannot just lash itself about aimlessly."

" Indeed no—the object will be there, never doubt that. Remember that as a little boy I saw hatred in action. I knew what fear meant, I heard the cries of women and the shouts of agony from men. Maybe I shall live to hear those things, to experience those things again—who knows ? "

" The Jews ! " Max exclaimed. " Why on earth should Germany wish to attack the Jews ? Germany has sheltered the Jews——"

" And so will have an excuse to say that the Jews have shown ingratitude towards the country which gave them safety. There is a saying that any stick suffices to beat a dog—if you wish to beat the dog. There are many very rich Jews in this country—their wealth will be counted against them. There are many rich Germans —they will be applauded for having worked hard and made money. Oh, believe me, reasons for attacking the Jews will be very easy to manufacture, Max."

" Attack ! " Max echoed. " You don't mean actually using violence, Father ? "

" I don't know—all that I am saying may be a dreadful mirage, which exists only in my imagination. I only tell you what I *feel*. I have no actual evidence to support my belief, nothing but a very few small, very trivial straws which show me, at least, the way the wind is blowing."

The following day Max met his brother Jacob for the first time since his return. He was reading the newspaper when the door opened and his brother walked in. Max glanced up and said, " Hello, Jacob—how are you ? "

Jacob did not move; his thin, rather haggard face was set into harsh lines, he looked older than his years. He made no attempt to come forward. He spoke in a voice which rasped, hard and unfriendly.

" Ah, my brother the foreign mercenary, eh ? " he said.

Max laughed. " Rather a strange greeting after so many years——"

" Many things have happened in those years. You—and your stupid English—may have forgotten, we Germans—remember."

" My good fellow, don't for heaven's sake be so portentous ! You're talking like some cheap orator. I don't think that in England they've forgotten much, you know, and I doubt if they are more stupid than the majority of people. They don't nurse hatreds, I fancy they are incapable of doing so. They won the war, they set out to do something and they did it—well, it's over ! "

" They set out to do something, they won the war ! That, my Englishman, is where you are wrong. They imagined that they won the war, they are hugging that belief to their hearts now—

well, they will have to be taught their lesson all over again—when
Germany is ready."

Max rose and walked towards his brother. He was determined
to keep his temper, though had he been anywhere except in his
father's house he would have found it impossible.

He laid his hand on Jacob's arm. "Look, old boy, you're
talking a lot of hot air. It's no use nursing hatreds and waiting
for revenge. It's waste of time and energy. It——"

Jacob brushed his hand from his arm as if it stung him. "Don't
touch me, you damned English Jew——"

"Jew! Damn it, what are you? You're as much Jew as I am!"

"I have the grace to be ashamed of it. As I have the grace to
feel proud of being a German."

"*Kelev!*" Max exclaimed. "You dirty dog, to talk in that way!
Be proud of being a German, she's lucky to have such a patriot!
But leave your own race alone. I'm no saint, I don't pretend to be
froom, but I'm proud of my race and, by God, no one, not even
my own brother, is going to speak slightingly of it."

The brothers stood staring at each other. Max's face was
flushed, his eyes very bright and angry; Jacob stood apparently
unmoved, his eyes looked curiously dead, like those of a fish too
long out of water. There was something inhuman in his expression of complete withdrawal. He stared at his brother as if he had
never known him, as if Max belonged to another world. He
looked cruel—not angry—but coldly cruel.

Max spoke first, trying to recover his temper. He hated scenes,
hated to grow angry, hated most of all the thought that his
beloved mother might come into the room and find her sons
quarrelling.

"What nonsense we talk," he said. "Have your opinions and
I'll have mine. Maybe I've lived so long in England that I have
become——"

Jacob interrupted. "That you have become a spy and a traitor.
I wonder why you have come to Germany at this moment. What
do you think you can discover? Take care, we are not blind in
Berlin. I wonder that you do not take your father and mother,
your smart, clever young brother and your sister to England with
you—make them English, eh?"

"When they wish to come to England they can do so." Max
shrugged his shoulders, it was impossible to talk to this brother
of his. "I shall welcome them, you can be sure of that."

"How long do you propose to remain in Berlin?" Jacob
demanded.

"Until I am ready to leave! Let me wish you—good-bye!"

He walked out, he was shaking and ashamed of doing so. That cold grey face, those fishy eyes, and that jaw which was set so cruelly had affected him deeply. He and Jacob had never been close friends, as he and Dan had been, but—damn it, the fellow was his brother, and they couldn't brawl in their father's house.

He made his way to the kitchen, and making a great effort, recovered himself. His mother was making pastry, she looked up and smiled.

" Did I hear Jacob come in ? "

" Yes, he's upstairs. Oh, little mother—give me a piece of hot pastry. You know you always used to when we were little ! "

" Ah, you remember, eh ? " She went to the oven and whipped out an oven sheet on which little cakes were baking. " Take one —no, you're not to look for the biggest. That's greedy ! "

" You used to say that too ! " Max said as he took the little cake. The warm kitchen, Truda's great bulk and wide smile, his mother's dancing eyes seemed to obliterate—for the time at least—the memory of Jacob's cold, unflinching eyes.

SIX

AT THE end of a week he remembered that he had promised to go to Italy—more, Elfa de Lucca forced herself into the forefront of his mind. He found himself wondering how her work was progressing, if Julius had placed more orders and made progress with the little shop—which was to be so elegant—in Bury Street. She had told him that Florence was the place to find materials which she would need. Max had never visited Italy, and the thought of going there pleased him. He would go to Venice and see San Marco. " All peoples go to Venice," he remembered her saying, and smiled.

Except for the encounter with his brother Jacob, the week had been a very happy one. Jacob he had seen once and once only. He had contrived to come to the house when Max was out, and Max had encouraged the rest of the family to visit theatres and music-halls with him to avoid Jacob. He found Berlin very little changed—to the outward eye, at least—but his father's ideas kept recurring and bringing with them a sense of apprehension and disturbance.

He looked for changes, and was relieved to find so few. Possibly there were fewer swaggering officers, more people begging in the gutters. There were still traces that the average people had been through privation—they looked too old for their years, their eyes were hollow. The children, too, were either painfully thin or flabbily fat as a result of bad feeding. The clothes of most people—except the obviously very rich—were shabby, though they were well kept and carefully brushed.

He thought, " In England—unemployed, a housing shortage, the rich too rich and the poor too poor. It's the same here—scarcely any difference. Yet England won the war ! What a farce it all is— this winning wars ! True, we've had a boom in England, but how long is it going to last—God knows ! "

He decided to ask his father if he might take Stanislaus and Miriam with him to Italy. He loved them both, they would be company and —they'd take his mind off all the things which worried and puzzled him. Isaac beamed his delight, and Rose declared that it was the greatest treat that Max could have devised for them.

Again he thought, " How unselfish they both are ! Here they have been all through the war, facing hardships, with three sons fighting and all kinds of other worries. Yet now their only thought is that a visit to Italy will be wonderful for the two children ! "

Isaac said, with that new gravity to which Max was scarcely accustomed, " It is very good that the children should both have passports. I have always attended to keeping your mother's and mine in proper order. A passport is always a valuable thing to have." He broke off and sighed. " At least, we like to imagine that it is."

So Max set off with his handsome young brother and his lovely sister. He took them to Venice, and stared at Saint Mark's, thinking that Elfa de Lucca must have seen it so many times; he thought the same of the Bridge of Sighs and the Rialto Bridge. In Florence he wondered what she had seen, of which buildings she had made pictures. He bought his materials, delighting Miriam by giving her presents and Stanislaus by buying him wonderful shirts and ties. They were both intelligent young people, and quite capable of amusing themselves while Max was engaged in business.

He spoke no Italian, but many of his business associates spoke either English or German. They discussed at great length—in the sanctity of their offices—the new régime. The March on Rome, the rise of Benito Mussolini. Had the King done right or wrong ? What would happen to the monarchy ? Mussolini had said, " I only come to Roma to make certain of your safety."

" A bloodless revolution, eh ? " Max said.

His friends looked dubious. " Not altogether so bloodless," they said.

Another, indulging in proverbs, as most Italians do, said, " It is impossible to produce an omelette without breaking eggs— this is agreed."

" A victory which was won because everywhere people were tired of a weak king, a corrupt Chamber of Deputies, of unscrupulous contractors and the threat of Communism. The new régime was welcomed—as law and order are always welcomed," another stated.

" The Fascist victory was won by something more simple— castor oil ! "

Several of the men glanced uneasily at the speaker; one said, " That is over."

He returned, " Memories—in particular memories of violence— are not soon forgotten ! Now Mussolini—Il Duce they call him— is a god. There have been historical counterparts—Julius Caesar, Napoleon, the Kaiser—where have they gone ? My friends, history is a slow book to write."

A grave-faced man with a spade beard wagged a forefinger at the speaker, saying, " My friend, remember that silence is golden."

Another, with eyes which seemed to burn in his pale face, murmured, " It is true that God pays all debts on Saturday."

" My friend, sometimes that particular Saturday is a long time arriving."

" Yet they say that Mussolini plans to drain the Pontine Marshes," a young man stated. His face was anxious. Max thought that he wished to make out a good argument for the new order. " He intends to build schools, many, many schools——"

" What will be taught in them ? " asked the man with the spade beard. " The doctrines of Fascismo sandwiched in with a little religion to make the Church content."

Max was puzzled, he felt that while there were evidences of returning prosperity, while the majority of the people raised their voices in praise of this man Mussolini, there existed a faction who hated all that he stood for. Trying very hard to be impartial, he suggested that with regard to the new party, " the proof of the pudding is in the eating ".

" Unless it gives you stomach-ache . . ."

" Or diarrhoea . . ."

" Castor oil will do that ! " someone said, and the whole company roared with delighted laughter.

He found them difficult to understand, these Italians; at one moment they were whispering together in conspiratorial secrecy, the next moment shouting with laughter at some slightly vulgar and usually very simple joke. Yet they were undoubtedly kindly, clever, and as business men he found them admirable to work with. Their smiles, like their tears, came easily, and yet he felt that their hearts were warm and kind, their brains clear and astute.

He visited Verona, and fell in love with the " peach-blossom city ". " One day," Max thought, " I shall come here and stay for a long time—I will get to know the place, to be familiar with it, allow everything to—sink into my consciousness." On the heels of that thought came another. With whom would he come to Verona ? He wondered if Alice really cared for old cities. She liked Monte Carlo, Cannes and Paris. He doubted if markets and old staircases—however beautiful—would appeal to her. It would be dreadful to come back to Verona with someone who found it dull and uninteresting. He knew, in his heart, who he wanted to walk through those narrow streets with him, to explore the old castle, the monuments—someone who could give him the knowledge for which he craved.

Impatiently he tried to banish even the vague thought from his mind. He called Miriam to walk with him down the Via Manzoni, where they would buy gloves and silk stockings for her mother and his own wife.

Back in Berlin he said good-bye to his father and mother, begging them both to remember that his home was theirs whenever they cared to come there. He held his father's hand a long time, looking steadily into his eyes, trying to keep his voice completely level and unmoved.

" When we talked," he said, " you told me that there might be changes. If such changes should come, in greater or lesser degree, leave at once. Never mind the business; your safety, that of my mother, brother and sister, are what matters supremely. I hope that you are wrong, I *pray* that you are mistaken—only, please, as you love me—remember what I have said."

Isaac nodded, his eyes misty with tears. " My good son, I shall remember."

Max's own home seemed strange and even a little bare after the house in Berlin; it was undeniably more beautiful, there were greater evidences of taste and elegance. He wondered if it were not just a shade too elegant, just a little . . . inhuman; it lacked something which made for comfort and homeliness.

The children were delightful. Alice was glad to see him and exclaimed with pleasure at the gifts he had brought for her. She wanted to know about " this man Mussolini ", about the shops and about the amount of business Max had transacted. She looked beautifully groomed, her hair shone, her complexion was perfect, the scent which she used was subtle and elusive. Max ate the dinner which was prepared for him; it was more elaborate than those served in his mother's house, the food was less heavy and served with greater care—the dishes were decorated, the silver was perfect, the glass shimmered and glittered. Rose Noller kept a good table, one which was ample and well flavoured; her pastry was light and flaky and all the appointments of the table were polished and well kept. It remained—simple. There was nothing simple about Alice Noller's table, or about Alice herself, Max thought. She was a product of an " elaborate " world, a world which had learned to scorn a little the old traditional dishes and ways of living.

" It is all a little—brittle," Max thought; " all rather like a scene in a play which has an admirable setting."

He appreciated the additional comforts. The bathroom at his father's house had been old-fashioned, a thing of mahogany surrounds and heavy brass taps; here his own bathroom was essentially modern. There was no question of asking, " Does anyone want a bath, because the water's nice and hot?" There were several bathrooms and the water was always hot.

The morning after his return found him entering his office, being greeted by Simons and Jepson, and seating himself at his big desk ready to begin his own work again. Simons laid everything before him, and Max dealt with all queries, trying to forget that he was waiting for the moment when Simons would say, " And Miss de Lucca, sir, about her work . . . ? "

When it came, Max opened his cigarette-case, took a cigarette and lit it carefully, then as he blew out the match, said, " Ah, yes, Miss de Lucca ? "

" Those pictures are going like hot cakes. I think—well, it's no business of mine, only a suggestion—I think we might screw the price up a bit. Mr. Berman's selling them—I got a friend of mine to go round—at ten shillings each, framed—oh, nicely framed, I'll admit—he said, for the little ones and fourteen for the larger type— framed. He's making a nice profit at that, sir."

Max said, " He is indeed. I'll go into it, Simons."

" The first agreement—kind of sample contract—has expired, you know."

" Yes, I'll attend to it. I'll get Miss de Lucca to come round. First, telephone to Mr. Berman. Say that I'm back and would like to see him. Yes, this morning."

He telephoned to Elfa de Lucca, would she have luncheon with him at the Papagallo at one ? She would. He said heartily, " That's good ! I shall have a lot of business to discuss with you."

He heard her laugh, and she answered, " Oh, and I am so bad at this busi-ness, Mistaire Nollaire. But I will try. One o'clock."

He dictated letters, talked to Simons about the new contacts which he had made in Italy, the new lines which Isaac Noller would be shipping to them shortly, and the various orders from his brother Daniel. At five minutes to twelve he went out to Julius Berman's. There, business seemed to be booming, the place was filled with buyers, travellers and the like. Julius, dressed almost oppressively like the late King, greeted him warmly.

" Ah, Maxie ! Have a good time, do good business ? You must come to dinner one evening, and tell me about this fellow Mussolini. I hear that the Italians are forbidden to mention his name aloud, have to refer to him as ' Mr. Black ' or some such rubbish. Now— let's get down to business."

" I'll have samples unpacked by tomorrow, can you come down ? "

" Yes, always ready to go after business. Hope you've something good."

" Tolerably, you'll find. Now, that little sideline—those pictures of the Italian girl's ? Going all right ? "

" Quite nicely—oh, quite nicely. Not setting the Thames on fire, y'know."

" You've had three repeat orders in three weeks——"

" While the novelty lasts ! Not stuff to hold in stock, Maxie. However, I'm a man of my word—as you know. I'll make a new contract—twenty shillings a dozen for the small pictures, and twenty-four for the larger ones. That suit you ? "

Max nodded. " That's all right. Now, the idea of the shop. I've thought it over, I'll put a thousand into it. I've brought back a lot of stuff, very nice—if you're still keen on the idea, sir."

Julius spread his hands wide, as if the shop meant nothing to him, and he even excused himself for having proposed the idea. " Keen —oh, well, I don't know that I'm so *keen*. I've had the place re-decorated, looks beautiful. Look, I've got the key here, go down and see it this afternoon. The workmen got out yesterday. Have a talk to these women, see what stock they've got, see what stuff you've brought back. Then we'll go into the financial side. I'll get Jack Cohen up to draw up something. That suit you ? A thousand, you said, eh ? I've spent six hundred on the place already ! "

" I might get Miss de Lucca and her mother to come down and see it with me."

" Good idea ! Then get in touch with me. I want to get cracking on this. Now, Maxie—what about a quick one ? "

Max drank his " quick one " and caught a taxi to Dean Street. He was a few minutes late and Elfa was waiting for him. He made his apologies, and when he had ordered wine and she had ordered the Italian dishes of which he scarcely knew the names, he told her his news.

The effect upon her was electrical. " As if someone turned on a light inside her," Max thought. Her eyes shone and her lips parted a little in delighted surprise. She looked younger, and very eager.

" I've brought you back paints and cards," he said. " I've brought back lawn and embroidering materials—I took my young sister to Italy to help me. Now when we've finished luncheon I want to show you the shop."

" It is finish ? Oh, how wonderful ! Mama and I have five friends who will be happy to work with us—Signora Nettis and her daughter, the Contess Ramoni and her sister Carlotta, Signora Nella Bertoldi—ah, her work is so beautiful—the finest *petit point*, like miniatures in needlework. So, when you wish, we can begin ! Mama is so excited, she talks of nothing else."

As they drove down to Bury Street he tried to talk to her about Italy. " I wished so much that you could have been there. You could have told me about things. As it was I just went stumbling along, taking sly glances at my guide-book because I didn't want everyone to know that I was visiting Italy for the first time."

She looked at him gravely. " It is a beautiful country, my heart is always there—but it has changed. The Italy in which I grew up, where my papa and mama were so 'appy, that is gone. Not for many years I can't go back."

" I thought that the whole country was set for prosperity——"

" Excuse—what is—set for ? "

" On the road to—under this chap Mussolini."

Her face flushed. " Ah, he is clevaire, he will do—what you call —conjuring treeks, and people will shout, ' 'Ow clevaire ! ' Then one day he will forget 'ow to do his treeks, or another man will come who does more difficult treeks—and the wind will change. I do not wish, Mister Nollaire, to talk about Mussolini. One day I will—talk to you. Now—please, the little shop ? "

It was charming. Max wondered how much of the decoration had been due to Murdoch's taste, and how he had managed to restrain Berman from insisting on hanging some half acre of painting in a huge gilt frame on one wall " to give tone ". The decorations were subdued, and it was obvious that expense had not been spared. The fittings were unobtrusive, and the two small fitting-rooms comfortable and practically soundproof. Elfa was delighted, and Max was surprised at her grasp of essential details.

" Now I want a list of your stock—with prices—and I shall have one ready tomorrow with my own stock and prices. Provided that you have sufficient materials and stock we ought to be ready to open on Monday next. You must decide who will be the best to sell, who to do the fitting, and who to merely do the making and embroidery. We'll have no private price marks—plain figures only."

" I shall be very stupid, I am afraid. Would it be possible for that kind little boy who blushes so easily to come and explain these things to me ? "

" Jepson ? What on earth does Jepson know about it ? I'll tell you what—with your permission I'll come to your house—tomorrow. I'll make all explanations. How would nine o'clock suit you ? "

He saw her to her bus and walked to Ryman's, where he bought everything he could imagine them wanting in the shop—tickets, billheads, order books, sales ledgers, pens, ink, carbons, even wrapping-paper and string. Later, when he had discussed the matter with Elfa, they must have boxes, and their own individual wrapping-paper, even their own particular string—the whole thing must be smart, different—tip-top ! He went back to his warehouse, thinking more of the little shop in Bury Street than of his own affairs. He had been happy with Elfa de Lucca, he had waited for her smiles and felt pleasantly amused at her small lapses into incorrect English. That evening as he drove home he asked himself if he were falling in love with her. He refused to allow the idea to occupy him.

" In love ?—what nonsense ! I've seen her three or four times. She's attractive, she's anxious to make a success—and, damn it, she's a pleasant change from so many of the dreary old buffers I have to see every day." As he ran upstairs to the nursery he smiled. " In love indeed ! What rubbish—the kind of thing a sentimental schoolgirl might ask herself ! "

That evening during dinner he told Alice about the shop. Told his story in a completely matter-of-fact tone, while admitting that he believed that he and Julius Berman were " on to a good thing ".

Alice said very calmly, " Oh, papa told me about it. I advised Murdoch about the decorations. You've seen it ? You didn't think they were papa's taste, did you ? "

He felt suddenly mentally " damped ", as if some of the sparkle had gone out of his venture. He said, " Well, they're very, very nice. I congratulate you. I hope to open on Monday, will you get some of your smart friends to come ? Give the thing a good send off ? "

" You ought to have invitation cards, Maxie. The printers can rush them through and I'll write the addresses—not too many—fifty is sufficient. The Press ought to come. Can you arrange to serve cocktails ? Make things go with a swing. In the room at the back."

" I'll attend to that," he promised. " Thank you, my dear, for being so helpful."

She laughed. " I'm dying to see this marvellous Italian girl."

" I never said that she was—marvellous."

" She's obviously made a great impression on you." Again she laughed, that rather high laugh which was faintly metallic. " Be careful, Maxie."

" What rot you talk ! I'm going tomorrow to initiate her into some of the elementary facts about making out bills. She lives in St. John's Wood."

" I thought that all Italians lived in Soho ! "

" Apparently not." With an effort to remain good-tempered he said, " I believe that the ice-cream vendors live in Saffron Hill."

He went the following evening to Wellington Road and found Elfa and her mother living in a maisonette. The place had obviously been let to them furnished, it was also evident that it had been let to many previous tenants. The room into which he was shown was shabbily comfortable, but seemed to bear the imprint of many people who had occupied it as birds of passage. On the mantelpiece Max noticed two photographs in frames which struck him as being " un-English ". One of a large house set in a wide garden, the balcony on the first floor being supported by pillars, and a wide terrace on which stood large stone vases filled with plants. The other was of an elderly man, strikingly handsome, wearing what appeared to be a court uniform and with some elaborate-looking order on a wide ribbon round his neck.

Elfa said, " Mama will join us presently, she is making the coffee."

Max said, " So I am to taste this famous Italian coffee ! "

" And then I am to have my lessons, no ? Mama and I are both very excited. We owe so much to you, Mister Nollaire—and believe me we are both very grateful to you."

The door opened to admit her mother: she was a tall, rather massive woman with beautiful white hair piled high, and a face which was colourless. Her eyes seemed to Max to blaze, and yet there was a warmth and kindliness in her expression. She moved with great dignity, and her daughter introduced Max.

" Mama, this is Mister Nollaire to whom we owe so much; this, Mister Nollaire, is my mother, the Contessa de Lucca."

Max, thankful that he had lived on the Continent, held out his hand; she laid hers on it, and he lifted it to his lips—without actually kissing it. When he raised his head, the Contessa was smiling at him, a singularly charming smile which reached even her strange eyes.

" I spik Ingleesh very badly, but I em gled to meet you, Mister Nollaire. My daughter hes spoke of you mooch. Carissima, bring the coffee, please. We 'ave no servant 'ere," she continued; " each day a ver' strange woman comes, she is called—char. Is that, you t'ink, a contrac-tion of Carlotta ? No ? She is ver' kind, but strange. It is wit' deefficultee I compre'end 'er. She call me ' Countess ', or at odder times ' mi ole pet '. W'at will thet mean ? "

" It's a kind of—affectionate—idiom," Max said.

" So ! This is 'ow I shall learn, no ? Oh, she teaches me many t'ings, my char—sometimes she tells me to ' back 'orses '. I nevaire see the 'orse, some friend of hers—she says—put it on. Another idiom, no doubt. Two weeks ago I won eight shillings, this week I lost six of them. She tells me to invest monie ' both ways '—I suppose to win or to lose, no ? "

Elfa brought in the coffee, a tin tray covered with a very fine embroidered cloth, and a strange coffee-machine which looked like two metal pots standing one above the other. The china was beautiful, and Max remarked upon it.

The Contessa, busy pouring out the strong fragrant coffee with hands which were immaculately kept and covered with old-fashioned rings which Max judged to be valuable but were in need of cleaning, nodded. " Yes, eet is good. For a long time it remains in my family. I believe your Regina Maria has some like it. She is ver'

clevaire, I 'ear, wit' old t'ings, a great judge. I remember 'er at
Livorno, wit' 'er 'usband. They stayed at the Netturno, she was
most dignified, but wit' nice smile—*affabale*. Your Royal Family
are mooch liked, held with respect. You take sugar ? 'Ow do you
like my coffee ? For me, all day I drink coffee—but nevaire your
English coffee—forgive me, eet is 'orrible ! ' "

When later Max set out his books, they sat one on either side of
him, and he found the Contessa astonishingly quick and receptive.
She kept saying, " Yes—yes—oh yes. 'Tis I compre'end. Ver'
simple—children could understand. Yes—yes."

He said to Elfa, " Your mother is a marvellous pupil. I think we
must leave the accounts in her hands, don't you ? "

She nodded. " Mama is very clevaire. She used to manage all
the accounts for the estate beautifully. All the *contadini*—peasants
—liked and knew they could trust mama in everyt'ing. *É vero*,
Mama ? "

" Oh, yes, eet is true. 'Tis when I t'ink of the books, accounts,
rents, everysing—t'is is the play of a children. Have no pre-
occupation, Signor, I compre'end perfectly. Now we shall make an
end, for t'ese t'ings are for offices, shops, not for the *salon*, no ? "

Max liked her, she was shrewd, he suspected that she could drive
a hard bargain, that even though her peasants might have liked her,
they went in wholesome dread of her ! There would be no mistakes
in the accounts of the Contessa !

During the days which followed Max worked long hours; he was
determined that this venture should be a success if his energy and
attention could make it so. Even Alice was filled with enthusiasm,
she sent out cards, she ordered flowers and found suitable vases for
them. Max took her down to the little shop, and found both Elfa
and her mother there.

The Contessa, her head tied up in a bandana silk handkerchief of
incredible brilliance, came forward. She was gracious and charming.

" Ah, Madame, you come to see the leetle jewel-box—for that ees
w'at eet is resembling—a jewel-box, no ! What *bon gusto*—'ow you
say, good taste—is demonstrated 'ere. We 'ave all workit ver' 'ard,
and we 'ave many beautiful t'ings to show you. Not only the
blouses, Madame, but 'andkerchiefs—so fine you might blow them
avay, dresses for the night—but they are poems, poems. The *petit
point* of *mia cara amica*, Nella Bertoldi, small pictures as made by
artist, after Watteau, Fragonard and Boucher. Oh, we do not stand
only upon one leg, we are like *centigambi*—we 'ave one 'undred
legs ! "

Alice smiled, said that she found everything delightful ; she begged
to see some of the goods, and Elfa—very quiet and subdued she

seemed to Max after the volubility of her mother—brought them. Alice uttered little screams of delight, she had never seen such work, such taste. Her friends would be enchanted—as she was.

Elfa said, " You are very kind, Madame."

As they drove home, Alice said to Max that the old woman was "a gasbag, but she's cute. She'd sell anything ! Contessa de Lucca ! Plenty of people will enjoy being attended to by a contessa ! Your young woman's a beauty, Maxie. Not much to say for herself, but she's quite lovely. What are the rest like—this woman who does *petit point*, for instance ? "

" I've not seen any of them ; there are, I think, five friends of the de Luccas working with them."

" All countesses ? "

" Quite probably, I imagine."

The little shop opened, the various agreements and contracts had been worked out by Berman's solicitor, Jack Cohen. They were signed and the whole business was settled. Berman said they'd never make a fortune, but that so long as the place paid it was " a bit of fun ". He came down to the opening resplendent in a grey frock coat, a white vest slip, a top hat carried in the crook of his arm and a buttonhole which put the finishing touch to his elaborate costume. He beamed on everyone, bowed over the hand of the Contessa and, having no Italian, spoke atrocious French to her friends. He remained only a short time—Max wondered if that elaborate " get up " had been worth it—then bowing again, assuring the Contessa that he was her servant and always at her disposal should she need advice, he departed.

Max stood leaning against the table in the room where cocktails were being served, watching Elfa moving among the clients. She moved slowly, always without apparent haste; her movements were quick without being hurried. He heard her voice explaining, commenting, giving information; the words did not reach him, but her voice fell on his ears gratefully, soothingly.

For the first time he was frank with himself. He thought, " By God, I've got to be careful ! I'm thinking too much about her. It won't do ! "

Only once did he speak to her during the afternoon. " Things going well, Miss de Lucca ? "

She turned and smiled. " I never dared to 'ope that they would go so well or that people would be so—charming. Already mama takes many orders, for nightdresses, underclothes. . . ." She laughed softly. " Mama would take an order for an elephant if someone asked for it. She'd find it some'ow ! "

" A woman of determination, eh ? "

Her smile died, she looked at him as if faintly disturbed. " So determined that sometimes I am afraid—*un rullo vapore*—t'ose engines which make roads level. . . ."

" Steam roller ? "

Elfa nodded. " Steam rollaire. But admirable, Mister Nollaire— she is most admirable, but sometimes—a small piece frightening." Speaking very softly, she added, " 'Tis confidence, you understand."

" Of course." But the idea of sharing a confidence with her sent him away with a feeling of pleasure, even though it were only concerning the Contessa being like a—what had she said ?—*un rullo vapore* !

The shop prospered; Max found himself calling there whenever he was in the West End. Elfa was not invariably to be found there, sometimes there was the Contessa, who appeared only to leave the place in order to snatch a few hours' sleep, and who, when not actually attending to customers, was never without some elaborate embroidery on which she was working.

Sometimes he found Signora Nettis there with her young and vivacious daughter Yolanda, or the tall, elegant Contessa Ramoni, and her sister Carlotta Bordoni. He had thought Carlotta Bordoni the ugliest woman he had ever seen, until he talked with her and realized the charming expression of her face and the brilliance of her smile. The Signora Nella Bertoldi he saw less frequently, for she worked at home and only came to Bury Street when she brought completed pieces of her beautiful work.

Very rarely did he find Elfa there alone, except for the two sewing-women who had been installed in the room at the back—Rosina and Teresa. One sunny but cold afternoon Max came in, and Elfa offered to get him a cup of tea. He said that it would be more than welcome, adding, " You can't come out and have tea somewhere, can you ? "

" No, that is impossible, I am in charge. Mama is working at home today. No, I will give you tea. Do you remember when I came first to see you, then you gave to me tea ? "

He nodded, then because he was not only cold but dead tired, he let his guard down for a moment and said, " I don't forget many things about you, my dear—they're all so important, you see."

She looked startled, then said nervously, " I shall get the tea." She returned with two cups and a plate of biscuits. " The biscuits are nice," she said. " Yolanda Nettis makes them—they are Italian biscuits."

" Do you miss Italy—all of you ? "

She shrugged her shoulders. " It is inevitable, no ? Oh, t'is life is quite good, amusing, people are kind, work is pleasant—but it is like making a long journey. However pleasant it is, you wait—expectantly—for the moment when you return 'ome again. Do you understand ? "

" Then you want to go back—all of you ? " he asked.

" We shall go back—w'en it is possible and w'en it is to be advised."

He said, " Advisable, you mean ? "

" Yes, advisable. Now it is not—when men are *ubriaco*—how you say, too much drink taken . . ."

" Drunk, when men are drunk . . ."

" Yes, they do violent t'ings, stupid, dangerous t'ings. Slowly t'ey *sobrio*—are sober once more. They can t'ink and maybe still do foolish t'ings, but not so foolish as in the first time. Do you understand, Mr. Max ? "

" I think so. I suppose that each one of you has a—story behind you ? "

" Someone—I don't remember 'oo it was—said nations were 'appy when t'ey had no 'istory. Maybe we are not 'appy—because we all have—'istories. Some not very nice stories. We laugh, people say, ' 'Ow gay t'ese peoples '; not really, we are not gay. Only, perhaps, some of the sunshine remains in our 'earts, some of the music in our ears, the scent of the flowers clings to our 'appy memories and so we smile. Also, dear friend, it may be that we laugh so that we don't cry ! Italians are an old race, but we are a new nation—oh, I don't mean the Fascist peoples—I mean—*the people*. A new nation, a united—or it should be a united nation. We are proud of t'is nation—we wish to see her grow and be strong."

He asked almost moodily, " You love your country ? "

Her smile was immediate. " W'at I t'ought was good for my country, in my deep heart, I would do. No matter w'at it was."

" Your King, how do you feel about him ? "

" Our little King ? Oh, we love him. He is not clevaire, he is—I don't t'ink strong, but—he is Vittorio Emmanuele of Italy, just the same, the head of the House of Savoia."

" And the other chap—this Mussolini ? It looks as if your King has given in to him all along the line, doesn't it ? "

For an instant she laid her hand very lightly on his arm. " In the Bible it says every 'eart knows its own bitterness. I don't understand all t'ings, I just try to believe that all t'ings come to those who know 'ow to wait. Mister Max, I must go. You have finish' your tea and my work is waiting for me. *Au revoir*, Mister Max."

At the end of 1924 Berman asked Max if he would object if he took Alice on a trip to America with him. Her mother hated the sea, the shortest sea voyage almost killed her. He was going on an important business trip, there would be a certain amount of entertaining to be done, and Alice longed to go.

Max said, " I don't mind, if she wants to go. The children will be all right with Nurse, I suppose. How long will you be away ? "

" About six weeks—possibly seven. Well, thanks, Maxie. You might talk to Alice about it, will you ? I'd like to sail early in January."

" Beastly time of year for an Atlantic trip, New York will be freezingly cold."

" Business, old boy, business. Anyway, in the summer New York grills you alive. You don't feel the rough seas on these big liners."

Alice, complete with the latest thing in suitcases and innovation trunks, departed for America with her father. Perfectly honestly, Max admitted to himself that he would miss her. He had long ceased to be in love with his wife, but he felt for her a genuine affection, though her " brittle " chatter and what he felt to be ill-timed remarks exasperated him at times. The night before she sailed she sat opposite to him at their handsome oval table and said, " Are you going to miss me, Maxie ? "

" My dear, of course I shall miss you."

" And not console yourself with anyone else while I am away ? Either your Miss de Lucca or the Nettis girl are charming ! " It was said with an air of gay badinage, but Max knew that he flushed with annoyance.

" Alice, I wish that you'd drop that rather outworn joke. Both those girls have in all probability got attractive and aristocratic young men waiting for them in Italy."

" They don't show any signs of wishing to go back to them. Muriel Purvis told me that she saw Miss Nettis at the opera—in a first-tier box—with young Wilford. Imagine it, the Marquis of Westerham's son ! "

Max answered shortly, " I might sit in the box with Queen Mary, it wouldn't make me Prince Consort."

" Really, Maxie, don't be so *silly* ! "

Alone without Alice, he felt relieved but not happier. He loved his two children, and both of them were growing to interest him more and more. But Nurse was adamant and he was not allowed to see very much of them. " They're both so intelligent, sir. Julius sleeps so badly if he gets excited and Gweneth's nearly as bad. It doesn't do to overtax their little brains."

His visits to the shop continued, his longing to see and talk with Elfa grew. He had no very clear idea what he hoped for, or even wished for regarding her. All that was in his mind was the wish to be with her, to watch her smile and to listen to her voice. He

4

proposed visiting an exhibition of modern Italian paintings and she agreed to go with him. He discovered that she cared very little for ultra-modern art, and suggested that she might like to see what the Tate Gallery held. She came with him and they spent a delightful afternoon; her criticisms were the result of keen observation and considerable technical knowledge. He asked the Contessa and Elfa to dine with him at his house and go on to a theatre. The Contessa was resplendent; she looked aristocratic and distinguished. Elfa looked as lovely as Max had ever seen her. His meetings with her on some pretext or other came to be almost daily occurrences. The shop was still very busy and eminently successful; Elfa's pictures sold steadily, and she had executed several profitable commissions. She never addressed him as anything but " Mister Nollaire " or " Mister Max " except on the rare occasions when she was deep in some argument and said, " my dear ". Never again did she say " *caro* ", and Max found himself wishing almost passionately that she would do so.

He was working very hard; Mallett, the traveller, still maintained that the boom was going to " peter out ", and Max flung himself feverishly into making hay while the commercial sun shone. He asked himself why Mallett should be regarded as an authority, and realized that he was only doing far more work than was necessary in order to prevent himself thinking too often of Elfa de Lucca.

He called to see the Contessa about some new designs one Sunday afternoon. The room was pleasantly warm, even a trifle stuffy. The Contessa showed her usual brisk shrewdness, and the business was soon finished. Max said, " It's such a lovely afternoon, Contessa—would you and Miss de Lucca care to come for a drive ? "

The Contessa shuddered. " To drive—on such a day of cold ! My dear Mister Max, w'at 'orrible 'tings you English t'ink of ! No, not for me ! I 'ate the cold, bare trees, wind like a knife. Elfa says that she enjoys it. Elfa can go if she wishes and you care to take 'er. You will not be too long time, no ? "

" No, possibly Richmond Park and back. Nothing."

" Then call Elfa and tell 'er to wrap up warmly."

" I'll bring you back some maids of honour, Contessa."

" W'at are t'ey ? Oh, cakes ! I shall be pleased. Why do t'ey 'ave this curious name ? "

" Honestly I don't know. Something historical no doubt."

She shook her handsome white head. " Oh, you English, you know nossing of 'istory—and appear not to wish to know. Disgraceful ! "

They drove through the quiet streets, neither of them talking much, Max filled with contentment that Elfa was seated beside him.

He could smell some very faint scent which she used, so faint that t was almost intangible. Once, when she moved to look at some building which he pointed out, her hair brushed his cheek for a second. He turned into the gates of Richmond Park and stopped the car.

Elfa said, " How cold it looks. Beautiful, but—cold."

Max slid his hand under the rug and found hers, it was soft and warm.

He said, " Look, Elfa, what are we going to do about it ? You realize what has happened, don't you, darling ? "

With her eyes still on the wintry landscape, the bare trees and the grey-green grass, she answered:

" *Caro* Max, I think I understand. I am very sorry. T'ere is not'ing we can do—except not to see each other."

" I couldn't do that ! I'd do anything for you—but not that."

She answered very softly, " I don't t'ink, *caro*, that I could do that."

Without speaking again he started the car and drove on farther into the park. The place was deserted; in the distance a few people wandered, seeking no doubt to shake off the effects of the British Sunday dinner. Again Max stopped, turned to face her and laid his arm across her shoulders.

" Elfa darling, kiss me. I've waited such a terribly long time."

In their embrace he felt that all the petty irritations, all the weariness of the past weeks, took flight; he felt young, hopeful, content. Nothing mattered—booms or slumps, successful sales or disappointments, customers who were too critical or those who were invariably satisfied. All that mattered was that he held Elfa de Lucca in his arms and knew that she was glad to have them round her.

SEVEN

THEN began for Max Noller a time which alternated between being the most blissful he had ever known or dreamed of and a time which frequently imposed upon him a sense of frustration which was almost unbearable. True, he saw Elfa very often, but rarely did he see her when they could rely upon being alone. At Bury Street, even if the sewing women were off duty, Elfa must be ready and waiting to receive customers. If she came to his office, the realization that if he took her in his arms he must listen for a knock on the door or expect an interruption by the telephone. In her own home the Contessa was immovable, and even when she was at Bury Street both Max and Elfa agreed that it was not advisable for him to call at Wellington Road.

The times which they could spend alone were restricted to picture galleries, meetings in museums, tea-shops or more rarely at an afternoon concert. While he was with her Max assured himself that he was content, that he wanted nothing more than to listen to her, wait expectantly for her low, full laugh, and to feast his eyes on her lovely face. The moments when he drove her home were precious, then he could hold her hand, sometimes even risk taking her in his arms for a brief moment.

When he returned home to visit his children and then look forward to a lonely evening his content vanished. He sat there listening, or half-listening, to the radio, pretending to read, but more often merely sitting staring into the fire, dreaming dreams, indulging in hopes which he began to doubt could ever be realized.

He begged her to come away with him somewhere into the country, for a week-end. She stared at him astonished.

" But, my dear one, w'at should I have to say to my mother ? "

" Say that you're going to spend the week-end with friends . . ."

" But, dear Max, I have no friends and my mother knows that."

" Say that you must go to Paris, Brussels—where you wish—to buy materials."

" My mother would never allow t'at. And also, Max, she would demand, if materials were to be bought, t'at she buy them."

" Then," he drew a deep breath, he was going to play his last card, " then let me take a flat where we can meet, and instead of going to art galleries and sitting at uncomfortable tables in damned tea-shops, let us meet there."

She looked at him not quite steadily, then shuddered.

" Max, my dear, I could not do t'at. For me it would be impossible. I am not ignorant, believe me. In Italy I 'ave 'ad friends who had lovaires. I 'ave 'eard of flats in Rome, Milan, Venice—and I 'ave seen what heppened. Not'ing lasted, every-t'ing—melted away. At first a big, fierce fire, then—only ashes. To come—almost guiltily to meet you at a flat—oh, Max, it is impossible. It would be the end of all t'ings."

He frowned and said sulkily, " I don't see why it should be."

" Dar-r-ling, because you will not see clearly. T'ink clearly—what is one of the chief reasons you suggest t'is flat—you know, I know also. I know peoples—I know myself, I know you, dear Max. For a few weeks, oh, all would be wond-er-ful, we should be divinely 'appy. T'en one day, you 'ave been very busy, t'ings 'ave not run smoothly. Per'aps you are worried over some con-tract, some delivery. You come to the flat, you are tired, your nerves are strung very tightly. I say, ' Dar-r-ling Max . . .' and you say, ' I say, Elfa, give me a cup of tea, I've got a dreadful 'eadache ! ' Or I am the tired one, my painting 'as not gone well, at the shop some woman 'as been tiresome. You are glad to see me, you tell me so, and I say, ' *Dio mio*, 'ow sick I am of t'is work —and of peoples. I shall make some coffee.'

" T'at, *caro mio*, would be the beginning. You would say in your 'eart that I loved you no more; I should say in mine t'at you cared most for your business. The music would die, the bright colours would fade, and one day we should remember, ' Why, it is nearly two weeks since we were 'ere together ! 'Ow time runs away ! ' No, dearest one, I love you too much. I love my love for you too much to risk t'is t'ing."

" You're colder-blooded than I am ! "

Elfa shook her head. " No, *caro*, Italians are not cold-blooded, but I t'ink sometimes that we are more—logical. We can see for long distances, not t'at always we *do*, but we *can*. It is not that I am cold or—what you say—prude. I long so much to give myself to you—completely. I am not t'inking of what is right—morally. I know t'at you are married, you have a wife, children, responsibilities—I admit I would forget—yes, willingly—all t'ose t'ings. But I am afraid to lose the smallest piece of your love for me. It is not my conscience, it is not that I am afraid to sin—if I 'ave to pay for it, all right, I will pay when payment is demanded."

" I'm not certain that you're not talking a lot of sophistry."

" Yes, you are quite sure, Max *caro*—you know that I am right."

He might fret and fume a little, but he knew that in reality he was happier than he had ever been in his life. He might smile a

little wryly at his reflection in the shaving-mirror and tell himse
that he *would* go and fall in love with a woman who possessed to
many scruples, who had no convenient friends and a dragon of
mother; but he knew that he had never loved so utterly an
completely before.

Alice returned from America. She brought numbers of ne
clothes and for a time, at least, affected a slight accent; she ha
enjoyed her trip and had never known that a steamer could b
so amusing.

" Glad to see me again, Maxie ? " she asked.

" Why, of course I'm glad, very glad." And he meant it too.

" Behaved yourself while I was away ? No call for me to extrac
confessions, eh ? "

" I'll try to make some up, if you like—strain my imaginatio
to please you, only you'll have to give me time."

Later in the year he went over to Germany to see his parents
He asked Elfa if she would come with him, knowing what he
answer would be. He only tried to nurse a faint hope, and i
died instantly.

Isaac looked tired, and his mother older. Jacob, it appeared
had left home and lived in rooms. They saw him very rarely
Max thought that Stanislaus at twenty-two and Miriam at eightee
were two of the most handsome youngsters he had ever seen. The
were intelligent, highly musical and charmingly affectionate toward
their elder brother.

Max had long talks with his father, conversations which agai
disturbed and worried him. Isaac was content concerning th
business, if anything it was doing better than a year ago, th
recovery was slow but sure. There was a great deal of unemploy
ment in Germany, people were restless and dissatisfied. Th
Treaty of Versailles had angered them, the introduction of Africa
troops on the Saar had added fuel to the flames of their fury. Th
English and Lloyd George were blamed, the French and Clemencea
were blamed, Wilson and the Americans were blamed.

" In fact the only people free from blame," Isaac said, " ar
the Germans themselves. They are innocent victims. They ar
angry with everyone—with all nations, and particularly there is
faction who is angry with the Jews. Always this cry of ' the ricl
Jews '—they appear to have forgotten how many poor Jews w
have. If they knew the cases which come before our Counci
they might think differently. This paper with which Jacob i
connected, I see it—or I should say that I *have seen* it, now I don'
read it any more. Always there are accusations about the Jews—
they are controlling the banks, they have procured for themselve

all the best positions, they have contrived to become professors in
the universities—these things, childish, illogical, are held against
them. Made into bogies to frighten credulous children. Ah,
people are very foolish. I remember how often my uncle, dear
Uncle Stanislaus, used to talk about the futility of hatred. Alway
he preached that love was a more—yes, *profitable*—thing, because
hate limited mentalities, and demanded great energy to keep it
alive. Let us forget these things for a time. Have you heard
from Daniel ? "

Yes, Max had heard from Dan, in fact Dan wrote pretty regularly.
He seemed happy enough, very attached to his wife and their
child. Maybe he wasn't making money at the rate he had hoped
for, but he was apparently content.

" Daniel was never a great one for money," Isaac said, " Daniel
never wanted money or to fill the upper seats at feasts. Jacob was
always ambitious. You are ambitious too, but not in the same
way, Max."

Max asked permission to take Miriam back to England, but
Miriam blushed and said that she was working hard at her studies
and could not miss the various lectures.

Her mother said, " Miriam works so hard, I sometimes think
she works too hard. She looks a little pale."

Stanislaus said, " Don't worry, Mama dear—that's only the worm
feeding on her damask cheek ! But she won't die of it——"

" Of what ? " Miriam demanded.

" Of love, beloved sister. ' Men have died and worms have
eaten them, but not for love '—that applies to the female of the
species as well."

" You talk complete rubbish, Stanislaus," she said with dignity.

Max said, " Next time I come over I shall take Stanislaus. I
shan't give you another chance, Miriam."

" I'll come like a shot," his brother assured him, and Max thought
what a success this handsome fellow would make, how Alice would
enjoy taking him about, showing him off. Vaguely he wondered
what Elfa would think of him.

He returned to England, making his parents promise that next
year they would visit him, and he would return with them.

His mother spoke to him one day when he wandered down into
the kitchen as he loved to do. She gave him a piece of cake fresh
from the oven and watched him eat it with affectionate eyes.

" I like to have my little boy again sometimes," she said. " Never
forget, dear Max, how deeply we love you. Every night I pray
to Our Lord to have you in His care, and each night I know your
father sends up the same prayer, though worded differently. I

never doubt that—like birds—those prayers find their way home—
and to the same nest. You're happy, Max ? "

" Why, yes, Mama. Particularly happy in this nice warm
kitchen with the heavenly smell of baking filling the air."

" I'm glad you're happy. The child of mine for whom I grieve
most is Jacob. To me he seems unhappy, as if his mind were
twisted, as if he was against everyone. He told me that he despised
me because I married a Jew. But Jacob is a Jew himself, Max !
Ah, well, it is all beyond me."

" Leave it like that—beyond you," Max said. " It's a phase,
it's a kind of idiotic slogan these disgruntled fools have adopted.
They'll tire of it."

He found that on his return to the warehouse Simons seemed
depressed. " Looks as if Mallett were right," he said, " trade isn't
what it was. Oh, we're *all right*, but the boom's over."

He called to see his father-in-law. Julius was gloomy.

" Oh, nothing actually to worry about," he insisted; " but
there are some queer stories floating about. I hear that Gillings
are very groggy and that Harwicks can't meet their obligations.
Harwicks ! Think of that—if it's true."

" Probably it's not true," Max said.

" Coster and Smurthwaites are closing. That's fact, not hearsay."

" Inevitable after a boom, it doesn't say that we're all going to
be ruined. Cheer up ! "

At Bury Street the Contessa greeted him warmly. Business
was good, it might not be *quite* so good as formerly, but they were
sufficiently busy. She showed him the order book, and it certainly
looked healthy enough.

" And how is Miss Elfa ? I hear that her paintings are still
selling quite well."

" She is well, I t'ank you. Busie, always busie. A leetle tired,
per'aps, I t'ink t'at we must tak' a small 'oliday. By the seaside, no ? "

" I don't know how much you would care for the seaside in
this country."

She shrugged her ample shoulders. " Ah, one must tak' what
offers."

Later in the week he saw Elfa. She looked, he thought, tired,
and seemed distrait. She assured him that she was really very
well, a little tired, too much work and not enough play.

He said, " I'm back now, darling, we'll find opportunities to
play."

She wished to know about the election, asked him questions
regarding policy and schemes which he could only answer vaguely.

Max was no politician, he was sufficiently immersed in his own business, his own affairs, to have little time for politics.

"A Labour Government means higher taxation," he told her.

"But they promise reduction of unemployment, no?"

"Parties promise anything before an election."

She asked questions regarding MacDonald, Snowden, Thomas—and Max was forced to admit that he knew very little of any of them. He knew that MacDonald was said to have a "golden voice", that Snowden had taken a strong line with the Communists and that Thomas was reputed to be astute.

Elfa laughed at him, "My dear ignorant Max! And the prospect of this possible new Government does not—excite you?"

"I don't think so. I'd rather the Tories got in, because—we've been taught, at all events—that they make for stabilization. I don't know. I expect that they're mostly the same. Doing the same things and calling them by different names."

Julius Berman was gloomy over the result of the election. He grumbled that the Labour Party would fling England into the arms of Russia, that the ministers would "line their own pockets" and that England's credit abroad would be weakened.

Alice said, "Of course, MacDonald's marvellous to *look* at, and he does say some beautiful things—in that nice Scottish voice. But some of them are so—common. I hear that both Thomas and that little man from the East End—Lansbury—drop their aitches."

"I don't know that it matters such a lot if they do," Max said.

"Darling, don't be stupid! How terrible for the King if he has to have them to dine!"

She still wanted him to go out with her to restaurants, tried to teach him the latest dances, and continually wanted him to play bridge. He was growing to hate the sight of a pack of cards. After her return from America Alice had tried to get their friends to play poker. Unfortunately, her own recollection of the precise rules were hazy, and her friends preferred to go back to the bridge which they knew and understood.

The Labour Government had a short reign, and again Max was forced to listen to discussions upon the merits and demerits of the parties, to arguments about some man called Campbell who edited a workers' paper. Unemployment was still considerable, but everyone had to admit that the figures had gone down since the Labour Government came into—place, though not, strictly speaking, into power.

Business was not good, orders had to be almost fought for, struggled for, angled for. Julius Berman gloomed and glowered, muttered curses against MacDonald and Philip Snowden; he seemed to nurse a personal grievance against both of them.

Then came another election, and the Conservatives were back. Julius rubbed his hands, Mallett cheered up considerably, Simons predicted a great rush of orders, and the little shop in Bury Street was really busy again.

Alice said, " Father appears to have taken a new lease of life since the new Government came in. Talks of a new boom——"

" Let's hope that he's right, we can do with one."

" Maxie dear, don't gloom, for heaven's sake ! "

Max thought, " Another few years and more than half my life will be gone. I must *do* something. I can't go on as I am doing. Would Alice divorce me ? I could give her grounds without dragging Elfa into it. I'd sell everything, get out, find somewhere quiet—get some rest. I'm tired of work and worry, planning and being civil to people who bore me unutterably."

The children were growing up, Julius had learned his alphabet, and Gweneth could talk—talk so that you knew what she said. He loved them, but he wasn't really important in their lives. How could he expect to be, when they only saw him for about an hour every evening ? He felt that his fits of depression only really lifted when he could snatch an hour to spend with Elfa. She seemed to —as he told her—smooth out the creases.

" I come to you," he said, " all creased and rumpled, and you send me away nicely ironed and tidy again. Only it doesn't last.'

In the early days of 1925 he went down to Bury Street and found her alone there. The day was wet and cold, and the little shop seemed delightfully warm and comfortable. Elfa came to greet him, her hands outstretched.

" My dear, I never expected you today. I'm all alone. I have sent Rosina and Teresa home, they had finished their work. Mama is at home with a little cold, and so I can make you some tea and we will talk."

He followed her into the small room at the back of the shop and laid his hands on her shoulders, leaning forward to kiss her.

" These are the snatches of real happiness that make everything else possible," he said. " To get away to you—to be alone with you—that is what is my *life*. The rest may be living—but it' not life."

She let him hold her close, kiss her cheeks, her lips, her eyelids —as he loved to do. He felt that she was happy to be with him, she was warm and kind, he knew that his passion communicated itself to her. Heard her long-drawn almost sensuous breathing as if she never wished his kisses and caresses to cease.

"Darling, my dearest love," he whispered, "don't let us go on like this. Life is running past us, the best years slipping away. Elfa, be brave. Let us make a life together, not a furtive business, not with some wretched little flat for occasional meeting—but always, always to be together—Elfa, you must, darling. This life is impossible."

She answered, her voice so low that he bent his head to catch her words, "I must t'ink. When you are wit' me, I see so clear that we cannot go on—t'is way. Only when you are away from me—it becomes so difficult. So many t'ings seem to crowd in on me. I grow afraid."

Max held her more closely. "Then the answer is that I must never go away from you. Elfa, the past—belonged to other people —the future can be ours. If we have sufficient courage."

"I know—oh yes, I know."

It was at that moment they heard a voice calling, a rather high-pitched voice, "Is no one 'ere? Elfa . . . 'oo is 'ere? 'As everyone gone a-way?"

Max felt Elfa slip out of his arms. She whispered, "Netta Bertoldi," and said clearly and rather loudly, "Ah, Signora Bertoldi! I am just about to make some tea—Mister Nollaire, please to light the gas-ring. So! In one moment it boils." She walked back into the shop, and Max—conscious that his hands were shaking and that in his heart he committed Netta Bertoldi to the nethermost hell—lit a cigarette and followed her.

Elfa was inspecting some work, praising it; she turned and held it out to Max as he entered. "Is it not beautiful? T'is is an order for Lady Mallingly. Netta, your work grows better—it would appear to be impossible, but it does—truly."

Max said, "It is a little masterpiece, Signora Bertoldi."

He knew that her bright dark eyes were watching them both, keenly and curiously. He hated her and her wretched *petit point*! She smiled her pleasure at their praise. Max thought, "She's only smiling with her lips—her eyes are darting everywhere like a lizard's."

"And you are 'ere a-lone, Elfa? I t'ought always Rosina and Teresa were 'ere? Oh, t'ey 'ave 'oliday, yes? And you—and Mister Nollaire are making tea—all so—w'at you call—*kosi*, like family, no? Yes, I shall like to 'ave one cup of tea. I shall sit down, I am tired. You, Elfa, look a little tired al-so."

Elfa smiled. "I'm not tired. I'll go and make the tea."

Signora Bertoldi turned to Max. "T'is is a fine girl t'is Elfa!"

"An exceedingly charming girl, Signora."

"I know all t'e family. In Italia t'ey are ver' important family."

"Indeed."

" 'Er cousin is *duca*! Almost—'ow you say?—*royale*. Duca
d'Ottaviano."

" Really, how interesting."

" At the beginning of Fascismo, all t'ings was deeficult. Now
—matters arrange themselves, I t'ink. Mooch better. Per'aps we
don' like mooch, but," she shrugged, " 'alf loafs is better t'an to
'ave no bread, no ? "

" Undoubtedly."

Elfa called, " The tea is—*pronto*! Come, Netta, come, Mister
Nollaire."

Max said, " I think that I must go. I only slipped in about that
new consignment of material—the lawn. I'll send the invoices down
in the morning. Well, just a cup—although I ought not to wait."

Netta Bertoldi said, " 'Ow mooch pleasanter are t'ings we ought
not to do t'an what is our duty, eh ? "

He smiled and felt his lips stiff. " Indubitably."

As he walked away up Bury Street he realized that his heart was
hammering, and that he felt breathless with a strange apprehension.
Had that wretched woman seen Elfa in his arms, or was she just
prepared to—hope for the worst ? That damned bell, how often
had he told them that it must be put right !

Because he was nervous and overstrung, the business of the
door bell began to assume enormous proportions, it obscured
everything else—whether Netta Bertoldi had seen Elfa in his
arms, whether she would take the story back to Contessa Lucca,
and what the results might be were all rapidly becoming of secondary
importance to the matter of the bell.

He had given orders a dozen times, there was a " handyman "
who could be sent for quite easily. Max was the owner of the
place—or virtually so—and his wishes were disregarded. So the
whole incident went on churning round and round in his brain,
until the whole world and its fate seemed to turn on the question
of a repair left undone to a shop bell.

Two days later the Contessa telephoned to ask if he could make
it convenient to go and see her at her house. Max knew that he
was conscious of a sudden chill. This was going to be the end !
Netta Bertoldi had taken her story to the Contessa, the result
was going to mean additional difficulties. He squared his shoulders,
contrived to keep his voice even, and replied, " Certainly, would
about four o'clock be convenient for you ? "

" Admirably, Mister Nollaire. I shall expect you then.
Good-bye."

Alice said, " Max, you look tired to death. I don't believe that
your trip to Germany did you a scrap of good. You want a real

holiday, not one of those ' combining business with pleasure '—
because that only means work all the time. Take a real holiday,
Maxie."

He shook his head. " Impossible, my dear. Things aren't too
good. It's going to be heavy going for a long time, I'm afraid.
The boom's over."

She laughed, " Darling, don't talk as if bankruptcy stared us
in the face ! It's not like you to panic ! "

" A good many people are going to have to face bankruptcy in
the near future. If some of us manage to get out, it will be more
by good luck than anything else."

" Then we shall have that beastly MacDonald to thank for it!
He's good-looking I admit, but I hate that common Labour crowd !
Why we can't have gentlemen to run the country I can't imagine."

Max shrugged himself into his coat. " Darling, don't talk rot.
Plenty of them are damned astute fellows."

All day the thought of his impending interview with the Contessa
remained in his mind; he was irritable at the warehouse, furious
over a delay in delivery, he snarled at Simons and was conscious
that when he announced that he was going out and would in all
probability not be back until the next morning there was a distinct
sense of relief in the place. As he drove to Wellington Road he
tried to think out some plan, to adjust his thoughts, to decide
how much this wretched old woman knew, how much he should
deny or admit.

The Contessa greeted him with elaborate courtesy. She was
not at the shop because she had been doing some work at home.
Elfa was there. Netta Bertoldi was going in to help her, but,
" Business is not—'ow do you call ?—br-risk, it is slow, and Elfa
can contrive ver' well."

She offered him coffee, and he drank it hoping that it might
steady his nerves. It was, as always, admirable.

" You wished to see me, Contessa ? Business ? " Max asked as
he set down his cup.

" Ah, indeed, and rat'er a sad business, Mister Nollaire. Our
ass-ociation 'as been so pleasant, always it will remain wiz me as
a—'appy memory. But now, alas, it 'as to come to an end. It
will appear t'at my nephew—the Duc of Ottaviano—'as made
arrange-ments in some way wiz t'ese Fascist monstairs. I myself
do not completely compr'end, but Ottaviano is a ver' noble per-son,
it is impossible for him to do anysing which is not correct, you
understand.

" He is again in his *castello*." She closed her eyes and bunching
the tips of her fingers, kissed them lightly as if in esctasy. " Oh,

w'at a place t'is ees ! 'Ow I wish that I might show you the gardens ! The fountains, the statues, t'ere are pictures of a magnificence—a Leonardo, a Tiepolo, at least t'ree Veronese. . . ."

Max said, " I am sure that it is a wonderful place, Contessa."

" Wonder-ful indeed. Also t'ere is 'is palace at Venice on the Grand Canal—the glass is beyond belief ! The glass of Murano. In Roma 'e 'as a fine 'ouse, a palace certainly, the staircase alone is to be marvelled at. In the mountains—ah, t'ere he 'as a beautiful place for summer time, wit' very much land, for sporting, you understand. The Duc is great sport-man."

" Really."

Again she raised her hands as if lost in admiration for the sporting proclivities of her nephew.

" Indeed it is so ! 'E rode at your Olympia—'ow long ago ? I forget, all papers were filled with admir-ation for 'im. Now 'e finds 'imself alone, for 'is mother—my beloved sister—is dead for t'ree years."

She crossed herself reverently, then continued with complete cheerfulness. " 'E write to me : ' *Carissima Zia* '—my dearest aunt —' no one can take the place of my adored mother, but you can make my life less lonely. Please to come with great quickness, you and my dear cousin Elfa.' It was a beautiful letter, Mister Nollaire."

Max said, " I am sure of it, Contessa. And when do you wish to go and take up residence in one—or more—of these magnificent residences ? "

" So soon as we can make ready all our *bauli*—boxes for travelment. The quicker the better it is, Mister Nollaire—you agree ? "

For the first time he heard the change in her voice, almost as if she challenged him. The smoothness had gone, and he felt that she had taken the buttons off the foils. Her eyes met his, those great dark, inscrutable eyes ; he watched her steadily, his face expressionless.

She continued, " You 'ave been very indiscreet, Mister Nollaire, I t'ink you ad-mit t'at, no ? "

" I admit nothing, Contessa."

" Do you deny t'at you 'ave 'ad an—*affaire* with my daughter ? "

" I deny nothing."

She shrugged her shoulders. " It is fortunate t'at my good friend Signora Bertoldi is a person of gr-great discretion, for it would be a disaster if any mention of t'is foolishness should reach the ears of the Duc. 'E and my daughter 'ave been under a *promessa di matriomonio*—an understanding, if you comprehend me—for

many years. For me—t'is has been a 'eavy and terrible blow—to
be told t'at my daughter——"

Max said, "Listen, and let me speak. I am in love with your
daughter. I have been—almost since the first time I met her. I
am perfectly ready to give my wife grounds for divorce, and at
the earliest possible moment to marry your daughter. That is
what I wish most sincerely and truly. I am not a poor man, I
can give your daughter all the comforts she needs. How can you
imagine that—loving me, and she does love me as I love her—
she will ever consent to marry this cousin? I don't care how rich
he is, I don't care how important, those things will not count
with Elfa."

She looked at him, her eyes wide with astonishment.

"Mister Nollaire—'ave you gone mad, please? Divorce—my
daughter is a Catholic, there is and never can be no divorce in our
Church. My daughter to marry—even if you were free—a merchant
and a Jew! I am sure you are honest, sincere, you 'ave shown
kindness to us, but—my good Mister Nollaire, my daughter is
aristocrat! The Ottavianos are great family. My own family
are noble also. No, you speak like a wild per-son. I 'ope we shall
leave England in two, t'ree, days and t'ere must be no at-tempt
to write to my daughter. That I forbid!"

Max felt the blood pounding at his temples, he wondered if
he could keep his voice steady, he knew that his hands were
shaking.

"I have a right—remember that, Contessa, a *right*—to see and
talk with your daughter before she leaves England. I shall ask
her if she will marry me—when I am free—Catholic Church or
no Catholic Church. If she decides to return to Italy——"

The old woman retorted, "*If* she decides! Please, t'ere is
no—if!"

"When can I see your daughter?" Max persisted.

"I have said that I do not think it is wise, not to be recom-
mended."

"And I say, Contessa, that with or without your permission I
will see your daughter before she leaves England. Please—without
any disrespect, take that as quite definite."

All through the interview Max had felt that he was living
through a dream, but a dream so fantastic that he could never
have imagined anything which bore the slightest resemblance to
it. Here in this small and rather overcrowded room he sat facing
the indomitable old woman with her keen dark eyes and her
tremendous personality. Her age did not appear to affect her in
the least; she was steel, iron, wire and whipcord. All her life—

until a system directed by a character of even greater strength than her own had driven her from her native land—she had organized and directed. Her ambitions had lain dormant, she had worked in a shop—and worked exceedingly hard, because that was part of her creed, to do everything as well as possible—now her old life was open to her again, and everything else sank into insignificance.

She sat staring at Max, then said suddenly, almost explosively, " Very well, I will telephone to my daughter to return home immediately. She can be here in a few moments."

" I have my car. I can go and fetch her."

The Contessa raised a thin yellow hand. " Pray do not'ing of the kind. I prefaire that she come 'ere. Remember t'at I am tr-rusting you, Mister Nollaire, when I leave you al-one with my daughter."

Max knew that his irritability overcame him. He had remained calm, temperate, but this last injunction was too much for him.

" I don't know what the devil you are trying to imply," he said. " I can only assure you that such a hint, suggestion, is an insult to your daughter and to me."

She rose, shrugging her shoulders. " Oh, I don't know—well, I shall telephone to my daughter. So I make farewell, Mister Nollaire. You will find all business matters in ordair." She resumed her air of social intercourse. " T'is has been a str-range time for us, Mister Nollaire, a time of interest. I must tell you 'ow you were—what do you say ?—a port in a tempest. I am gr-rateful. So—we shall say ' good-bye ', no ? "

He bowed. " Good-bye, Contessa."

Max closed the door behind her, heard her voice screaming— all these foreigners appeared to scream on the telephone—to Elfa. He sat down, and buried his face in his hands. It was over, finished, done with. Elfa would go out of his life, he would fade into being a vague memory. Their association had not always been easy, there had been times when he had suffered from an acute sense of frustration, when he had longed with a desperate intensity to make their love complete in every possible way. Slowly he had come to accept Elfa's decision; he had been grateful for her companionship; he had loved her beauty, and his meetings with her had been like sudden breaks in a sky where clouds are lowering and dark.

The old woman—detestable though he found her—was right. He could not expect Elfa to wait until he rearranged his whole life, until Alice divorced him. In addition, the Contessa was right when she said that they belonged to different worlds. They were bred under different traditions, they had been accustomed to

lives which bore little or no similarity. Circumstances had flung
Elfa into his environment, and the turn of the wheel would
remove her from it—for ever.

What his life would be like without her Max scarcely dared
imagine.

Life was going to be difficult, markets were falling, firms he
had always regarded as being " as safe as the Bank of England "
were, to say the least of it, tottering. There were rumours that
England would go off the gold standard. Daniel wrote to him of
a slump in America. True, Daniel made light of it all, but Max
understood his brother and realized that things with Daniel
were in a parlous state. Life had not always been easy; now—
as Max saw it—it was likely to be almost insuperably difficult. In
Germany, too, things were coming to a head. There was a
sinister underground stir, a kind of bubbling as if the world
waited for the great simmering, stinking pot to boil over.

Things had been difficult before, not insuperably difficult but
bringing plenty of worry and a certain amount of apprehension.
Only, until now he had been able to talk to Elfa, had been able
from time to time to feel her arms round him, her kisses on his
cheeks, and to hear her voice say softly, " Dear, Max be br-rave,
all will come r-right. Cour-rage, dear, dear Max. So precious, so
dear—ah, my loved one, what you mean to me ! "

That was over . . . he had his children, and he loved them
both ; he had Alice, and he possessed a great admiration for her,
an admiration which amounted to deep affection, but with Elfa's
going the one intimate relationship in his life would go. He would
be cast for certain rôles—to the children a kind, amusing, affectionate father who generally had some sweets in his pocket; to
Alice the successful man of business, able to dress well, to take
her to dine at expensive restaurants and to pay the household
bills without question or protest.

The small gifts which were all that Elfa had allowed him to
give her would seem childish and ridiculous to Alice—a bunch of
early violets . . . " Dear Max, how nice of you, where on earth
shall I put them ? " Small intimate dinners at some little-known
restaurant, carefully planned. Alice would stare round such
places and comment, " It's sweet, Maxie, but . . . I mean . . .
well, why come *here* ? "

He lifted his head and sighed, felt that a weight lay on his
shoulders. He heard a taxi drive up, rose and knew that his heart
missed a beat. This was—the last time. Standing very upright,
he waited.

EIGHT

MAX held his breath as the door opened and Elfa came into the room. She was pale, and without speaking held out her hands to him. He took them and drew her into his arms. She lay there quiescent and tranquil, then gently slipped out of his embrace and stood watching him.

" You have talked with mama ? "

He nodded. " Yes, I've heard everything. There is no need for you to explain anything. Only let me tell you what I am ready, anxious, to do. I can give my wife grounds for divorce; once that is through—finished—we can be married. I can't offer you half a dozen houses, but I can offer you all the love of which I am capable, tenderness, and I have the ability to work hard—you should have—everything."

She watched him, her beautiful eyes very steady and tender, then shook her head.

" Max, my dear, my dearest dear, it is not possible. First, I am, as you know, Catholic. Per'aps not very good Catholic, but—t'ere it is. We have no divorce. You have a wife, a beautiful home, two nice children—'ow can you t'ink I could let you leave be'ind you all that—even if it were possible ? "

" Then," he said heavily, " this is the end ? "

" Always we 'ave memories, Max."

" They won't help much, my dear."

" They can help, dear." She smiled. " They will *have* to help me."

" When you're a duchess, with half a dozen houses, and——"

She laid her hand on his shoulder. " Don't speak t'at way, my dear. It is all too difficult. If I cannot be with you—and I cannot— then w'at does it concern us with whom I shall be ? My cousin Nino is not bad—after you, I shall find him stupid; he will not laugh as you do for silly t'ings, he will not make charming, small present . . . he is very—'ow you say ?—elaborate. But, dear, dear Max," she came nearer and put her arm round his shoulders, " not'ing and no one can tak' from us w'at we have had. T'ose t'ings are ours, for always, for ever."

" If only—if only . . ."

She laid her cheek against his. " I know, you t'ink—if only I had been your mistress *in fact*, not only in my heart ! You r-regret t'is so much. If t'is means so much, then if it had existed it would have made our parting more difficult. You t'ink I am so cold, fr-rigid; no, dear one, many, many times I have found it so difficult; not alone because I am a ver' passionate woman, but it has been so difficult to say no to you, who I love so much. T'ere, come and sit down near me, let me talk to you. Put your arms round me, so ! It has to me been so beautiful, the love, brightness, companionship. I once tr-ried to explain to you—about that flat. No ! It was impossible. It would have been like putting dirty water into a vase made by Cellini himself. Sacrilegious. I have held our love against my 'eart as I might have held a child of yours—trying always to keep it safe, unharmed, secure, beautiful. Dear Max, please try to understand . . ."

He twisted round so that he could stare into her eyes. "This cousin—this duke, you'll love him ? "

" My dear, nevaire as I love you. The rest—what does it matter ? *Fa niente !* Life comes, life uses us, circumstances catch us. Each one has a secret life, like a garden. Wit' high walls and a closed gate, for which only we—each one has the key. T'ere in t'at garden, my be-loved Max, I shall walk wit' you sometimes. Dar-rling, t'is all too difficult for us. Once, take me in your arms, hold me tightly, make me feel t'at nevaire shall I forget—always be able to remember."

He held her to him, whispered words which tried to convey his love to her; she clung to him, and he realized that she was crying—unrestrainedly. He said, " Elfa, it's not too late. Let's leave it all. Take trains, boats and get away—somewhere, any-where, if only we can be together."

She raised her head, he saw the tears streaming down her cheeks.

" My dear, it is not possible. In t'ese days of passports, of permissions, of business—life is too complicated, my dar-rling. You must go. My mother is waiting, listening, wondering. If we have done ver' wrong, *possibile* God will forgive us, because we 'ave made sacrifice. My love goes wit' you, my dear love, for always. Not today, not tomorrow—but always."

Max said, almost gruffly, " Let me wipe your tears away. There ! Don't let your mother know that you have been crying. Good-bye, my love, my wonderful Elfa." He kissed her, quietly and without passion, then held her at arms' length and looked at her as if he tried to make a mental picture which would never fade. "*Shalom.*"

She said, " Max—dear Max—go with God."

Without turning to look at her again, he walked out of the room, closing the door very softly behind him.

Three days later Signora Bertoldi told him, when he visited the shop in Bury Street, that the Contessa and her daughter had left that morning. She was voluble, recounting at great length the amount of luggage which they had taken, the precautions which the Duke had taken for the comfort of their journey to Milano. She also announced with a certain satisfaction that she and her sister were leaving for Italy very soon.

Max said, " That is something of a relief, signora, for I wish to close this establishment. The takings are not sufficient to reimburse me."

She flung up her hands and protested that this was a disaster. Mister Nollaire had always been so kind, so good, so considerate, it was terrible that his ventures should not prove profitable.

Max said stiffly, " The fault does not lie with my kind assistants. They have always given me work which was perfect, and I can never be sufficiently grateful. Times—I speak financially—are difficult, and I cannot afford to lose money. I trust that in closing the shop I shall not cause any—er—inconvenience to you or your kind and skilful friends."

She assured him that he must not disturb himself. Matters, she said, in Italy, had to a great extent " arranged themselves "; she would speak to the rest of what she called, smiling broadly, " our leetle colonie ".

Max walked away, thinking, " Good. That door's shut, or will be damned soon."

Months dragged on. Everywhere he heard stories of firms who could not meet their liabilities, firms—long regarded as prosperous—who were now known to be " tottering ". A spirit of unrest was abroad, a sense of uncertainty. His own business was doing sufficiently well, but it was an effort to obtain each order. No longer people came begging to hear of the latest importations; customers bought, as Simons said, " cagey, with an eye all the time on the price list."

Julius Berman, growing hollow-eyed and haggard, said, " Look, Maxie, I'm getting out. I've made enough to live on— live well. The bottom's dropped out of the whole market. Who wants ' fancies ' in these days ? It's taking them all their time to buy necessities. Half my stuff—at the moment—is no more than *junk*. I've my eye on a place at Croydon, bit of ground, and if things pick up I might start again—in a small way. I'm getting out while the going's good."

Max said, " The going isn't good, that's the trouble. I'm hanging on."

If matters were bad in London, all over Britain, it was evident that they were worse in America. Max thought that you could sense the tenseness in the commercial atmosphere. He had never been through such a time of mental unrest in his life. Elfa had vanished out of his life, and he missed her companionship

terribly; at night he lay awake thinking of her, speculating and
wondering, falling asleep when day was breaking, to wake again
heavy-eyed and dreading the new worries which the day might
bring. He confided to Alice some of the difficulties which beset
him. She was sympathetic, but confident that " everything will
be all right. This is just a passing phase. I've known you depressed
like this before, Maxie."

" We must try to cut down on everything," he insisted. " Your
father realizes the gravity of the whole situation, he's getting out.
I want to hang on—if it's possible."

That startled her; she stared at him, her eyes wide in astonishment. " You don't mean that—that your business might—fail ! "

" My dear, the way things are going, anything might happen."

" What about your father ? "

" I fancy things are pretty difficult there."

" And your brother in America ? "

" I should think that he's standing in the breadline from what
I can gather."

" I'll economize all I can, Maxie, but it's difficult, you know."

She tried and tried hard, but Max realized that such trivial
economies as she was able to effect made very little—if any—
difference in the general state of his affairs. Finally, when he found
her " doing the books ", a frown puckering her smooth forehead,
he said gruffly, " Don't worry yourself about the wretched accounts.
If we're going to smash—well, we might as well be hung for a
sheep as a lamb."

Early in 1929 he began to think that the worst of the depression had passed, began to look for small and hopeful increases in
trade, and almost fearfully allowed himself to believe that the
worst was over.

Daniel wrote that " things are looking up ", and added that
they'd had a rough passage, and although it would take a lot of
hard work before they could count on being into smooth water,
yet the skies did seem a little brighter. Next year, if it were possible,
he planned to visit Europe.

Max thought, " I'll go to Germany, too. It's so long since I
saw them. I've lost count of time during this awful depression."
On the morning of his birthday he stared at his face as he shaved,
and realized that the years had taken their toll of him. He was
thinner than he had ever been, his cheeks were hollow, making
shaving additionally difficult. There were pouches beneath his eyes,
new lines engraved at the corners, his hair was rapidly turning grey.

He thought, " She'd scarcely know me—if she met me now. I
wonder where she is, if she ever wonders how I am, where I am,

if I've managed to survive these lean years ? " And with the thought of Elfa de Lucca came the old longing for her, the sense of desolation that he was no longer able to hear her voice, watch her walking towards him—so slim, so poised, so incredibly lovely.

When he went into his wife's room to bid her good morning Alice was sitting up in bed, her pillows stacked behind her, looking particularly cheerful and charming. She was an attractive woman, and even now when she was nearing forty retained practically all her good looks.

" Happy birthday, Maxie—and here's a present for a good boy."

He opened the small parcel, thanked her, assuring her that he had been on the point of buying himself a new fountain pen, but that this one was far superior to anything he had planned to buy.

" I'm so glad, Maxie—can you be home in good time ? I've some people coming to dinner. Some Americans I met when I was in New York—nice people, you'll like them. I meant to tell you last night, but I forgot."

" I'll be home in good time."

He came home early, wished that he felt less tired, " played out ", not in the mood to entertain guests and make himself pleasant. They were pleasant enough people, Alice's American friends; Mr. and Mrs. Harry Crown, their daughter Marybell, and a tall, angular man called Lewis Carrick. The dinner was excellent, and it appeared that both the Crowns were great talkers, and the conversation needed no stimulation from Max Noller. He leaned back in his chair, content to listen to Mrs. Crown's account of the " slump ". He let his eyes wander round the table, wondering if his own daughter would grow up to be as pretty and as confident as Marybell Crown; what Crown did for a living—he must make plenty of money to allow his wife to dress like that. The other man, Carrick, what was he ? He wasn't a bad-looking fellow, bit gaunt, and with a nose that looked as if it might have been broken sometime. Good eyes, and a firm chin with a cleft in it. As Max watched him, he saw Carrick's eyes turn towards Alice, saw Alice's lips part in a small but strangely intimate smile, saw something flicker for a moment in her eyes, then both the smile and the flicker died, and she turned to speak to Harry Crown.

Max could not have said how he knew, in what exact way the realization came to him, but he both knew and realized that at some time Carrick and his wife had been lovers. The look which Alice had given Carrick seemed to convey that there existed a secret between them, a secret known only to themselves; it was as if they had silently admitted that they shared memories—

memories which were possibly of a time long past and over, but which still held a charm for them both.

Max listened to Mrs. Crown's vivacious chatter, his mind working, he felt, in two distinct halves; one which heard every word she said and which worked sufficiently smoothly to allow him to make suitable replies, the other which turned back to Alice and Carrick. He did not feel either outraged or shocked, his relationship with Alice had been always temperate, and now they had even ceased to share a room. He had been sleeping badly, and had often sat up until the small hours working at accounts, trying to make things seem a little less black.

Alice must have met Carrick in America. Max wondered if she had seen him since, or was this their first meeting since she left New York? Queer to think that in all probability Alice " belonged " to this stranger more than she did to him; strange, but not particularly disturbing. He felt a vague sense of annoyance that Elfa should have been so circumspect all the time they had loved each other. If Elfa had known, if he had known about Alice—would it have made any difference? Anyway, what did it matter now? That was all over, finished, done with.

" Don't stay down here too long," Alice was saying. " Mr. Carrick will play for us. How long is it since I heard you play the piano ? "

Carrick said, " Why, not since that time you were in New York, Mrs. Noller—a long time ago."

Again Max saw that queer intimate glance flash between them, and again he thought, " I'm right ! Well, I hope they were happy."

Crown said, " I must say, Noller, this port is some of the finest I've ever tasted—it's re-markable."

" A present from my wife's father. You met him in New York ? "

" Why, yes, we did quite a little business together. We're planning to run down to see him at—where is it ?—Croydon. Yes, grand old fellow. We liked him a lot, eh, Lewis ? "

" We certainly did. If I may say so, Noller, your wife doesn't look a day older. She tells me that your son is going to boarding school in the summer. Doesn't seem possible."

Crown gave it as his opinion that time certainly did fly.

When they had gone, Alice said, " Nice people, aren't they ? "

" Very. That man Carrick plays wonderfully."

" He's practically a professional pianist," she said. " Has a beautiful *appartement*, I imagine that he's very wealthy. He's aged a lot, I think."

" He told me that you didn't look a day older," Max said.

"Maxie dear, Lewis Carrick says those things almost automatically."

He didn't attempt to persuade her to talk of Carrick, he didn't want to know. The whole thing was over, and to dig and delve into the past could serve no good purpose. He might have satisfied his curiosity, if he had felt any curiosity to satisfy. He hadn't. She kissed him good night, as she always did, warmly and affectionately. As Max fell asleep he wondered if he ought, by all conventional standards, to have felt angry and outraged.

During the days which followed he knew that Alice went about a good deal with the Americans, lunched and dined with them, and seemed to be enjoying herself. Then they sailed for America, and the whole incident faded from Max's memory. He was very busy, immersed in trying to get his business back to its old state; he was no longer worried about Daniel, but there were times when letters from his brother Stanislaus made him definitely uneasy. One storm might have blown over, but Max felt that another—perhaps a much greater one—was blowing up from another quarter.

In the New Year he went over to Germany. Daniel was to join him there, and Max looked forward with an excited expectancy to meeting his brother again. He found both his father and mother looking older; there was, he felt, hanging round them a nervous tension. They were cheerful, too cheerful he felt, they seemed to him to be "putting on an act". His father confided to him that his mother had been ill, and the specialist had told him in private that her heart was in a very bad state.

"There must be no shocks, no disturbances in her life," Isaac said. Again and again he repeated, "Tranquillity is necessary. How can I guarantee that for my beloved wife ! She has suffered with Daniel in his fight against adversity, she has suffered because Miriam lost her chance of what she imagined might be happiness —because the young man would not marry a Jewish girl. She suffers continually because of Jacob—ah, that is perhaps the worst blow of all—Jacob. He is the friend of men who are monsters, who swear openly that they will rid Germany of the Jews—how, in what way, they admit they do not care. And my son, your mother's son, is one of them. He is a close friend of a man named Streicher, who boasts that one day he will be known as ' The Jew-baiter '. How can I find peace for your dear mother, Max ? "

"Bring her to live in England. Sell your business, leave Germany behind you for good. Stanislaus can find work, Miriam will find happiness, you with my mother will find peace and tranquillity," Max said.

Isaac shook his head. "I don't know. It is very difficult."

Stanislaus was away when Max arrived, he was doing some travelling for the firm; everywhere he went, Mrs Noller told Max, he was a success. His quite remarkable good looks, his charming manners, were talismans, keys which seemed to open all doors to him.

"He has the goodwill of everyone," she said.

Daniel arrived, by far the tallest and most heavily built of all the family; his shoulders were immense, his hands, as he said himself, "like hams". His face was ruddy and his expression one of complete good temper. He sat talking to Max long into the night.

"That slump has been—still is—quite—something," he said. "Every day you heard of some big business tumbling down. Every day fewer and fewer people came into the shop, and those who came spent less and less money. From dollars you came to be thankful to take cents. My poor old father-in-law, he couldn't take it. He'd worked hard, worked dead honest, and he saw his business dwindling to nothing. I kept it quiet, my wife—say, Max, she's a woman if you like, got the courage of a lion!—still don't know what happened. The poor old boy—well, he got out, took a jump in the dark. I guess he threw himself out of a window on the fourth floor. I managed to make out it was an accident. Poor old feller, —not so old either, only sixty.

"We started to try to carry on the business. Gosh, Max, there *was* no business. I've known times when we've been hard put to manage to give the little girl—gee, she's as pretty as a picture, that kid!—enough to eat. What Lena and I lived on—I hate to think! Stock—why, I'd no money to buy stock, so I used to dress the shelves to look like they were full, while actually there'd be one line of cans and not a thing behind them! Rosie came in one day—mind, it's not a swell neighbourhood where we live, mostly small shops kept by small people—it was something at the school next day, I forgot what—Thanksgiving or Independence Day, I'd not remember. She'd seen a little dress in a window, just a rather scruffy cotton thing, but it had taken her eye. How she wanted that dress for this jamboree at the school!

"I looked at Lena, Lena looked at me; darn it, we'd got about half a dollar between us. Rosie kind o' cuddled up to me. 'I can have it, Pop, can't I?' I said what would it cost, because I'd just loaned the Ford works a coupla million dollars to keep them going, and I was a bit short and the banks 'ud be closed in the morning on account of the holiday? The kid said, 'It's only a dollar, Pop, that's all.' I thought how, when times had been good, neither Lena nor I'd have let Rosie wear a dress that didn't cost

five or six or seven dollars. Lena was very nearly crying. Rosie
said, ' It's in the window at Mheerbeyers—oh, Mom, it's so cute ! '
Mheerbeyers—a nasty, lousy kind o' shop, mostly junk !

" I winked at Lena, said, ' Guess I'd better go and take a look
at it, eh ? Just wait until I come back.' I had a pair of cuff-links,
just about all we hadn't sold. Not awfully good they weren't."
He threw back his head and laughed. " Come to that, Max, Jacob
gave them to me when I was twenty-one, so you can guess they'd
not cost a fortune. I got a dollar and a half on them, got the
dress—boy, it was the trashiest thing !—and took it home. With
the half dollar we managed to make a little feast for the next day.
To see Lena going out with that half dollar next day you'd have
thought she was Mrs. Rothschild going out to fix a banquet for a
hundred guests at the Waldorf Astoria !

" Well, Max, slowly—so slowly it was painful, the tide began
to turn. Not running very swift, but moving in the right direction.
I dared scarcely believe it, kind of held my breath when I had
four customers in the shop all in one morning ! I took the takings
to Lena, shouting, ' Listen, we're on the up and up ! I've taken
four dollars thirty this morning ! ' Poor old Lena just burst out
crying. We're not on Easy Street, I have my doubts if we ever
will be. I doubt too if things will ever be like what they were
once; but—it's a great country, and you can't keep a squirrel on
the ground. No use of talking about ' easy money ', there ain't
any ' easy money ' to be had, it's all got to be sweated for. My
place is doing nicely, I can say that. It's not a big swell place, but
folks know that Henniker's—yep, I kept the old man's name—
can be relied on. We got a nice little *appartement* above, three
bedrooms, a parlour, kitchen and a fine bathroom. I got a radio
and—well, I've got pretty well all that it takes. Maybe next year
I'll get me an automobile. We keep the shop clean as a new pin,
everything shines ! I've come over to see the old folks, and you,
Max, came over tourist class and first rate it was. Take it all in
all"—Daniel leaned back in his chair, a beaming smile on his
broad, rather plain face—" I reckon I'm a lucky guy. I'm an
American, and darned proud of it ! Lots of folks think they're
just playboys, lots of folks imagine that America's filled with
financiers blown up with riches. Folks say, ' They're a young race.'
Sure they are a young race, and they'll take particular care they're
not going to copy all the mistakes of the old races ! No, sir !

" They like a good time, they're good spenders; but deep
down, Max, they can be tough, darned tough. A good kind of
toughness, too, the kind that doesn't know when it's licked.
Germans, when they're licked—like we licked 'em in '18—just

sit back on their fannies and say, ' We were licked ? Not on your
life. We've been badly done by, we've had a rotten deal, we're
the little boys that nobody loves—barring ourselves. We love
ourselves plenty and then some.' Americans say, ' Gosh, that was
a nasty right hook ! Had me down on the canvas for a count of
seven, but—gosh, here I come back on my feet before they can
count me out ! Now take that and that, and there's plenty more
where they came from.' See what I'm getting at, Max ? " He
started, sat bolt upright in his chair, listening intently. " Say,
Max, who's this ? Pop and mom are in bed hours ago ; so's Truda
and Miriam."

They heard the front door open, heard it closed again very
carefully; there were stealthy steps in the hall, and as Max sprang
to his feet the door opened and Stanislaus walked in.

Max said, " Why, Stan, where have you come from ? God,
what's happened to you ? "

Stanislaus blinked his eyes, looked from Max to Daniel as if
he were half dazed. Then he smiled, " Hello, both of you. This is
nice. Nicer still if you'd have the decency, either of you, to give
me a drink."

Daniel said, " Sure, I'll fix one. For heaven's sake, where've
you been ? "

Stanislaus lowered himself in a chair. His clothes were dis-
ordered, his hair hung over his forehead, one eye was blackened
and his lower lip was cut and swollen.

He said, " Thanks, Daniel—ah, that tastes good ! I've come
from Leipzig. In that delectable town I had a few words with some
gentlemen who have a profound dislike for the whole of our race.
Max—it's started ! The cauldrons are all bubbling and boiling in
hell's kitchen, the new era is on the point of being launched upon
the world. Thanks, Max, I will have another, then I'll tell you."

Under the discolourations, the blood which marked his cheeks,
Max saw that his face was white, his eyes bloodshot. He handed
him the second drink and waited. Daniel moved impatiently.
" Get cracking, Stan."

" I was in Leipzig, nice town, supposed to have the finest
station in Europe. Well, something's happened to that town. I
heard things, very nasty things indeed. I didn't actually believe
them. Then I saw notices on the windows of restaurants : ' Jews
keep out ', ' Jews forbidden to eat here ', ' Jews not wanted ', and
so forth. Gave you a queer feeling. A kind of cold shudder. I
thought, ' It's here, it's started ! ' "

Max said, " And I imagine that you—very promptly—entered
one of those restaurants, eh ? "

Daniel said, " You bet he did, so would you have done ! Go on, Stan boy."

Stanislaus smiled, then said, " Ouch, that hurt ! My face is stiff, damn it ! Yes, I walked in. Everyone was very civil, one or two quite nice-looking girls stared at me. Blue eyes, fair hair, pink cheeks—they didn't imagine that I was a Jew. I ate my dinner, remarkably good one too. Then the real amusement began. The doors opened and in came a small crowd of—men, youths, wearing brown shirts—one had a green one on, I'd never seen that before. They began to question the people sitting at the tables. The girls—tarts, I imagine—sat back and giggled.

" 'Are you a filthy Jew swine ? ' Two middle-aged men and a very old man admitted that they were Jews; they were forced to show their papers and practically kicked out. Pretty roughly too. The girls went on giggling. The old man got a kick on the backside that sent him spinning into the street, landing on his hands and knees on the pavement. I waited.

" Then another man came in, tall, thin, wearing a rather dirty raincoat with the belt far too tight. He was pale-faced, a long pale face, and a jaw set like a trap. He stood near the door, watching. I realized that he was the boss of this charming outfit. More . . ." He leaned forward and stared at them both, his eyes filled with horror. " More, I recognized him. He didn't see me, he was too busy watching them hustle out an elderly man and woman; as he heard the things they called them—these charming young Germans—his mouth twisted into a smile. I'd seen that smile so often, seen it all my life . . ."

Max half started from his chair. " Great God ! It wasn't—Stan, you don't mean it ! "

Stanislaus nodded. " It was our estimable brother Jacob."

Daniel said, " May God damn him ! "

Stanislaus answered equably. " I have no doubt that He will do so. They continued to make their rounds, asking questions, offering insults. When they reached me they asked if I lived in Leipzig. I said no, I was only there on business. I said it very pleasantly, very politely, you understand, and was rewarded by brilliant smiles from the two tarts. They were preparing to pass on when I said, ' Have you no questions to ask me, pray ? '

" One fellow with a scarlet jowl and a face like a pig laughed and said, ' If you were a filthy swine of a Jew, we'd ask you questions,' and laughed—quite a friendly laugh.

" I said, ' Excuse me, a mistake. I am a Jew—but not a filthy swine of a Jew. He '—and I pointed to Jacob— ' is both, and many other things.'

" He started forward at the sound of my voice, shouting,
' This man is a pig of a Jew, fling him out ! He pollutes the whole
place ! ' That was when it began. They rushed at me, but I am
very quick and in good training. I hit two of them—and as you
see they hit me. Tables were knocked over, the tarts screamed,
the men shouted. Only Jacob remained apart, cold, detached.
Finally I forced my way into the street—and ran ! "

Daniel pulled out his handkerchief and mopped his forehead.
" Jeze," he said, " Jacob ! I always disliked him, a low-down
rat."

Max asked, " Yes, and then . . . ? "

" To the station. I saw a goods train just about ready to steam
out. The driver was in the cab—big, broad-shouldered fellow. He
looked down at me, grinned and said, ' Been in trouble ? ' I
nodded. ' Pretty bad trouble too. I want to get away. Where are
you bound for ? ' He looked at me, frowned, then asked, ' Those
bastards at it again ? God damn them ! They'll let hell loose in
this country before they've finished. I'm bound for Berlin. Jump
in, plenty of places to hide in the trucks. Look sharp.' I ran
back down the train, found a truck loaded with bales of wool—it
felt like wool, covered with a tarpaulin. Hauled myself up, and
here I am. Gosh, the longest journey I ever took in my life ! The
driver came along when we stopped, whistling. I whistled back.
He brought me some bread and sausage . . ."—Stanislaus laughed
—" may have been pork, I'd no idea; and later a bottle of beer. I
went with him to an all-night café when we got here, place used by
railway men. He told me things. In Leipzig—listen to this—over
thirty Jews have been beaten up and over twenty killed, he said,
' already, mind you—already ! ' That ' already ' is significant, eh ? "

Max went to the kitchen, brought back warm water in a bowl
and a clean towel. Stanislaus bathed his face and smoothed his
hair. Max took back the bowl and returned with bread and meat.
Stanislaus ate it as if he were half famished. Then the three
brothers sat and talked. They agreed that nothing must be said
to their father or mother. If they asked questions Max must make
up some lie to meet the case. Max stipulated that if anyone came
to see Stanislaus, if anyone asked him questions as to where he
had been or mentioned his brother Jacob, he was to assume a
complete ignorance. He had never been to Leipzig, he knew
nothing of his brother's whereabouts, he had not set eyes on
Jacob for months.

It was Daniel who made the suggestion which satisfied Max.

" See, why not take Stan over to England with you, Max ?
Maybe Miriam could go along too. They've not been there for I

dunno how long. Get Stan away until this bit of bother and
devilment has blown over."

So Max returned to England, taking with him his sister and
brother. The two young people charmed everyone. Miriam was
so lovely and Stanislaus so handsome that they won all hearts.
Alice was only too glad to take them out, and slowly the look of
strain and horror died from Stanislaus' face, and Max, watching
him, felt that the abominable incident had faded from his mind.

Daniel sailed for America, and Max, who saw him go from
Southampton, was conscious of a sense of content that he had
such a brother. He still felt the existence of that dark shadow
coming ever closer and closer, and it had been a relief to confide
his anxieties to Daniel. He had begged his father and mother to
sell the business and come to England. Isaac refused.

" My roots are here, it is difficult to uproot old trees. Why
should anyone wish to harm us ? We are peaceable people, we
take no interest in politics; and although there are many, many
things concerning my son Jacob of which I disapprove and on
which I look with horror, yet I cannot believe that if there were
any danger his natural affection for his mother and me would not
assert itself. No, Max, we shall stay; we shall do very well. I
have heard rumours, but what are rumours ? Two men quarrel,
they fight, one is hurt—immediately it is noised abroad that there
has been a riot in which much blood has been shed ! No, no; be
assured. If any danger should threaten I should never hesitate a
moment, but send for my good English son, God bless and
keep him."

Daniel, who had spent two days in London, where the elegance
of Max's house had impressed him greatly, was incapable of
feeling even a spasm of envy. He was completely happy to be
returning to his own *appartement* in New York where his buxom
wife and his pretty daughter would be waiting for him. Admit-
tedly the *appartement* was situated over the shop, and in summer
there was always a hint of the smell of cheeses, Bismarck herring,
sauerkraut, making its way into the living-room. Neither Daniel
nor his wife found it objectionable, and little Rosie had grown
up with it and never noticed it.

There had been a time, Daniel remembered, when he had
dreamed of a chain of stores, of a time when he and Lena would
live in a splendid *appartement* or maybe a luxurious penthouse on
River Drive, when a yearly trip to Europe, travelling on a great
liner with a whole suite to themselves, would have been taken
for granted. He told himself that his grandfather had been a
schneider, and that to cut his coat according to his cloth must be a

traditional strain in his blood. " If we can't snow white then we'll snow as light a shade of grey as is possible," he told Lena.

Lena beamed at him. " I'm satisfied, Danny; s'long as you and Rosie are well, that's all that matters to me. After all, we gotta whole lot of things that *are* luxuries—my electric cleaner, what d'you call it ?—a vacuum; and that frige you got me. It's the last word, pretty well does everything except play tunes ! And say, Danny, just bear in mind we *did* survive the slump, an' if we didn't just come out on top of the world—well, we managed to keep our feet on solid earth. I don't say it might not have been fun to live like swell folk, but maybe we'd have got pretty bored with having to entertain a whole lot, with you having to get into a white shirt and a tuxedo and me into a dress with bare arms every night to eat our suppers."

A grand girl, that Lena of his ! Next year he'd planned to get a car. It wouldn't be one of those great powerful things, just a nice little machine to take them out week-ends. They might leave Lena's brother and his wife to look after things and take a real holiday—not just the odd day, but pack trunks and go off to the mountains some place for a couple weeks.

He wished that he could have transplanted his father and mother to America, but maybe Pop was right and old folks didn't uproot easily. Then they might miss their own home in Berlin. Dan still thought of it as " old fashioned " but " pretty good ". He liked his own home, he liked steel furniture which could be kept clean so easily, he liked to know that the beds were the most hygienic that could be bought, and what he liked best of all was that it belonged—every stick of it—to him and to Lena, and he'd never bought anything on the instalment system. His father might have beautifully-polished silver on his table; Dan hadn't any silver and didn't really want any, the plate he had was good and Lena kept it shining and bright.

He realized that Max wore better clothes than his own, that Max spoke with no trace of an accent; Max was, in short, a real swell. Stanislaus would be the same, with easy manners and capable of making light conversation without " wise-cracking " in order to interest folks. As he saw the ever-changing outline of New York against the sky, Dan knew that a wave of sentiment swept over him.

" That's my home town," he said softly, " that's where I belong, where I've got my wife and kiddy. That's where I've got my work and where I've got to make good—and, by God, I will too ! Gee, I'm glad I'm an American—boy, am I glad ? "

NINE

THINGS were better, business was apparently pulling up again, but Max wondered how far the apparent return to reasonable prosperity was artificial. The unemployment figures were still terribly high; then on August 19th, 1931, England went off the gold standard. The Labour Prime Minister had taken the first step towards the fate which was to destroy him. Max, who had for so long regarded himself as completely British, shared with the rest of the nation a state of almost incredulous dismay and horror. The pound—recognized everywhere for so long as something having a solid, real and unchangeable value, had lost its former worth. Max felt that it was an admission to the whole world that Britain's house had not been set in order, that she with her allies might have won the war and had to admit that they had lost the peace. "The Old Lady of Threadneedle Street", who had contrived to pay her way for so many years under circumstances which had been hard and even bitter, had, Max felt with thousands of others, lost face before the world.

Germany and Austria had faced terrible inflation, they had known when money lost its value, when notes bearing enormous figures were so much waste paper; now England had admitted that her pound sterling, her twenty shillings, could no longer be offered in the markets of the world as unchanging and unchangeable.

Daniel wrote:

Keep your chins up, anything is better than inflation. I reckon it's been the square thing to do. Hard to understand, but these guys must know what they're doing. Keep on saying, " There's a sun still shining in the sky."

Max wondered, worried and depressed. Stanislaus had returned home, and Max had warned him to keep out of all political embroilments. Stanislaus stood there watching him while he talked, his handsome head held very high, his eyes defiant.

" Just sit down under it all, eh ? " he asked.

" Just keep out of political matters. Get on with your own work and don't concern yourself with other people's affairs."

" In other words, shut my eyes and swear that because my own backside hasn't been kicked, no one else has had theirs kicked ? "

" My dear fellow, your father is growing old, your dear mother

must not be worried for the sake of her own health; surely to know
hat you were taking any active part in—well, in anything political
would be an additional worry to them both ? ''

Gravely Stanislaus said, '' I will do my best to safeguard them
both.''

With that Max had to be content, and Stanislaus returned to
Berlin. Miriam remained in London, she was enjoying herself, and
Alice enjoyed having her about the place. There was also a young
man who made no secret of the fact that he was completely in love
with her. He was a good-looking successful wool manufacturer
who came from Leeds. His father and grandfather had both been
in the same trade, both had been successful. Charles Hare at
twenty-five was an exceedingly eligible young man.

He was a Jew and proud of his race, but like the Nollers themselves, he was not deeply religious and paid little attention to forms
and ceremonies. With permission from Max and Alice he took
Miriam to stay with his father and mother. She returned declaring
that everything had been delightful, that in spite of the grime and
dirt she liked the wild country, liked the kindly open-hearted people,
who might be blunt and outspoken, but who emanated a sense of
trustworthiness and solidity.

'' Charles would like to come back to Berlin with me to meet
mother and father. I've told him that after his father's house ours
will seem very modest and simple. Their place is immense, Max,
they have cars and grounds like a park, and masses of servants.
They've two hard tennis courts. . . .'' She sighed. '' I hope
Charles won't find our home too modest.''

Max watched her, thinking what a beautiful creature she was and
how he longed that life might give her nothing but happiness.

'' I take it, then, that you and Charles are in love ? ''

Miriam blushed. '' Oh, Max dear—of course we are.''

'' He wants father's consent to marry you, eh ? ''

'' Why, yes, his own father is quite willing,'' She laughed. '' I
think they all rather liked me.''

'' Then it only remains to get father's approval and you can be
married and live happily ever after ? ''

'' Something like that. If people do really ever live happily ever
after, Max.''

'' Wise people take the rough with the smooth, my dear. Even
if life is not and can't be one long, glorious, slightly over-coloured
honeymoon, it can bring content, companionship and great
affection.''

Miriam made a small grimace. '' That sounds dull, Max. Dull
and just a little disillusioned, don't you think ? ''

5

" Maybe most of us grow rather dull and a little disillusioned."
So Miriam Noller went back to Berlin with Charles Hare, an
Isaac and Rose beamed on them both. Charles asked for permissio
to marry Miriam. Isaac shook his hand and cried, " With all m
heart—and may joy be yours," while Rose smiled and wiped he
eyes, suddenly dim with tears. Her only daughter was to leave hom
and go to England to become an Englishwoman. Rose looked bac
on the last time she had been in England, on the time when she ha
gone over taking Stanislaus and Miriam with her to attend Max'
wedding. They had been small children then, and here was Miriam
going to be married and—one hoped—have children of her own.

Life had been very happy, very peaceful, in those far-off day
when Max had married Alice Berman. Business had prospered
people had been friendly, the Nollers had enjoyed entertaining i
a modest yet sufficiently gracious way. Now—Rose sighed—
things were so different. She missed the frank greetings, sh
found eyes averted from her—not only on the part of her Christia
friends, but many of the Jewish persuasion as well. Did the Jew
know of the activities of her son Jacob ? Did they perhaps know
more than she did ? Her own knowledge was small; Jacob wa
the assistant editor of a paper which was acknowledged to b
anti-Jewish, a paper which Isaac had forbidden any of them t
bring into the house. Perhaps her Jewish friends distrusted he
because of Jacob, and in distrusting her, distrusted also her dea
Isaac, her lovely daughter and her handsome young son.

The Christians—could they dislike and distrust her for n
better reason than that she had married Isaac Noller ? She shrugge
her shoulders. The whole thing was too difficult for her. She ha
never been a very clever woman, she had merely been a very kin
one, a woman who loved and lived for her husband and her family

That night Isaac said to her, " My dear one, you are please
about our daughter ? You are glad that she will marry this nic
young man ? "

She said, " I am glad that she is to marry an Englishman, tha
she will live in England. I used to love your Germany, now I am
growing to hate it. There is suspicion everywhere; of what ar
people suspicious ? There is no friendliness left, why are peopl
unfriendly ? I find only hate, distrust and fear—of what I don'
know; but these things exist in the minds of people. I am thankfu
that Miriam will live in a land where people do not go about with
hard, angry eyes and tight-lipped mouths."

Isaac, taking off his tie and hanging it carefully as he
always did on the pillar supporting the mirror, smiled at his
reflection.

" My dearest Rose, even in England Miriam will not find everyone kind. I admire your nation, I respect them, but surely they are not the only perfect people in the world ? " He spoke lightly, trying to make her smile, to take her mind away from things which were obviously distressing her, things which Isaac Noller in his business had found only too evident during the last eighteen months.

She answered gravely, " I don't know, my dear. No, not perfect, but they have certain fundamental traits which are— fundamentally good. They make mistakes, they do foolish things, it may be that often they are wrong in their political instincts— but they are not . . ." She hesitated, then went on firmly, " cruel, Isaac. Adversity makes them determined; adversity makes Germans sullen, bitter, vindictive. Our dear Daniel, he is American, I know, but with him it is the same. He has been through a difficult time, and he smiles and says, ' Atta boy ! ' The last time I saw our son Jacob, his eyes, his thin lips, frightened me. I felt that I was no longer his mother—I was a woman who had married a Jew, and he hates me for it. There, it is late— you must sleep."

Isaac did not sleep, he slept badly in those days, lying awake thinking, listening for the step of young Stanislaus who came home so late. He never asked him where he had been, never showed any trace of curiosity, but he wondered. There were strange stories going round; everywhere it was known that a certain party were determined to get rid of the Jews. Streicher declared, " No matter how, that will be our business, but it shall and will be done—Germany will be Germany once again, purged of these swine, these bloodsuckers."

Lying there, listening to his wife's even breathing, for Rose was a person who could never remain in a state of tension for very long, he would try to puzzle it out. As a little boy—so many years ago—he had heard of the *pogroms*, he had heard the clatter of horses' hooves, the screams of women, the hoarse cries of suffering men. Then there had been a time of peace in Germany with Uncle Stanislaus and his kind aunt. Then he had heard Germany spoken of as " the kind, patient mother of nations ", as " the Fatherland "—they never seemed to decide whether the country was a kind mother or a great father, Isaac thought. In those days his aunt had spoken of the Russians with tears running down her cheeks. How well he remembered it, and Uncle Stanislaus had come in and announced that he was going to take them to listen to the music of Herr Mozart. In those days it had been the Russians who hated the Jews, who sought to exterminate them. Right back down history first one nation then another had hated the Jews, had persecuted them, driven them from pillar to post. Spanish, Dutch, hundreds of years ago, even the English had joined against them. Dimly he remembered a Jewish massacre at York, was it in the reign of Richard the First? —he had forgotten.

Now the hatred had come to Germany, and as always with Germany they tried to justify themselves. The Jews were bankers, were financiers, were moneylenders—well, so were plenty of people who were not Jews.

He had said to old Father Muldoon, " Now they say that we killed Christ ! "

The old man nodded. " Well, possibly you didn't do anything much to help Him—but in these days who does do anything to help Him? Jesus Christ, my dear friend, can never be killed, yet men are trying to kill Him every day in the year. I am very sorry for this poor Jesus Christ."

The Jews were no worse than any other people, Isaac reflected. True, there were bad Jews, there were bad Germans, bad Christians, bad Protestants. The people who were ready to persecute the Jews were not doing it in the name of Jesus Christ. Isaac had read about Him, rightly or wrongly, and he could not, would not, believe that this kindly man, with His thoughts for birds, lost sheep, children and sick people, could approve of persecution " in His name ".

Did Jews wield too much power? Were they a danger to the state? If so, in what way? They were not planning a revolution, they were not organizing a crusade. He had said as much to his friend Herr Bauer.

Bauer said, " Noller, we are friends, I hope, but all you Jews are schemers."

Isaac replied, " I have never schemed in my life—except to keep secret some surprise for my wife for her birthday ! "

" You have fingers in every pie——"

" My own pie occupies all my time, Bauer, my friend."

" You have an uncanny faculty for making money . . ."

" Oi, oi, and how many poor people do we have also? If you were on some of the committees on which I sit you would know. There is great poverty—and, thank God, great charity."

" You only help your own people ! " Bauer, usually so quiet, was growing indignant.

" But that is natural, surely? I am a little man of no importance, but for many years I have given such help as I could to many people who were not only Jews. Tell me, what do you do for us ? "

" There is a great society, a world-wide society, for the propagation of Christianity among the Jews."

" I cannot understand you, my friend. We don't want to be made Christians. It would be great impertinence on our part to have a society for the propagation of Judaism among the Christians."

Bauer, a heavily built man, nodded pontifically and spoke with careful temperance. " Listen, my dear Noller. Why is it that you Jews have always been persecuted ? Why is it that no nation has wanted you in their country—not for long ? "

Isaac said, " I think that I am right that in the Middle Ages Italy was very glad to encourage us, to allow us to open printing presses——"

" Tut, tut, you are being frivolous. I must speak frankly. In adversity you are humble, you are law-abiding, you work hard at trades and professions."

" Only recently—comparatively—have we been allowed to enter many trades and professions, Bauer."

" Yes, yes," impatiently, " but allow me to continue. Once you are established, what happens ? You begin to work for power. You gather riches. You enter the political field. In short, you become—too strong, too great a power in the land which has given you protection and hospitality. Then you grow proud, arrogant, even oppressive. For that reason Germany has turned against the Jews. They can have no real part in the—New Germany. If I have spoken too plainly, forgive me. I have a great respect for you, my friend Noller, but you are the exception."

Isaac smiled. " I know of many men who are like me, but much better. Men who are consistently kind, charitable, hard-working— so," his smile widened, " for the sake of four or five just men the Jews may be saved, eh ? "

He sighed. Life had once been so simple, and now it was a mass of complications. He remembered how Uncle Stanislaus had spoken always of love being so much stronger than hate. He had never been tired of begging his wife and his nephew to keep hate from their hearts. Dear Uncle Stanislaus, what would he have made of things in this world of 1932 ?

He heard the careful footsteps of his son ascending the stairs— so Stanislaus was back ! Isaac wondered where he had been, then decided that Stanislaus had a right to go and come as he pleased. The boy was a boy no longer, he was twenty-nine. At his age Max had been married, so had Daniel.

When they discussed Miriam's wedding it was Stanislaus who proposed that she should be married from Max's house in London. He had many reasons to bring forward—the house in London was larger, it would be more convenient for Hare's relations, there were a dozen reasons which he gave, and every hour some new one seemed to suggest itself. It might even be possible to make a grand reunion of the occasion—with Daniel and his wife over from America. Miriam listened gravely, and young Hare agreed with Stanislaus. His father and mother hated travelling, his sister was not sufficiently strong to take a long journey, and so on.

Later, when Miriam was alone with her brother, she said, " What is the real reason, Stan, dear ? "

He smiled. " The real reason for what, darling ? Be more explicit."

" Wishing me to be married from Max's house."

" I've given them all. This house is too small, mother would worry herself into a nervous breakdown. Truda is growing old; it will be a splendid opportunity for us all to meet——"

" Max and Alice could have come over here; if Daniel comes with Lena they can come to Berlin as well as to London."

" My dear, don't let's go over it all again. It's settled, and everyone is pleased. I hope that you are too."

" Pleased, but puzzled . . ."

" Puzzled at what ? "

" Your tenacity and secrecy, Stan, dear."

" You were always imaginative, Miriam."

Miriam Noller's wedding was celebrated at the Great Portland Street Synagogue in July 1932. Everyone agreed that the bride looked beautiful, that a more handsome young couple never stood under the *choopah*, and that the Nollers, while they might not be people of actual wealth as accounted so by the Hares' West Riding standards, certainly had distinction and good looks.

" Germans, eh ? " asked Henry Burns, who might be a Jew but spoke with a pronounced Yorkshire accent.

" Nay," the elder Hare replied, " Poles, I believe. But then, no one knows really where we Jews came from——"

" And, by the road things are going, won't know where they're going if this racket goes on in Germany much longer. There's trouble coming, Hare, big trouble. No use saying—well, what about Palestine ? Palestine wouldn't hold a tenth of them, and how much chance will they be given to *get* to Palestine, tell me that ? "

" Look, Henry "—only Hare said " luke " as became a good Yorkshireman—" we're at a wedding, not a funeral. Stop croaking, for heaven's sake ! "

Burns replied, " Never mind ' croaking ', take a look at that

young man's face. That young Noller, the handsome one. You're
not going to tell me that young chap hasn't got some inkling of
what's waiting."

Max had booked seats for *Cavalcade* at Drury Lane; as he
dressed he gave a sigh of satisfaction. Everything had gone off
well, Miriam had looked beautiful—better still, she had looked
happy; Daniel had told him that business was picking up, he
looked well, and if his wife was just a little " overblown " she was
obviously kindly, and it was equally obvious that Daniel adored
her. Stanislaus—well, Max smiled more broadly, it was evident
that every woman in the place regarded him as exceptionally
handsome and charming. Queer how Stanislaus, with his looks,
his charm and his one-time love of laughter had grown so grave,
so serious. There was a kind of aura which seemed to Max to
envelop him. Not that he was a dull dog, the fellow could never
be that, but he had lost that youthful gaiety, that light-heartedness
which had been so attractive.

Max was determined to enjoy himself; he was content to have
his father and mother with him, and for this evening at least he was
going to banish dark thoughts, speculations and nameless fears.
Drury Lane, supper at the Savoy, he might even dance—he hadn't
danced for a long time; no, it was to be a real gala night.

The theatre was crowded; all Max's party were punctual and
he flattered himself that you could not have found prettier women
and better turned-out men anywhere.

Alice said, touching his hand with the tips of her fingers as they
stood in the foyer, " Going to enjoy it, Maxie ? You're looking so
much better, less tired."

He said, " I'm feeling fine. I've wanted to see this show." The
next day he realized that he did not remember a line of it, had no
idea of the plot and that the whole production had made not the
slightest impression upon him.

The place was crowded, and one of the programme-girls whispered
to Max as he bought a bundle of programmes, " They say that the
Ambassador's coming tonight, bringing a big party."

" Which Ambassador ? " Max asked idly.

" I'm not certain, either the French or Italian—no, really I
forget."

He seated himself in his stall next to Mrs. Hare, and when the
orchestra was playing the overture she touched his arm. " Look,
Mr. Noller, have you ever seen such jewels ? That must be the
Ambassador's party."

Max turned and stared up at the first tier of boxes; a woman
entered magnificently gowned, wearing jewellery which was

catching the lights from the great cut-glass chandeliers and flinging back a thousand glittering sparks of colour. Another woman, taller, slimmer, followed her, and Max wondered if his heart had ceased to beat. She looked older, more mature and completely mistress of herself; she moved—as he remembered that she had always done—easily, smoothly and effortlessly. As she entered the box she turned to speak to a tall, excessively thin man with a dark moustache which made his pallid skin look unnaturally white. Max remembered that movement so well, that trick of speaking over her shoulder, so that the long slender line of her neck and throat showed so delightfully. She sat down and stared round the great house, turning to speak to her hostess from time to time.

Mrs. Hare said, " Oh, what a beautiful woman—what do you think she is—French ? "

" Possibly—or Italian."

" She's the most lovely woman I've ever seen. She's—well, she's unbelievably beautiful."

Max did not speak because he felt that his mouth was too dry. There she sat, Elfa de Lucca, Duchessa d'Ottaviano, the woman he had loved, the woman for whom he had been ready to leave everything—home, wife, children. He wondered with a sudden sense of panic if she might see him, and what he would do if their eyes met; wondered if he could make some excuse and slip away, leave the theatre and only return when he knew that the play was over. . . . Then mercifully the house lights dimmed, and he heard Mrs. Hare sigh in happy expectancy, " Ah, I'm going to enjoy this ! "

To Max the whole play was a confused mass of fleeting impressions, each one having superimposed upon it some memory of Elfa and the hours he had spent with her. He saw people dancing, and remembered how he had longed to take her out to supper and dance. He saw soldiers embarking, and remembered that now the sea divided them, and that only on brief visits was she in the same country as himself. Words about homes, children, love, reached him through a haze, every sentence being twisted in Max's mind to something Elfa had once said to him, or something he had said to her.

When the curtain fell on the first act he leaned across and said, trying to keep the urgency from his voice, " Anyone coming for a drink ? You, Hare, Stan—you'll come, Daniel ? Father—what about you ? "

Then scarcely waiting for them to reply, he made a quick apology to Mrs. Hare, and leaving his seat walked rapidly along the gangway. It wasn't likely that the two Italian women would come out for drinks, and if the men did—well, they didn't know him from Adam.

He was talking to Hare, agreeing that the show was wonderful, the acting first rate, when a commissionaire came up to him. Again Max felt that his heart leapt into his throat.

" Excuse me, sir—Mr. Noller ? "

Max licked his dry lips. " I am Mr. Noller."

" Lady in the box—box A—told me to give you this, sir."

" Oh, thanks. Wait a minute—thanks."

He took the card, rather larger than those which were usual in England which bore the name, surmounted by a ducal coronet, " Duchessa d'Ottaviano ".

I saw you in the stalls. Won't you please come and say " how do you do ? "

E. d'O.

He said to Hare, " Most curious thing. This lady used to work for me. Yes, sounds fantastic, eh ? She and her mother—Italian aristocrats—fell foul in some way of the Fascists. She—this lady "—he tapped the card with his finger—" used to paint pictures —very pretty they were too. Will you forgive me if I go and pay my respects ? "

He made his way to the box still holding the card in his hand. He felt that he was moving in a world which was completely unreal. In a moment he would speak with her, listen to her voice, see her eyes and the smile which he had loved. There was no sensation of actual pain, no passionate emotion, rather he felt as some thirsty traveller in a desert might feel at the realization that an oasis was within reach. He would assuage his hunger, slake his thirst, find rest and delight for his eyes.

He reached the door of the box and knocked lightly. A voice cried, " *Avante!* " Max turned the handle and entered. Elfa was standing looking down at the audience with the woman Max took to be the Ambassadress. She turned and their eyes met.

She came towards him, her hands outstretched. " Mister Nollaire—how kind of you to come ! 'Ow fortunate t'at I caught sight of you. Madame, may I present a ver' kind friend—in adversity—Mister Max Nollaire." Max bowed over the plump hand, heavy with rings, and entirely forgot to listen for the name. He only longed to be able to look at Elfa again.

She walked with him to the back of the box. Again he caught his breath as he watched how easily, smoothly, she moved.

" I am so anxious t'at you should meet my 'usband. I 'ave told 'im of all your kindness to my dear mother and myself. 'E is most grateful. 'E asks if you can per'aps take suppaire wiz us after the t'eatre. No? Then another time. Tomorrow—will t'at be possible?" She spoke more softly, moving almost imperceptibly nearer to him. " T'ere are t'ings which I wish to speak wit' you—important t'ings. Please, make it possible." Her voice sank still lower. " You are German, no? German Jew?"

Feeling that he was speaking in a dream, Max said," I'm British. My father is a Polish Jew—we came from Poland. I changed my nationality."

" Your father?"

" No, he is officially a German; he left Poland when he was a very young boy—six years old, I think."

" Luncheon tomorrow? Claridge's, we 'ave a private room. One o'clock. I 'ave so many t'ings for which to be grateful, my 'usband also feels t'is. Tell me, are you well—Max?"

He said hoarsely, " Yes, I am well."

He knew that his eyes never left her face, this was the woman he had loved, desired, dreamed of; now she was married to someone else.

She said, " T'en tomorrow at Claridge's. Good-night—Max."

As she said his name, her voice dropped, taking on a softer tone. He wondered if she—like himself—was remembering so much.

" That will be delightful. Good-bye."

He never remembered anything of the remainder of the play; from time to time when he heard Mrs. Hare either laugh or applaud he followed her example, but all the time his eyes were turning, while the house was still dark, towards the box where Elfa sat.

They went on to the Savoy. Max danced with Alice, with Mrs. Hare, with Daniel's stout, pleasant wife, and complimented them all on how well they moved, observed the rhythm or something equally futile and commonplace. Later he told Alice of his meeting with Elfa.

She said, " Really, Maxie—and she's a Duchess! And she used to work for you in the little shop at Bury Street. I remember that at one time I thought you might find her very attractive—too attractive, perhaps."

He answered with a kind of offhand stubbornness. " I still think that she is attractive."

" Yes, but—well, it's different now, isn't it? And she wants to see you?"

" I gather that her husband wants to see me. It may be some

business. These Italian landowners—they often dabble in exporting wine, fruit, a dozen things."

Max slept very little, the thought of meeting Elfa again excited him and drove away sleep. He was tired to death, the day had been a long one and he wanted so much to sink into oblivion, to relax and rest. Instead his mind went on churning round and round, speculating, probing, wondering. Was he still in love with her? He admitted that he didn't know. Certainly her beauty made an appeal to him, it was delightful to hear her voice with its unusual modulations. Anyway, what did it matter if he were in love with her? Tomorrow he would see her, in all probability, for the last time. Aristocrats—Italian dukes and duchesses—did not keep up friendship with German-Jew tradesmen, however successful they might be.

Morning came, Max felt no less tired than when he had gone to bed.

Alice, looking as she always did, fresh and sweet in the early morning, smiled, saying, " Maxie, dear, late nights and festivities don't suit you. You're looking played out."

He nodded. " Champagne. I ought never to touch the stuff."

.   .   .   .

At five minutes to one h e was at Claridge's, carrying' a huge box of flowers which made him feel embarrassed and a trifle awkward. He was taken up to the suite; he wondered during the ascent in the lift if other people could hear his heart beating as he heard it himself.

He was ushered into the sitting-room, which was filled with flowers. He set down his box and waited. A door opened and Elfa came in. She held out her hands as she came towards him. " Max, how nice t'is is ! "

" It's a wonderful surprise. You look more beautiful than ever."

Elfa laughed. " All men say t'ese t'ings. I am much oldaire. So are you, dear Max. There is more grey in your 'air."

" We've been through a difficult time—even now we're not really into smooth water."

She moved to a table where bottles and glasses stood. " W'at shall it be ? Cock-tail or—what was it you used to say ?—I remember, ' a man's drink ', t'at meant a visky-and-soda."

" A man's drink, please. How nice of you to remember, Elfa."
She handed him his glass and said gravely, " I forget ver' little."
" You're happy ? "
" Yes, I am ver' 'appy. Nino is the kindest husband imaginable

He is ver' important man, but he has re-tained—yes, re-tained—his simplicity. He is anxious to talk wit' you. He will be here in a few moments. Now he is wit' the Ambassador."

Max felt a certain surprise that he did not experience an irresistible longing to catch her to him and hold her in his arms, if only for a few brief seconds. He knew that he experienced no such impulse; it was sufficient to stand here, in this luxurious room filled with the scent of flowers, to watch her, listen to her, and realize that after their long separation they were together again.

He sighed, " Ah, Elfa, it's so good to be with you again——"

" I do not feel t'at we have ever been separated, Max."

" You haven't felt the separation as I have done, my dear."

" Yes," eagerly, " indeed I have suffered from being separated from you; now we are toget'er I am not conscious t'at t'ere has been any separation. Now it is as it all was—what do you say in the tales you tell children ?—as it was—once upon a time. So I t'ink it will always be between us, Max. Ah, here is my husband —Nino, here is Max Nollaire."

The Duca was tall, elegant and very thin. His skin was tinged with yellow, his dark eyes looked as if the brown pigment had run a little, discolouring the whites. His clothes were admirable and his manners perfect. He spoke English a trifle stiltedly, with care and ease. He greeted his wife, then turned to Max. " I have waited for a very long time to have this pleasure. Many times my wife has assured me of your consistent kindness to her and to my dear aunt. I am very much pleased that you could make it convenient to take luncheon with us. Elfa, shall I telephone to them that we are ready ? I am afraid that I was a little late—I was detained."

The luncheon was served, and Ottaviano dismissed the waiters. " We shall wait upon ourselves. If anything is needed I shall ring."

The Duca, Max noticed, ate very little, and when he laid down his knife and fork turned to Max, twisting a little in his chair to 1ace him more easily.

" Mister Nollaire—oh, excuse, it is Noller ! You must blame my wife, who has given me wrong instructions. I am in your debt for many things—kindnesses, consideration, understanding, to name only a few. I like to—in so far as it is possible—to pay my debts. Please listen. We live in strange, unquiet times. I suspect that they may grow still less quiet. You have interests in Germany ? "

" Scarcely; my father and brother have. Buisness in Berlin."

The Duca leaned back in his chair, he nodded very gently. " I should advise you if it is possible to persuade your father to—get rid of his business—soon."

Max laughed. " You don't know my father ! He is stubborn, he lives a life in which politics play no part, he is not interested in them."

Ottaviano leaned forward towards his guest. " The time might come, Mr. Noller, when he would be forced—in a very disagreeable manner—to take an interest in the political developments of Germany. Time will show us. Now, I have not so much influence as might be expected, perhaps. Yes, I have very large extensive estates, but I have never . . ." He paused and repeated the word, " never been actively concerned with the—the present system of government in Italy. Nevertheless I have still for various reasons some small power. In case of need . . ." he shrugged his shoulders, " shall we say for the sake of taking an example—in case someone needed quickly—what shall I say ?—new papers, a new passport, addresses to which they might go for safety and shelter—I might, I repeat *might*, be able to be of assistance. I shall hope with great sincerity that never will it be necessary for you—or yours—to need to ask me for such help. But," he smiled, " how shall one know in these difficult times ? Elfa, my dear, we have that small present for Mr. Noller; would you enhance its value—to him, I am sure—by giving it to him ? "

She went over to the writing-table, and unlocking the drawer took out a note-case of leather with gold corners. Smiling, she handed it to him.

" A *ricordo* from us both," she said.

Max turned it over, it was obviously expensive, beautifully made. Why should they wish to give him a joint present after all this long preamble ? What had this thin, elegant fellow been talking about ? He said, " That is very kind of you both, I shall treasure it."

The Duca nodded gently. " We refrained from having initials put on it—sometimes initials are tiresome things. Perhaps when you are alone—completely alone—you will investigate the case. I have put in one or two visiting-cards, cards of good friends of mine, warm-hearted people, always ready to—to oblige other friends of mine. I hope that you will never be called upon to use this information, but—as you say in this country—it is better to be forewarned, then you become forearmed."

Max stared at him. Dimly he understood that Ottaviano was wishing to help him, was even running a grave risk by so doing. His old sense of a great, dark cloud drawing nearer oppressed

him. He pushed the case into his breast pocket, saying again,
" Thank you—both."

Then, " What do you think——"

Ottaviano held up his hand. " I never allow myself to speculate.
Think, possibly, but speculate—never. I have talked too much. I
am afraid that you have eaten nothing. Elfa, my dear, are you
willing to give me a great treat, and Mr. Noller also ? " Again he
turned to Max. " I hold the unshakable belief that no one can
make coffee like my wife. Even here she makes it for us. It is
delicious."

They drank coffee, sending Max's thoughts flying back to the
room in Wellington Road, to the old dark-eyed Contessa, and to
the hours which he and Elfa had spent together.

The duca sipped his coffee with appreciation, smiling beatifically.
He talked easily and well; he was even amusing, Max thought.
Elfa spoke very little, but again and again he saw her watching
her husband and thought, " I don't know how much she loves
him, but they're great friends, these two. I'd trust him—he's
clever, subtle and he's straight."

The Duca finished his second cup of coffee, glanced at his watch
and begged them to excuse him. He had an appointment, and
was almost late for it already. He reminded his wife that they
were meeting—Max did not catch the name, or, if he did, forgot
it—for cocktails at six.

Max sprang to his feet. " I must go. I have stayed an un-
conscionable time."

" One other cup of coffee, Mr. Noller. We leave in the morning,
this is your last opportunity. Good-bye, Elfa my dear, *au revoir*."

As the door closed, Max said, " And so you go tomorrow ? "

" Back to Rome and then to the mountains—oh, Rome will
be so hot ! "

" How wonderful it has been to see you again ! To know that
you're well, happy."

She nodded. " Yes, I am happy, Max. Not the happiness of—
those first days, when we met. Not happy as I used to be in
R-Richmond Park when we drove t'ere, or E-Epping Forest,
but happy—in a way that is quiet and peaceful and filled with
tranquil t'ings."

Max held out his hand. " Good-bye, my dear, and thank you."

She leaned forward, kissed his cheek very gently, then said,
" Dear Max—always—*dear* Max—go with God."

TEN

DURING the months which followed his visit to Elfa and her husband Max felt unusually soothed and contented. Strangely enough he suffered no great sense of deprivation, he was not even quite certain whether he really wished to see Elfa again. The sight of her, the realization that she was—if not wildly happy— at least fortunate and satisfied in her marriage gave him—because he loved her and always would love her—a sensation of calmness and definite happiness.

He understood that she had for him an affection which was built on a firm foundation, that so long as she lived she would think of him with kindness and without regret. Their meeting had stabilized him, had given him the assurance which he needed; the glimpses of her as one of the loveliest women he had ever seen, and her last affectionate and essentially affectionate kiss remained with him as thoughts and recollections to be treasured and remembered.

Alice scarcely mentioned his visit to Claridge's, and Max wondered a little if she suspected him of visiting Elfa alone. She did not ask any definite questions and he volunteered no information. Alice was changing, he thought; she was more gentle, less demanding, she rarely begged to be taken out to expensive places or grumbled about life being dull and monotonous.

He began to feel that whereas during the first years of their married life they had felt an almost overwhelming physical attraction, they had passed through a second period when they were both—frankly—slightly bored and dissatisfied with each other. Now their true companionship, their friendship and their affection had blossomed and developed; they understood themselves and each other, saw life more clearly.

Previously Alice's interest in his business had been perfunctory, limited to brief questions as to how business was going, but actually implying no anxiety to know any details. Then " Max's business " had been the source which supplied the money for the household bills, for the children's clothes and school fees and a certain amount of amusement. Now, Max felt that she was actually feeling an interest in his work, not merely simulating one in order to please him. Although the physical side of their life together was practically non-existent, they were actually more intimate than they had been for years.

She never mentioned either Carrick or the Crowns, and for a

time Max wondered if she wrote to Carrick; he allowed the speculation to die, and knew that he was grateful that Alice and he were able to find life together such a pleasant and warmly friendly affair.

Alice, for her part, was convinced that Max had discovered in some way her affair with Carrick. She had realized it after that dinner-party, and had respected Max because he had never attempted to probe into the matter. The whole thing had been over after she left America; for a time Carrick had written, sent her presents, and she had replied that she wished for neither.

The whole thing is over (she wrote). *It was very foolish, probably very wrong, but as far as we ourselves are concerned I don't think that either of us were badly hurt at the parting.*

When Carrick came to England with the Crowns he had done his best to achieve a sentimental atmosphere once more; he had taken Alice out to luncheon, they had driven together, and he had seen to it that her rooms were always filled with flowers. He found her still quite delightfully attractive and was quite prepared to indulge in a brief love-affair during his visit.

" Come and show me some of the beauties of the countryside —for a week-end," he suggested. " Harry and Minnie often go away on their own with Marybell, to visit friends or distant relations."

Alice refused. " I've no intention of doing anything of the kind," she told him. " I should hate it."

" At one time you liked being with me," he reminded her reproachfully.

She smiled. " My dear, years and years ago. I've grown up since then."

" Are you in love with your husband ? "

" I doubt if two people remain *in love* when they've been married as long as Max and I have. I love Max, and I respect him; he's one of the finest men I've ever met—probably *the* finest. Oh, he's not spectacular, I should hate to have married a spectacular man; Max is good and real, and—well, if my son grows up as good as Max I shall be very proud of him."

Carrick had smiled, assuming an expression which she remembered as his " worldly smile " and which years ago she had admired and felt that it stamped him as a man who assessed the value of most things very low, who had tasted life, savoured it, and was prepared to give his verdict to his friends and acquaintances. " And do you believe," he asked now, " that your husband

has never had any—affairs, never felt an attraction to other
women ? "

Alice said calmly and equably, " I've never known if he had.
I doubt that Max has ever kept a mistress. If he has done so, all I
know is that he has never failed in kindness and consideration
towards me. Then too—who am I to blame—if he has done—
for what I did myself ? "

Carrick changed his tone, lowered his voice a little, stared at
her, his eyes moody and—he hoped—wistful.

" And now, what you once felt for me—is dead, Alice ? "

" Completely," she said cheerfully, " as yours is for me, if
you'd be honest and admit that all you want is—a companion
while you are in England."

" Why do you suppose that I came to England ? "

" Because you wanted to see me again—for one reason, I don't
doubt. Then, people from America *do* come to England. It
couldn't have been any overwhelming desire to see me again—
you'd waited a good many years. No, Lewis, don't try to flog
dead horses. It's a stupid pastime after all."

She remembered the night they were at Drury Lane, after
Miriam's wedding, that she had fancied that Max looked pale; but
he had seemed to enjoy himself at the Savoy, and she had long ago
ceased to wonder if he found that lovely Italian girl—who painted
pictures or embroidered blouses or something of the kind—really
attractive or not. She doubted if she had ever been Max's mistress,
and now—well, she was married to some Italian aristocrat, and
was as far removed from Max as Lewis Carrick was from herself.

Now Max seemed happier than she had known him for a
long time; he told her that he was sleeping better, that business
was improving steadily. He was satisfied that things were going
well with Daniel in America, and certainly when Dan and his
wife came over for the wedding they had looked very flourishing.
Just a little ordinary, Alice thought, lacking Max's finish and
cultured speech; certainly Daniel had none of the good looks of
Stanislaus. Max told her that he was delighted at his sister's
marriage with young Hare; he had seen Charles several times
when he came up on business to London, and said that the fellow
could talk about nothing but his wonderful wife and his own
amazing good luck in being her husband.

Stories filtered through to him from Germany, dreadful
stories, things which made Max's blood run cold and which
served to render him depressed and disquieted; but letters which
he received from his father and mother served in a great measure
to reassure him. They both wrote very cheerfully, and referred

very often to their intention to come over in the Spring to visit Miriam.

On January 13th, 1933, news came of the installation of Hitler's Government in Germany. Max frowned; he had heard of the fellow, who had written some book or other, or was threatening to write a book; it was to contain his ideas for putting the world to rights. Was this the man who had instigated the " beating up " of Jews, the man [whom his brother Jacob followed and for whom he worked? Max waited, his fears and disquiet growing.

The pictures in the Press of the unpleasant-looking man with his forelock and his moustache grown on the lines which had once been affected by Charlie Chaplin, his tightly belted raincoat, looked too insignificant to be able to dominate a nation.

He told Alice, " I think that I shall slip over to Berlin to see if everything is all right."

She tried to reassure him. " Maxie dear, don't panic. Nothing's wrong, both your father and Stanislaus wrote only a few days ago. They were quite cheerful."

" I know—but—this new Government——"

On February 3rd, Charles Hare and Miriam arrived in London. He had to go over to Italy; it appeared that Mussolini was trying to develop the Italian wool trade, and Charles wished to ascertain " what there was in it ". He was taking Miriam to Berlin and calling for her on his way back.

After dinner Max began to ask questions. Did Charles think that it was wise to take Miriam?

" Honestly I do. She's a bit worried about her mother. After all, I shall be coming back in under three weeks. I don't believe that anything can happen. The Germans after all are a pretty solid, level-headed race. This screaming fellow Hitler isn't going to do anything to set the whole world against him when he's only just got established, is he? "

" Possibly you're right. I hope to God that you are. You'll leave Miriam addresses that will always find you, and plenty of money. Tell her that—if anything should go wrong——"

Charles laughed. " My dear Max, nothing *will* go wrong ! "

Max continued doggedly, " If anything should go wrong, she's to send a telegram to me at once. Say anything she likes —Mother not so well, or something of that kind. Anyway, Stanislaus is there—only he's been up against that swine of a brother of ours before . . ."

They left England two days later. Miriam was excited at the thought of seeing her mother and father, and Charles was delighted to be taking her to Berlin looking so well, so smart and so evidently happy.

He stayed with the Nollers for three days, and on February 9th left for Italy. He had written to Max that Berlin was quiet, but that there was a great deal of unemployment, many people were begging in the streets, not begging only for money but for food, they looked nearly starved. There were a great number of restaurants where Jews were forbidden to enter.

Makes you feel furious (Charles wrote), *all the Yorkshireman in me comes to the top and I long to—have a bash at someone. There are plenty of swaggering young men, wearing black leather coats, breeches and boots, moving about. They appear to be sufficiently well fed. It's not a particularly pleasant city somehow, although it's quiet enough. I can't quite say what it is—probably I imagine things, though an over-active imagination has never been one of my failings.*

Miriam found her brother Stanislaus more changed than the rest of the family. Her father was still cheerful, radiating kindliness and anxious to help anyone who needed assistance. Her mother looked frail, she thought, and Miriam fancied that there was a faint blue tinge round her lips, but she was cheerful and talked excitedly about her visit to England in the Spring. The great change was in Stanislaus; he had always been slim, with narrow hips and a waist which—she had teased him—was like a girl's. His blue eyes had always danced with expectancy and amusement, a dozen times a day he found some incident which was worth recounting as humorous. Now his fine-featured face was set into grave lines, she felt that his blue eyes no longer danced. He was preoccupied, ready to sink into silence and to indulge in thoughts which—judging from his expression—were not too pleasant.

She went down into the kitchen to speak to Truda about something and found him there talking gravely, impressively. She asked what their confabulation was about, and Stanislaus laughed.

" Do you imagine, my dear sister, that Truda and I are going to discuss our private secrets with a mere child ? "

She smiled, " You and your old secrets ! Trying to persuade her to make you a special cake or something ! "

He nodded. " I shan't say that you are wrong, wise child."

When they went out together, Truda, growing old, very stout and filled as always with complete devotion to her beloved Noller family, took out a piece of paper and smoothed it carefully. In Stanislaus' clear, exact hand was written the address which Truda knew was that of his brother Max. Then, " Family affairs your presence required Father."

He had come down to the kitchen laughing. " Truda, do something for me. I'm growing old and silly and—nervous about nothing. This is a dead secret just between us. This is a telegram to Max. You know how to send off a telegram ? "

" I've sent off hundreds, don't ask silly questions ! "

" Now, these "—and he lowered his voice, his tone lost its lightness—" Nazis, these brown-shirted chaps, don't like Jews. They might try to loot my father's warehouse. They might—oh, do lots of things. I might be away on business. If there should be any . . . trouble—well, that's too serious a word, for Germany is still a law-abiding country, let's say *bother*—for my father or my mother, send that telegram to Max if I am away. Look, here's money," and he pushed a huge wad of notes into her hand. " God knows what it will be worth in twenty-four hours' time ! "

He stared at her earnestly. " Have you any money saved, Truda ? "

She nodded. " Don't you worry, Stanislaus. I've been with your family too long not to have salted something down. My brother—Marcus—in Switzerland has it banked there for me. Not that now it's worth banking, it's cheaper to light the fires with notes than with wood ! Stanislaus, do you think that something is going to—to happen ? "

He answered. " As God judges me, Truda, I don't know ! You won't forget what I have said ? "

" If I have to tear the damned post-office down that telegram will be sent, and please God that it never needs to be sent, because if——"

It had been then that Miriam walked into the kitchen and their talk had been interrupted.

Miriam received her letters from Charles daily, her mother watched her read them eagerly, almost avidly, as if she wished to savour every word which he had written.

Rose said, " You're very happy with Charles, my sweet ? "

Miriam sighed, a deep sigh of contentment. " Mama, I never knew that I could—that anyone could—love anyone as I love Charles. It's so big, so all-consuming that there are times when this love almost hurts. All my life I have known love—from you, dear papa, Max, Stan and Daniel—though I don't know Daniel so well. I've had a lovely life, a life filled with love and kindness, and now it seems that the culmination of it all is—Charles. You see, you do love your husband differently from other people, don't you, darling ? "

Rose nodded. " Yes, indeed, that is true—if it is a real, true marriage."

" So, loving him as I do doesn't make me love any of you less," Miriam went on. " I think that husbands and mothers have a very special place in people's hearts. I know that you and Charles have in mine ! " She glanced again at her letters. " He will be back on the first of March. His trip has been very successful—but," she laughed, " he is longing to get back to me."

" Then I shall lose you again, eh ? "

" Only for a month, two months at the most—then you're coming to see my home, coming and bringing papa. Oh, darling, isn't life exciting ! "

On the evening of February 27th they had finished supper—which they always had early because Stanislaus and Isaac returned hungry from the warehouse. It had been a particularly good supper, for Rose had felt very well all day and had insisted upon helping Truda in the kitchen.

The room was warm and cheerful, and even Stanislaus seemed in good spirits. Isaac complimented his wife on the rice soup and again on the *junger puter*—everyone neglected to suggest that the bird was rather too small and excessively thin—and the sweet was exceptionally good.

They had just finished their very small cups of coffee, for it was at a premium and Isaac hoarded it carefully—it was one of the things which were good for his dear Rose's heart—when the bell rang. Stanislaus went to the door, calling, " Don't come up Truda, I'm going."

He returned a moment later, his face drained of its colour. " The Reichstag is burning ! "

Isaac repeated, " The Reichstag ! "

Stanislaus answered, " Indeed yes—the Reichstag."

Isaac sprang to his feet. " Let us go——"

Rose said, " Isaac, don't go. Stay here ! To see a building burnt, what is it ? You are not a boy to stand and stare ! Isaac, don't go."

Miriam, watching her father edge towards the door, laid her hand on her mother's. " They are both boys, Mama, they want to see a bonfire ! You and I will stay here and wait for them to come back with fantastic tales."

The night was cold and there was a slight drizzle falling; together father and son made their way to the Reichstag, where already flames could be seen licking window-frames in a dozen places.

Stanislaus frowned. " Where is the fire brigade ? It has scarcely caught hold yet ! "

A young man with a heavy jaw, wearing a black leather jacket and a peaked cap, turned and snarled at him, " What do you know about it ? All is being done that can be done ! Kindly mind your own business."

The rumour ran along the crowd. " The work of one man ! " " Some dirty Jew——" " They won't get away with it ! " " It is said that the Leader himself is coming down to see it." " He is beside himself with fury ! " and so it went on. There was a sudden stir among the crowd, a great car drove up, followed by another and another. Men descended, the first among them an insigni-ficant-looking fellow with a putty-coloured face and a black smudge of moustache. His hands were clasped before him in an attitude which struck Stanislaus as sanctimonious and yet nervous. He stared at the increasing flames, turned and spoke to a fat man with a face which at first sight seemed to radiate good-nature, who wagged his head and in his turn whispered to a smaller fellow with a lame foot. Then, shrugging their shoulders, they turned to return to the waiting cars.

The flames had gathered strength, the roar of the heat and conflagration were growing in intensity, when suddenly there was a shout of triumph and a detachment of young men rushed forward. Their shouts reached the Leader and his friends. They turned, watched eagerly.

" We have him ! " " He is caught ! " " Catch him ! Hold him ! He'll suffer for this ! " Stanislaus saw a man rush from the burning building into the Koenigsplatz. He was of medium size, looked young and wore a checked shirt—with no coat over it. He had a heavy, stupid face, his expression was dazed, Stanislaus thought, but not unduly filled with terror. The group of important men, which now included Vice-Chancellor von Papen, watched the young man being bundled into a huge police car. A cheer went up from some of the black-leather-jacketed young men, and the Leader was heard to say in that high, hysterical voice which was to become so familiar to the world, " This is a God-given signal. This fire is, I believe, the work of Communists, then there is nothing now shall stop us crushing out this murder pest with an iron fist." He was turning again to the car, when he added, " We face a new epoch—this is the beginning."

The police car drove away; the fat man, Captain Hermann Goering, was being very busy and doubtless very efficient. Isaac touched his son's arm.

" Come, let us go home again."

They walked home in silence, to find Miriam and Rose waiting. Miriam said, " Tell us, how did it happen ? "

Stanislaus answered, " Some vile creature—a Communist—no doubt he will prove to be also a Jew in the morning, contrived to rush into the Reichstag and set it alight. Alone, unaided ! One has to admit that the fellow was pretty active, for it's a large place."

Isaac nodded. " And old Bismarck, standing on his plinth, watched it all. I wonder what his thoughts must have been ! "

Stanislaus said briefly, " Unrepeatable. The Leader came down himself. He announced that this is the beginning of a new epoch. Chubby-faced Goering ran—well, no, he didn't actually run, but he made himself very busy. Goebbels was there and von Papen. Oh, they were all there—only the fire brigade were very late."

Rose said a little breathlessly, " And the man who committed this crime ? "

Stanislaus answered, " Dear Mama, you mean the man who was arrested. He looked quite young and rather stupid. Judging from the way he walked—oh, they didn't manhandle him—I should judge him to be a pronounced homosexual."

Rose said in mild protest, " Stanislaus, my dear—please ! "

" Sorry, Mama. Evil communications corrupt good manners —I've been among the brownshirts."

Isaac held up his hand, Miriam saw that it shook a little.

" Listen," he said, " it will be necessary for us all to walk carefully. We are peaceful people, we are not Communists. I myself hate and dread Communism. But remember that we are Jews, and all Jews will be suspect. Do not discuss this matter. Shrug your shoulders and say that it was a terrible thing, though " —and for a moment a smile hovered round his lips—" the loss of the Reichstag is not a great calamity. Architecture in 1884 was not at its best and Wilhelm the First was not the greatest judge of architecture. Now, it is very late; Rose, my dear, you must rest. To bed, all of you, and may the Lord our God protect us all."

The day which followed seemed to Miriam one of the strangest she had ever spent. There was a sense of apprehension and suspense in the air. It had begun to circulate that the man who had set fire to the Reichstag was a Dutchman called Van der Lubbe. He was quite young and had already been interrogated. Some doubts were expressed regarding his sanity. On the whole, people went about quietly; there were the same number of beggars in the streets, but Miriam fancied that there were more storm troopers than usual and that they watched everyone with bright, cold, suspicious eyes. Beyond whistling as she passed to do her daily shopping—beyond making remarks of an unpleasant if flattering nature—they did not attempt either to question or molest her. She remembered that she was fairhaired, and that in all probability not one of them suspected her of being a Jewish woman, she passed as a pure-blooded Aryan.

"How I hate them all!" she thought as she hurried along. "How loathsome they have become! I shall be thankful when Charles is back. He must use all his influence with papa and mama to persuade them to come back to England with us." Then she asked herself again, "After all, of what am I afraid? The Reichstag has been burnt, they say by a Communist. We have heard of Jews being ill-treated, but not in sufficient numbers to make me feel this dreadful sensation of cold fear."

That evening, when he came home, Isaac appeared to have recovered his good spirits. He told them that this young man, Van der Lubbe, had confessed everything. Carefully he had smuggled incendiary materials into the building.

Stanislaus asked, "How—exactly, Papa? The place is always filled with janitors, policemen, guards and the like."

Isaac shrugged his shoulders. "I admit that I do not know. There is some talk that he managed to make his way into the house of Captain Goering, and from that house there is a passage leading to the Reichstag. This young man admits, too, that he enjoys setting fire to buildings. It is a form of mania with him. It appears that they are very satisfied by the enquiry." He smiled at them, and Miriam wondered if there was not a hint of malice in his expression.

He suggested that they should go out, to take coffee at a café where Jews were allowed and indeed welcomed. He said that it was unwise to cling too closely to the house "as if we were afraid".

Stanislaus asked, "Aren't we, then, afraid, Papa?"

"No, my son," Isaac replied, and it seemed to Miriam that he held himself more erect, looked taller as he spoke; "we have done nothing wrong—not one of us. We are Jews, but not Communists. We have lived decently, behaved well, done our duty to the State. I have always treated everyone with *derech erets*—and I shall continue to do so."

Again Stanislaus spoke. "*Derech erets!* How much do these young hooligans know of good manners, and what do they care for them?"

"Perhaps more than we realize. Well, my son, are you coming with me?"

Miriam said, "I'd like to come too. Mama, will you be all right with Truda? We shan't be very long."

"My dear, of course. I shall get Truda to come and talk to me here."

They walked to the café, one where Jews were still permitted. It was a pleasant, bright place kept by a man called Josef Zimmer. He was a big scarlet-faced fellow, no one could have looked less like the typical idea of a Jew. He beamed at Isaac Noller and came to attend to him personally.

He glanced round the café; it was almost empty, except for a young man and woman at the next table and two elderly men seated near the door. Zimmer, after seeing that the Nollers were served, sat down at their table.

" Ah, Herr Noller, what do you think of last night ? "

" A dreadful thing indeed."

" The work, they say, of one scoundrelly Communist—think of that ! "

Isaac smiled. " I do, I have been thinking about it a great deal. The Reichstag is a very large building. The young man must be very active."

" And," Stanislaus added in a low voice, " he must have known the interior of the Reichstag very accurately. But possibly he had obtained a plan."

Zimmer said, " I hear that they were all there—Hitler, Goering, Goebbels and von Papen. How did Goebbels strike you ? "

With a low chuckle Stanislaus said, " He didn't—I have no doubt that sooner or later he will ! "

" *Gewalt!* " Zimmer exclaimed in horror. " Never even think such a thing, Mr. Stanislaus. God forfend ! "

They left the café; the two young people had gone, but the two old Jews were still there, indulging in a long argument about some exact translation of the Hebrew into German. Stanislaus caught a phrase as he passed uttered in a calm, scholarly voice.

Outside the streets were quiet, once or twice they passed a party of storm troopers, but except for turning their heads to stare at Miriam they appeared to take not the slightest interest in the three Jewish people. At home—and Miriam thought what a *safe* place " home " seemed—Rose and Truda were seated on either side of the fire, talking of some particular pickle. Truda's sister had written from Switzerland speaking of it highly. As they entered, Rose said, " Yes, the secret, I can see, lies in allowing it to stand in a cool place for forty-eight hours——" She broke off and turned to them, smiling, " Ah, you're back."

Miriam stooped and kissed her. " Tomorrow is the first of March. I've not much longer here. I had a letter from Charles this morning, he is trying hard to get here a day or two before he promised. Almost my last night at home ! "

Isaac said, " Then let us all drink a bottle of wine together. Yes,

you will enjoy a glass of wine, Truda. I shall get it, if you will set
out glasses."

Together they drank the good German wine, Truda with
particular appreciation, Isaac thoughtfully, as if he savoured it with
care. They finished; Isaac said, " Now we shall sleep well . . .
don't forget your night prayers, children." He had said that every
night since Miriam could remember.

It was Rose who did not move, then she said in that gentle
voice which they all loved, " I have never asked you to share in
my prayers, but now I do. There is nothing that can offend any
of you. Please," she smiled, " to do your mother a favour."

Isaac watched her, blinking his tears away. Stanislaus answered,
" Darling, sweetest mother, I'd say any prayer to please you."

" Then please say—with me—' Lighten our darkness, we beseech
Thee, O Lord, and of Thy great mercy defend us from all perils
and dangers of this night. Amen.' There—I shall sleep very
soundly. Thank you all."

It seemed to Miriam that the night passed very quickly; she
woke to find Truda by her bedside with a cup of tea. Truda
despised tea, but since Miriam had married an Englishman she felt
that it was incumbent to conform to what she knew to be English
ways.

Miriam rubbed her eyes. " Is it morning already ? "

Truda beamed down at her. " Indeed ! One day nearer the
return of your dear husband. There, drink the tea—ugh, how
nasty it smells !—while it is still hot."

She went down to breakfast to find her father and Stanislaus
waiting. Rose, since her illness, always had her breakfast taken to
her by Truda. Isaac smiled at his daughter. " How is my dear
one; you slept well ? "

She kissed him affectionately, thinking as she had done since
she was a little girl, " How nice papa always smells ! So well
washed—and yet people talk of—dirty Jews ! "

Stanislaus laughed. " When these family greetings are over,
might a poor hard-working fellow have his coffee ? "

Miriam kissed him good morning. He looked better, less
strained this morning; his eyes were very clear and bright, his
skin looked as if it still glowed with the application of soap and
water, a pale gleam of sunshine filtered through the windows and
touched his smooth fair hair.

She said, " Yes, I'll give you your breakfast, Mr. Lord of
Creation, just because you know how good-looking you are !
Oh, Papa, it's not like the breakfasts we used to have, is it ? Still,
porridge is good for us, they say that it makes bone and sinew.

Do you miss your real coffee, Papa ? I suppose one gets used to this—mixture.''

" We're thankful for what we can get," Isaac said; " it's not what we used to have, but so few things are as they used to be. Ah, well, so long as God grants us health and strength, we must not——"

" What's that ? " Miriam interrupted sharply. She sprang to her feet and ran to the window. There was a sudden hammering on the door which rang through the house. " There's a big car at the door—and "—her voice became a shriek—" men in black uniforms. Papa—what is it ? "

Stanislaus, his face suddenly white, said evenly, " I'll go and see. Sit down, both of you, go on eating."

They obeyed him. Miriam was shaking, her father's hands trembled. They heard a voice demand, " Is this the house of Noller, the Jew bastard ? "

" The house of Isaac Noller, a law-abiding citizen," they heard Stanislaus answer.

The rest of the words were drowned in shouts and hoarse laughter, then the room was filled with young men wearing the black leather jackets they had come to know so well. A man with a long pale face and small burning eyes went to where Isaac sat.

" You are Isaac Noller, the Jew swine ? "

Isaac replied very quietly, " My name is Noller and I am a Jew."

" Stand up when you speak to me, you filthy dog ! D'you hear, stand up ! "

Isaac rose and Stanislaus wrenched himself free from the hands of the two young men who held him by the arms.

" What is this ? " he demanded. " We are decent people, we are not concerned in political matters. This is an intrusion—illegal."

The white-faced man glanced at him and said, " Shut his mouth for him ! " A third man who might have been pleasant-looking enough except for his loose wet-looking mouth rushed forward and struck Stanislaus over the face. Miriam saw the blood trickling from her brother's lips; she screamed, tried to reach him, but she was held fast.

" Shut up, Jew sow ! Behave yourself or you'll get something you won't like . . ." he guffawed, showing long yellow teeth, " though we might."

One of the men holding Stanislaus panted, " God, he's strong as an ox ! "

The white-faced man said, " You fools, you know your job, don't you ? Hit him—go on, hit him."

Isaac had not moved, he stood as if carved in stone, his face completely blank. Miriam saw that his lips moved, and when Stanislaus slipped to the ground, unconscious after repeated blows on the head and face with rubber truncheons, she noticed the beads of sweat on her father's forehead.

The horse-faced man turned back to him. " You dumb beast ! " he screamed. " You and your damned son and your whore of a daughter sit here guzzling while honest people go hungry." He picked up two of the cups and hurled them into the fireplace, dipped his hand into Miriam's half-empty porridge-plate, and scooping out some of the oatmeal, daubed it on Isaac's face. " You would sit in a café and give your opinion of the Reichstag fire, make criticisms, discuss the leaders ! The work was done by Communists and well you know it, for you're a stinking Communist yourself. Two of you . . . soil your hands by touching the dirty Jew—it's necessary, one of the sacrifices you have to make for the Leader ! Take him away, he can tell his lies to the court in due time. As for the other Jew—kick him until he stands up, he's only shamming; they're all damned cowards, every one——"

It was then, as two troopers leapt forward to hold Isaac, that Rose Noller appeared in the open doorway. She was wearing a blue dressing-gown over her nightdress, her hair was still in the plaits into which she put it every night. She looked curiously young and innocent, she stared round the room, her eyes wide with horror.

" What are you doing here ? " she demanded of the man with the clay-coloured face. " Isaac, what does all this mean ? "

" It means," said the fellow, " that you—you Jewish sow, and your filthy swine of a bastard husband—will do as you're told or it will be worse for you. Go on, boys, take the old Jew away to the Hedemannstrasse. He can tell his lies there ! Keep hold of the girl and kick the son to his feet—lying there shamming ! Kick him where it hurts most, Hans ! "

Two troopers began to hustle Isaac towards the door. He made no resistance, he only spoke to Rose, saying quietly and calmly, " Do not distress yourself, dear one. I am innocent—I shall be back with you very soon."

She stared at him, her eyes filled with horror, then swayed a little and fell in a crumpled heap at his feet. Isaac, filled with sudden strength, tore himself free from the great red hands which held him, and dropped on his knees, crying, " Rose—speak—my dear, all is well. Rose . . . ! " His voice rose to a wail, he looked up at the two stolid faces above him and said, " My God, she's dead ! You've killed her ! "

The man like a horse knelt down and touched her still face.

"The Jew's right," he said, "the sow's dead. Two of you carry her up and lay her on a bed somewhere. I'll take care of the old man. Get that long lump of Jewish refuse to his feet and look sharp. We don't want to be here all day."

The two men carried Rose's body upstairs; they were a considerable time, and when they returned the grey-faced fellow said, "Hand over what you've got! The things these lice have—a gold watch, gold brooch, what else? Gold studs! There you are, plenty of money while honest folk go hungry without boots to their feet. Take the old man down to the car, make him move. So! You're on your damned feet, are you?"

Stanislaus stood supported by two troopers. His face was bleeding, his mouth dripped blood, one eye was closed and already turning black. He seemed only half-conscious, unable to comprehend what was taking place. Miriam called, "Stan—Stan—they've killed mama!"

He turned his head towards the place from which her voice came as if he was searching for her and could not locate her position. Isaac had gone, they began to push Stanislaus towards the door. Miriam screamed, her head thrown back, her mouth wide open. The dreadful sounds seemed to fill the room. She looked like a lunatic, from time to time she uttered some noises which might have been made by a wild animal. Once she screamed, "Stan—don't leave me! Stan—oh, God, don't let Stan go!" then slumped in the storm trooper's grasp like a half-filled sack, and kneeling, her head swinging senselessly from side to side like the pendulum of a clock, remained.

One trooper said to the other, "Mind you, she's a good-looking whore."

The other grinned. "She won't be much longer, I reckon."

The grey-faced man was examining the table, picking up spoons and forks and stuffing them into his pockets. He muttered, "The Jew swine use silver!" He smashed a couple of plates in his righteous annoyance, then began to open drawers and to search for papers. Isaac's desk proved to contain nothing but neat piles of paid bills, one or two documents stating what rates were due and a few receipts for contributions which he had made to various charitable societies.

The storm troopers had allowed Miriam to drop sprawling to the floor and were smoking cigarettes, their faces bored and impassive. The man at the desk flung a handful of papers into the grate, muttering as he did so.

" Artful old swine, too cunning to leave anything about !
Damn him ! "

There was a sound outside, one of the troopers turned and
looked out of the window. He said to the man at the desk,
" Here's someone ! An officer—he's coming in."

The tread of feet grew nearer, and a young officer entered the
room. He was tall and admirably groomed. His expression was
arrogant and he stood staring at the three men, his grey eyes like
flints. He was strikingly good-looking with a fine straight nose
and a mouth which, while well shaped, was a trifle too full. His
round, obstinate chin was cleft deeply.

The storm troopers stood to attention. The officer barked,
" What's this ? "

The man by the desk replied, " Orders, Captain. This is the
house of the Jew Noller. He and his son have been taken to the
Hedemannstrasse. The old woman fell down dead—two of the
men carried her body upstairs. Laid her on one of the beds.
That's the daughter—collapsed on the floor."

Captain Erich von Kessel turned and looked at Miriam as she
lay there. He was a sensual young man, and over a year ago when
he had seen Miriam Noller in the street he had stared after her
enviously. He had made enquiries, had ascertained where she
lived, and she had come to occupy his thoughts to an almost
unbearable extent. He had heard that she was married, had gone
to live in England; in a kind of fury he had flung himself into an
orgy of sexual adventures. Then, only a few days ago, he had
seen her again, lovelier than ever. All his old desire for her had
flamed, he was consumed by it. She had been walking with a
young man so like her that it was obvious that he was her brother;
he had seen her too with an old man—doubtless her father, Isaac
Noller, now on his way to be examined.

He forced his eyes away from her as she lay in a crumpled heap,
only saying, " Lift her up and lay her on that sofa." Then to
the third man, " Have you found anything ? "

" Nothing yet, Captain. Too cunning, probably got everything
hidden under the floorboards. They'll get the information out
of them at the Hedemannstrasse, never fear."

Miriam's eyes were open. Von Kessel walked over to her and
looked down at her; her face was drained of all colour, her eyes
looked wild and distraught.

He said, " You are Miriam Noller, eh ? "

She said, speaking thickly as a half-drunken woman might
speak, " They have taken away my father and brother. My mother
is dead."

" You're married ?   To an Englishman ? "

" He is coming soon.   We must bury my mother."

" Soon ?   How soon ? "

" I don't know.   One day—tomorrow, next week—I don't know."

Von Kessel was not a particularly clever young man, except when his sensuality took control of his rather dull brain as it did now.   He said to the eldest of the troopers. " Great care must be exercised here. Her husband is an Englishman. They like Jews in England, even the aristocracy mix with them ! Leave this in my hands. There is a telephone here ? Find out then ! Get me the Adelaide Sophia clinic in the Kurfurstendamm. I wish to speak to the matron. Give my name—Captain von Kessel. Move, man —d'you hear ! "

A moment later he was speaking to the matron. She knew him very well, he was exceedingly rich, and several times young ladies—very beautiful young ladies—had come to the clinic for some trivial operation, and Captain von Kessel had paid the exorbitant bills with calmness and courtesy. He had closed the door of the dining-room behind him, and even though the horse-faced man listened with his ear to the keyhole he could hear nothing, except such words as, " Yes . . . indeed. Well, many thanks . . . yes, immediately," which were of no help or interest to anyone.

Von Kessel returned to the dining-room. Miriam lay with her eyes closed, the storm troopers stood stiffly to attention.

Von Kessel said, " Everything is arranged. I have the matter in hand. You may continue your search. I shall take the lady with me to a clinic. As I say, she is a British subject and care must be exercised. I advise you," he repeated with emphasis, " I say that I *advise* you to keep your mouths shut as much as possible. Two filthy Jews are one thing, but a British subject is quite another. Help her down to my car."

A moment later Miriam, who had sunk into a stupor again, was being driven in von Kessel's handsome Buick towards the nursing home.

The great silent black car passed a stout old woman who with a basket on her arm was evidently going shopping. She was not hurrying unduly, but she covered the ground at a smart pace. Her face looked like a crumpled white paper bag. Her lips moved as she walked, she clutched a piece of paper in her hand. She whispered to herself, " I shall send it to Max—just that—Max. I won't use the name Noller. Max will be sufficient."

Truda was on her way to the General Post Office.

ELEVEN

ALICE said, "Maxie, you're eating nothing. The wretched old fire has nothing to do with us. It says here in the *News Chronicle* that to say that it was the work of the German Government is just nonsense. The Communists must have done it."

Max nodded. "It doesn't matter who did it, my dear—in Germany at the moment all Jews are regarded as Communists. Whoever burnt the damned Reichstag, the Jews will be blamed. I wish to heaven Miriam was back and the rest of the family. I tell you, Alice, it's all going to be very ugly."

He started, listening intently, and heard the quick knock of a telegraph boy; he looked very white, his eyes widened with fear.

"I'll get it," he said, and returned a moment later holding the open telegram in his hand, "It's come," he said, "trouble of some kind. This was sent to 'Max', not to 'Noller'. It says *Family affairs your presence required Father*. I must go. . . ." He sat down heavily in his chair, propping his chin on his hand. "The quickest way—'plane, I suppose. I must get on to Herbert Borridge, hire one somehow. Alice, put some things in a bag for me, will you? Send someone to the bank—yes, I'll write a cheque." He pulled out a cheque-book and wrote a cheque for an amount which seemed to Alice to be staggering. He must have noticed the expression on her face, for he smiled miserably, saying, "I know, my dear, but it may have to buy their lives. I've no illusions. I'll get on to Borridge."

Yes, a 'plane was possible, sufficiently difficult, but possible. Borridge reminded him that he must have the necessary papers. "They're very hot on documents, Noller, remember that. Passport in order? Right—I can get you off in an hour. Drive straight down to our place at Borley, ask for me. Hope everything will be all right, old man. Don't panic."

Max drove out of London, Alice seated beside him. He drove, as he always did, with care, but faster than was usual for him, she thought. He scarcely spoke, and when she turned to watch him she saw that his face looked grim and set.

Once he gave a short barking laugh. "Too many houses," he said. "London's too big." Then relapsed into silence again.

She said, "It's not going to be dangerous for you, Maxie, is it?"

"Not if I can help it!" Again that queer laugh. "I shan't take

156

any chances, but—I'm going to *do* something, if I have to set the whole damned lot of Nazis by the ears."

" You don't know that . . ." she hesitated, " anything—has actually happened, do you ? "

" I know," he answered in a low fierce tone, " that unless something had happened, or was on the point of happening, that telegram would never have been sent. There, Borley airport ! Thank God ! " He stopped the car and sprang out.

A man said, " Mr. Noller—private 'plane ? Ready, sir, on the runway. Mr. Borridge is waiting for you."

Max nodded. " Take my bag, will you ? Alice dear, don't wait. Just drive right home again. No use hanging about. Don't worry, I'll get in touch with you—somehow." He put his arm round her shoulders and pulled her to him. " Don't worry, nothing to worry about. Bless you, you're a grand woman ! "

She felt a sob rise in her throat. " Oh, Maxie, Maxie, do be careful ! "

" Of course. God bless you."

She watched him break into a run as he followed the man who carried his bag, and then sat staring at the airfield, surely of all places in the world the most dismal. The light was fading, the whole place looked cold and unfriendly; the 'plane—which looked so ridiculously small—was waiting. Max reached it, she saw him shake hands with a big burly man in a heavy coat, then he turned and waved. A moment later he had climbed into the 'plane. The sudden roar of engines broke the stillness; she watched men running here and there; slowly the 'plane began to move, taxi-ing along until she saw its nose begin to rise. Higher and higher, circling round, until it seemed to take a definite course away from the airport. She watched until it was lost to sight, then started her engine and drove back to London.

Max disliked flying, it had always bored him, and this 'plane was particularly uncomfortable. His knees felt cramped, and as they flew night began to fall and he could see nothing except here and there lights far below twinkling and sparkling. The words of some poem which he had learned as a child kept running through his brain:

" In peaceful homes he saw the light
Of household fire gleam warm and bright——"

He wished they were shining " warm and bright " in this wretched 'plane, for he felt chilled and wished that he had brought a heavier coat with him. He quite consciously continued to think of trivial

6

things, anything to prevent his mind from indulging in speculations regarding what he might find in Berlin. He even felt in his
coat pocket for a daily paper, and unfolding it tried to do the
crossword puzzle. " Swords are bright when——" Seven letters.
How the devil did he know ? " I am Sir Oracle and when——"
Something about " my mouth let no man bark "—or was it " no
dog bark " ? He stuffed the paper back into his pocket and felt
that of all things in a hateful world, crossword puzzles were the
most hateful. Berlin—the Reichstag fire. Jew-baiting. That devil
Streicher, who boasted that he would be " Jew-baiter Number
One ". Papa, mama . . . with her weak heart . . . Miriam,
waiting for Charles, and young Stanislaus—were they all right ?
Could his abominable brother Jacob have had a hand in something
infamous ?

Borridge—decent fellow, Borridge—had said, " Hope there's
no trouble."

Max had answered, " God only knows. I've had a telegram to
say that I'm wanted."

Borridge pursed his thick lips. " I don't trust the bastards—
these Nazis."

" We saw them in the war, didn't we, Herbert ? " Max said.

" You're not taking a gun, are you ? Good," as Max replied
in the negative, " far better not to. Only gives them a handle
against you. Civilian with arms ! All that stuff. Well, old man,
over the top and the best of luck."

He dozed and woke with a start, his legs cramped and aching.
In his pocket he found his big silver flask, Alice must have slipped
it there. He stared at it, a fine flask—his father-in-law Julius
Berman had given it to him years ago. He unscrewed the bayonet
cap and poured some brandy into the cup. It seemed to go right
down to his feet—warm, grateful. Someone's cocoa had been
called that—" grateful and comforting ". Again he dozed, and his
sleep was made fearful by dreams; horrid shapes, sights, dreadful
noises. He woke dripping with sweat, crying, " Where are you ?
For God's sake, where are you ? " He felt that he must have yelled
so loudly that the pilot must have heard, then realized that the
noise he had made was scarcely more than a squeak.

The second pilot said, " Berlin in ten minutes, Mr. Noller."

He looked at his watch, it was twenty minutes past seven.
What were his plans ? He had made none. He had tried to prevent
himself thinking about what might be waiting for him at Berlin.
Home—that was obviously the first thing to do—home, to discuss
—whatever there was to discuss with someone—whoever was
there to talk with him.

Yes, home first. Bergmannstrasse—number twenty-five. Even the thought of going home soothed him. Nothing could have happened there, the place was always so peaceful, so bright—not, possibly, furnished in the taste which Max preferred, but there was something almost lovable in the things on which his father and mother set such value. Furniture which had belonged to Uncle Stanislaus, things which they had bought when they were married, to practically everything some small personal history was attached.

The pilot said, "We're going to land, better slip your belt on, sir."

Lights coming nearer, the ground coming up to meet them, flares, the dark figures of men running towards them. They had touched down, they were taxi-ing rather bumpily along the runway. He was in Berlin.

Max unloosed his belt, stood up flexing his stiff knees. He thanked the two men who had brought him over, using the usual formula. "Thanks for a good trip. Have a drink with me, will you ? Good luck ! "

He climbed down from the 'plane and spoke to the man who was waiting, holding the ladder, in German.

" Can I get a taxi immediately ? "

" I'll try, sir. There might be one."

There was a taxi. Max prepared to get in. "Twenty-five, Bergmannstrasse."

The driver said, " It's a long way——"

" You'll get well paid, don't worry, and drive as quickly as you can."

" All right. Heil Hitler ! "

Max asked sharply. " What's that ? "

" Heil Hitler ! Everyone says that—a tribute to the Leader."

" I see—I've been away for a long time. Drive on."

The streets as they reached the town seemed strangely deserted. Max saw the dark shapes of storm troopers parading along, pushing everyone out of their way, as in the old days German officers had shouldered mere civilians off the footpath. The car stopped, he was home.

There was no light in the window, and Max felt his heart hammering against his ribs, knew that once again his forehead was damp. He paid the driver, an amount which was extortionate.

Mechanically he said, " That's far too much."

" Petrol's dear in these days. Heil Hitler ! "

He turned to enter the house; he remembered how his mother

always insisted that they should have latchkeys. Even Daniel in New York had his old key.

His mother had said, " I like to know that all my children—no matter where they may live—can get into their own home at any hour. It would be dreadful if one of you came and we were all out—away on holiday. No, keep your keys."

A dim light was burning in the hall and the door of the back sitting-room opened as Max entered, closing the front door behind him. He saw a very old, shabby-looking priest, small, rotund, with steel-rimmed glasses. He recognized him, it was his father's old friend the Catholic priest Father Muldoon.

He blinked his eyes behind their thick lenses and said, " Ah, Max—you are here. Come in and sit down for a moment. Truda will bring you some coffee." He called down the stairs, " Truda, here is Mr. Max."

" But where are the others ? " Max asked. " My mother . . . my father . . ."

The priest laid his hand on Max's arm. " I shall tell you—ah, here is the good Truda."

The stout old woman flung herself into Max's arms; she was sobbing, unable to speak. She uttered disjointed words, scraps of sentences.

Again the priest spoke. " Poor Mr. Max has been travelling for a long time. Now don't you think it would be kind to give him some coffee ? "

" Dear God, forgive me—poor Max ! Yes, I'll get it."

" Now," Max said, " tell me, please."

Very gently the old man told him as much of the story as he had been able to gather. Max listened, his face deathly white, motionless.

" Then my father, Miriam and my brother—where are they ? "

" God help them, we don't know."

" My mother——"

" The funeral was this morning. What had to be done had to be done quickly. I made what arrangements I could. Rightly or wrongly, I am not concerned with that—I performed the service; she is buried in the Catholic cemetery. I don't think that she suffered, Max."

" No, no, we must hope that. But the others—where are they ? How can I find them ? Miriam—with those devils ! " He sat without speaking, only rocking himself backwards and forwards. Truda brought in the coffee, he looked at her gratefully. " Truda, what is going to happen ? Is this the end of everything ? How

THE MORNING WILL COME   161

clever you were to get that telegram to me—it was you who sent it, eh ? "

" Stanislaus told me to send it—if anything happened."

" Then he expected—this—something . . . Stanislaus knew ? " She sighed. " Always a clever boy he was."

Max sat staring at the room, the familiar furniture, the ornaments which his mother had always admired. An ordinary room in an ordinary house, where ordinary people had lived together, worked hard and honestly and where they had been happy. He had no illusions concerning himself or his family; Isaac was a clever business man, never sufficiently clever—or sufficiently unscrupulous—to make a fortune; his mother—he shivered—sweet, the essence of kindness, living for her husband and her children. Daniel, himself—just two average men, ready to work and make their way in the world to the best of their ability. Only, perhaps, Stanislaus and Miriam were different. They were both so much more handsome than the rest, their colouring was brighter, he had often thought that Stan's brain was clearer than his own. There was something so clean-cut about them both. And now—this pleasant, modest home was broken up, ruined, filled with terror, horror, speculation as to what had happened in that other room. Something that had been essentially good, wholesome, warm and decent was destroyed, trampled in the filth and muck of Nazism.

Soon Charles Hare would come, eager to greet his wife, and he must be told that she had—gone, and that none of them knew where to find her. The thought of Charles, with his pleasant, fresh face, his clear eyes and his devotion to Miriam, which he never troubled to hide in the least no matter in what company he found himself, filled Max with a new and dreadful sense of apprehension.

He stared at old Father Muldoon, at Truda—with her face swollen from the many tears which she had shed—and suddenly covered his face with his hands and began to cry. He cried as if his soul were being wrenched from him, great tearing sobs shook him, again and again he caught his breath as if he were choking. Truda rushed to him, put her arms round him and held him as she had done when he was a small boy suffering from some unhappiness or disappointment.

" Max, Max," she murmured, " you must not cry. You are the person we depend on, you're our hope, you must be our strength. We look to you—you will not disappoint us. Somewhere is your father, your brother, your sister—you must find them. Thank God we have no need to be anxious for your dear mother—on her be peace—she is with God. The others—Max, this is where

you will forget everything except your duty. There, there, how
often has your good father said, ' Now we shall consult Max ! '
That is what he is saying now—he is waiting to see what Max, his
first-born, will do."

Max raised his haggard face. " Yes, Truda—yes. Father, I
am sorry."

" Now don't be sorry, my son," the old man said. " That is
Nature's way of helping. That is how she—wise old lady that she
is—lessens the strain. Now—you must think—here we have the
Abomination of Desolation standing where it ought not, now
we have the Temple of God—for all good homes are temples of
God—laid waste. You must think what is best to do."

Max nodded. " Yes—yes, Father Muldoon. First this house
must be kept open because my sister's husband will be here any
day. He must not come and find it closed. Then . . ." He paused,
his face changed, his eyes shone suddenly. " I've remembered. My
dreadful brother ! Jacob ! He shall find them for me ! Is it too
late ?—what, only half past eight ! I must go at once, Father, I
shall see you tomorrow. Truda, lock the doors and wait for me.
I have my key." He gave his strange, new barking laugh. " Now
we shall begin to move. Where do these scoundrels have their
headquarters ? "

Father Muldoon said, " The Hedemannstrasse . . . but tonight . . . ? "

" Now," Max said, " now."

Truda said, " Yes, tonight, Max. But first you must wash, put
on a clean collar, shave if it is necessary. You must go to these
filthy dogs as a very important English gentleman. Come, I shall
show you where I have put your bag."

The little priest nodded. " Truda is right. I wish you good
night, and go with God, my dear Max—go with God."

Ten minutes later Max left the house, and walked swiftly in
the direction which Truda had given him. The streets were almost
empty, except for the black-coated storm troopers. They scarcely
glanced at him. He was forced to ask one or two people to direct
him, but at last he found himself outside the headquarters of the
Nazi Party. He stood staring at the building for a moment, then
walked in briskly. He thought as he did so, " I've got to act !
They can't do anything to me. I'm a British subject ! God damn
them all ! "

A tall, thick-set young man with a pimply face sprang
forward.

" What is your business ? "

Max stared at him insolently. " None of yours, I should say. I

wish to know where I can find my brother—Herr Jacob Noller.
Direct me to him if he is here, immediately."

The young man scratched his head, repeating, " Noller—Noller
—Jacob Noller ?   Let me enquire."

He returned and asked Max—with marked respect—to follow
him. He was shown into a small overheated room, where a very
small thin man sat at a huge desk. He rose as Max entered and
said, " Heil Hitler," in a tone which was almost conversational.

Max said, " Good evening. I wish to see my brother—Jacob
Noller."

" Kindly sit down, Herr Noller."

" Thanks, I'd rather stand.   I have no time to waste."

The thin man smiled, showing a number of teeth stopped with
what appeared to be silver; he bowed politely. Max longed to
drive his fist into his face.

" Herr Noller, we waste little time here. Allow me to compli-
ment you on your German. You speak it like a native. Your
brother—a man who is held in the highest respect by all the Party,
who has received signal favours from the Leader himself—has for
patriotic reasons changed his name."

" Seems to be a habit," Max said.   " I hope that he has not taken
the name which a certain—exalted—person cast off. Well,"
sharply, " what does he call himself ? "

" Brusch—Klaus Brusch. He is an Honorary Aryan, in fact it
has been proved that he is only fifty per cent Jew. Forgive me,
Herr Noller, I have no wish to be offensive. It would appear that
his mother was—an Englishwoman."

Max, feeling suddenly cold, replied, " That is correct. Now I
wish to see my brother, if you please."

The thin man continued to smile. " Herr Brusch is not in the
building. He has his own office, and we shall be honoured to
send you there in a car. Herr Noller, please believe that we
welcome visits from Englishmen; we have nothing to hide—
nothing. So long as you remain in Berlin you are at liberty to
go where you please, to see everything. We are not—not," he
repeated with emphasis, " against the Jews, but there are times
when the Jews make matters very difficult for us—for our noble
Leader."

Max said, " Good ! That's nice to hear. Now this car, if you'll
be so good."

The official touched a bell on his desk, a young man—they
were all young—entered and saluted smartly. He raised his eyes
for a moment to the large photograph of the Leader which hung
above the desk, saying as he did so, " Heil Hitler ! "

" The trouble with them," Max thought, " is that the damn'
fools have no sense of humour ! "

The car was ordered. " And be quick about it, this gentleman
is to be taken to the Minister Brusch immediately. Report when
the car is here." He turned to Max again. " You have accommodation for the night, Herr Noller ? If not, it can be arranged.
The Adlon would perhaps be convenient for you ? "

" I have accommodation, thank you."

" Then here is your car, and oblige me by giving my compliments to Herr Minister Brusch. Good night, Herr Noller, good
night."

They drove in the great silent car through dark streets. Max
wondered where they were going, the wretched little creature
seated there below Hitler's picture had not told him. When the
car stopped he said to the driver, " I see that we're in the Charlotten-
strasse."

" Excuse, sir, the Wilhelmstrasse."

" Of course, how foolish of me. Good night."

" I was instructed to wait, sir."

" Very good."

He walked into the big hall with its black-and-white-marble
pavement; again he was asked his business by another young
man with fair hair and blue eyes. Max thought, " Ah, no doubt
the true Nordic type, blast him ! " He said, " I wish to see Herr
Brusch. There is my card. Immediately."

He waited, his heart hammering. He must control himself.
Jacob was necessary to him, it was vital that he got the information which he needed. Yet to talk to his brother, to ask favours—
the idea revolted him. He remembered that Truda used to say,
" Those who sup with the devil must use a long spoon." He'd
use a long spoon !

" This way, Herr Noller."

An immense staircase. He wondered who had lived in this
great house before the Forty Thieves took possession. Probably
this had been the home of some rich, well-born German family,
a place where music had been heard, where people had gathered
to talk of art, literature and the like. Now, here it was overrun
with these usurpers, these criminals.

The young trooper knocked on a door, was bidden to enter,
and did so announcing, " Heil Hitler ! Herr Noller, Minister."

Max entered the overheated room; it was large, the desk behind
which his brother stood was immense; there were telephones,
dictaphones, electric bells and, over the desk, the inevitable picture
of Hitler. Jacob did not move, he waited until the door closed

behind the trooper, then said in the rasping voice which Max remembered so well, " Well, Max, what is it ? "

" I think you know the answer to that question as well as I do. Where are they ?   Where are my father, Stanislaus and my sister Miriam ? "

" Sit down—let me explain to you."

" I don't wish to sit down and there can be no explanation."

Jacob shrugged his narrow shoulders, his cadaverous face looked haggard and drawn, his eyes were sunk in his head.   Max thought, " Damn him, he looks like a skull ! "

" I was not informed of this—arrest," Jacob said, " it is scarcely my province.   This happened two days ago, and things move rapidly.   I hear—on the evidence of two trustworthy people—that your father and his son, accompanied by Noller's daughter——"

Max's irration and anxiety got the better of him, he rapped out, " For God's sake can't you say ' father ' and Stanislaus instead of using all that circumlocution ? "

His brother continued as if he had not heard what he said. " These Jews visited a café where they expressed themselves very freely concerning the fire at the Reichstag.   They spoke slightingly of the Leader, of Vice-Chancellor von Papen and of Captain Goering.   It has long been known that Stanislaus Noller is against the Party and that his father is always ready to argue—not openly, mark you—against the present Government."

" He never cared what the Government was so long as people had work and food !   And you know that as well as I do."

" He was heard to say," Jacob continued inexorably, " that he wondered what Count Bismarck thought as he watched the Reichstag burn.   It is well known that Bismarck was a friend of the Jews !   Oh, there is plenty of evidence against Isaac Noller ! "

" All right, if you call that kind of childish stuff—evidence !   I want to know—where is he ?   I've come to take him away.   Now listen, Jacob, I am a British citizen, whether you like it or not; all of us—except my father—are fifty per cent British—by blood. I am not without influence—in very high places indeed.   Your brother Daniel, an American citizen, is also a man of tremendous importance in New York.   Oh, he is modest—that's his way— but his influence is very great."   He slipped his hand into his coat pocket, and inside the pocket pushed forward the stem of his pipe.   He kept his eyes on Jacob, saying, " Don't move ! There's no need for you to get hurt, only, believe me, I am going to know where my father is—if not—well. . . . Now get cracking, Jacob."

" What do you want ? Remember that I have only to press one of these bells and I can have you pretty badly handled——"

" No, you can't—oh, no, you can't. I'm a British citizen and never forget it. Now—where is he ?—and I want a note from you giving him safe conduct out of this blasted, infernal country. Get moving, Jacob, I might get nervous—something might go off ! Write what you like—tell what lies you like—only no monkey tricks. I can read German as well as you can write it."

For the first time Jacob Noller looked actually worried. He said nervously, " Put down that gun, Max. There'd be trouble if it was found on you. I can't release Isaac Noller on my own. You must give me until tomorrow. Come back here—in the morning —at ten o'clock. I swear to you that by that time I'll have a permit —I swear it."

" I wonder what your oath's worth ? Not much——"

The grey eyes met his, they were hard and cold, and yet Max saw in them something which was disturbing. Under the coldness, the hardness, lay—madness. This brother of his, like the rest of them, was crazy with a lust for power, with a hatred for the Jews and with a longing for persecution. Jacob rose, it was obvious that the interview was over.

Max said, " No, no, stop a minute. Remember there is not only my father, there's Miriam and Stanislaus. I want information about them. I don't ask for information about my mother—may her soul rest in peace—for these brutes virtually killed her. It might interest you to know that she was buried early this morning."

He watched Jacob's face closely, and fancied that he saw a sudden flicker pass over it ; was it regret, distress ? Max couldn't tell, for it was extinguished instantly, and the same expressionless face was before him.

" Remember—Miriam and Stanislaus."

" I shall do my best, that is all I can say. Good night."

Max turned without another word and walked out, past the heavy-bodied young men who stared at him insolently, into the wide street where the car allocated to him was waiting. He gave the address, and leaning back allowed his sense of exhaustion to take possession of him. So far he had accomplished nothing— there were three of his family in Nazi hands, probably suffering ill-treatment, and he had done nothing. Jacob promised to arrange matters for the morning—how far could he trust him ? His brother had assumed the character of a malicious devil to Max ; he was dangerous, a man without heart, a man possessed of only Nazi ideas and plans. It was his mission in life to carry out those plans, to impose those ideas; that was his creed, his religion.

The car stopped, Max got out and offered a substantial tip to the driver. The fellow took it readily, his thanks were obsequious, his face became creased in smiles, he poured out thanks extravagantly.

Max said, " No need for so many thanks—my name is Noller. I am a Jew."

The chauffeur continued to smile. " Herr Noller—there are Jews *and* Jews. Heil Hitler ! "

Rather childishly Max answered, " God save the King."

Truda came to meet him, wringing her hands. " Max, Max, thank God you have come ! The husband of Miriam has arrived. I think that he is going out of his mind. The poor young man— Max, go to him—try to comfort him."

Max stared at her with his heavy tired eyes. " Comfort ! " he said. " ' Of comfort no man speak, let's talk of graves . . .'— what am I talking about ? Yes, I'll go to him."

Charles Hare was sitting on a low chair—a chair Max remembered which his mother had always liked; she had said, " It's such a *cosy* chair "—his head in his hands. Max walked over to him and touched him on the shoulder. Charles started, raised his tear-stained face and gasped, " Max—thank God ! Where is she— when can I go to her—when can I take her away from this damned place ? Max, tell me—I'm going crazy. Miriam in the hands of those devils ! "

Very gently and carefully Max told him, recounted his interview with Jacob—" now Minister Klaus Brusch "—and his promise for the morning.

" And she must stay another night with these devils ? "

" There was no alternative, Charles, remember that these people are in power. They are Aryans—or pretend to be when it serves their purpose—we are Jews, yes. Yes, even if we are English Jews, even if Miriam is married to a man who was born British. True, we might be able to make strong representations to our own Government, but these things take time. Machinery has to be set in motion. Meanwhile . . ." he shrugged his shoulders, " life might not be made very pleasant for those we love—we must go carefully."

Charles rose and began to walk restlessly up and down the overcrowded room. Max could hear his laboured breathing, see the veins standing out on his forehead. Finally he stopped his pacing and stood before Max.

" If they don't find Miriam for me tomorrow—tomorrow,

mind—I shall go straight back to London—I'll fly back—and things *shall* begin to move ! By God, they shall ! I daren't think what may have happened to her—it's ghastly, horrible—my wife in the hands of those brutes. Max, for the love of God, is there nothing we can do—now, tonight ? "

Max shook his head. " Nothing, Charles, without causing additional danger to the very people we want to help—to save."

He gave Charles a drink, in fact several drinks, until he realized that the young man was fairly drunk, and—felt glad of it. The chances were that the spirit might have dulled his brain, might make him sleep. Later he helped Charles upstairs, assisted him to undress and saw him safely into bed. He himself scarcely slept at all, but lay with his mind twisting and turning, wondering, planning, trying to devise plans, should Jacob have lied. They met at breakfast, both with reddened eyes, and refusing anything but the strong coffee which Truda had made.

Charles scarcely spoke, except to ejaculate questions.

" Ten o'clock you said, eh ? "

" Yes."

" You know the place ? "

" Yes, I know the place."

" Max, it's going to be all right ? "

" I pray so, Charles."

They drove to the Wilhelmstrasse. Max stated that he wished to see Minister Brusch. The trooper jerked his head, indicating that they should follow him. Jacob was sitting behind his desk under the picture of Hitler. He rose, saluted stiffly and said, " Heil Hitler ! "

Max said, " Now where's my father ? "

" Sit down, won't you ? "

" No. Where's my father ? "

" Who is this man with you ? "

" Your sister's husband, a British subject——"

" A Jew ? " The lips curved into a sneer as he spoke the word.

" Yes," Charles said loudly, " and proud to be one until I saw that the race can include scum like you, Jacob Noller."

Jacob sat down, picked up a pencil and began to play with it. " That kind of abuse will not help you, whether you are German, Jew or British. Kindly remain civil or the guards shall put you out. I have the permit for you to remove Isaac Noller, it is a very special concession—made thanks to the services which I have rendered to the Party. It appears that Isaac Noller, instead of going quietly for his examination, became both abusive and violent——"

Max said, " You know as well as I do, my father has never in
his life been either.   Go on."

" It was necessary to—restrain him—to restrain him forcibly,
otherwise he would have inflicted bodily injury on the guards who
were treating him with every kindness and consideration."

" *Aich mir a chiffush!* " Max said.   " Ah, I beg your pardon,
perhaps you no longer understand our language.   I meant to say
that your story was most novel and interesting.   Pray continue."

" You may find him—not quite himself.   The doctor has seen
him and he will be fit to travel in a few days.   I recommend you
to get him out of the country as quickly as possible.   There "—he
flicked a sheet of paper across the desk—" is your permit."

In a hoarse unnatural voice Charles Hare said, " And—
my wife ? "

" Enquiries have been made—we can find no trace of her
at all."

" No trace ! "   His voice rose to a scream.   " No trace of Miriam !
What in God's name do you mean ?   A girl can't disappear !   You
damned beast—where is she ?   By God, you shall find her—or the
British Government will !   I'll raise hell !   I'll make you and your
loathsome, stinking party *reek*.   I'll force people stronger than you
to take steps—my wife is a British subject—remember that, you
dog, curse you—rot you all——"

Max laid his hand on the younger man's arm.   " One moment,
Charles."   He turned back to Jacob.   " But surely someone took her
from the house—she wasn't allowed to run out into the street !
You must know something ! "

" All that I—we—can discover is that she drove away with an
officer in a large Buick car.   Where they went, what happened to
her then—we have no knowledge.   His name, we are told, is von
Kessel, but he denies ever having been in the vicinity of your
house.   His alibis appear to be quite watertight.   Stanislaus—who
was terribly violent, uncontrollable—dangerous, like a madman
—has been taken to Heuberg.   I shall at once institute enquiries
concerning him."   He leaned back in his chair, his face a mask,
and said, " That is the best I have been able to do."

The room seemed to Max to be swamped in tragedy.   There
was his brother, cold, inhuman; and before him stood Charles
Hare, his face drawn, lined like that of a man who has suffered.
He was breathing heavily, Max could see his chest heaving, hear
the breaths which he drew, laboured and difficult.   He swayed a
little where he stood.   From the wall the representation of the
man who had evolved these schemes, who had gloried in their
inception, who had gathered round him men who would help to

plan tortures, burnings, imprisonments. Men who gloried in
their work, who boasted of it. One had said, " We shall make
the hemp industry flourish," and another declared that until Jews
were seen running about the streets with their ears and noses
missing there was no cause for excitement.

Charles broke the silence. " Then you won't tell me where
my wife is ? "

" I do not know where she is."

" And you can't find out ? With your spies, your paid agents,
snoopers, you can't find out ? You lying bastard ! See here, she's a
British subject, she's only fifty per cent Jewish, anyway—and
you've bloody well *got* to find out. I'm leaving for England today
—but I shall be back—and very quickly. I'll find a whip to make
you squeal, Herr whatever you call your damned self ! "

Jacob said, " You have the permit ? Then this interview is
ended. I repeat that we shall do our best. Good morning."

Charles shouted, " I'm not sure that I've finished yet——"

Jacob's hand went to one of the bells on his desk, two troopers
entered. It struck Max that they had been waiting immediately
outside the door.

" Heil Hitler ! Show these gentlemen out."

With his hand on Charles' arm, Max led him from the room.
Charles burst into tears, muttering as they made their way from
the building disjointed phrases and exclamations which were
almost unintelligible.

TWELVE

CHARLES staggered out of the building, the troopers watching him with a disdainful amusement which they did not trouble to hide. Max, holding his arm, whispered to him to pull himself together; with a violent effort he did so, squared his shoulders, and although the sobs still shook him he walked firmly, looking neither to the right nor the left.

Max said, " I'm going to get my father. Are you coming ? "

Charles shook his head. " Don't think that I'm unfeeling, but only one thing matters to me—I've got to find Miriam." He paused and repeated, " I've got to find Miriam—or I shall go mad."

" That's all right. Only, Charles, be careful. These people are dangerous. They have spies everywhere. Don't be too outspoken or they can just—liquidate you quietly and unostentatiously. That won't do either you or Miriam any good."

" I'll mind my step," Charles said. " I'll be back tonight. Don't worry, lad."

Max drove off to the address given on the paper which he held as a kind of talisman. Leaning back in the taxi he wondered if he were dreaming, if it was possible that he was living, breathing in a real world, or was he going through a hideous nightmare from which eventually he must wake ?

Everything he had known in his youth in Berlin had changed. He remembered it as a quiet, orderly city—always a little vulgar with regard to its buildings—but inhabited by people who were hardworking and, superficially, at least, reasonably kindly. Now everyone appeared to regard everyone else with suspicion, their eyes were watchful, and if you asked them where to find this street or that, they answered briefly and half unwillingly.

He put thoughts of Miriam and Stanislaus from him so far as was possible and concentrated upon the fact that he was going to take his father out of the clutches of these Nazis. Charles must do what he could concerning Miriam—he, Max—would deal with Stanislaus later, Isaac was the first objective.

The taxi stopped, and again he went through the same procedure; he entered a bleak hall, filled with troopers, who stared at him with cold, unfriendly eyes. He stated the reason for his visit. The man stared at him, sucking a hollow tooth as he did so.

" Let's see your permit ! "

Max held it towards him, and he made a movement to take it.

Max said, " No, you don't . . . read it from here, while I hold it."

" All right.   You're not very trustful, are you ? "

" Not in the least.   Take me to the man whose name is written there."

Again the same long corridors, the same marble steps, the same doors with names and numbers inscribed upon them. The trooper stopped and knocked, a voice called to him to enter. There again, the same type of office, a huge desk, the picture of Hitler hanging on the wall behind it. The same salute, the " Heil Hitler ! " and the salute returned.

The man who rose, saying, " Herr Noller, I was expecting you," was a stout, round-faced individual. Had you met him at a children's party, you would have believed that he was incapable of anything but loving kindness and friendliness. His eyes beamed at Max from behind gold-rimmed glasses, and he held out a large, fat, well-kept hand. Max disregarded the hand, and handed him the paper which Jacob had given him. The fat man read it with grave attention, then said, " Herr Noller, I beg that you will be seated."

" I prefer to stand.   Now ! "

He bowed, " If you wish, Herr Noller. I wish to make some small explanation to you. There is a belief that we—under the direction of our great Leader—are against the Jews." His voice was well-pitched and his German beautifully spoken. " Nothing —nothing could be further from the truth. We wish to live at peace with all men, so that our Leader may carry out his great designs. Unfortunately a certain section of the community are against us— violently against us. The Communists. Now," his voice took on a slightly more conversational tone—" unfortunately again, the Communist Party contains many Jews. They are arrested . . . not, I repeat, *not* because they are Jews—with whom we have no quarrel, but because they are members of the Communist organization and as such are a danger to the great new Germany which is rapidly rising from the ashes of the old. Do I make myself clear ? "

Max said, " Go on."

" Your father, Isaac Noller, is a man respected by all who know him. His arrest was unfortunate, terribly unfortunate. He had been grossly unwise. He had permitted himself to utter criticisms against our leaders in a public café, he had spoken slightingly, he had questioned the origin of the terrible burning of the Reichstag— a disaster which every true German felt most keenly. Information was lodged against him, by two staunch supporters who were seated at the next table. His arrest was inevitable. It was necessary to make certain that he was not a Communist. You follow me, Herr Noller?"

Again Max said, "Go on."

"He was treated with all respect, he was not threatened in any way. He was brought here. On his arrival he became—as did his son—abusive. He attacked his guards, he was so angry, so beside himself that they were in actual physical danger. It was necessary to restrain him."

"And so—what?" Max barked.

The fat man shrugged his shoulders. "We restrained him. Now, we find on investigation that Isaac Noller is not connected with the Communist Party, he was merely unwise, ill-advised. We understand too that he had suffered a shock in the unfortunate death of his wife."

"Leave my mother out of it, if you please."

"As you wish, I was merely attempting to explain. You are at liberty to take your father away, and—if I may be allowed to give you a word of advice—I should recommend that you take him back to England with you as soon as possible. I advise you for his own good and yours, Herr Noller."

Max stared at him, the kindly expression, the impression that this man whould be the life and soul of children's parties had faded, some new expression had crept into his face. The flabby folds of flesh seemed to have hardened, the fat hands which at first had seemed to be fitted for caressing the downy heads of young babies looked different. Even the smooth voice with its meticulous German had become charged with a steel-like quality.

"And my brother Stanislaus? What about him?"

The voice rapped back, "I can answer no questions concerning Stanislaus Noller. He was brought here and behaved like a fiend"
—the voice rose to a shriek—"a fiend from hell! I regard him as a dangerous man."

"One day I'll find out what he thinks about you. And my sister—— ?"

"I know nothing whatever about your sister, Herr Noller. Now I will send for your father. Remember what I have said, if you wish to be wise."

He rang one of the electric bells, and a trooper appeared.

"Bring the Jew, Isaac Noller, here immediately."

Max waited, he was trying to brace himself to meet whatever shock was waiting for him. This story of his gentle father attacking his guards was nonsense, childish nonsense. His father had never attacked anyone, anything, in his life!

He turned to the man behind the desk. " It's not all going to end here, you know. Someone is going to pay——"

The voice was smooth and almost persuasive. " Herr Noller, life is filled with mistakes, that is inevitable. No good ever came of nursing grievances, encouraging hatreds. There is a saying in your country—I was at school there—that it is impossible to make omelettes without breaking eggs. It is impossible to found a great new régime, a great nation, without mistakes being made. It is unfortunate, regrettable, but it remains a fact. Take back to England—what a beautiful country !—the assurance that Germany —the new Germany—Hitler's Germany, has no quarrel with the Jews. I say that in all sincerity."

" I've a brother in America," Max said; " he taught me this expression, ' Oh, yeah ! ' I like it. Ah ! " He swung round to face the door, it swung open and two troopers brought in an old man, supporting him by holding him under the arms.

He was dragging his feet, his head hung down, and when he managed to lift it Max covered his face with his hands. The eyes were bruised and blackened, the ears were swollen like the cauli- flower ears of a prize-fighter. The face was bloodless. The mouth hung a little open.

Max cried, " Papa—Papa—what have they done to you ? My dear papa, I've come to take you away. You know me—it's Max —Max, your son."

A strange old voice, which seemed to come from a great distance, reached Max's ears like a thin thread of sound.

" Ah, Max ! come for me, good boy—take me away."

Max went forward, he stared at the impassive faces of the troopers, saying:

" Let him go ! I'll take care of him ! " Then putting his arms round the bent and broken figure he said again, " Papa, it's all right, we're going home now—now."

The fat man was wiping his eyes with a very white, exceedingly fine handkerchief, " Very affecting. I should like you "—to the troopers—" to take notice that even among Jews there exists this family affection. That is one reason why the Nazis could never persecute them. That family affection is one of the strongest emotions which exists in our splendid country, we are proud of it in ourselves, and we admire it in others. There is——"

Max turned, his face scarlet with fury, and said, " Oh, shut up ! One of you fellows get me a taxi and look sharp about it ! "

" One moment, Herr Noller. Will you sign this paper to state that you have removed your father, and that he was—er—in good health ? "

" God ! How do I know ? I'll sign that I removed the goods, but that's all I'm prepared to do. Give me the paper——" He pulled out his fountain-pen and wrote, " *Received my father, Isaac Noller, considerably damaged*", and signed it with his name, and a flourish which he hoped looked defiant.

He flung the paper on the desk and going to his father helped him with great tenderness to rise from his chair, then nodding to the trooper to open the door, he walked out, supporting the trembling, shattered body of his father.

At home he called for Truda to help him; together they almost carried Isaac upstairs. Laid on his bed he groaned, and between them they undressed him, cutting off his clothes where necessary to save him pain.

" Telephone for a doctor, Truda," Max ordered, " and I want a lawyer here as well."

Isaac lay there, tears forcing their way through his closed lids. Max did not speak, but sat holding his hand—he noticed that the nails were bruised and blackened as if they had been struck with a heavy instrument. Presently Isaac opened his eyes and stared at Max, then a slow smile curved his lips.

" It's Max, eh ? "

" It's Max, Papa. You're all right. Safe at home again. How do you feel ? "

" My back—that hurts—ah, how they beat me ! My head, my ears, it was a nightmare. Max, they are not sane ! They said things to me—so horrible, so—so *dirty* that I could never speak them myself." He was speaking with greater strength now. " There is something *obscene* in all this. It is not only that they wish to exterminate the Jews . . . they enjoy exterminating anyone. It is perversion—and perversion of the most terrible kind."

Max noticed that he did not mention his wife, did not ask after either Miriam or Stanislaus, and he judged it wiser to allow him to speak of them in his own time. The little Jewish doctor came, nervous and worried. He was a stout man who had attended the Nollers for many years; his distress at seeing Isaac was obvious.

Max said smoothly, " My father has had a bad accident. He was set on by some roughs in the street. They were, no doubt, after his wallet. Please do what you can to make him more comfortable."

The lawyer followed him, a young Jew with a clever, astute face; he listened to Max's story and nodded, his face twisted into an expression of horror and disbelief.

" I want you," Max said, " to make out an account of what Doctor Maydek finds. I wish you to sign it—also the good doctor, Truda and myself. I will give you my word that it will not be used in this country, neither shall your name be brought into the matter at all. Are you satisfied with that ? "

" Perfectly." The young lawyer sat down and prepared to write. The stout little doctor began his examination, working as he did so. His quiet voice, filled with sympathy, murmured on as he did his work. Truda stood near him, her wrinkled face like something carved out of stone, handing him such swabs and bandages as he needed.

" My poor friend—tut, tut—your back, the marks of rubber truncheons, of steel rods. How many strokes ? Ah, you lost count. At least fifty. *Oi, oi, oi!* This rib—it is broken, was that a kick, my friend ? Truda, this must be strapped—courage, Isaac, courage. Yes, a broken rib, caused by a kick. This I can tell from the contusion, the bruise around it. Umph, your ear, like you have been in a prize-fight ! Yes, a pad with cooling lotion—we must trust that the drum is not broken. Your eyes, they will be all right, the discolouration will go in time. Your hands—*oi, oi*, look at these nails ! I am afraid that you may lose some of them, they are so badly bruised. How was this done, Isaac ? A billet of wood—*tach!* So that is the best that we can do, and rest. Truda, some of your good broth, to put heart again into our poor friend. *Alle kloles af sein kop!* Yes, whoever did this—may he be cursed for ever and ever ! Now, my friend, rest; you are safe, you have your good son, and Truda; all will be well."

Isaac closed his eyes, he was very tired, so many things were going on inside his head. There were things which had become dimmed, hazy, indistinct, others which remained clear as bright daylight. Rose—his dear Rose—he remembered that clearly. Rose in her blue dressing-gown, he had given it to her for her birthday, because he liked to see her in blue. Her hair in plaits—like a young girl. She had died, he remembered that, he saw her clearly. Rose had died. Miriam, he could see her face, white and strained, her eyes looking wild, her mouth distorted. Not like his lovely Miriam. Stanislaus lying on the floor, with blood on his head and face. He shuddered and then lay very still because it hurt to move, even such a small movement as to shiver. He opened his eyes a little. Max was leaning over a table, writing, then Truda took his place, and finally the little doctor—he'd known him for such a long time, Rose had liked him—Moses Maydek.

The doctor came back to the bed and pulled up the sleeve of Isaac's nightshirt—he had never taken to pyjamas. He had always said, " I take off my trousers to go to bed, I don't put on another pair ! "

Maydek said, " It won't hurt, Isaac . . ." It didn't hurt, and

Maydek pulled down the sleeve and said, " Now sleep—you hear me ? Sleep, relax and let sleep take possession of you . . . Sleep, forgetfulness, quiet sleep—think of nothing, my dear friend—only sleep."

Isaac's eyelids felt heavy, so heavy that they dropped over his eyes, his breathing became slower, deeper ; the little doctor, his finger on his lips, tiptoed from the room, followed by the others. Isaac Noller went wandering through quiet woods, where wild flowers grew, with Rose walking beside him. They were both young, she was lovely, and the world was a delightful place for young lovers.

Charles Hare went through the streets of Berlin, trying to evolve some plan. His wife, his beautiful wife, was missing. All that they knew was that some storm trooper had said that she drove away with an officer called von Kessel. Now von Kessel denied that he had ever seen her, and had alibis which were accepted as being water-tight. The first thing to do was to find von Kessel whoever he was, whatever he knew or didn't know. Charles' German was sufficiently good, not perfect as was that of Max or his beloved Miriam, but fluent enough.

He walked into a café, ignoring the notice that Jews were for-bidden to enter, and sat down. He didn't suppose that they would suspect him, he was sufficiently fair, and his clothes were obviously those of a foreigner.

" The stuff they wear here," Charles thought, " we'd be ashamed to turn out in Yorkshire. It's all ' shorts '—no wonder their clothes lose their shape ! Half of the stuff is ' dog's wool and okum '—damn them anyway."

He sat down, ordered strong coffee, drank it and felt better, though he doubted if it was pure coffee. He decided to be very much the Englishman who spoke German passably well.

He beckoned to the waiter. " See, I'm here on holiday—yes, that's right, on holiday. I want to meet some officers, see ? One of them went to school with my brother. I've a letter to introduce me. Where'd I find officers ? I mean the real high up kind. Some-where where they might go for drinks, cocktails, see ? "

The waiter considered ; there were various night clubs which he knew were frequented by the smart officers, but this man was evidently English. The English were strange, narrow-minded, lacking in humour ; he doubted if things which were screamingly funny, things which he himself longed to see, would appeal to these dull clods of English. This fresh-faced young man with the red-rimmed eyes looked as if he might have been on the *bummel*, and yet he didn't look the gay kind.

He said, " There are handsome cocktail bars in the smart hotels. Many officers go to the Adlon about six in the evening. Then there are night clubs——"

Charles nodded. " I've heard of the Adlon. It's good, eh ? "

" Magnificent ! As is also the Victoria, and the Koningberg—oh, Berlin is not without fine hotels, *mein Herr*."

" I'll bet that it's not. Well, thanks."

The waiter looked at his tip and grinned. " Rich and stupid. They'll always be stupid, these English, but they will not always be rich ! "

Charles continued to pace the streets; as he walked he whistled—and he whistled particularly piercingly and loudly " Charlie is my darling ". People stared at him, he didn't appear to care, but continued to stride along giving vent to his ear-splitting whistle. In an expensive nursing home a girl lying half drugged heard the sound, it seemed to cut through her dreams, through the clouds which enveloped her. She stirred restlessly.

A nurse, said " What is it ? "

She shook her head. " I don't know—a tune, music. Someone is whistling for me. Nurse, look out ! Quickly. A man—tall, young, is he whistling ? "

The nurse, a big buxom Saxon girl, went to the window and looked out.

" There is no one there," she said, " the whistling has gone, finished. Now go to sleep again."

The clouds and haze descended again, and the girl slept.

Six o'clock found Charles, very well shaved, well brushed and generally immaculate, standing in the cocktail bar of the Adlon. He was terribly tired, he had walked he felt for miles, whistling, always whistling that tune, " Charlie is my darling ". Miriam had learned it to sing to him, and he had called it " our own special tune ". Miriam, Miriam, Miriam—Charles was not a particularly literary young man, but he tried to put the thought of her from him, thinking, " No, ' that way madness lies '. I must keep sane."

He sat there on a high stool, sipping his cocktail and a very good one, too. People drifted in, and went out again, he watched them idly. He was waiting for uniforms, people wearing civilian clothes meant nothing to him. Suddenly four of them arrived, fine upstanding fellows, with uniforms which fitted their excellent figures like gloves. Good-looking fellows too, except for a slight heaviness about the jaw, and the fact that their necks looked too thick, and in several cases were pressed into rolls above their high collars. They crowded to the bar, glancing at Charles as if they felt he ought to make way for them; then at a second glance, noting his admirable clothes, his beautifully polished shoes and general air of affluence, they looked less arrogant. Their voices were loud, and Charles could hear everything they said.

They laughed, even shouted with laughter, and then he heard the name for which he was waiting spoken.

" *Ach*, that von Kessel ! A success, of course he's a success—he's got everything——"

" Money, any amount of it, good looks, and remember that *Brigade-fuehrer* is his uncle ! "

The third said sourly, " That might or might not be an advantage."

The others laughed. " The old fellow leaves other people to hunt his game, then he comes in for the kill——"

The man with the sour voice said, " Which kill ? "

Charles slipped from his high stool, and said, " Gentlemen, pardon me, please. I was unable not to overhear you mention a certain officer—von Kessel."

The tallest of the group spun round. " And if we did ? What then ? "

" I am anxious to meet this officer, gentlemen. I have every reason to believe that he was at an English public school with my elder brother. It appears," he laughed, " that my brother—when they were at school—borrowed money from this officer—he wasn't an officer then, of course—and having lost touch with him, he begged me—my brother, that is—to try to find him to repay what he owes him. I hope you forgive my intrusion. Might I—in order to atone for my apparent rudeness—beg you to join me in a drink ? "

The most arrogant of the group stared at Charles, then said, " Who are you ? "

" An Englishman; my name is Charles Hare. My card, gentlemen."

The second officer asked, " Might one ask—what are you ? "

Charles' smile widened, he felt that he was acting the " silly ass " fairly well. " I am afraid that I am—well, nothing. I am one of those despicable people who enjoy life too much to wish to spoil it by working."

They exchanged glances, it was evident that they thought him a fool, which, Charles reflected, was exactly what he wished them to think.

" Thanks, we'll have a drink. What ? "

" Whatever you wish, gentlemen. It's not often I have the honour of drinking with officers." He stared round the cocktail bar. " This is a marvellous place, isn't it ? Luxurious, eh ? "

They ordered champagne cocktails. Charles admitted that he

had never tasted one. " Only drink champagne at dinners and weddings, of course," he added.

As he sipped his cocktail he let his mind rush forward. They were actually expecting this von Kessel. Von Kessel was implicated somehow; that damned Jacob Noller said that he had proved alibis, so even they must have suspected him if they had interrogated him regarding his movements. Anyway, he might know something, and as he was the only clue which presented itself it was worth following. As he thought, keeping his mind clear, and trying to act his part perfectly, he marvelled that a human mind could so—apparently at least—overcome the torture which was inflicted upon it. It was like some music he had once heard, where all the time, under whatever was played, you could hear a steady rhythm, a kind of subterranean melody flowing, submerged but still moving strongly. That was how he felt. Everything was divided, sharply, clearly. These detestable young men, in their immaculate heavy coats, their supercilious expressions, their contempt for him which they took so little trouble to conceal, and yet their willingness to allow him to pay for drinks —were in one compartment. Presently this von Kessel would arrive, and slip into his compartment; and always, always, always there was Miriam, waiting somewhere for him to come and find her.

One of the officers tilted back his glass and set it down, saying, " Ah, here is Captain von Kessel ! Now you can stand another round, Mr. . . . what's your name ! "

Charles said, " Yes, willingly, it's a pleasure," and thought, " You dirty dogs, you cadging swine ! " He turned and saw a good-looking young officer coming towards them. He was about the same height as Charles, fair, with bright eyes, or they might have been bright had they not been slightly clouded; Charles fancied that he had been drinking. One would have called it a distinctly pleasant face, even a handsome one. He walked with a slight swagger towards the group.

One man called, " Hello, von Kessel, here's some good news for you ! "

A second added, with a laugh, " An Englishman who wants to pay you some money."

Von Kessel smiled. " This sounds most unlikely. Where is this miracle among Englishmen ? Oh, this gentleman ? "

Nervously, Charles said, " My name is Hare, Charles Hare. My brother Maurice knew you at school, you lent him twenty pounds——"

The sour-looking officer added, " To buy a secondhand motor-bicycle ! "

Von Kessel said, " Your brother—what's the name ? Hare—at Cluddingly with me ? I don't recall anyone of that name."

With delight pictured on every line of his face Charles said, " Yes, that's right—at Cluddingly. I went to Sedburgh. Oh, that was a hard school, you know, they didn't pamper you there. But it's a grand school. I'm glad that I went there. I was——"

" Hare—Hare—Maurice Hare ? You know somewhere I have a vague idea that I did know a chap called Hare—or was it Hart—no, I believe that it was Hare. I'm not certain that his name was Maurice, we didn't use Christian names, not being a pansy school ! Well, I call it damned nice of him to have remembered, and damned smart of you to have found me. Let's have a drink."

Eagerly Charles said, " Oh, please, this is mine. Yes, I insist. It's a pleasure, it is indeed. I like this place. Yes, steward, another round."

They drank, Charles paid, he fancied that the last drink hadn't done von Kessel a lot of good. His eyes looked decidedly glassy. The sour-faced man leaned forward, and said something in a low voice to him. He shook his head.

" You promised to come along ! "

Von Kessel continued to shake his head. " My boy, I've finished with the Butterfly Club, I've other fish to fry. No, no, take Hare with you if you like. Fancy seeing something of Berlin night life, Hare ? "

Charles caught the look of disgust at the possibility of his accepting the offer pass between two of the men ; he said, quickly, " Well, no, thanks, not tonight. Another night I should like to, like to very much. I'm a bit tired. Only arrived this morning, y'know."

" Staying in Berlin long ? "

The tone implied that the speaker hoped that Charles might be leaving very soon.

" Just as long as I find it amusing."

" Then we're pushing off. Might slip round to Mufflings for a bite. If you feel like it, come along, von Kessel."

Charles noticed that he was not included in the invitation. Von Kessel nodded abstractedly, and the other moved off.

He glanced at von Kessel, and said in a tone full of anxiety, " I say, don't think that I'm being intrusive, but are you feeling all right ? You looked all in to me. Anything I can do ? "

The other stared at him with heavy eyes, and answered with the portentous gravity of a partially drunken man, " To tell you t'truth, I've gorrer lot on my mind." Then, impulsively, " Loo' here, I like you. Those other bastards didn't, thought you weren't grand enough

f'them. Who the devil are they? I ask you Hare—who 'tdevil
are they? They had you f'a mug, paying f' their blasted drinks!
Damn' shame. Not genner'men! Cads, thatch w'a' they are—
cads."

" Oh, don't let that worry you," Charles assured him, " I didn't
mind. I was waiting to see you. They were a type you do meet
sometimes. Look, let me give you that twenty pounds or would
you like a banker's draft? "

" Marrer o' complete indiff'rence to me. Look, let's go and have
some dinner. Yes, here. B'lieve I'd feel berrer if I had some dinner.
Not eaten musch all day. Lot to think about—worry. Yes, let's
have dinner."

" I'd like to. I suppose you can't tell me your worry? They say
that a worry shared is a worry halved. I'm a careful fellow, if it's
anything private, I don't talk. Let's have another drink, eh? "

" Shertainly. Let's siddown over there quiet. Damn it, I like you,
you're an honest kind o' chap. Sticks out a mile. Steward, bring
two drinks over there." Carefully Charles piloted him to the seat.
He told himself that he knew nothing, he had no facts, nothing on
which to draw a conclusion, and yet he had a " hunch " that he
was " on to something ".

Von Kessel stretched out his long legs and frowned. Charles
longed to urge him to speak, but managed to control his impatience. At last von Kessel hiccoughed violently and said with
elaborate courtesy, " I beg your pardon. Please excuse."

Charles answered, " Don't mention it, I often do it myself."

Von Kessel twisted round to face him and began to speak in a
low voice.

" It's the damned police—storm troopers—particularly that
swine who calls himself Klaus Brusch. Had me interrogated—me!
I had to prove an alibi, dozchens of alibis, hundreds of 'em. Cost
me the devil of a lot of money. Even brought in a sergeant of
storm troopers—a sergeant, mind you! I'd squared him first, but
what the swine wanted! They know I'm rich, and they take
advantage of it. I'll get even with that brute one day."

" By jove, what a shame! " Charles said. His heart was beating
so heavily he found it difficult to speak. He just added a few noises
which he hoped sounded sympathetic.

" What I shay is," von Kessel continued, " is this. When a man's
in love he'll stick at nothing. I've been in love with this girl for
months, more—over a year. Didn't know her, she's a Jewess.
God, is she lovely! "

He sighed, and Charles again uttered his sympathetic noises.

" Look, I b'lieve in you, Hare, b'lieve in you. That's why I'm

going to do three things. Dine with you—ask your advice—and
show you a photograph of her. Ver' clever, t'way I got that photograph. Schaw it in a photographer's window, went in—schaid I
was an English journalist—wanted some good German types for an
English paper. I chose four, burnt the others, only kep' hers." He
fumbled about in his inner pocket and dragged out a small leather
case. " Never shown it to a livin' schoul, never will."

Charles wiped his forehead, thankful that von Kessel was too
busy with his precious case to notice him. He moved his head
nervously, felt that he was being stifled. He remembered that in
his own case was a photograph of Miriam, taken in Berlin, which
she had had taken for him when they were first engaged.

Von Kessel opened the case, gazed at the picture, then pressed
it to his lips. Finally he handed it to Charles.

" Ever scheen anything so lovely ? D'you wonder that I'm
frantic for her ? "

Licking his lips Charles managed to say, " Never—no, I don't
wonder."

He handed back the case; it had been a strange experience to
see Miriam's face looking at him from a case which belonged to
another man; to realize that in some way he must find out her
whereabouts, must get her away to safety. Miriam, his Miriam,
in the hands of this half-drunken sot ! God only knew what he
was like when he was sober, but drunk he was damnably boring
and probably, to a decent woman, disgusting.

" Is she—with you now ? " He hoped that his voice didn't shake
or that von Kessel was too drunk to notice it.

The other wagged his forefinger. " Not likely. It was this way.
At the house where she lives—lived—there wasch some bother.
These Jews can be damned annoying, damned annoying. Nec-
chers'ry to take action. I was passing—I've always gone past the
place as often as I could to get a look at her—saw the car, door
open, and walked in. Mother had died—heart, the old father they
took off, the son lay on the floor senseless, posshibly shamming—
she was in a faint.

" Now I'm a man of action, saw my chance. Gave my orders
and made them carry her out to my car and drove off to a nursing
home I know of. It's a first-class place. I've taken girls there before
—when—well, when it was necessary to have anything put right.
You're man o' the world, you understand. I've been to see her
every day—nothing wrong—just a friendly visit—flowers, sweets
and so on. Now, today she seemed upset, didn't scheem happy,
if you know what I mean. She'd told the nurse that someone had
been whistling underneath her window. Something's up ! It's that

devil Brusch—blast him, he's her brother, though the family don't own him or he them, come to that.

"Nach'urly I want her in my flat—gotter lovely flat, luxurious. Real love nest. I b'lieve once I gotter there, I could make her fond of me. Besides, that bloody Brusch might take it into his head to have all the nursing homes searched ! Let's have 'nother drink, Hare. I'm glad I met you. You're a help—sympathetic, unnerstandin'. I can schee farther than mos' fellers. T'minute I schaw you, I knew—that's a good fellow ! Gerrer drink, Hare, ole man."

Charles got the drinks, he felt that he never needed one more in his life. Again that strange feeling that his brain was working in different compartments; everything appeared to have taken on an almost startling clarity, the decorations of the cocktail bar, the creases in the steward's beautifully laundered jacket, the slight gathering of sweat round von Kessel's well-cut nostrils, the setting of the ring which he wore—all incredibly clear and distinct.

Von Kessel took the drink with the overdone gratitude of a drunken man.

"Shan't forrget this, ole man. W'arrer friend ! No one says a word against Englishmen before me again. B' God, if they do. I'll say, ' Shut up ! Best feller I know—Charles Hare of ' . . . where d'you come from ? "

"Near Bradford."

"Charles Hare of near Bradford. Who insults Hare—insults von Kessel. Now, what'd you do about this girl I told you in the nursing home ? "

"Do you want to marry her ? " Charles asked, wishing to gain time.

Von Kessel stared at him. "Marry her—God, I'd not mind, but it's not possible. Jewess. Ruin my prospects. Anyway, her father's a dealer in something or other—fruit, groceries——"

Losing complete control for a second, Charles said, "Not even a traveller in champagne ? "

The other wagged his forefinger said. "B' careful, old man. Not safe to say things like that, schee ? That feller's no right to call himself ' von '—'s a bloody insult to decent people. No, I can't marry her, but I'll give her a damned good time, give her lots of clothes, look after her. Afterwards, I'll find some chap who'll marry her. No, she'll be all right. Mind "—with awful gravity—" I confesch that if it were possible I would marry her. Hare, I'm in love ! Been in love before—not like thisch ! S'terrible ! "

Charles leaned his head on his hand. This was Charles Hare, who used to meet his friends in the American Bar at the Queen's at Leeds—nice chaps the stewards there—who used to meet other friends in the Grand at Bradford, who had a few drinks after business was finished, told the odd story, then got into his car and went home to Miriam. Here he was with this drunken libertine, being asked to decide what should be done with his wife ! His own wife, his adored Miriam ! The very fantasy of the whole thing made him feel giddy.

Von Kessel said, " C'm on, wha' d'you think ? "

Charles raised his head and said slowly, " Take my tip, get her away from that nursing home now ! Don't wait until the morning no time like the present. You don't know what this fellow Buch——"

Von Kessel said, " Brusch's his name."

" Well, Brusch, you don't know what he's up to. Get a bite of dinner quick, and then get her away." He laughed, a high snickering laugh which, had he realized it, was faintly charged with hysteria. " Make hay while the sun shines. You stay there, have another drink, while I go to the ' gents '. I'll be right back. Steward, another drink for the Captain."

Von Kessel said, " B' God, you're right. Been feelin' it in my bones all day. Now I got my friend, trusty friend, to advise me. You get along, then we'll have a quick bite. I'm longing to see her."

Charles rushed away to where he knew the telephone boxes were and called for the number of the Noller house. Max answered and Charles, almost breathless with excitement and nerves, said, " That you, Max, my valet ? "

" That's me, sir."

" I'm at the Adlon, bring down my bags and leave them here. Staying the night." Then *sotto voce*, " Not likely."

" Very good, sir."

" Tell Truda that I am going to see her sister, Miriam, who will leave with me for Switzerland tonight. How is the old gentleman ? "

" Better, sir, better."

" Listen, go to the doctor, I've got one of my nervous fits. Shan't sleep a wink. Get him to give me something, tablets, anything, but something that will get me to sleep fairly quickly." He laughed, " I don't want a—a lethal dose, just something to get me a good sound sleep on the train. Bring down the bags, and better get Truda to put in some things for her sister—oh, I don't know what ! Clean stockings, any jewellery she values, you know . . ."

" Quite, sir, and I ask for you ? "

" Yes, muttonhead, who else would you ask for ? And look sharp about coming down."

He rang off and tore back to von Kessel, who stared at him, saying,

" Where the devil have you been ?   The toilets are just round the corner ? "

" I missed them, landed on the first floor.   Sorry.   Let's have some food, eh ? "

Arm in arm they wandered, a trifle unsteadily, into the large and elegant dining-room.   Various head waiters bowed to von Kessel, who nodded back.   Charles said, " Civil lot, eh ? "

" They'd berrer be civil !   I sphend a devil of a lorrer money here."

Von Kessel ate very little, although the food was good, but he ordered a bottle of champagne, and drank thirstily.   Charles forced himself to eat, wondering where he would have his next meal. The food seemed to have no taste, he thought that Dead Sea fruit must taste like that.

A page came to their table, saying, " Mr. Charles Hare ?   Your servant is here, sir."

Von Kessel stared, " D'you run to a personal servant ?   Whew ! "

Max was waiting, with his two suitcases; his attitude was correct and deferential.   Charles nodded and said, " Hello, Max, everything present and correct ? "

" Everything, sir.   You'll let me hear from you, sir ? "

" Of course, then you can follow.   What's this ?   Oh, some things for Truda's sister—damned nuisance these people are.   What is it ? Oh, her passport !   Good.   And this ? "

Max spoke in a manner suitably ingratiating.   " A friend of mine, sir, in Zurich.   If you had time to call and give him my regards— well, his sister is rather a friend of mine too.   I had hoped that we might be going there."

" Right !   I must get back, I'm dining with a friend—Captain von Kessel.   Then collecting Truda's sister, and . . . well, I'll see what she's like ! "   He laughed again and winked.   " Got plenty of money, Max ?   Sure ?   Then wait until I send you a telegram. Good night."   He walked towards the door with Max, saying very low and without moving his lips, " It's all right.   I've found her." Then more loudly, " I didn't know that the wool in Italy was of such good quality."

" That's good, sir.   Good night—good luck."

THIRTEEN

THE revolving doors turned and Max vanished from sight; Charles felt that he was terribly alone. In all this huge town there was not one person to whom he could turn for help if he needed it. Max and Isaac Noller were both suspect, he must trust to his own mother wit and common sense. Being Charles Hare, he would have hesitated to use such words as courage or determination, either of those words would have savoured faintly of " showing off " or " swank ". Max had brought a small bag which had been left with his own larger ones, evidently he had judged it wiser not to bring too much luggage. Charles felt suddenly exultant, once they were home again he'd spend all the money he could find on new clothes for Miriam ! Something to look forward to—Marshall's, Copé's at Harrogate, all the shops where they sold pretty things for women.

He held the packet which Max had given him, weighing it in his hand. The sleeping tablets, Miriam's British passport—where could he open the thing ? In this confounded country the only place where you could be reasonably safe from prying eyes was the lavatory ! He dashed into one of the compartments and tore open the packet. Yes, her good, dark blue, dignified-looking British passport, and a small envelope which rattled when he shook it. In Max's neat, rather precise hand was written, " *Tasteless—three should do the trick in ten minutes—try four if in doubt, deep, peaceful rest essential.*"

He tipped them into his waistcoat pocket, flung the envelope down the lavatory along with the paper in which the small packet had been wrapped, pulled the chain with a sense of elation, and returned to the dining-room feeling that he was one step nearer his goal.

Von Kessel said, " Been a hell of a time with that servant of yours ! "

Charles smiled. " He's something of a talker——"

" Don't let's wait for coffee here, have it in the cocktail bar. God, so excited ! Hope that everything's looking nice at the flat. Better get some flowers, women like flowers, don't they ? And food ! There's only coffee—well, by this time she'll have had her dinner at the clinic. Say, Hare, b'lieve I'm a bit over the mark ; hope that you drive, can you ? 'S a Buick."

" Don't worry, I have one at home. Is she filled up ? "

" Always keep her filled—'s a rule of mine. Always filled—
petrol, oil, warrer—that's wha' I say."

Very heartily Charles said, " A jolly good rule—pity more
people haven't the sense to stick to it. Never mind the flowers—
it's getting late."

Von Kessel nodded. " Gerrin' too damn late. C'on."

The big black Buick was there. Charles looked at her with
satisfaction. She'd eat up the miles. He'd only got to keep his
head. His hands were sweating at the palms, he felt that his breath
was not quite under control. Von Kessel stumbled in and Charles
got into the driver's seat. He hadn't a Buick, but his father had
one, he knew all about them.

" Straight ahead, third on the right."

Past the lights, the shops which were still illuminated, past the
beggars standing at the kerb, the swaggering officers, the Nazi
troopers, turning into streets which were less brightly lit, where
the traffic thinned. " T'clinic's at the end of thisch street, las'
house on the left." The car slid to a standstill, the clock showed
that it was half past eight. Von Kessel got out and said, "Come
wi' me. I want her to know my besch friend."

" Is that all right, won't Miss Noller object to a strange man
in her bedroom ? "

Von Kessel turned and grinned, a drunken grin but indicating
amusement, and something else which Charles tried hard to ignore.
He mustn't lose his temper at this moment.

The German said, " Misch Noller 'ul get used to a lorrer things
in her bedroom before she's through. C'on, Charles."

They entered the building, their feet rang on the polished tiles,
a woman in uniform with a clever, vicious face met them. She
smiled at von Kessel.

" I've come to take Misch Noller away wi' me," von Kessel
said. " I've brought my besch friend, wonnerful fellow. I'll pay
the bill now, Matron, an' manny thanks for all you've done. I
feel that I can rely on you. Just wait there a minute, Charles,
shan't be long."

He disappeared into an office, and Charles sat down on a hard,
highly polished bench to wait. He kept repeating softly, " It's
going to be dead easy—dead easy. We won't go by Holland or
Belgium, we won't try for France either—we'll go the long way
Dresden, Chemnitz, Nuremberg, Munich, then Innsbruck and on
to Zurich. They'll all rush for the easy routes, they'll watch those
frontiers ; besides, we shall get away in the night. I'll drive all
night, I've done it before. I've plenty of money and before I leave
this damned flat of his I'll have his money as well. And papers—

I must remember—papers, money, some food if there is any." He
was growing nervous, and kept saying, " Steady, Charles, steady
the Buffs ! " while his eyes kept turning to the closed door of the
matron's office. What were they doing in there ? He had a sudden
feeling of panic. Had von Kessel said, " Oh, Matron, give me
something to pull me together. I've had one or two too many " ?
Would he emerge perfectly sober, and make everything hideously
complicated ?

Then the door opened, and the German stalked out. He looked
no more sober than when he had entered. Charles breathed a sigh
of relief. They went up to the first floor, in a small but efficient
lift. Again Charles thought, " Damn them, they *are* so efficient."
Von Kessel gripped his arm as they left the lift, and whispered,
" Wait until you see her ! " He knocked on a door, a voice—
Miriam's voice—called to them to enter. Von Kessel flung upon
the door and Charles hung back, laying his fingers to his lips,
enjoining silence. Miriam started to her feet, and for the first few
seconds did not notice Charles, who, as he told her afterwards,
was " trying to make myself look as small as possible ".

Von Kessel said, his voice thick, " My Miriam, I have come
to take you home to our love nest. I have brought my best friend,
Charles 'Are, to drive us. Dear heart, I have been so happy at the
thought of seeing you t'at I hev perhaps taken too musch to drink.
You will forgive . . . you will be glad to come with me, yes ? "

She was standing staring at von Kessel, while her eyes flickered
backwards and forwards to Charles, standing very still, his finger
on his lips. Her eyes were wide, her breath came quickly and
for a brief second she seemed to hesitate. Charles nodded his
head, almost imperceptibly.

" Yes," she said. " Yes. I want to come home, Erich. I am
tired of being here. Take me home—now, immediately."

Von Kessel moved towards her and put his arms round her,
holding her to him; over his shoulder her eyes met those of Charles,
and in them he saw all the fear of those things through which she
had passed, all her despair, and all her hope and expectancy which
she believed his presence could make reality. He still stood with
his finger on his lips, then allowed himself to remove it and send
her a very small, quick smile of encouragement.

Von Kessel released her, laughing, " My angel dove, you are
shy. Shy because my good Charles is here. Charles, come and meet
my dear sweetheart, Miriam Noller. Charles, meet the mosch
beautiful woman in'sch world. His brother, my angel, wash wi'
me at school. He was another splendid fellow."

Charles stepped forward, took the hand which Miriam offered

and said that he was delighted to meet her. He turned to von Kessel. " It's getting late, we'd better get cracking, eh ? "

Miriam wrapped herself in a huge fur coat, a present from von Kessel, Charles judged. Well, what did it matter, " spoil the Egyptians ", and the more spoil you collected the better ! Von Kessel was still fairly drunk, and when they reached the waiting Buick, Charles said, " Look, sit here with me, I shall miss the road if you don't. I'm completely lost."

Von Kessel in the front seat twisted back to face Miriam, saying, " What does it matter ? Only a matter of minutes and we shall be in our love nest." Then to Charles, " To the right—now left, and left again."

A huge block of flats, a gilded lift—obviously a luxury building. Von Kessel fumbling with a key, swearing under his breath ; the door swinging open, an impression of heavy carpets, central heating, modern furniture and the atmosphere heavily charged with scent.

" Here, in here," von Kessel said, throwing open a door and admitting them into one of the ugliest rooms Charles had ever seen. Often he had wished that his parents in Bradford had better taste, but at any rate their furniture was made of good honest, well-seasoned wood. This room was filled with what Charles stigmatized as fake.

Von Kessel, swaying slightly on his heels, said, " Scharles, my dear friend, here I leave you. I go with my angel to show her the room which I have prepared for her. That is schomsing I cannot schare." Turning to Miriam he said, " Darling, will you go and make ready for your impatient bridegroom ? "

Her eyes met Charles', flickered, and she replied, " Yes, Erich. But don't hurry me, I must have the bath, the baths at the clinic are very lacking in luxury." To Charles, she held out her hand, saying, " I hope that we may meet again."

He bowed over her hand, " Very soon, I hope."

Von Kessel went with her, and Charles again felt cold sweat break on his face ; he wiped his forehead, then squared his shoulders. This was when he must keep his head, when, if it were necessary, to be ready to kill von Kessel. He glanced at the bottles standing on the little steel table and poured out a large brandy and soda, dropping in two of his precious pellets. For himself he merely poured a few drops of brandy and a bare squirt of soda. He tiptoed to the door and listened. He could hear Miriam's voice, pitched higher and louder than he knew it. She wished him to hear, wanted to reassure him.

" Ah, thank you, Erich, you have thought of everything " ;

then, " Happy ? And how could I help being happy ? " " This room is beautiful; now go, Erich. I will take this beautiful scented bath and then call for you."

Von Kessel came back, his eyes were shining, his mouth looked slack and damp. He seized Charles' hands, crying, " My dear friend, she is happy, she longs for the moment when we shall consummate our love ! Ah, you have a drink ready for me ! And for yourschelf ? Good." He raised his glass and drank. " To my happinesch—give me another ! "

Two more tablets. Charles didn't care if they killed him, there were still three left and he should have those before Charles and Miriam left. He stood before von Kessel, smiling, he hoped that it was a crafty smile, but he doubted it.

" Look, von Kessel, you don't want to be disturbed in the morning. Let's take off the telephone receiver, eh ? Let me write a note and pin it on the door—' Don't disturb.' That means you'll have peace and quiet, eh ? What d'you think of the idea ? "

" S'wunnerful ! " He leered at Charles. " 'Can schee you've played thisch game before, no ? Take off the damned receiver—there ! Now write that card, stick it on'er door. 'S against orders, musch be ready when wanted ! Who the devil cares ? Not me ! Gie me 'nother drink, Charles."

In went the other three tablets, Charles gave the glass a twist to make them dissolve. He thought, " Gosh, if they don't work I shall have to kill the bastard ! They will work, Max would never make a mess of things." Von Kessel took the glass, saying, " One night of love—ah, an' not only one night either ! I shay, Charles, is thisch room hot ? Feelsch hot to me. Long time she is taking that damned bath." He opened his mouth and yawned prodigiously. " God, I'm tired ! Won't do to be tired . . . gi'e me 'nother drink."

With the fresh drink in his hand, he suddenly rolled from the sofa on which he was sitting, breathing noisily. His face was palid, his eyes not quite closed, his mouth hung open. Charles stood and stared at him. He was " out " all right. Charles fell on his knees, opened the tight tunic, feeling for the inside pocket. He had the wallet; quickly glancing through it he found all that he wanted—papers, a passport, various pieces of stamped paper which he took to be permits. The sweat was pouring off him, falling on the German's grey uniform, leaving little damp patches. The other pockets—a wad of money, cigarettes, matches. Charles muttered, " I'll have the lot ! " He rose and went over to the dreadful little gimcrack, over-polished, over-decorated desk, and continued his search there. More money. Gosh, the fellow had plenty—some tickets for the opera—Charles tore them in pieces. "You'll have difficulty in getting in you so-and-so!" In one of the drawers a revolver and a cardboard box of cartridges. Charles turned again to the unconscious von Kessel. He stooped down and loosened the belt.

Then walking over to the door of the bedroom, he knocked. Miriam called,

"You can't come in, I'm still in the bath!"

He replied, "Go on, you hussy! It's me, Charles! Come on, we're off—be quick, darling!"

The door opened, she was there, fully dressed, her eyes shining. She flung herself into his arms, crying, "Charles, my Charles!— oh, I've been so frightened! Darling, take me away!"

"That's exactly what I'm here to do. Now is there any food in this damned 'abode of love'? There's a big box of chocolates, take that. I'll look in the kitchen." He glanced quickly round the luxurious bedroom. "Gosh, what a disgusting place! Brothels are decent compared with this place!"

He collected a bottle of brandy, found four small rolls, and some butter; took a coat with a magnificent fur collar from a wardrobe, and taking Miriam's hand, said, "We're ready. You've got Gerda's passport? No, of course I have it . . . and your own. We're set!"

"And von Kessel?"

"Drugged to death . . . he won't die, but he's liable to sleep for hours. Miriam, darling, come on!"

Half past nine, they drove out of Berlin. A dark night and chilly. Charles was grateful for von Kessel's coat, still more grateful for his methodical attention to his car. It was wonderful to feel Miriam seated beside him, to feel her hand on his shoulder, her breath on his cheek. He shivered once when he remembered what might have happened to her, and she seemed to read his thoughts, for she moved even closer to him and kissed his cheek, saying, "Don't worry, Charles, everything is all right. I'm with you, I'm safe. Oh, I'm so happy."

Charles, with his eyes on the dark, straight road, said, almost gruffly, "I was half crazy . . . no, I *was* crazy. Did you ever hear me whistling 'Charlie is my darling?' I whistled it up and down every damned street in Berlin."

"I did hear you. I couldn't believe my ears. Where are we going?"

"We're going to Munich, and then to Innsbruck, and then to Zurich. With luck, we'll be home in a few days."

All through the night he drove. He wasn't sleepy, wasn't

ven hungry. He was just completely content. He had Miriam
ack with him, he had left von Kessel safely accounted for—
nd if he knew anything of the man it was no rare thing for him
o sleep late and resent disturbance. Miriam, leaning against
im, dropped off to sleep. Charles judged that she was exhausted
y what she had been through and was glad that she could relax.
he Buick, he told himself, behaved like an angel. Von Kessel
ad not boasted, the tank was filled, the oil had been checked;
he was running easily and powerfully. Charles regretted that
omewhere he would have to leave her. No one appeared to be
urious about them. When he had stopped for a moment at the
dlon on the way out of Berlin they had brought his bags and
he little one which he supposed held Miriam's things without
omment. He had said, easily, " We're going back to spend the
ight with Captain von Kessel. Good night—oh, reserve a table
or luncheon for four tomorrow. Yes, in his name—I almost
orgot. One o'clock. Good night."

On and on, through silent towns, over bridges, past old churches
vhich stood shadowy and almost ghostly in the dim night. There
vere stars, and Charles tried to reassure himself that they were
' stars of hope ". He didn't know one star from another, but
t was pleasant to think that they twinkled away, taking a personal
nterest in the two young people in the big, tearing Buick. Through
Dresden, where he could see the Elbe like a wide silver ribbon,
hrough Chemnitz, and then taking the open road again, a road
vhich looked as if it might never end. Queer to think that in
hose farmhouses people lay sleeping, happy people who knew
othing of persecution, violence and torture. People who went
bout their daily work, quietly, contentedly; who never experi-
nced the horror of losing those they loved by brutality, by
bduction.

He thought, " That's how they sleep away on our moors near
Bradford. It may not be an exciting life, may not have many
hrills, but it's a good life, a worthwhile life. That's because in
England we don't go in for wholesale political parties, we'd never
olerate all this ' Heil Hitler ' stuff. We're too sane, too matter-of-
act . . . too solid. We've got both feet on the ground. These
Germans may think they have, but they've no real balance."

It was growing light when they neared the frontier. Miriam
voke, yawned and said, " Poor darling, you must be dead. Now,
vhen we get there, get out and begin to get petrol or look into
he bonnet. I speak better German, I'll take the passports and
apers."

Charles nodded, " God, I'm nervous ! "

" Only because you're dead tired—ten hours' hard driving."

" I'd love a drink—hot coffee, whew, that would be some thing."

" We'll see. Leave it to me."

It was all almost " frighteningly " easy. The passports were accepted, they came out, the Customs officer to ask in slightly hushed tones if Charles required any help. He smiled and shook his head, merely thanking them briefly. When Miriam returned Charles was demonstrative towards her, kept slipping his hand through her arm and looking, so he hoped, unutterable things. When they climbed back into the car, one Customs man said, " A happy holiday, Herr Captain."

Miriam giggled, Charles grinned and leered, nodded and gave the man a tip, then the car glided away. Miriam sighed. " It will be very pleasant to be treated as your wife and not your ' bit of home work ' again."

He nodded. " I'd say so. Makes me feel quite sick. I'd like to punch their heads."

" Poor devils, they think they're being pleasant."

The Austrian Customs were more formal and less expansive. They stamped papers with an air of desperate efficiency, handed passports back with a snap of the cover; they clicked heels, bowed and were altogether very correct and slightly aloof.

" Now, my sweet, you shall have some coffee," Miriam said, and they stopped at a small inn with gaily painted shutters and clean-scrubbed tables. The coffee was not perhaps of the finest quality, but as Charles said, it was ' hot and wet ', and when he began to eat the fresh rolls he realized how hungry he was. He was tired to death, his clothes felt stiff and uneasy against his body, he wanted a shave, wanted to have a bath and wash away the grime—it might be spiritual grime—but he felt as if he had been rolling in dirt, and that a good deal of it had stuck. Charles hated telling lies, and when he remembered that after he met von Kessel he had told nothing else, he felt disgusted. He tried to explain to Miriam, who said, " But, darling, it was in a good cause, he deserved to be told lies."

Charles said eagerly, " Oh, I know—I know, I wasn't alto gether thinking about him, I was thinking about myself. It was all so incredibly *nasty*—what it must have been for you I daren't think."

" I'd got to the stage when I kept planning how to kill myself," she said calmly. " That seemed the only way to get rid of von Kessel."

He laid his hand on hers. " We've got to forget it—forget it all."

To his surprise she replied with a sudden fierceness, " Forget it all ! We've got to forget nothing—nothing—nothing ! We don't know what the future will hold, what we may be forced to do—from motives of expediency—but we must never forget."

As she spoke, he saw that her lips were drawn back a little, showing her teeth, as if she snarled. The sight half frightened him, it was so unlike the woman he knew.

They drove on, checking only for a quick meal, petrol or a wash, and Charles knew that he was growing horribly exhausted. He didn't feel that he wanted sleep so desperately, but that he wanted to be able to sit down quietly, to not have to watch that black ribbon of a road, to know that his hands were free of the steering-wheel, and his feet not concerned with brakes.

He drove in silence and at last said, almost defiantly, because he was so horribly tired, " I'm going to give Zurich a miss. There'll be plenty of Germans there, and I'm not risking it."

As he spoke he felt that if Miriam did not agree to the change of plan he might easily hit her, shout at her, swear at her, tell her that he was in charge and not she . . . Then the very idea seemed laughable. He could never grow angry with Miriam.

She said, " You're right. Let's make Innsbruck, find somewhere outside the town. You've got to sleep and rest. In the morning we'll go over the Brenner and make plans when we're rested."

He glanced at her for a second, his eyes bloodshot and heavy, and nodded, " You're a grand lass," he said.

Through Innsbruck, taking the steep hill which led towards the Brenner. A little village, with an hotel which looked bright and cheerful. The Rosa. Miriam said abruptly, " This will do—stop, Charles."

It was spotlessly clean, simple and unpretentious. Charles left everything to Miriam. She arranged everything while he sat slumped in a chair, a tankard of beer on the table beside him, smoking a cigarette as if he savoured every draw as something precious. His eyes followed her, he listened to her voice, hearing it hazily, for his brain was too weary to understand completely what she was saying.

She came back to him. He thought how well and easily she moved, how beautifully she carried her head, and how proud he was that she was his wife. She sat down and held his hand.

" Everything is arranged. I have even got an envelope and sent poor Gerda back her passport. There is a man here . . . oh, didn't you notice him ? I'm sorry, he was so obviously attracted by me ! —who is going into Innsbruck and will post the letter there to save time. I explained that I had taken my maid's passport in

error. They are preparing dinner for us now, and then hot baths
—oh, my dear, to think——"

But Charles was fast asleep, his head had fallen forward a little,
he looked, Miriam thought, singularly young and unprotected.

When he woke next morning, as the light was filtering into their
bedroom, he scarcely remembered the events of the previous night.
He had eaten something, yes, something which was quite good, he
had drunk some wine, that also was good. He had taken a bath
and dimly remembered that Miriam had sat near the bath smoking
a cigarette, and saying, " Now don't be long, I want to get you to
bed, my dear." He could recall the exquisite sensation as he
pushed his feet down between the good coarse linen sheets, felt
his whole body relax, as if he distributed its weight evenly all
over the bed. Miriam had leaned over him and kissed him . . .
the rest was a long, dreamless sleep.

Now, when he turned his head, he could see the early morning
light growing stronger with every moment, touching the mountains,
bringing colour to them. He looked at his watch—Miriam must
have wound it last night—the time was seven o'clock. She awoke
as she always did, as if she flung off the mists of sleep in an instant.
She smiled and said, " Yes, we'll be off. I'll ring for coffee."

Before eight they were over the Brenner and heading for Merano.
Merano was accustomed to foreigners, and pleased to see them
when they travelled in large and expensive cars. They ate and
drove on south.

" Where are you making for ? "

Charles said, " Milan, and then the train for England." He
heard her catch her breath, as if the prospect seemed too good to
be true. He went on, " We leave the car in a garage at Milan,
they'll look after it for my wife's cousin, Count von Kessel. I
only hope that he finds it ! "

Milan, big, sprawling, in many parts distinctly ugly, but bringing
to them a sense of security and safety. The Italians might have
joined the Axis. Charles said, " If they joined it a hundred times
that would never make them behave like Germans ! "

Charles went to Cook's; he talked, and talked persuasively.
They were able to get sleepers, they could leave the following
morning. He emerged with neat little books of tickets, grinning
like a schoolboy and saying, " Look, here are our magic carpets."

The car was placed in a garage. Charles was most punctilious
about it all being in order. The Count would arrive in a few days,
a week at the most, the car would have to be cleaned, checked
over, filled up with petrol. They would be careful that they
handed it over to no one except the Count, " with these car

thieves one must exercise care ". He gave a minute description of
the Count, a short, stout, elderly gentleman, going slightly bald,
wearing horn-rimmed glasses. He tipped them most generously,
asking anxiously if they objected to taking German marks. They
did not mind—they exclaimed at his open-handed manner of
tipping.

Miriam said, " You infant ! And that money you were flinging
about ? "

" Oh, his ! Certainly not mine. I shall need all mine for new
clothes for my wife."

They slept in a bedroom as luxurious as the one the previous
night had been simple. Charles sighed with content.

" Darling, I'm something of a dumb ox, and I can't tell you
how proud I am of you . . . you've been quite wonderful. Ah,
it's heaven to be able to hold you in my arms again. Miriam,
Miriam—you're everything to me."

Max's pleasant home in Kensington, with Max, looking old and
strained about the eyes, but rejoicing that he had been able to
bring his father home again. The old man was in bed, the shock
had been very great and he would need constant care.

Max added, " Now it only remains to find Stanislaus. I have
cabled to Dan, he is coming over. Together we shall find him."

Alice sighed, " Oh, it's all so dreadful, so dangerous. I shall
never know a moment's peace until Max is home again."

Suddenly Miriam began to speak, telling them about her incar-
ceration in the clinic and von Kessel's daily visits. Charles listened,
thinking how wise she was to have turned them from the subject
of Stanislaus. Then his half-smile of approbation faded, and
he leaned forward, watching Miriam closely. She was speaking
very quickly, her voice, he thought, pitched higher than usual,
and rising with each sentence.

" Every day he came. Flowers, chocolates, a fur coat—yes,
Alice, a magnificent fur coat. I hated it all—though I admit that
I brought the fur coat with me, didn't I, Charles ? " She threw
back her head and laughed, then continued, " But I was frightened
all the time ! I was growing more frightened with each day, with
each night." She was screaming now, her mouth wide open, her
eyes rolling.

Charles said, " Darling, forget it all—don't talk about it."

She yelled at him, " Forget ! Who is to forget ? Me ? Not me,
Charles, not me—don't come near me, how do I know that you're
not Nazi—how do I know that you didn't kill my mother—how
do I know . . ." The awful, screaming voice continued, she

was flinging herself about, tossing her head, there was a little accumulation of froth on her lips.   Charles kept saying :

" Darling, you're tired, don't excite yourself, you've been so wonderful."

Outside, Max's quiet voice could be heard speaking on the telephone.   " Yes, at once—most urgent.   Within five minutes ? Thank you."

Miriam caught Charles' hand.   " That's Max, telephoning to the Gestapo ! "

" No, darling—we're in England, there's no Gestapo here."

Leaning forward so that her face almost touched his, her expression furious, even vile with concentrated fury, she hissed at him, " Ah, so you're one too, eh ?   You want me to sleep with you, I suppose—want me to——" and she slipped to the floor, where she lay writhing and twisting.

For days and weeks she lay tossing feverishly, when she was not kept under the influence of drugs; the only person who seemed to be able to calm her was her father, Isaac Noller, who, frail and still unable to walk firmly, would sit by her bedside and hold her hand, murmuring gentle, loving and always simple endearments to her.   Then Miriam would lie still, turning her head with its great sunken eyes to watch his thin white face, and to listen intently.

One day she asked suddenly, " Why are you wearing gloves, Papa ? "

" I have hurt my hands, my dear one.   They are getting better."

" How did you hurt them ? "

" I dropped a heavy piece of wood on them——"

" On both hands, Papa ? "   For the first time he saw a flicker of interest and understanding show in her eyes.   " You could, *yourself*, drop a heavy piece of wood on *both* your hands, darling ? No, no, one day you shall tell me—I can imagine."

Slowly, painfully, with setbacks, she regained her mental health.   She laughed less, she disliked being left alone, she was nervous of going out by herself, but she realized these things and set to work to find a cure.   It was nearly six months before Charles was able to take her back to Yorkshire.   As they drove towards Bradford, where the great pall of smoke hung over the town, she turned to him and smiled.

" We're back, Charles.   I think that we'll go no more a-roaming, eh ? "

" Not for a long time, darling, and then only when you want to go."

" You've been so good——"

Gruffly he said, " Nay, don't talk so daft, lass."

Dan Noller arrived from America; Dan was huge, bulky and obviously prosperous. He exuded success and yet had contrived to remain the same kindly, simple person Max had always loved.

" Why, Maxie," he said, " you look kinder peeky——"

" Life hasn't been exactly easy, Dan. Miriam's getting better, but she gave us a fright. Papa's more like himself, even comes down to the warehouse now and then, but he's had a bad time too. Then there's Stanislaus—that's driving me crazy. Not a word. I didn't expect anything from that swine of a brother of ours— not really."

Dan wagged a great hand. " See, Maxie, you don't have to worry. You and I are going to find Stan all right. I've gotten the best of most things in my time, and if I can't get over the lousy bum of a brother of ours, well, I'll get the surprise of my life. If we've got to we'll kidnap old—what's his name—Stickle-grubber, and hold him to ransom. Now we'll get cracking. Tell papa you're putting him in charge of the business what time you're away. It 'ul do him good ! Yeah, it will. Mentally. How's business, anyway."

" If everything was as good, life would be easy, Dan," Max said.

" Fine. Now we're going over to find out what's happened to papa's property. That's our reason for going—on paper. The rest," he winked largely and impressively, " well, we can keep our mouths shut about that."

Max found comfort in this American brother of his; there was a solidity about him, a conviction that with sufficient effort and common sense there were precious few things which could not be accomplished. He might not be particularly cultured, his clothes might seem strange to Max's eyes and to those of his son, but there was a drive about Dan which gave you courage, and a sense of satisfaction that he was standing shoulder to shoulder with you.

" I've forgotten most things I learned at school," Dan said, " but I still quote a bit of Shakespeare I learned. ' Come the four corners of the world in arms, and we shall shock them . . .' That's the line, Maxie—we'll shock them before we're through."

Dan was armed with numerous documents on which he seemed to place great value. They certainly looked impressive, and Dan gave Max to understand that they were signed by Senators and Congressmen who were his personal friends. " Other guys too —heads of the police here, and a general in the Army there— I dunno what they can any of 'em *do*, but the seals and fancy

writing look impressive. These damned tuppenny-ha'penny Govern-
ments, Nazis and the like, mushroom affairs, *live* on papers and
documents and what will you. Flourish these under their dirty
noses and they think you gotten something . . . they don't know
what, but it's exactly what they do themselves. Bluff, Maxie,
bluff. We're going to call that bluff ! "

On the journey over Dan talked to his brother seriously. His
big round face, which Max always thought looked so un-Jewish,
grave and intent.

" We live in pretty bad times, Maxie," he said. " I'm not all
that *froom* but I'm proud of being a Jew, and anyway, this persecution doesn't make sense. Go back to that Shakespeare of
yours—a wise guy that; look at the picture he draws of Shylock,
the Jew. Why, if you read the play, read it with a little sense and
intelligence, who was the hero of the whole thing ? Why, Shylock !
In that court scene, with the Duke, and that wingeing Antonio
and Bassanio, with that impudent baggage Portia, and Jessica—
that one was a floosie if ever there was one—who stands out ?
The Jew. D'you know that line, ' I pray you give me leave to
go from here . . . I am not well.' I think I gotten it right, but
there's dignity ! He don't care about the half of his gelt being
taken from him, even with half of what he has—he's rich. It's
the having to change his faith . . . to feel that he's betrayed his
own people. That's what hurts, Maxie. I don't reckon Shylock
was so *froom*; pretty well like me, I guess, not being all that
mindful of fasts and feasts. But . . . deep down, he was a Jew,
first, last and all the time.

" That's why this Hitler damnableness is going to hit every
single Jew in the world, it's going to bind them together, make
them that solid that they'll stand as one people. Not all in the
same place—there isn't room in Palestine for them, but mentally
standing solid. In a way this dirty rat and his henchmen have done
the Jews a service; he's welded them together ! They've been
sheep without a shepherd, they've wandered about the world,
some of them—lots of them—have forgotten to be proud. Clean
pride, Maxie, not just being high hat. Well, he's given them back
their pride, established them. I don't say they're all saints—
nothing like it. Too many of them run around worshipping the
Golden Calf, what they call ' Strange Gods '—maybe this will
teach them—that kind of thing don't pay, not real solid dividends.

" A feller said to me over in New York not long ago, ' You are
a Jew, Noller. . . . Gosh, I'm sorry for you.' Meaning he hated to
think of what was going on in Germany. I said, ' See here, don't
be sorry for any of us because we're Jews, but be sorry for a hell

of a lot of us because we were born Germans ! ' Well, we gotten papa home, and Miriam, and, please God, we'll get Stan. That's three less for Old Man Hitler ! What we can do and will do thousands can do, and will do.

" It's a bad time, Maxie boy, but d'you remember ' Watchman, what of the night ? The morning will come . . . ' ? Remember that ? There's something papa used to say . . . ever struck you, Maxie, what a gentle voice he has ? He used to say, ' Always remember—" Be still and know that I am God." ' That don't mean, I reckon, sit still and fold your hands ; it means don't get into a flap, don't lose your head and run wild—just remember that ' I am God '."

Max said, " I wish that He'd *do* something, that's all."

" How d'you know He's not doing a hell of a lot of things ? I reckon He's there, same as He's always been. He's got plans, and He'll work them out in His own way. I'd not know how much filth, blood, beastliness and that like we've got to go through yet—not only Jews, the whole world. But, if it's part of His plan, then we've got a lesson to learn—the blasted damn' futility of hate ! Waste of energy, waste of time, waste of every damn' thing you can think of.

" Jews have got to learn a heck of a lot, Maxie boy. They've got to learn not to go making difficulties, imagining that the length of this border or the way something's killed, or things that have got to be done when folks die make all the difference to life. It's essentials that matter—those things aren't essentials ! No more'n a Catholic dying without a priest, maybe miles from anywhere, is going to be judged a bad feller. Oh, say, let's give God credit for being at least as intelligent as we are . . . we all underrate His intelligence, His decency, His kindliness. . . . Yeah, Jews, Catholics, Protestants, Latter Day Saints, the whole boiling, Maxie, we're going to have to tramp through hell, I believe, in the time that's coming. We shall come through, we'll not find Heaven on the other side, but we'll have had such a sickener of hell, we'll get out some charts and plans, some leaders and captains to set us on the track for—if not Heaven—su'thing a bit better'n hell. Say, Maxie, can we get a drink ? I'm dry as a desert. . . . Gosh, hope I've not talked too much ! "

FOURTEEN

Dan sniffed as they walked into the Adlon, saying, " Say, this town an' everything about it—stinks. Folks 'ull tell you Noo York's vulgar . . . gosh, it's the essence of refinement in every way compared with this burg. Now the curtain's up. Let's telephone to that prize bastard, Herr Obergruppenfuehrer Klaus Brusch or whatever his filthy rank is. Got the number, Maxie ? Right, you speak, your German's better'n mine. You're the Jew, Noller, come to find out about his father's property."

Max's voice was quiet. Dan thought that his voice made even German sound musical. Yes, he was the son of Isaac Noller. He had received kindness at the hands of Herr Brusch and hoped that Herr Brusch would grant him an interview. " Ah, Herr Brusch will speak to me. I am glad."

" Yes, I have just arrived from England. No, I know nothing about a Buick car—nothing. I have brought from England my brother Daniel—he is highly influential in America, he has documents, recommendations, requests—all signed by the most important people." He turned and smiled at Dan, who was sitting leaning forward in an armchair, a glass of whisky-and-soda in his hand. " I have brought nothing—— Oh, you will like Daniel, he has one fault, he has such a *loud voice*. Yes, his Embassy knows of his arrival, the British Embassy knows of mine. Of course. Of course we can come to your office, but might it not be more pleasant if you could make it convenient to call in here on your way home ? The room number is 175, yes, 175. Oh, that is most kind, and wise. Daniel is effusive, and we want no scenes of greeting before your fine troopers. No, quite. Within an hour. I am glad; thank you."

Daniel said, " Gosh, he's coming ! The fellow has more pluck than I gave him credit for. Once we get what we want, it 'ud not be difficult to tip him out of the window, eh ? Nice long drop."

Max shook his head. " No, we can't kill the swine. He's our brother."

Dan grinned, " Mere accident of birth."

They bathed, talked, and Daniel had again poured out drinks when the telephone rang to announce that Gruppenfuehrer Brusch was on his way to their room.

Dan said, " I didn't get it quite right. Now, are your nails clean ? Got your handkerchief—is that clean ? Behave like a little gentleman ! "

Dan swung open the door, and standing in the corridor said in his loudest and most hearty voice, " Well, Herr Brusch, this is pleasant, I will say ! Long time since I seen you; you don't change, just the same old friend, eh ? Why, who are your smart boy friends ? "

Max heard his brother Jacob make some explanation regarding the two troopers.

Daniel shouted with laughter, " Why, we can't keep the poor fellers hanging around. Send them down to the bar to have some drinks. Boys, it's all on me, tell them—room 175. Come right in, here's another old friend to meet you—Max Noller. Yeah." As he closed the door quietly, he lowered his voice. " All Jews together—and all brothers ! Say, you can't bring those stiffs snooping round my door, with their ears glued to the darned keyhole. Maxie, see if they've vamoozed. They have, eh ? Now, you big bum, sit down, and mind your manners, or I'll take care of them for you. Where's Stanislaus ? "

" Why should I tell you ? You can make enquiries through the usual channels, can't you ? "

Daniel grinned and drawing up a chair sat down beside his brother.

" Max, stand over by that door. Now, Jacob . . . Brother Jacob, you'll tell me because otherwise I'm going to take you over to that window, just to show you one of the windows opposite. You always were a clumsy fool, and you'll overbalance. That's why you're going to tell me. Now, get cracking, you stink ! "

Jacob's face was always an unhealthy colour, but Max saw his big lantern jaws working as if he were grinding his back teeth —the upper against the lower.

" And if you did such a foolish thing," he asked in his rasping voice, " what do you imagine would happen to you, both of you ? "

" Well, that needs some consideration," Dan admitted. " Give me another drink—highball, Maxie—I think better when I'm drinking. I'll go and spill the beans. Yeah, good headlines in the *New York Times*. ' Jew-baiters employ Jews who are renegades " —something better'n that but that's the rough idea. I don't believe you'd be killed, Jacob, just badly, nastily, messily hurt. Crippled, shockingly crippled. Oh, you'd better come clean and tell us where Stan is—better for you, easier for us. Have a drink, Jacob. Give him a glass, Maxie, we'll be all pals together, barring drinking to Hitler. Now, Jacob, where is Stan ? "

Max drew his breath sharply. Something in the atmosphere of the comfortable, unimaginative hotel bedroom, with its highly polished furniture, its well-kept carpet, and its general air of being part of an ordinary world, made him shiver. This wasn't an ordinary world in which they were moving, it was a world from which old values, old beliefs and ideals had been banished; a world where, instead, only power had any value. Power, ruthless power, old family affections had gone, decency had gone; that was why his own brother Daniel was standing, glass in hand, staring down at his other brother with eyes which were deadly cold and filled with hatred.

Max had not the slightest doubt that if Jacob refused to give the information which Daniel demanded he was quite capable of putting his threat into execution. What was happening? The very thought that Daniel, kindly, easy-going, good-humoured Daniel, could contemplate killing his own brother . . . and still appear to be enjoying his highball seemed to Max to be fantastic. They were living through some nightmare.

How had it all happened? He remembered Germans—kind, friendly, hard-working people. Holidays which he had spent with his father and mother in little villages, where the houses might be simple but which gleamed with cleanliness and were filled with goodwill. It was all inexplicable. Surely the whole blame could not rest with this undersized, dynamic, half-epileptic Hitler; there must have been some soil ready to produce this terrible harvest.

Max closed his eyes; he heard Daniel's voice, he heard Jacob's harsh replies, he felt too tired to listen. Either they got Stanislaus' location or they didn't. Either he was dead or alive, and if alive, then he and Dan must find him, if they worked for the remainder of their lives. He heard Dan say, " Well, c'm on, I've hung around long enough. Do we hear where Stan is, do we get a permit, Herr Ober—whatever the devil you are—or don't we? I like a joke, but times I get tired of joking and this is one of them. Come clean, Jacob, or I swear—out you go ! We're all set with passports . . . one British, the other American—no matter what you try to do to us, there'll be a stink. Now, what's it to be ? "

" You may ruin me ! " Into the rasping voice a note of self-pity had crept. Max heard it and spoke for the first time.

" Cut out that whining. Never mind what we may do to you, what have you done to plenty of better people ? Do as Daniel tells you. Where's Stanislaus ? "

Jacob licked his lips, took another sip of his whisky-and-soda.

" Stanislaus Noller is in the Stadfeldt prison at Macitz. Thirty miles out of Berlin, going south-east. He is detained there as a political prisoner. Now—are you satisfied ? "

Daniel shook his head, " No, brother, that's not enough. We want a letter from you to the Governor of this prison, pesthouse, morgue or whatever it is, just saying that it's all a mistake and that Stan has to be set free at once, and handed over to his two brothers—*pronto* ! "

He rose and walked into the bathroom, returning with a scent-spray. " You might think it's a bit cissy, but I like eau-de-Cologne. I've a fancy this room is getting a bit stuffy." He opened the first of the doors which led on to the tiny lobby and inserted the nozzle of the scent-spray into the keyhole, pressing the bulb. There was a smothered oath from the corridor, and Daniel, returning, replaced the spray in the bathroom.

" Listeners never hear any good o' themselves. I *hope* that he got it in the eye, I'm afraid I only washed his ear out for him. Now, c'm, Jacob, get cracking." His big hand came down on Jacob's shoulder. Daniel lifted him to his feet and propelled him to the writing-desk. " Make a sound," he said, " an' by God, you're going to take a long look outer that window. Sit down and write."

His hand had slipped round the back of Jacob's neck, and Max knew how that particular pressure could hurt—they had used it sometimes when they were children, and the victim invariably cried " Pax ! " That had been when they were playing, there was no playing about this; Jacob squirmed, his face was purple and congested. Max heard his hoarse whisper, " Don't . . . let me go ! "

" Begin to write," Dan said. " Max, c'm here, tell him how to word it. Yeah, it's hotel notepaper, cross that out, write the address of your damned hellhole of an H.Q. Now . . . go on, Max, make it tony."

Max dictated slowly, carefully. An order to release Stanislaus Noller immediately and to hand him over to his two brothers, Daniel and Max Noller. " Without let or hindrance," Max said.

" Grand," Dan murmured, " sounds real official, good old Maxie."

" The imprisonment of the said Noller has been due to a complete misapprehension, which is deeply regretted. Proper compensation will be made to Herr Noller in due course. Then, if you know this fellow, add your compliments and a few Germanic flourishes. Now sign it and see that you don't start faking your signature."

Jacob finished writing, then pushed the sheet of paper away

from him as if the sight of it revolted him. " Between the two of you, I am in all probability ruined."

Daniel said, " Now that's good hearing ! Have another highball."

" I swear that from now on, until the whole of Germany is purged, I shall work against the Jews, in every possible way. I shall stick at nothing, nothing ! I hate the lot of you—cheats, liars, usurers, bloodsuckers——"

Dan smacked him lightly across the face and said pleasantly, " Say, don't he know a lot of nasty words ? Get along with you, Jacob, and don't try any funny business; it won't pay." He opened the two doors and speaking in a loud hearty voice said, " Well, it certainly has been a treat to have a chat with you, Herr Brusch. We got the goods, you want them ! Right, you can count on us. We'll make the first delivery quite soon. Oh, we'll keep in touch. Good-bye . . . carry on the good work ! "

Jacob moved almost mechanically. At the door he said, raising his arm, " Heil Hitler ! "

Dan bawled, " What say ? Oh, pardon, Heil Hitler ! Why sure ! He's got what it takes has your Herr Hitler ! "

He closed the door and came back, his face very grim. He poured out another drink, then, catching sight of the glass Jacob had used, took it to the waste-paper basket and flung it in. Max heard the crack of breaking glass.

Dan said, " I'd not wish anyone so badly that they'd have to drink after that lousy bastard brother of mine."

" The dirty renegade," Max said; " and now ? "

In under an hour Daniel had hired a car and they were driving out to Macitz. Neither of them spoke very much. Max was trying to imagine Stanislaus' delight when he heard he was free. Stanislaus with his fastidious ways, his intense sensitivity, his love for everything that was fine and beautiful. Max did not suppose that any prisons were particularly comfortable, but he was certain that discomfort for Jewish prisoners was organized to a fine art. He shuddered when he thought that the authorities might have inflicted actual physical pain on his brother. He remembered his father's bruised and broken fingers, his lacerated back—and that had been the result of a mere " examination ".

Dan said, " Not particularly pleasant country, eh ? I'd not choose it for a summer vacation."

It was ugly country through which they were passing, flat, grey and uninteresting; fields stretched away to the horizon with no hills to break the monotony. The trees were infrequent and stunted.

In the midst of a dead, dull flat plain stood a great square building. It looked forbidding, unfriendly, as if dreadful secrets were locked within its walls. Max asked the driver if this was Stadfeldt. He nodded. Round the building itself was built a high brick wall, and as they came closer they could see that the summit was not only covered with broken glass but festooned with barbed wire. At each corner of the walls was a raised platform where an armed soldier stood, commanding the whole of the ground inside the walls.

They drew up at a gate, heavily studded with huge nails, and fitted with a grating which was opened when they knocked. A bullet-headed soldier demanded what was their errand.

Dan spoke, his German was fluent but heavily tinged with an American accent. Max wondered if he wasn't exaggerating it a good deal. He said, " Now get that damn' door open. We're here to see the Governor. We're from the American and British Embassies, an' we've no time to waste. Get cracking, you big stiff ! "

The grill closed, they waited and the great door swung open. Max saw their driver craning forward eagerly to catch a glimpse of the courtyard into which they passed; then the door swung to again.

A paved courtyard, the paving-stones broken in many places, with shallow pools and puddles of water formed in the spaces. Before them stood the prison itself, a big towering building, divided into two parts, or sections. All the windows were barred, and there was an air of secrecy and suppression, of something which was sinister, cold and completely dreadful. The place was full, Max felt, of horrid hidden things, of fears, cruelty and destruction. Again Max shivered.

They followed a trooper down a long corridor which smelt of disinfectant and lack of air, and were shown into a room furnished as an office. There was the usual desk, a telephone, filing cabinets and the inevitable portrait of Hitler, looking insignificant and unpleasant as usual. At the desk sat a young man, who rose, and said, " Heil Hitler ! "

Dan said, " And God save the President of the United States; glad to know you, Governor."

" Will you sit down, please ? Smoke if you wish."

He was a man of possibly thirty, or even less. His hair was very light, and waved, his skin was fair, his eyes large and blue. They were strange eyes, eyes which Max felt should have been wide and rather childish, and instead were wide and frightened. His hands were beautifully kept, with polished nails, and very white skin. His uniform was immaculate.

" You, gentlemen, have come from the British and American Embassies ? "

Dan said, " Why yes—more or less. Actually we've come from Herr Ober something-fuehrer Klaus Brusch. Know him ? "

" Indeed, yes." He spoke eagerly, as if he were anxious to ingratiate himself with them. " Indeed, yes," he repeated. " My name is Captain Franz Kestner. I am, you must think, young to hold this position, but I am very proud of the confidence which has been reposed in me by our great Leader. He is personally interested in such appointments. We are glad to have visitors from other countries, because," he smiled, although Max saw that his full lips were not quite steady, " we have nothing to hide, gentlemen, nothing."

Max asked, " Have you been here long, Captain Kestner ? "

Again that queer look of fear, and then the answer, ingratiating and mechanically impulsive, " I have been here since July, 1934."

" Ah, you were in Munich ? When Roehm was killed ? "

" I was in Munich, but I had nothing to do with Roehm, nothing. I only knew that our Leader took a great and courageous attitude on that occasion. He has no sense of fear."

Dan asked pleasantly. " Did you know Roehm ? "

" I *knew* him, but he was not a friend of mine. I didn't like him at all. No, I hated Roehm ! " His voice rose, it held a certain hysterical quality.

Dryly Max said, " Very interesting to hear about these great happenings but we must get on with our business, I'm sure that you are busy."

Smiling, the young Governor said, " Busy—oh, I am always busy. There is so much to attend to, so many things to arrange— oh, I never have a minute. What can I do for you ? "

Dan held out the letter written by Jacob. He did not hand it to the Governor, but held it out for him to read. For the first time Max saw something which pleased him in the young man's face; a look of genuine pleasure, a trace of real happiness in the eyes, even the full mouth looked firmer and happier.

" Oh, Stanislaus Noller ! I am so glad ! I know that he is a Jew—not that we have anything against Jews, of course, gentlemen. But Noller is so handsome, so tall, straight like a fir tree in the forest—he might bend but he would never break. He is so—educated. Now, we will send for him, how happy he will be ! " He rang a bell on his desk, his expression changed; he looked, Max thought, rather like a small boy " playing soldiers ".

" Bring at once Stanislaus Noller here," he ordered the trooper.

He turned back to the brothers. "I knew that it was all a mistake. I knew that he was never guilty of planning against our great Leader, of attacking our gallant troopers and causing them bodily harm. Oh, believe me, this is such a happiness for me."

Suddenly his voice changed; his hands were clenched so that the knuckles showed white. He leaned forward and spoke rapidly but very quietly, "I should like to see them all go! Dear God, how I hate and loathe this life! It is death in life for me. There is a woman who is in charge of the female side of the prison—ah! I can hear them scream. I don't know what she does, she is a devil, a fiend. She laughs at me because I don't find myself able to do these things.

"I should not be here, I am not fitted for this. It was after Munich. . . ."

"He's half mad," Max thought, "taking drugs to keep himself sane, poor wretched boy. What in God's name can we do to help him?"

"It was after Munich—there had been so much talk—talk that we were all homosexuals. Suddenly it was denounced. That was why Roehm was shot, he knew too much—poor Roehm. I, too. My family are rich, industrialists. I am only twenty-seven. I was sent here as a concession, you understand! A concession! I am waiting for one of two things—either I shall be—liquidated, or I shall go mad. It was so nice to meet Stanislaus . . . he is not like I am, but he is gentle and kind. He can understand, sympathize, he tried to stop me taking drugs. How can I? How can I?" His voice rose to a scream. "How is it possible to sleep when I hear women's cries in the night, when that she-devil, that whore is there, standing by, watching . . . experiments!"

He stopped and wiped his ash-coloured face with a very fine handkerchief. "Gentlemen, I don't know what I've been saying. Please forgive me," He shook his head as if it ached unbearably. "If I have said anything which . . . might be used against me, . . . please try to forget it. I—I am afraid of living . . . but I am terribly afraid to die."

Max leaned over the desk and laid his hand on the German's. His voice was very kind, almost tender.

"My poor boy, you have my sympathy and that of my brother here. It is terrible—horrible. Give me the names and address of your parents. There might be some way—some way in which you can escape, find a country where life is . . . safe."

Kestner stared at him. "You mean it . . . and your name is—— ?"

"Max Noller, I am a Jew. This is my brother, and Stanislaus also.'

" And you would try—try to save me ? I am a Catholic; we come
from Bavaria, but——" he closed his eyes and the tears forced
themselves through the lids. He looked, Max thought, like some
frightened schoolboy, who longs only for his home and the comfort
which his family can give him.

Kestner said softly, almost reflectively, " You are three brothers.
All good friends, loving each other. That is finished in Germany.
If you are a Nazi you must spy on your brother, be ready to
denounce him; spy on your mother, father, sister. Home life—
kind life—is finished. Everything is filled with Nazi ideals, Nazi
plans, Nazi plots. You mean that I may give you my name,
you mean that you will try to help me ? Look ! " He snatched
a piece of paper and wrote his name and address. There was
still something of a flourish as he—this young man—wrote
" Captain ". Max took the paper, folded it carefully, and put it
away in his pocket-book. He looked round the ugly room,
wishing that the guards would bring Stanislaus; he wanted to
get away. He hated these drab walls, the rather dirty floor, hated
most of all the preposterous picture of a half-lunatic creature
which hung on the wall, and which must be saluted on every
possible occasion. He thought, " Insignificant swine; all these
photographs, these salutes, are only to keep him before his
wretched Nazis. He is nothing in reality, only a thing of gas, wind
and wickedness. Fighting to keep his foothold, determined to
impose his mentality on the world. . . ."

The door opened and two guards entered, uttering their familiar
" Heil Hitler ! " Kestner stared at them; their faces were the
colour of clay, they appeared scarcely able to meet his eyes.

" The Jew—Stanislaus Noller ? " Kestner asked.

" Captain—he has escaped ! "

" Escaped ! " There was less surprise than concentrated horror
in the man's voice. " You have allowed him to—escape ! You
swine, you pigs, when—how ? "

Dan shouted, " Stan's escaped, eh ? Why, that's certainly
something ! "

Max asked, speaking quietly and with authority. " How did
this man escape ? "

" It must have been before the first light this morning, *mein
Herr*. We have had a new issue of uniforms, and this Jew was
given the work of checking them, placing them in order in the
store."

The second guard interrupted, " At the roll call some other
Jew must have answered for him—for this Noller—that is
evident."

" There is a guard placed at each corner of the exercise yard,"
the first guard continued; " one of them remembers how a soldier
in uniform came to the guard at the south-west corner and, giving
him a paper, took his rifle and assumed the guard. The other
returned to the prison, and it is reported handed in an order to
take immediate leave, the reason being the grave illness of his
mother—that is the mother of the guard."

" Go on," Max said, " go on."

" The order was signed by the Deputy Governor—Oberleutnant Grosser. The guard, the one who presented the paper,
is now on his way to Hamburg to visit his mother. When light
broke, it was found that the look-out of the guard in the south-
west corner was empty. Search was made; it was thought that the
guard had been taken ill—attacked . . ."

Kestner, his face drained of every vestige of colour, said, " Why
was this not reported to me ? "

The guard, a scarlet-faced fellow, who had been clay-coloured
when he entered, but into whose face the blood was trickling
back answered:

" Captain, it was tried. You were—you were asleep, Captain.
Oberleutnant Grosser said that it was better to continue the search;
he did not wish to disturb you without actual necessity."

Kestner said, " I understand. You may go, send the Oberleutnant to me."

They saluted and stamped out. Kestner covered his face with
his hands.

Max said, " Come along, tell us——"

" Grosser has succeeded. He hates me. He accuses me of being
too soft with prisoners, particularly the Jews. He is in love with
the she-devil in charge of the women's prison. Now he will ruin
me ! I have heard him boast that he and this Susanna Doight
would make this place a hell on earth for all Jews."

" I'd keep your powder dry if I were you, son." Dan said.
" Let's have a look at this Grosser. Well, what'd'you know, Maxie
—old Stan well away. You bet he had a decent suit under his
uniform." He turned to Kestner. " Ever give my brother a suit
of clothes, Captain ? Ah, you did. Good for you. Once we get
you purged of this damned Nazi filth you might make a real
healthy feller."

" I think that I shall be killed quite soon," Kestner said.

Again the door swung open and an officer stood there. He
was tall, beefy, and every line of his face was coarse. He gave the
usual salute, and glanced at the two strangers, his eyebrows
raised.

Kestner, making a valiant effort to keep his voice firm and even, said :

" So Noller has escaped, eh ? "

" It was reported to you—you were—" he grinned—" asleep."

Dan pushed his big head forward. " See here, Captain, kindly allow me to investigate this. I am in charge of this business, Leutnant Grosser. I come from the American Embassy. How came you to sign that permit ? "

" My signature was forged—forged by this Jew swine, Noller."

" Well, we've only got your word for that. Captain, I'd like to see that permit, if you please. Oh, well, have you got it, Leutnant ? "

" In my anger, rage, I am afraid that I destroyed it."

" O-o-oh, that's bad. That's very bad. I don't quite know what's going to happen now, upon my word I don't. You've got yourself into a mess."

" I reported the matter to my "—his thick lips twisted into a sneer—" my commanding officer ! He was asleep."

" That's no excuse for destroying evidence. None whatever." He turned to Max, " Very bad, eh ? "

" Unforgivable—I hesitate to think what Herr Brusch will say when I tell him. He'll take a particularly grave view of it. He particularly wanted to interrogate this man Noller."

The heavy-faced young man wilted visibly; he breathed hard, the sweat gathered on his forehead, and his hands with their big, swollen-looking fingers were unsteady.

Dan spat out, " Well, what have you to say—what explanation to give ? "

" *Mein Herr,* I was frightened when I saw my name. I didn't sign the permit, it was a forgery, I swear, I swear. But it was a good forgery, and—yes, I was afraid. I promise you that was why I did this foolish action—that was the sole reason. If I might ask that you would not report this to Oberfuehrer Brusch, I should be so very grateful . . . so very grateful. It was a foolish impulse —I swear."

Dan looked at Max and shook his head. Max, who had not the slightest idea what was in his brother's mind, nodded. Dan cleared his throat and, taking out his cigarette-case, offered one to Kestner, to Max and then with elaborate care lit his own and theirs. Grosser stood there, sweating and shaking.

" As I am here," Dan said, " with this gentleman "—he pointed to Max—" who is a very exalted member of the International Red Cross, he comes from The Hague, let's talk a little more.

Captain Kestner, just see that those guards clear off, and then lock the door. That's right. Now, Grosser, do you know a dame—a lady called Susanna Doight? You do . . . so does Captain Kestner—yes, no doubt he does, but he's not working with her. You, you swine, you stinking limb of Satan, you bit of disgusting offal left to poison the air—you do! Now, I've got here in my breast pocket all the information I need, and this gentleman"—pointing to Max—" has all he needs. Now, you've got your damned Gestapo all over this benighted country. What you poor silly idiots don't know is that there are other Gestapos —yes, others—and *mine's* one of them. They don't wear uniforms, they might look like butchers and bankers and candlestick- makers, but, by God, they've got ears, eyes and they've got money! Would it surprise you to know that in this very prison there are—seven——"

Max said, " Excuse me—eight."

" Eight, that's right, all watching. D'you know who they're watching? I'll tell you! You and that flaming doxy of yours, this Doight. If you comb the whole place through with a small-tooth comb you'd never find them! You're clever—or you think you are, but we're clever and we *know* that we are. Grosser, you and your doxy are for it . . . not today, not tomorrow, but it's coming. You'll never know when or where; you can get a transfer, but we're on your trail. It might be a knife in the back, in a dark street; it might be you'd just feel ill, and the doctor would shake his head and admit that he couldn't give it a name—but you'd die." He flung back his head and laughed, " God, how you'd die! That chap I saw die in Chemnitz . . . I'll never forget it, how he——"

Again Max said quietly, " Don't, it's too horrible . . . those hours! "

" All right." He spoke to Kestner. " You'd think that he was squeamish; he's the coldest, most calculating, hardest of the lot when he's on the work. Got your revolver in your pocket? "

Max nodded. Dan said, " Then cover Captain Kestner. Now, Grosser, I'm going to give you something to be going on with, you damned hog. Kestner, make a sound and he'll put a bullet through you. Now . . ." he sprang to his feet and swung his fist into Grosser's face. " Put them up—go on." The big German was flabby. Dan was hard as nails. For the next five minutes Max watched his brother " beat up " a man. It wasn't a pleasant sight, it wasn't a particularly noble one. Dan's great fists swung like flails. Grosser fell, Dan stirred him with his foot, " Get up, you've not had enough yet! Get on your feet! " Up and down—

the man's face was streaming with blood, it ran from his nose, his mouth, from below his eye where again and again Dan's fist landed. Finally he dropped and lay, his mouth open, breathing noisily. Dan settled his tie. " C'on, Maxie. Kestner, keep your head, plug that Gestapo of ours for all you're worth. Make a getaway if you can. We'll get in touch with you."

Max said, " Listen, take a pull on yourself. If you think they're going to liquidate you, make a getaway. You're the Governor of the place, have a call to Berlin. I'll do my best to help. Leave those damned drugs alone. I'll send you an address—someone who might help you. Good luck."

The young man, with the corn-coloured hair, the blue eyes and the weak mouth, smiled at them both a little tremulously. He shook his head.

" You're kind, but it's no use. They'll get me. I shall be out of the way before you reach—wherever you're going—The Hague or where it may be. Good-bye. . . . It's all gone too far. They know too much about me. Good-bye."

They walked out, heard the great gates swing to behind them. Dan said to the driver, " Gosh, we're hellishly late ! Stamp on the gas and get us back to the Adlon."

He leaned back in the car, reflectively licked a broken knuckle, and sighed. " So Stan's made a getaway—good old Stan. He'll get through. They'll not try to do much; all that Grosser wants to do now is keep everything quiet. Now it only remains for us to pack and get out, I've began to wonder who and what I am—a fairly decent American citizen, some kind of underground spy boss or part of the American Secret Service. As for you, Maxie boy . . . you played that Hague part darned well. Now don't worry about Stan; if I know Stan he'll turn up smiling any day."

" I shall be glad to get out of the bloody country," Max said. " It was pretty horrible watching you knock hell out of that fellow——"

" G'wan," Dan said, " he'd got no guts ! That's their trouble, no bloody guts, just arrogance and bounce."

FIFTEEN

STANISLAUS NOLLER snuggled down into the hay and laughed softly. All his life he had longed for adventure; as a small boy he had imagined himself the hero of wonderful escapes, thrilling escapades —well, now his dreams were coming true. He was out of the prison, that hateful place which had filled him with such unutterable horror. When he first regained complete consciousness he had felt abysmal despair; he had been flung about by the guards, left so that the blood dried on his wounds and made them ache unbearably. It was then that other prisoners had crept to where he lay and had done what they could for him.

He had found kindly people there, people who, in spite of their own precarious position, were ready to give him help and assistance in any way which lay in their—very limited—power. As he regained his strength he had admitted that he was going to make an attempt to escape.

Old Elias Gottlieb had shaken his head. " It is almost impossible. Poor Marcus tried, so did Moses, and Joseph—they were all killed. Only one—Phineas—escaped."

" Then if this Phineas escaped—so can I," Stanislaus said.

Slowly his wounds, cuts and bruises healed; he was able to take the routine exercise without flinching with pain, and so calling down the stream of coarse invective from his guards. The food was horrible, but he forced himself to eat; he was determined to keep up his strength so far as was possible. He choked down the dreadful messes which were issued to the prisoners, even though again and again his stomach heaved and he longed to spew it up and be rid of the foul stuff.

Old Elias, a well-known painter and engraver, talked to him in his gentle, soft voice. Always about his escape, always about ways and means by which he might get free.

" Papers—you must have papers," he said. " One of us has managed to hide his, here in this hellhole. I shall make a copy, so good, so exact, that only under a microscope will anyone be able to find fault with this passport. I am not an artist for nothing, my Stanislaus ! It is useless for me to attempt to escape. I am too old, I am crippled with rheumatism and my leg was broken when they —interrogated me. But I can still work . . . still contrive to give a little help. This is the only life left to me."

And what a wonderful imitation the old man had made! Stanislaus, lying among the soft, scented hay, smiled. " I shall be quite sorry when I have to relinquish it."

Then there had come what Stanislaus—who knew his Sherlock Holmes—thought of as " The Strange Case of the Prison Governor". He had seen Stanislaus when he first arrived at the prison, but the memory in Noller's mind was dim and hazy, he had been scarcely conscious. His first recollection of Captain Kestner had been when he came out to make an inspection of all the prisoners. Grosser— how they all hated Grosser !—came out first, and warned them that the Governor was coming. They were to make an attempt to look less like Jew pigs and more like decent Germans, " if that is even remotely possible ". The guards, to show their appreciation of his humour, had stuck the butt of their rifles into the ribs of the Jewish prisoners nearest to them, saying, " Listen, you Jew swine, to what the officer says."

Then Kestner had walked out, tall, elegant and immaculate. His attitude was aloof, as if he felt himself removed from the sights and sounds around him. He halted before one prisoner, Grosser at his side, and looked at him in disgust.

" Oberleutnant, this man is—dirty ! "

" He's a Jew, Captain. They prefer to be dirty."

" I don't care what they *prefer*, I prefer them clean. What is your name ? "

" Horowitz, sir. Michaelovich. Sir, I have no soap—how then shall I wash ? "

Kestner turned to Grosser. " Are they given an issue of soap ? "

" Yes—sometimes they waste it, sell it."

" Kindly make an issue today. I will sign the order."

" Very good, sir."

He had moved on, and when he came to Stanislaus their eyes met. Like a flash the thought had come to Stanislaus that this man was an invert. At the sight of Stanislaus' fair hair, clear, pale skin and broad shoulders a light of sudden interest had shown itself in the young Governor's expression.

" Who are you ? I have not seen you before——"

" I believe that I was brought to you, sir, when I was—admitted."

" I don't recognize you."

" That is scarcely surprising, sir. I had been recently— interrogated."

Grosser said, " Sir, this man is a trouble-maker, a bad character. His manner is insufferable."

The Governor asked Stanislaus, " Why is this ? "

" I regret, sir, that I was unaware of this shortcoming."

" You don't dispute, I hope, what the Oberleutnant says ? "

" I should never dream of doing so, sir. Undoubtedly the fault
is mine. I shall do my best to correct it."

In the prison they said—and the place was like a whispering
gallery—that Kestner took drugs, that he was often unconscious
for hours at a time. He had come to the prison after the Munich
Purge; it was said that he had only escaped with his life because
his father was tremendously rich and that Goering had interceded
for him. Stanislaus felt a kind of pity for the man. He looked so
young; he was obviously nervous of that great Grosser. He flushed
easily, his beautifully kept hands twitched, his full mouth looked
tremulous. Grosser, and the terrible woman in charge of the
woman's block, both hated and despised him.

He sent for Stanislaus and asked him if he thought that he could
look after uniforms, shoes and boots—in fact, act as his valet.
Stanislaus met the wide blue eyes very steadily and shook his
head.

" I regret, sir, that I have no knowledge of these things."

" Can you keep accounts, write a good hand; you appear to be
a man of education, Noller."

" I can write and do accounts—tolerably, sir."

" Would you like to work here, in my office ? "

" If you felt that I could be useful, sir."

Their eyes had met, and they stared at each other in silence; it
was Stanislaus who spoke first. He knew that he was literally taking
his life in his hands. He realized that this attractive-looking young
man longed for companionship, and a greater intimacy than Stanislaus knew he would ever consent to, even if by so doing he might
gain preferential treatment.

He said, " Look, sir, for one moment try to imagine that we are
not in this prison. We are both free men, chatting in a hotel in
Berlin. I am a very normal individual. I am no judge of what other
men may do. I do not understand their point of view. I am neither
in a position to condemn or condone. Had we met in the world
outside we might have been good friends. I like to think that we
should have been. Anything more, sir—no. And, sir," he dropped
his voice to a whisper, " don't take drugs. You weaken your own
position, *others* watch you. They are envious, they would welcome
an opportunity to—trip you up."

The fair skin flushed painfully. " They know ? "

" Everyone in this place knows, sir."

" I can't stop—I daren't stop ! "

" Try ! I beg you. To go on is too dangerous."

He remembered how the muscles of Kestner's throat had

contracted, how his long, white-fingered hands had twitched before
he answered, " Thank you—try to help me, Noller."

In a strange fashion a friendship had existed between them
Stanislaus knew that many of the prisoners thought that a senti
mental attachment existed between himself and Kestner; he ever
heard whispers. They said that he was " making his own be
comfortable ", as Fluther and Bauer—two of the troopers—wer
reported to be doing with the assistance of Grosser and the horribl
Doight.

Grosser had sent him over once or twice with messages for her
He suspected that Grosser had gossiped about him. She was a tall
heavily built woman, with a tremendous bust and a jowl like a prize
fighter.

She sat lounging in her office and stared at Stanislaus boldly. He
felt that she was undressing him in imagination.

" Are you the Jew Noller ? "

" I am a Jew, fräulein, and my name is Noller."

" I've heard some pretty tales about you."

" I can only hope, fräulein, that they were amusing."

" Not bad. You look damned well fed. That Governor o
yours pampers the Jews! Makes pets of them ! I sometime
wonder if he's not a Jew himself. Has he ever admitted it to you
Jew ? "

" My conversation with the Governor, fräulein, is restricted t
his giving and my taking orders."

She laughed, showing great yellow teeth like those of a mare.

" You lying Jew sodomite ! Well, you'd find that it paid bette
to keep on the right side of Oberleutnant Grosser—and myself
I've got some nice-looking women here, y'know. They won't be s
nice-looking by the time I've finished with them ! Make hay whil
the sun shines, Jew."

" Fräulein, will you allow me to return to my work ? Is there
reply to the message which Herr Oberleutnant sent, if you please ? "

She stood up, leaning across the desk, pushing her face toward
his, so that he caught the stale reek of her breath. " Yes, go an
tell him that I say you're a mealy-mouthed, slimy Jew—that you're
a liar, as well as everything else ! "

Stanislaus clicked his heels together, saying, " Very good
fräulein."

" You all ought to be exterminated—if justice was done ! "

" Yes, fräulein."

" Get out of my sight; the look on your damned Jew face make
me want to vomit."

Strange days, Stanislaus reflected. Those two devils, watching

planning, doing everything they knew to undermine the authority
of Kestner. Not that he exerted his authority overmuch, he was
under the influence of drugs half the time; but he was kind. He
ordered more blankets, he tried to improve the food, and from time
to time he received parcels of clothes which he distributed among
the prisoners who were most in need of them. He sent for old Elias
and talked to him about his work. He gave him materials with which
to paint, and bought two pictures to send home to his mother.
Elias laughed softly and said, " Stanislaus, look, he has given me
money ! Poor silly boy, what can I do with money here, except try
to bribe the guards ! You plan to escape. We shall hide it for
you, no ? "

That money was now lying hidden in his belt. That and some
more which he had stolen from Kestner. He had left a note saying:

Dear Captain,
I could not ask you to loan me money. The fact that I did so
would have told you that I intended to try to escape. I have taken a
hundred marks from your wallet which you left on your desk. If I am
caught, you will be able to reclaim the money ; if not, then I shall send
it to you from England. I thank you for many kindnesses to your
friend,   *Stanislaus Noller.*

Kestner had given him a suit of clothes. Stanislaus had been told
by Grosser to tar some of the wooden buildings; his own suit was
ruined in the process. He remembered how Kestner had given him
the suit he was now wearing, saying, half pathetically, Stanislaus
thought, " It's a nice suit, Noller. I had it made in Berlin. It's
good stuff. They swore that it was English wool."

Then the consignment of uniforms and stores had been delivered,
and Kestner had detailed Stanislaus and old Elias to sort, docket
and lay away the things in their proper places. Stanislaus wondered
if the fair-haired fellow had not tried to co-operate with him in
making a getaway. One complete guard's uniform short—what was
that with old Elias able to alter any figure so that the change could
not be detected ?

Old Elias had chuckled as he wrote out the permit for the guard
on duty—they had found out from the rota what his name was—
Heinrich Ulhman. Elias had examined his work with satisfaction.
He had contrived to engrave a piece of metal—they had extracted
acid from the electric light batteries. The work was beautiful.

" My masterpiece ! " Elias said. " To think that I wasted time
on painting pictures, when I might have been making banknotes !
Now, who shall sign this document ? Ah, the Oberleutnant !

Splendid ! His signature is on all the notices, and an uneducate
handwriting it is too."

It had taken some time to discover that Ulhman had a moth
who lived in Hamburg, but the fact that Stanislaus sometim
worked in the office of the administration made it possible. T
wretched Kestner was more often under the influence of dru
than not, and Stanislaus worked quickly and deftly.

The day came; Stanislaus had his exquisitely forged passpo
and the note for the guard. He dressed in his stolen uniforn
old Elias wished him " God speed " and his eyes were mois
Stanislaus strode out into the exercise yard. It was late afternoo
most of the guards were resting after their heavy mid-day mea
prisoners were locked in. Grosser had been seen striding over
the women's quarters to join his she-devil.

Poor Kestner had been nervous and inclined to be hysteric
all the morning; he had cried a little and said to Stanislaus the
he only found life bearable because of his presence at the prison
By now he was probably unconscious. Stanislaus reached the fo
of the steps which led to the guards' look-out perch.

" Hey, Ulhman ! " he cried.

Ulhman, long, lanky and dyspeptic-looking, leaned down an
replied, " What is it ? Who are you ? I don't know you, do I ?

" Only arrived this morning. By train from Essen. Obe
leutnant told me to bring this to you. I'm to take over from
you. Hope that you find your mother in good health—she
ill at the moment."

" My mother ! Dear God, my mother is like a horse for strength
Show me ! " He read the permit and whistled, " Must be serious
All right—take over. What's your name ? "

" Mine ? Fritz Helden. Good luck, Ulhman."

The rifle in his hands, Stanislaus stood stiffly on the look-ou
perch and glanced at the height of the wall. The light was fading
leaving that half light which is so confusing and deceptive. He ha
no time to waste; at any moment they might come running
Fifteen—sixteen feet ! Whew, a nasty drop ! Then he saw the tre
Not a remarkably fine or strong tree, but growing not far from th
wall. That was what he must jump for, even if the branches brok
they would break his fall. How far ? Not more than four fee
Surely he could manage that. He laid his rifle down, moved to th
very edge of the wall, bent his knees—and sprang to the tree.

The noise of breaking twigs and small branches sounded lik
artillery fire in his ears. His fingers closed on a branch, close
and clung. It held; slowly, carefully, Stanislaus lowered himsel
to the ground. He had memorized the various directions on

small map which he had copied in Kestner's office. His way must
be dead south. He made his rapid calculations and set off, walking
very fast over the flat, lonely country. Night was falling fast, and
it was dark when he reached the bank of a river. There he removed
his guard's uniform and sought for stones to put in the pockets
before flinging it into the river. He walked on until he found a
place where the water ran dark, and he felt that it was of considerable depth. Then he flung the clothes into the flowing river, and
with great satisfaction watched them sink.

Then he continued his walk. How long he walked, or how far, he
did not know. He skirted several villages, where the lights were
few, and he judged that the inhabitants were going to bed early. He
was very hungry. In his pockets were a piece of chocolate, which
Kestner had given to him several days before, and a piece of black,
very sour bread. He nibbled the bread and felt even more hungry
than before. He went on walking; it was imperative that he put as
great a distance as possible between himself and the prison. Later
he could take things more easily. He found a shed; inside were
piles of dried fern, probably used for the bedding of cattle. He
threw himself down, burrowed deep into the fern and fell asleep.

The first daylight woke him, and he roused himself, doing his best
to get rid of the dried bits of bracken which clung to his clothes.
He had a tiny piece of comb in his pocket and straightened his hair,
then he set out again. His mouth felt dry and sour, his tongue thick
and coated. At a small stream he knelt and drank, and using his
scrap of soap with great care, managed to wash his face and hands.
Back on the high road again, for he judged that if they were seeking
for him they would be beating the woods and thickets.

He ate his chocolate and thought that he had never tasted
anything nastier in his life. As Stanislaus stood for a moment
wondering whether his stomach would retain the stuff, a lorry
came along the road. It was a removal van and he hailed it.

" Give me a lift, mate," he called. " I can pay for my ride—
and I'll stand you breakfast."

The driver stopped. He was a rotund fellow, with a face heavily
powdered with freckles. He grinned, showing white teeth widely
spaced in his head. He answered in a dialect so broad that
Stanislaus found it hard to understand him.

" Where are you making for ? "

" Kameny, then on to Dresden."

" Get up, I go past Kameny. I'll hold you to the offer of
breakfast."

" I'll be pleased if you do."

" Been sleeping out ? "

8

" No, at my uncle's—his house is away up there." Stanislaus waved his hand vaguely in the direction from which he had come. " I had to leave early because I want to get on to Dresden. I've a job waiting for me. I just had a drink of milk and a piece of bread."

The freckle-faced fellow grinned. " I'll get you something better than that. We'll be there in about twenty minutes. Just off the road. They know me. It's a little farm; we'll get new-laid eggs, maybe a bit of pork and bread. How'll that suit you ? "

" Fine—barring the pork. My digestion's weak."

" That's bad. I've an aunt who suffers that road. Always taking stuff, nothing does her any good. They say it's an ulcer. Fine big strapping woman, but can't digest what a baby could take easily." He was a friendly fellow, and in fifteen minutes had told Stanislaus about his family, the girl he hoped to marry, his hours of work, how much he earned a week, in fact by the time they pulled up at the little farmhouse, up a side lane, there was very little that Stanislaus did not know about Rudi Phiffenhauer and his family.

The kitchen was warm and very stuffy; it was not particularly clean, but the farmer's wife was ready to provide them with food and some very bad coffee. It was made tolerable by plenty of new milk.

Stanislaus ate two eggs and a considerable amount of bread-and-butter. He asked if he might have some eggs hard boiled to take with him. The driver told her that Stanislaus was on his way to get a job at Dresden, that he suffered from stomach trouble and that he came from Essen. She immediately recounted her husband's ailments, which appeared to be that he could not touch fat in any form, it was " death to him ". She advised Stanislaus to get his mother—if he had one—to make a concoction of dandelion leaves, boiled and sprinkled with salt.

The driver said, " This chap's promised to pay for breakfast, mother."

" I shan't rob you," she assured him. " I've boys of my own."

Money was safely hidden in his belt. He kept in his pocket only sufficient for immediate necessities. He glanced round the room, his eyes seeking the usual portrait of Hitler. The driver caught his eye and laughed.

" You'll not find it here ! " he said. " Will he, mother ? "

" He'll not find it today, nor tomorrow, nor yet in twenty years' time if he came this road again. That's all I've got to say."

The drive on to Kameny was distinctly pleasant. Stanislaus felt that with every moment he was putting a greater distance between himself and his possible—and probable—pursuers. He sat there with the early sunlight filtering into the cab of the camion,

warmed, well fed and content. The driver talked without ceasing
and appeared quite happy if Stanislaus merely interjected at
intervals a " Yes ", " No " or " Imagine that ".

At Kameny he pulled up. " Well, chum, best of friends must
part. I've liked having you with me. Good luck and all that's
good."

Stanislaus held out his hand. " You don't say Heil Hitler,
then ? "

The other man laughed, showing his queer widely spaced teeth.

" No, chum," he said, " I don't. What's more—I never will,
neither."

Speaking quietly, Stanislaus asked, " Are there many who
feel as you do ? "

There was silence for a few seconds, then the driver
answered, " Thousands, thank God. Good-bye, chum. God go
with you."

Stanislaus watched the camion drive away and pondered on
what he had heard. Into his mind came the story of Sodom and
Gomorrah. " For the sake of five just men, the Lord would
spare the city." Might it be that in Germany those five " just
men " might be found, and that salvation, freedom, might come
through their efforts ?

That night he slept very happily and contentedly in a barn
filled with hay; beyond the fact that the stalks tickled his neck,
he told himself that he could not have wished for an easier bed.
As he lay there, recalling all that had happened since he left the
prison, he tried to continue his journey in his mind, and formulate
some definite plans. One thing was certain, that if he managed
to evade his pursuers he must waste no time in getting back to
England. There was work waiting in England; he must make
plans, find some way by which he could join with others to help
some of the prisoners of the Nazis to escape—America, England,
no matter where, so long as they could get out of the clutches of
fiends like Grosser and Doight.

Stanislaus Noller realized with something of a shock that he
was over thirty, and that for the first time in his life he felt a
definite urge to plan his life. He had worked hard, and well, he
had been diligent and painstaking; but to work with his father,
to earn sufficient money to make life enjoyable, had been his
chief aim. Now, with the memories of what he himself had
suffered, with recollections of what he had seen inflicted upon
others, it seemed to him that the whole purpose of his life had
become crystallized.

How he was to accomplish his purpose, his heart's desire, he did not know, but that he would and could find some way in which to help those unfortunate prisoners he had no doubt.

He woke in the morning, refreshed and very hungry. His hard-boiled eggs had been eaten last night, and now he must search for food. The morning was clear and bright; he stood at the door of the barn and filled his lungs with the good air. No matter what lay before him, this would have made everything worth while. To stand there, a free man ! Small wonder, Stanislaus thought, that throughout the ages men had fought and striven for freedom—freedom of action, freedom of speech, freedom to go and come as they pleased.

It was as he stood there that the sound of motor-cycles reached him. He drew back into the shadow of the barn and watched. As he expected—Nazi soldiers. They checked their machines, the roaring of engines died and they began to walk towards the farmhouse which lay two hundred yards away from where Stanislaus stood. He could hear their loud arrogant voices interrogating the farmer, a fellow with tow-coloured hair and an expression of complete stolidity. They seemed to be talking for a long time, the farmer pointing towards the direction in which the troopers had come. They consulted together, then turned and ran back to their machines, turned them and with a roar of engines rushed away back the road down which they had come.

Stanislaus waited and decided to take a chance. He made his way to the farmhouse and knocked. The door opened and he stood face to face with the fair-haired farmer.

Before Stanislaus could speak, he said, " *Ach,* so it was you they were after ? "

" I don't know what you mean, *mein Herr*—— "

The man nodded. " You know all right. They've gone back to the woods round Kottbus. Miles away ! I said that was where you said you were making for. You'll want something to eat, eh ? We've not much, but you can have what there is. I'm a German, a good German, I hope, but I've an idiot daughter— thanks to fellows like those. I don't forget. Come in, and I'll keep a lookout, but they won't come back. They think I look so stupid that I couldn't make up a lie ! "

They gave him milk and black bread. The place was poor, but clean, and presently, as Stanislaus ate, a girl of about fourteen sidled into the room. She was fair, with large vacant blue eyes, and a mouth which hung open a little. Had her face held any intelligence she might have been pretty, for her skin was very smooth and her colouring good.

THE MORNING WILL COME   225

The farmer nodded towards her. "That's her," he said. "She was the cleverest child at the school—until two of them met her coming home through the woods." He spoke to her very gently, "Come, *mädchen*, sit down. This is a friend—nice man, good man." The girl sidled to her seat at the table, her eyes watching Stanislaus as a timid animal might watch a stranger. She did not speak, but when he spoke to her she gave him a slight, wavering smile and nodded.

Stanislaus noticed how both the man and his wife were inordinately gentle with her, lowering their rough voices, even making their movements quiet and restrained. They gave him food to take in his pockets. He paid and they stared at the amount which he insisted upon giving them.

The farmer whistled, "*Himmel*, you must be rich!"

Stanislaus said, "No, but one day I shall come this way again. I shall come with money, maybe food, and I shall show my gratitude. If other men—like me—should come this way, please treat them as you have treated me. I shall come back."

"So you will come back?" The farmer asked, "When you come, perhaps I shall be able to tell you, *mein Herr*, that I have achieved my ambition. To be revenged—for her, my daughter."

They gave him directions for his journey. If the guards were out it was wiser not to go through Kameny again—there was a road through the woods, not easy going, too difficult to find.

"*Gott!* I'll show you the way," the farmer volunteered. "Come."

It was a bad road. After the farmer left him Stanislaus stumbled on, his body growing weary with climbing stiff slopes and slithering down steep crags. His boots were not very good either and his feet ached, and he felt certain that they were blistered. For three days he walked, sleeping where he deemed it to be fairly safe, getting food at farmhouses, and going for long hours hungry. The days were fine, but the nights were bitterly cold, and by the time he finally reached Dresden he felt chilled to the marrow, was so desperately hungry that he scarcely dared glance in the windows of food shops, and was conscious that his boots proclaimed him to be a tramp. His beard had grown, and his fair hair looked dirty. He made his way to the public baths, longed to take a ticket for the first class, but realized that it was safer to go to the lowest grade. The hot water revived him, and gave him fresh courage. He visited a barber, told him to shave his chin and cheeks, but to leave his rapidly growing moustache.

"My sweetheart wishes me to grow a moustache," he explained.

He bought a pair of boots. " Strong boots, suitable for a working man." He bought socks and a cheap shirt, and a tie, very cottony and cheap. He had a meal, and thought it the most delicious thing he had ever tasted. Rich, heavy and more than a little greasy, but he ate it with real enjoyment. Hot coffee too, not the pure coffee they used to drink at home, but it was hot and warm and sweetened until it was almost thick.

When he walked out into the streets he looked with great attention to all the public notices, seeking to find if there were any regarding his own escape. He found nothing, and his courage asserted itself. He held his head high, and, after eating another meal, found a cheap lodging-house and slept in a bed which was reasonably clean and comfortable.

The following morning, wearing his clean shirt and socks, his new boots, and having had another shave, he boldly took the train for Kitzbuhel. Kitzbuhel, that brought back memories. He had been there for winter sports when they had been a party of young, happy people, when they had laughed and joked, and found life a splendid business. They had never imagined that it might all end, that a new world of suspicion, hatred and intensive spying might be inaugurated with the coming of the Nazi régime.

At the frontier his passport caused no comment, and he blessed old Elias for his almost uncanny skill. " May he have the opportunity to make many other such passports," Stanislaus thought, " to help many others to get away as he has helped me."

He found a very modest lodging for the night, and wandered about the little town remembering other days, other nights filled with music and singing which he had spent there. The next day he walked; the new boots were hard and stiff, but the train journey and the hot bath had eased his feet and he made good progress. Again he caught the train, and again no comments were made on his passport when he crossed the frontier into Italy.

Italy ! As he stood on the station platform at Bolzano, Stanislaus felt a great sense of relief. He had done it ! He had put miles between the prison and himself; he had felt that luck was on his side all the way, and now he knew that he had friends— that beautiful woman who had worked for Max. She had married a Duke—Duca—was it ?—Ottaviano. She and her husband had told Max that if he ever needed help it would be forthcoming from them. Max had given Stanislaus their address in Rome, saying, " In these days you never know. They're good people, people one can trust."

Rome then should be his objective. A long way, and Stanislaus knew that he did not look the kind of person to call upon the aristocracy. He would pretend that he had come to apply for the position of—what?—valet. He had been offered one he remembered by Kestner, and had refused it. Poor unhappy Kestner, to whom he would return a hundred marks as soon as possible.

Again he had a bath, again he was shaved, and felt some of his self-respect return. He changed his marks into lire and felt that he had left the last of Germany behind him.

Auto-bus—another auto-bus, night spent in an inn, where he drank the good rough wine of the country, and ate mounds of *pasta* with tomato sauce; another auto-bus, and finally a train which carried him to Rome. The address was safe in his memory, his spirits were rising with every mile that flew past. Perhaps tomorrow he might be speeding on his way to England, to his family—it was then that his heart gave a queer little contraction, as he remembered that he knew actually nothing concerning his beloved mother, his father or Miriam.

That was what this cursed system did: separated families, severed all ties and made life so difficult that you forgot to worry about the people you loved best. Life ceased to be a thing of charm, dignity and affection, it became instead a wild, concentrated fight to keep alive.

Stanislaus knew that he was terribly tired, that the strain of the past days—was it days or weeks, he had lost count of time?—was telling on him, making him feel uncertain and light-headed. He felt that he had been playing a tremendous rôle in some fantastic play, and that now the play was nearing its end he had barely sufficient strength to finish the performance.

He watched the passing landscape with eyes which had lost interest. He had been delighted at first in the beauty of Italy, now all he longed for was to know that his journey was ended. Slowly the long, heavy train drew into the station at Rome. Stanislaus roused himself. He found a taxi-cab, gave the address, telling the man to drive round to the servants' entrance if there was one. The man nodded, and the taxi, which seemed as if it might fall to pieces at any moment, rattled off. Stanislaus leaned back, closing his eyes, and felt tears force themselves between his closed lids. He was safe!

The taxi stopped; he roused himself, got out and paid the driver. He was admitted and shown into a very clean, rather bare room, where a tall man who seemed to be a major-domo or butler was waiting.

Stanislaus asked that he might be permitted to speak with the Duca or the Duchessa.

The man looked doubtfully at Stanislaus' dusty and crumpled clothes.

" Have you a letter of recommendation ? " he asked.

" No, signor, but both the Duca and Her Grace know my family."

" And the name ? "

" Noller, signor. Stanislaus Noller."

" I will make enquiries. Sit down."

He returned a few minutes later with a tall, thin man with a yellow-skinned face and large melancholy eyes. He looked at Stanislaus intently, then said, " Ah, I am pleased to meet you, Mr. Stanislaus Noller." He smiled very pleasantly, the whole expression of his face became curiously gentle and sympathetic. " I shall be glad if you will come with me. I wish you to meet my wife, and—some friends."

Stanislaus said, " Your Grace, I am not dressed to mix in society. I have come a very long way, and my clothes——"

The Duca held up a very thin hand with long, rather knotted fingers. " Please come with me. All will be explained. I am grateful," and again that pleasant smile, " you have saved me a great deal of trouble by arriving at this moment. Please be so good as to follow me."

Up a wide marble staircase, where the heavy nailed boots made walking difficult, Stanislaus was afraid that at any moment he might go sprawling. Along a vast corridor, where treacherous though beautiful rugs again threatened his safety. From time to time the Duca turned and smiled encouragement. They halted outside double doors; the prince very deftly flung them both open, saying as he did so, " Elfa, my dear, may I present—Mr. Stanislaus Noller ? "

Stanislaus had a vague impression of a tall woman wearing a white dress turning to him. He heard a great shout of " Well, what'cher know—it's Stan ! " and his brother Max's voice saying, " Now, now, my boy, you're all right—oh, thank God ! "

The room seemed to grow dark. He was pushed into a big chair and he felt the cool rim of a glass on his lips, and heard someone saying, " There . . . drink that—slowly—there. You're better."

SIXTEEN

STANISLAUS lay in the big comfortable bed, with its fine linen sheets and huge pillow-cases all embroidered with the monograms of the Duke and Duchess intertwined, surmounted by a beautifully worked coronet, and from time to time he shivered. He did not shiver because he was cold, the palazzo was centrally heated and delightfully warm. He was given the choicest foods and wines. He luxuriated in the steaming baths, which he took in the bathroom adjoining his bedroom, a room as big as a moderately sized drawing-room, with countless taps, showers, jars of sweetly smelling salts and a whole collection of towels of all colours and sizes. Yet—he shivered.

He knew why. During the time of his escape he had been excited, he had known that he was making progress, he was able to go where he wished—always admitting the danger—and the fear of capture had receded in his conscious mind. Now, lying here in quiet and extreme comfort, he had time to think. He lay there and wondered what they would have done to him had he been taken. He wondered if his escape would have brought down reprisals on the other Jews in the prison, if the " she-devil " Doight would have used his escape as a reason for administering further tortures to her wretched victims. Would Grosser have reported his escape as due to the neglect of the unfortunate Kestner, and what would have happened to that poor, unhappy, pretty, fair-haired fellow. For these things and many others—Stanislaus lay and shivered.

The Duchessa came and sat by his bed, talking to him in her soft, finely modulated voice, assuring him that the time of terror was behind him, and that all he had to do now was to get strong and well, so that he might return to England with Max.

Stanislaus watched her with his big sunken eyes. How attractive she was, how serene and apparently unmoved ! He shook his head.

" Forgive me," he said, " but you're wrong. I've not left it all behind. I've brought so much of it all—the shame, the dirt, the cruelty and the hideous violence—away with me. When you were —inside—somehow everything was part of the horror—it fitted in —you almost accepted it. Now, in a civilized life, surrounded by all the evidences of your thought and kindness, with the attention and affection of my two brothers, I look back and understand that one of the most dreadful things about this Nazi attitude is its complete—artificiality. It begins by all this worship of a dictator. If he were some splendid, intelligent, noble-hearted individual—well, one might be able to find some justification. As it is—small, second-rate, obviously not one of the great intellects of the world—and you ask yourself, why?

"That's where all the terror begins. Look at the men he has gathered round him. How many are men who would have made a great success of life, have left a great mark on the world? He has put—*put*, mark you—power into their hands, a power they never hoped to have. They have sprung like mushrooms from nothing to great obscene growths. But—and here is the snag—they have to justify their existence. They must make an impression; they must gather round them a whole army of servants, a great flock of carrion crows; they must show ingenuity and ability to be ruthless. More, they must even *enjoy* being ruthless. They must be cruel—but effectively. They must devise new methods of torture, of the ' means of liquidation '.

" These are the thoughts that make one—shiver, Duchessa."

She nodded. " Yes, I know. Here—and I speak to you very intimately now—we are more fortunate. Our dictator is a blustering, shouting man who was—I repeat—who *was*—filled with energy and many ideas which were sound common sense. How those ideas were enforced at the inception of Fascismo is regrettable, because cruelty and violence are always regrettable. There were—there are injustices, terrible and dreadful injustices—but no Italian has the capacity for what one might call organized cruelty. I don't say that men have not been beaten, manhandled, abused, even wrongfully detained in prison—for they have.

" Dictators are stupid people, or they would realize at this point in the history of the world they have no real permanence. They are like rockets; very bright, brilliant, even attractive, but they can only rise so far, and only remain at that height for a certain time. Then—they come down, with a thud! You will see—in ten years, twenty years—it will be as if the waters had passed over them and they exist no longer."

Stanislaus moved uneasily against his pillows. " I know—I am willing to believe these things. But now—in this time—with prisons overflowing, with innocent people being beaten, ruined mentally and physically, what can *we* do ? "

She smiled at him, and laid her strong, well-formed hand on his.

" You are not a Christian boy," she said, " but I can still say to you, ' Oh, ye of little faith . . .' Do you think that nothing is being done ? Do you think that all over the world people are being idle, unmoved, unstirred ? No, Stanislaus, this is not the truth.

Everywhere men and women are working, striving, going into danger, using their brains and their cunning to save the lives of innocent people against the attacks of these dreadful men. This is what your brother sits and talks to my husband for—night after night. This is what he is explaining, proving; this is what they listen to with interest, hope and with determination in their hearts. All cannot be saved, but some can be and shall be. So dream of a band of men and women working together, Stanislaus, and let that drive away your thoughts of what has been, of what still is—with the thoughts of what *will* be."

He almost whispered, " Can I help too ? "

" But, of course, that is what your brothers, what my husband—and what I hoped to hear you ask."

Dan was sailing from Genoa on March 11th, and on the tenth of that month the news came that Germany had annexed Austria. The " little Chancellor " had been wounded, left to bleed to death, refused the last offices of his Church, and Austria lay firmly under the Nazi jackboot.

Dan said, " Well, for sheer cast-iron, triple-riveted, copper-bottomed audacity, this beats everything. Now, Dook, your Mussolini's on the side of Austria, he says. What 'ul happen now ? "

The Duca smiled his wintry smile. " My friend, men involved in a fight for power are on the side where they believe their bread to be buttered."

" Gosh ! Looks like all the gangsters and twisters in the world are trying to run Europe ! "

" Run not only Europe, my friend, but the whole world."

Before he left, Dan talked to Max and Stanislaus in the big luxurious bedroom where Stanislaus lay in the wonderfully carved and decorated bed.

" Looks like our little jaunt on the continent of Europe's coming to an end," Dan said. " We've got information from the Dook—say, that's a great guy, a real feller. Keep in touch, if we can only save one—two—well, we shall have freed at least a couple more people who can come out into the world and speak their little piece about what dictators lead to. And "—his big fresh-coloured face looked suddenly grim—" and maybe one of us 'ul get a chance one day to avenge our dear mother—on her be peace."

" I don't believe, Dan," Max said gently, " that she'd want us to take revenge. She is at peace and her soul is with God. Let's leave it at that, and do what we can for the living. Mama wasn't a revengeful kind of person; she'd rather have said what the Jesus Christ of the Christians said, ' Father, forgive them, for they know not what they do.' That was how mama would have spoken."

Dan shrugged his shoulders. " I dunno—anyway, folks, I'll be moving. My love to papa and Miriam, and—let's get on with the job. I'll be over in time for the next war ! Hope you folks in England have your eyes open, and your minds on the job. Go home—tell 'em the truth—same as I'm going to do over home. This Austria business is only the start. Oh, he'll promise anything—so'd most folks if they'd gotten their hearts really set on anything. Get well, Stan—Maxie, you've been grand. *Mazeltov. . . .*"

Max kissed his brother on both cheeks. " *Sholem Alaichem.*"

Dan grinned, his friendly warmhearted grin. " Peace be unto you —why, yes. All over the world people are saying that—Jews, Christians, all of them—asking for ' peace on earth '—but we shan't get it, Maxie, not yet. There, Stan, get well, and—I'll be seein' you."

Max and Stanislaus were travelling to Marseilles overland and joining the boat there; Max felt that the sea voyage might be good for his brother. Stanislaus was stronger; he seemed to have improved daily since Elfa Ottaviano had talked to him. He asked Max innumerable questions, made tentative suggestions and declared his willingness to go anywhere and do—or attempt to do—anything."

Max said, " It's going to be dangerous, Stanislaus, damned dangerous."

His brother met his eyes steadily, there was no hint of bombast in his words; he spoke quietly and with deep sincerity.

" It is sometimes expedient that a man die for the people," he said.

Before he left, Max had a last interview with the Duchessa. She was, he thought, more beautiful than ever; there was an added serenity about her, a steadfastness.

She said, " It has been so nice to see you again, Max, although the reason for your coming here was not a nice one. I am glad that you will work with Nino—he is a very good, very honest man, a man to be trusted."

Abruptly Max said, " You love him, Elfa ? "

She smiled. " Indeed I do. Not, dear Max, as I once dreamed of love, that was full of brilliant colours, dancing flames, nearly all the time one stood in sunshine." She shook her head. " This is not the same. At first it was not easy. Nino is not simple to understand; he is the product of generations of intellectuals, of the aristocracy to which he belongs. Nino has—his code, and nothing would make him deviate from that code. Now, we both understand very well, we have mutual love—yes, and respect. Still," and she laughed softly, " it has been so pleasant to see you again, dear Max."

He took her hand and raised it to his lips. " I shall always be very grateful to you, my dear. God bless and keep you always."

He spoke the truth; the old sentimental feeling was gone, all that remained was the consciousness that she belonged to life when he had been young, when this dark cloud might have threatened, but had not yet stretched its vast darkness over the European sky. He was going home, taking his brother Stanislaus with him; he was to see Alice—how dear to him she had become in the past few years—his beloved father and his two children. Then, recalling Dan's last words, " I'll be seein' you," he felt a sudden chill. If Dan were right, if war should come, if the intolerable attitude of the wretched Schickelgrueber should become too much, and Europe embarked on a war—his son Julius was eighteen this year—old enough to serve as a soldier, Stanislaus would go; if Max knew anything of Dan, Dan would be coming over to serve for the second time.

Max thought, " I'm fifty past. Damn it, I'd make them accept me ! "

London seemed very gloomy, very homely and wonderfully safe. There was a certain tension, Max felt, everywhere. A sense that everyone was waiting for something—something to which they would not, dared not, give a name. Under that strange tension was a kind of substrata of unspoken confidence. An unvoiced belief that whatever happened—" we "—the British nation, with her Commonwealth and America working with her, had no real need for fear. Perhaps the attitude was expressed by a man Max heard talking to another in Covent Garden Market as he passed through one morning.

" 'Ow's fings, 'Arry ? "

" Orlrite. This 'ere b—— 'Itler tri'ng ter make things difficult. Mind yer, *and* 'e mai. We can 'andle 'im, 'andle the whole b—— German nation come ter thet. What metters is *why* ? B—— it, we don't want ter 'ave ter tike the trouble ! Upsettin' trade, upsettin' prices, upsettin' every b—— thing. Let 'im stop messin' the map o' Europe abart, thet's wot I sez."

Max had found his father better than he had dared to hope. Isaac had, Max felt, actually enjoyed running the business, and running it well. He had liked the sense of responsibility, the feeling that he was achieving something. He spoke rarely of Rose, and when he did it was with a gentleness and obvious deep love which was very touching. Charles Hare came to London, bringing Miriam with him—a Miriam who had regained all her old beauty and poise. True there were moments when, Max fancied, a faint shadow crossed her face, but Charles was always watchful, and at the first sign that she was going back, in her mind, to what had happened in Berlin, he was ready to turn the conversation into other channels.

He and Max sat talking late one evening. Charles said, " You know Miriam is going to have a baby ? Oh, I thought, maybe, she'd told Alice."

" That must please you both very much," Max said.

" I don't know—it's not much of a world to hurl kids into, is it ? God knows what's going to happen ! Make no mistake about it, that Nazi tiger has tasted blood, and he'll want to lick it again. A war—and hell, what a war ! Last time, some statesman said, ' All over the world the lights are going out.' This time, it will be, ' The old order changeth, giving place to new . . .' but there won't be much of ' God fulfils Himself in many ways.' D'you see, Max, that so many of us will go into this war not only because we think that it's right to defend our country, not only because we're anxious to do our duty, but because so many of us will carry into it a wish for personal revenge. You and I, Daniel and plenty of others, may not meet the man or men on whom we wish to be revenged, but the spirit will be there. I want to meet von Kessel; well, the chances are that I never shall, but there'll be the wish in my heart to make someone—to make several chaps—pay the debt von Kessel owes. You and Dan will remember your poor mother, Miriam, and what Stanislaus suffered—and that will go on all over the world, wherever men are fighting—and they will fight all over the world. Oh, men will go into this war with hard hearts ! "

Rumours, whispers, reports, speculations—and then the whole thing developing suddenly, coming to a head like some obnoxious boil and " Czechoslovakia " in everyone's mouth. Many people had no very clear idea where the place was, many more had no idea how the word was pronounced, but everyone knew that Britain had promised to defend the country, had given a guarantee. Those who troubled to get out maps and find where Czechoslovakia was situated frowned and wondered how in Heaven's name the British could get there anyway.

September, and the cauldron began to boil. Max and Stanislaus had worked without ceasing ever since their return; they had worked in conjunction with Dan over in the United States, with Nino Ottaviano in Italy, and they had been successful in saving the lives of many of their co-religionists. More, Dan had written, *Not only Jews, but anyone. Get that straight. We can't pick and choose. Any guy who is suffering, persecuted, is fair game for us. Ottaviano's a Catholic, and if he can take trouble over Jews, well, it's up to us to take the same trouble over just anyone who comes along.*

Max had been over several times to the German frontier.

Stanislaus had gone over and even entered Germany itself, using a false passport and forged papers. Julius Berman had helped them with money, so had Charles' father. Getting prisoners or political suspects out of Germany, particularly when they happened to be Jews, was an expensive business.

Max remembered once in July, when Stanislaus returned from one of his visits to Germany, how he sat down, his face very white, his hands clenched. Max asked if he had been through a difficult time.

"Not more than usual. It's always a bit nerve-racking. No, your father-in-law gave me a letter when I came back last night. You remember when we sent Kestner back the hundred marks I stole from him? Well, we gave Berman's address. I'll read the letter to you. Listen! *We regret to inform you that Captain Kestner died three months ago. We take it that the hundred marks enclosed were intended as a small donation to the Party funds. They have therefore been handed to the proper administrator in Captain Kestner's name.*" Stanislaus stared at Max. "Damn it, if it wasn't so completely insupportable, it would be laughable. The blasted impertinence of the swine! Poor fellow—either he was liquidated or he shot himself."

Then came Munich, and all Europe sighed with relief when it was known that Chamberlain was flying to meet Hitler, meeting Daladier and Mussolini in conference. Chamberlain was a public hero; the typical middle-class politician who had never flown before was going—with his umbrella—to beard the lion in his den.

He returned and with him came reports, rumours, stories. Chamberlain and Mussolini were the two who had received the loudest plaudits from the crowds who watched them pass. Hitler and Mussolini had scarcely spoken, it was obvious they loathed each other. The spirit of the Axis was dead! The "scrap of paper" —"Peace in our time".

Isaac listened and said, "I remember once before, in 1914, that a German showed to the world what he and his thought of—a scrap of paper. Don't you remember, please, Max? That was Kaiser Wilhelm; now here is this devil making an imitation of him. We shall see. Mr. Chamberlain may as well use it to light his pipe, this 'scrap of paper'."

Alice expostulated, "Oh, Grandpapa dear, don't be so pessimistic."

"No, never have I been pessimistic! I am only trying to see an inch farther than my nose, Alice, my dear."

Bohemia and Moravia were annexed, Memel followed; each time Hitler announced, "This is my final demand!" Italy annexed

Albania, choosing Good Friday for the work. Men shook their heads, and muttered that " The Duce's slipped up this time—after all, Italians are Catholics, and they think a lot about Good Friday "—they added hastily—" as we do."

" Possibly." Max suggested, " Mussolini worked on the assumption of the statement being true which says, ' Better the day, better the deed.' "

One man stared at him, then said very firmly, " Well, I for one am thankful that we have given a guarantee to Poland ! "

" I expect," Max said, " that the Poles are excited and pleased about that too."

" I don't care much for your tone, Noller ! "

" I can't say that I altogether like it myself. Let's leave it at that, shall we ? "

September 3rd, and Isaac said, " Now again the world has gone mad, but it was inevitable. I have always distrusted old men who, when a war begins, say, ' I wish to God that I were young enough to go and fight ! ' They don't mean it ; most times they mean, ' Thank God that I am too old to be called upon to fight.' I say that I would give a very great deal to be able to become a soldier in *this* war. I shall take care of your business for you, Max."

Alice exclaimed, " Max, you're not going to offer to go ! "

He smiled, " Indeed I am, my dear. There is nothing else to do."

" And Stanislaus . . . and Dan and "—her voice shook a little —" Julius ? "

Max nodded, " Yes, all of us, I hope and trust. You know that in your heart you'd not have us do anything else. Be honest, darling."

" And Charles ? Oh, dear, it is like the end of the world ! "

" Or maybe," Isaac said softly, " once it is over—the beginning of a New World."

So the war came to them all. Isaac held himself more upright, and immersed himself in the business. It was very difficult, for so many of their sources of supply were closed, and people could not buy easily, food was short and likely to become shorter, they were told. Max, grumbling a little, went to the R.A.S.C., Stanislaus and young Julius into the R.A.F., and Dan cabled wildly and excitedly, *I'm on my way stop reckon war as good as over now I'm in it stop I'll be seeing you Dan.*

Gweneth was promised that she could enter the W.R.N.S. the day that she was eighteen, and swaggered about it abominably. Miriam declared that as soon as ever Charles the Second arrived, and could be left to the care of a doting grandmother and an efficient nurse, she was joining the A.T.S.

The house seemed very quiet, and Alice knew that it was an effort to keep her spirits from falling. The New Year brought disaster after disaster—Narvik, the Dutch surrender, the Belgium surrender—Dunkirk. Isaac spoke gently, with sympathy, and Alice felt herself coming to rely upon his patience and steadfast faith more and more. Max came back from Dunkirk; he looked thin, haggard, but his eyes were bright and his spirits high.

Alice said, " It must have been terrible——"

" Terrible and stupendously wonderful. They *can't* lose with that spirit. Gosh, Churchill puts guts into people; not that they didn't have them already, but he makes them realize just how good, how sound, those guts, those hearts, those ' lights and livers ' are."

He only wanted to get back; she cried a little and clung to him.

" Max, must you ? Oh, Max, you're so precious. You mean so much to me. More than even when we were first married. Then, for a time, I don't think either of us mattered a great deal to the other, but that's all changed. Now, you're my world. Oh, Max, can't you apply for a home job ? "

He kissed her very tenderly, " Why yes, I could; and run the risk of my son asking if I'd got cold feet, of my great hulking brother Dan, saying, ' Something of the cissy about you, eh, brother ? ' And you . . . trying very gallantly to believe that you were glad, that I'd done the right thing, and because of that essential honesty of yours—failing. No, no, Alice darling, it wouldn't work. God, you don't think that I *like* it ? I've grown accustomed to comfort, my sweet, to hot baths and soft beds and decent food. But then I've hated plenty of things in my life—how I hated checking invoices when I first worked with my father. I never got used to the smell of tea in the chests—sickly, and unpleasant, to me at all events. Stocktaking, that was the end of everything. Still, they had to be done, though I went on hating them all the time, all my life. I shall go on hating this blasted war all the time. We're none of us heroes, except possibly Stanislaus has a trace of the heroic in him. I loathe it all. Dan, well, Dan likes a scrap anyway, and Julius is young and it's exciting to be in Canada and learning to fly, and to think of the grand things he's going to do." He laughed and drew her nearer. " Believe me, when we hear this business is finished no one will cheer more loudly, more sincerely, more heartily than your husband—and his chief reason for so doing will be that he—wants to get home."

August 8th until October 31st were filled with the daylight raids, and then began, too, the night raids, making the hours of darkness terrible and filled with apprehension and the presence of death. The warehouse was hit, reduced to a mere ruin. Isaac went down to inspect it, calmly and apparently unmoved.

" Bad business, Mr. Noller," Simons said.

Isaac nodded. " Yes, indeed. It might have been worse. Thank God our stocks were very low ! " and diving in among the rubble and ruins he returned smiling with a large jar of *pâté*—unbroken. " This we shall keep for when we make a festival—when all this is over, no ? "

Simons said later to his family, " Talk about taking it on the chin ! Wonderful old gentleman, if you ask me—wonderful."

The years dragged on; the Battle of Britain came to an end, and the hated Blitz took its place; England lived to the thunder of roaring 'planes, read each morning of new disasters—and then that, too, came to an end, and the enemy retired to devise some new form of destruction.

Alice felt that she was only able to hold on, tenaciously, but with fear in her heart. At night she lay staring into the darkness, asking herself how they could hope that their own men could survive. How could they believe that Max, Dan, Stanislaus, Julius and Charles Hare could all come through this terror unscathed ? When she heard that Charles was being sent home after being wounded she almost sighed with relief—so it wasn't all too good to be true, and Charles seemed like a hostage given to Fate.

Periodically the men returned on leave, a leave which always seemed to vanish like smoke, to be gone in a flash. She watched them and felt that they were very tired—fatigued—mentally and physically. Max went with her to see this play and that, assured her that he had enjoyed them all, but she never quite believed him. He looked old; his hair was quite white at the temples, and his eyes had lines at the corners and pouches beneath them.

Max said, " Due to too many late sessions and Italian gin, darling."

Her own son, returning fully trained, had grown in stature, and, she felt, self-reliance. She told him so and he laughed.

" If I have self-reliance, Mummy, well, that's what the Government has been spending money on me for."

Gweneth, unbelievably smart, had been engaged twice in two years. Now she declared that " this is serious, Mummy. He's grand ! Naval type. No, not handsome, but oh, he's grand ! You and Daddy will let us be married just as soon as we can both get leave, won't you ? "

Dan had changed least; he came into the quiet house like a whirlwind and announced his determination to " have a swell time ! "

His energy was inexhaustible, his vitality tremendous. He thought that Italy was overrated, their wine poor stuff, their spirits worse.

"This sun we've heard about—blue Italian skies. Alice, don't you believe it. It just exists on picture postcards. Can it be cold ! Oh boy ! I've never been so cold, not in the middle of a New York winter. I'd like to show 'em how to raise decent chickens; you never saw such scrawny things in your life. I reckon they come along and just give themselves up, because they're sick of life ! Naples—you've heard about see Naples and die—I tell you, after you've seen some of the things in Naples that I've seen you darned well *want* to die ! Still, they say the first ten years are the worst, after that I b'lieve you get quite fond of the war ! C'm on, Alice, let's go dancing ! "

Stanislaus had changed, she thought, more than the others. He was very quiet, spending a great deal of time talking to his father. They would sit together in the room which Max had furnished for his father—like the sitting-room in their home in Berlin. Not the best sitting-room which had been furnished in heavy silk with satin stripes, where the furniture had been so tightly stuffed and so heavily " buttoned " that no chair was really comfortable. This room was like the " ordinary sitting-room ", and Max had taken infinite pains over it. There Stanislaus would sit and talk to his father. Alice could hear the sound of their voices gently rising and falling as if they spoke of tender, intimate things.

Stanislaus was even thinner than Max, and the brightness had faded from his hair; he had refused a commission, and his hands were roughened with work, his great clumsy boots looked too heavy for his feet.

"You'd have been more comfortable if you'd taken a commission," Alice said.

He smiled, shaking his head.

"I suppose that I funk the responsibility," he said. "It's as much as I can manage to give orders to Stanislaus Noller and to see that he obeys them. Tell me, has papa heard anything about Jacob ? "

"I don't think so. He has never mentioned him to me. Why ? "

"I saw a German newspaper—months old. It said that Klaus Brusch had died and been given a magnificent public funeral. All the ' high ups ' had been present, and Streicher—this is amusing—had spoken a funeral oration. Funny that the newspaper should come into my hand, wasn't it ? "

She said gravely, " Oh, Stan, how dreadful ! Didn't you feel anything ? "

"Yes, a deep satisfaction, my dear. I suppose that he was

liquidated, or advised to liquidate himself. They always give them magnificent funerals when they die—unnatural deaths. It's part of the set-up. I shan't mention it to papa."

Then, when she was beginning to believe that Dan was right, and that the "first ten years were the worst", the tide began to turn; the current at first was almost imperceptible, then it grew until she imagined she could hear the roar of it in her ears if she listened intently.

She fancied that she could hear the thunder of the tank transporters, the tramp of feet, the dull roar of the tanks themselves, the scream of falling bombs and the noise of aeroplanes. Names which had stood for disasters now became towns marking the victorious progress of the Allies. May 4th, 5th and 7th of 1945, surrenders everywhere.

Alice held out her hands to her father-in-law, her eyes filled with tears. "The last Germans have surrendered, Papa," she said. "It's over——"

He smiled back at her. He looked what indeed he was, an old man, tired and bearing the marks of suffering. She had not thought of him as being really old when the war began; now—she thought —why, he was nearly eighty.

"I am glad to have lived to see this," he said. "I wish that I might hope for many more years to see—to see things put right again. War is an untidy thing, my dear; there will be a great deal of setting houses in order. You, who keep your own house so well, know what a great deal of work only one house demands. Here are thousands, millions, to be cleaned and swept and garnished. They are not houses built with hands—that will make it so much more difficult."

Slowly the men came home, and talked of taking up their own lives again. Dan had gone to America at the earliest possible moment, he had paid a brief visit to take farewell of his father. He had promised to come back.

"Just let me see how they've come through over there, and I'll be right back and bring my family to see you all." Only when he was leaving did he clasp Max's hands very tightly and say, "Gosh, I didn't like saying good-bye to him, Maxie. He looks kinder frail to me—old—worn out. We've forgotten how old he is while we've been over there. Take care of him, Maxie."

"Can you doubt that I shall?"

SEVENTEEN

THE family had gathered, as they did so often, in Isaac Noller's comfortable, slightly overheated, ugly room. He sat with his light rug over his knees, his head covered by his black velvet skull cap, and smiled at them. Nothing pleased him more than to realize how, in spite of the other beautiful and charming rooms in the house, they invariably gravitated to his sitting-room.

He looked at them all in turn, looked with a satisfaction which was reflected in his kind, intelligent old face. There was his grandson, Julius, seated on the arm of his mother's chair, swinging one beautifully shod foot. Isaac reflected that he had feet like his grandmother's, rather long and very slim. Isaac always thought of them as " English feet ". Julius had done well, his record was excellent. Now he was content to be wearing his good and highly expensive civilian clothes.

He turned his eyes to Alice; he loved Alice more now than he had done when she and Max first married. She had matured, had lost that superficial hardness; something, which had been sparkling and rather brittle, had been replaced by a warmth and serenity which was very pleasant to watch and experience. She was still a handsome woman, though the war had left its mark on her, had robbed her hair of much of its colour and had traced new, fine lines round her eyes and mouth.

And Max—his so-dearly-loved Max. He was too thin, and Isaac could remember when he had warned him against allowing himself to grow too stout !

" For an old man excessive stoutness is an additional burden and even a danger; for a young man it is a disaster, Max," he had said.

There was no excessive weight about Max now; his figure was lacking in an ounce of superfluous fat; his hair was grey, not only at the temples but all over his well-shaped head. Isaac knew that Max had tremendous reserves of energy; those reserves would grow now that he was home again and able to live a regular normal life. No, he had no need to worry about Max. Max with his loved wife, his daughter happily married, and his son back from those terrible days when the sound of 'planes always sent their thoughts flying to him, and their eyes met in the unspoken thought, " Is Julius safe ? "

Stanislaus sat in the chair next to his father, his long legs stretched before him, his hands thrust deep into his trouser pockets. Stanislaus had changed, changed perhaps more than any of his children. He did not laugh easily as he had done only a few—or comparatively few—years ago. Isaac remembered that when you grew old you thought of " a few years " because they seemed few to you, whereas to younger people they covered an appreciable period. The gold had faded from his hair; he was still handsome—he would always be that because the bones of his face were so good—but after all, Stanislaus was no longer very young, he had long since ceased to be even a young man, he was on the verge of being distinctly middle-aged.

Max said, " Well, Papa, now that we are all together again, ready to begin to live again in the piping times of peace, shall we celebrate ? "

Young Julius laughed, " To celebrate with father means only one thing—champagne ! I'm right, Father, eh ? "

" You're right," Max agreed. " How people imagine that they can ' celebrate ' by drinking cocktails—poor, trivial things which may make you drunk but which never make you light-hearted. I belong to the spacious days when celebrations were carried out with dignity and a certain pomposity ! Papa, I have some 1920—time that it was drunk, don't you think ? "

Stanislaus said lazily, " A good year, Max, eh ? "

" Time that it was drunk," Isaac agreed, " in fact even now, to my mind, it will have lost something. Twenty years is sufficiently long. Still, you are right, Max, let us celebrate."

Isaac went back to his own thoughts; he could hear the voices of Julius and Alice, the sound was like a running accompaniment to his thoughts. They were going to celebrate. The war was over, and people longed for a return to a normal and secure existence.

He had heard that morning from his daughter Miriam, how happy she seemed with her good, steady British husband, and her lovely baby. It seemed impossible to believe that the woman whose letter had so delighted him that morning could be the same half-demented creature who had returned home, and while recounting what had happened, had begun to scream crazily, hideously.

" Young people are resilient," he thought, " and thanks be to God for it. They gather so many new impressions, develop new interests, and the old, bad things are, if not blotted out, at least overlaid by the brightness of the present. Dan too, he has faced difficult times, but then Dan was always able to ' come to the top ', dangers and anxieties never submerged him. No, they will all enjoy life, in their individual ways. Stanislaus will find the greatest difficulty in adjusting himself to new conditions. He feels too much. They all have good hearts, but his is so tender. Only that other son failed, not me, not his brothers and sister, but himself. Poor misguided Jacob. Maybe, now, he had learnt greater wisdom. Max, Stanislaus never mention him, and perhaps that is well, it is bad for brothers to speak ill of brothers, better that his memory should be obliterated, forgotten ! "

Max entered, crying, " Julius, you lazy ruffian, can't you get glasses ? Skip to it, or I'll get them myself, and there'll be one short—yours ! "

Julius swung himself to his feet. " What a life ! I imagined that returned heroes were waited upon hand and foot, petted, made much of, regaled on fatted calves."

" Damn it, Stan and I are returned heroes, aren't we ? " Max demanded. " And as for fatted calves, remember we're rationed."

" I've not eaten veal for months and months," Alice said.

" The glasses, as good as any your father has, are in my sideboard," Isaac said. " Max envies me those glasses ! " he chuckled.

Their glasses filled, they turned towards Isaac for a toast. Max raised his eyebrows enquiringly. " Yes, Papa ? "

His father smiled. " The only possible one, surely. Peace and the Future ! "

He sipped his wine with appreciation. " Very good, Max, it has survived the war as well as any of us. And Julius, tell us, what is your future to be ? "

The young man looked from one to another. " I shall stay where I am," he said. " It's a good life, I like it. They're quite pleased with my record."

His mother interpolated, " So they should be ! "

He laid his hand on her shoulder. " I don't believe, Father, that I'd stick to a strictly routine job. I'd not settle. You wouldn't mind ? "

Max said, " I'm afraid that your mother may——"

Julius turned to her. " No, Mummy'd not mind, would you, darling ? You must have got used to the idea of my flying by now, eh ? "

She smiled up at him, a smile which was not quite steady. " It is quite evident that you have grown up, Julius. That was a typical grown-up man's remark. Getting used to it ! Here's Gweneth living somewhere in the north of Scotland, so that she can be with her husband—and quite right too—but, oh, well . . . Max, we shall have to make the best of it, be thankful for small mercies when either of our children can pay us short visits, and " —she laughed, and pressed her son's arm as if to reassure him

that she was not completely serious—" expect to be waited upon
by their ageing parents, eh ? "

Isaac turned to Max, " And you, Max ? "

" You and I, Papa, will set to work to build up the business
again, shall we ? "

" With the help of Stanislaus, eh ? "

" Stanislaus may have plans of his own, Papa."

" So ! Tell us, please, Stanislaus."

Stanislaus rose and went to stand by the fireplace, his arm
resting along the mantelpiece. He looked very tall as he stood
there watching them, a little smile curving his lips.

" I am going back to Germany, Papa. That is what I want
to do."

Julius cried, as if in protest, " Uncle Stan ! You don't mean it ! "

" Indeed I do, Julius. You see, dear Papa, you were not born
in Germany, you were brought up there by a particularly good
and kind man, and his equally good and kind wife. You had, in
spite of the tragic beginning of your life, nothing but goodness
and love taught to you. These things were inculcated into you
from the beginning of your life in Germany. Max came over and
became an Englishman, and a damned good one too. Dan "—
Stanislaus laughed—" is more American than the Americans.
Miriam has married an Englishman, she is an Englishwoman.
I—well, I was born in Germany, I lived there all my life, I am a
German."

Almost truculently Julius said, " You fought against Germany
in the war, Uncle Stan ! You fought for England, surely ! "

" I fought for what I believed to be right. I fought against
Nazism, Julius. I hated the tyranny, loathed the Nazis as I think
few people have loathed them. I know that all decent-thinking
people hated the régime, the abominable Party ; that was inevitable among people who had a sense of right and justice. In me,
there was an added reason for fury, for hatred."

" And that was——? " Max asked.

" The fact that I was a German, they were makingt he whole
nation stink in the nostrils of decent men and women. This affected
me closely and personally."

" I don't quite see how going back to Germany is going to
help," Julius said; he was frowning, as if the puzzle were too much
for him. Max felt that had he been speaking to anyone except his
Uncle Stanislaus, Julius would have lost his temper, only his
innate affection for him restrained the young man. " It looks to
me like deserting England," Julius went on. " After all, life
isn't going to be all roses for the British. They've stood by the

Jews pretty well, and if I know anything about it they'll have to hold the dirty end of the stick when it comes to getting the world on its feet again. England will need young men——"

Stanislaus smiled. "But I'm not young any more, Julius. We're none of us really young, not even you. You've left some of your youth behind. That's one of the things that war does—it robs people of their youth. Let me get back to my explanation——"

"Yes, yes, I want to hear," his father said; "I am waiting eagerly."

"When I was escaping from that damned prison, wandering about Germany, I met Germans who were kind to me—essentially kind, and for no reason except that they *wished* to be kind. They were people who—without any great demonstration—were firmly and solidly opposed to Nazism and all that it meant. How far that awful infection has spread we can't tell; how long it will take to purge the infected people we don't know—only time will show. Now, all Germans are suspect; now it is taken practically as an axiom that all Germans are liars, brutes, devils in human shape, models of Hitler, Goering, Hess and the rest. They're not, they can't be—no nation can be composed completely of fiends. To believe this is to deny God.

"Let me give you my own limited experience; when I was escaping—one man, remember, with thousands against him—I met a farmer's wife, maybe a farmer's widow, I don't know. She was kind to me, she had no fear of admitting to me, a stranger, that she hated the Nazis, hated their works, detested Hitler and his gang. I met a farmer—very poor; to save me he lied to two storm troopers, put them off my track, and who, at the risk of his life, showed me a path through the woods. I met a young man driving a truck; a cheerful fellow, with freckles and widely spaced teeth, I remember. He took me into his truck and asked no questions. I'm afraid that I told him a good many lies, and I believe that he knew they were lies. He felt the same—there was no ' Heil Hitler ' there. I asked him, ' Are there many who feel as you do ? ' He said, ' Thousands ! ' "

"They didn't do very much, did they, these thousands, did they ? " Julius said.

Max answered, " My dear lad, what could they do ? And how do we know that they didn't do a great deal ? There were resistance movements in all countries, except possibly this one, and we were never invaded here. Now what are you going to do, Stan ? Go back to Germany, yes, and then ? "

" Acknowledge myself to be a German, a German who took the oath of allegiance to the King of England because he wanted

to fight Nazism.   Then, I want to visit those people who were
good to me. I want to know what happened to old Elias, who
forged my beautiful papers ! I want to make my way back, along
the road I took to escape right back to Italy, and there to get in
touch with the Duke. He will be able to advise and direct me.
There is so much work waiting, in so many forms. Personally, I
should wish to work in Germany, to associate myself with the
life there—perhaps I could reopen your business there, Papa ?
There are homeless people, dispirited people, heartbroken
people, and such people are a danger, for they will grasp at
anything which seems to offer better conditions of life and
living. As they did with the Nazis. They heard promises, they
were patted on the back, they were stuffed with lies—they
swallowed everything, because in many cases it was all the poor
devils *had* to swallow."

Isaac was leaning forward, his fine face eager and alight.

" Yes, Stanislaus, reopen the business ! Your great-uncle was
held in high respect, I believe that I was also—and people have
longer memories than we often care to believe. At first it will of
necessity be only a small business, that will give you time to work
at the schemes which you and the Duke may evolve. Kindness,
integrity, sincerity—these things may not breed quite as fast as
the wickedness which enveloped Germany, but they spread.
These things and faith which never wavers no matter how dark
the horizon may look. To find homes, however poor, however
small, for the homeless, to ease the burden which lies heavily on
people's hearts, to smooth a little rough roads, and to show a
light in darkness—these are good things, and nothing but good
can come of them."

" And money ? " Alice asked.   " How will you live, Stan ? "

" I have some left to me by Great-uncle Stanislaus——"

" I'm not completely broke," Max said, and smiled.

" And I," Isaac added, " can spare something from my plenitude,
so we shall all feel that we are joining in this work, no ? "

Alice said, " Well, in my opinion Max and Stan have already
done work which is magnificent, but if Stan wants to go on, well,
I don't doubt that my father "—she laughed—" would like to
invest something in the reopening of the firm of Noller in Berlin.
He can never resist a good investment, can he ? "

Stanislaus smiled back at her.   " Trust you, Alice, silently to
disapprove and then to weigh in, heavily, on the right side,
bless you."

Isaac leaned back in his chair, his face very happy in its expression.

" Max, fill my glass, and if that bottle is empty please get another ! ' Wine to make glad the heart of man,' eh ? I feel that we must get rid of labels, and not prejudice people because they were born in a certain geographical area. Good people are good people all over the world. I admit that there are certain nations who are more easily swayed, influenced by bad and foolish doctrines —even so, many remain who stand steadfast and who stand for decency.

" Jews have not *always* been wise, but sometimes they have been much wiser than other men. Unfortunately, ' the evil that men do lives after them,' and so today there are many Christians who are really uncomfortable and distressed if you remind them that their God was a Jew. I have read a great deal about this Jesus Christ of the Christians. He was good, completely good, a man would long for Him to be a friend, a counsellor. He was born a Jew. He might as easily have been born a German, a man with a yellow face, a black skin. He had no nationality, save only that He belonged to the International Nation which is composed of Good People.

" Silly labels bring silly qualifications—mean Scots, lazy Italians, immoral Frenchmen, cunning Chinese, brutal Germans, bombastic Americans, and so forth. What rubbish ! How men incline to limit the intelligence of God. You are right, Stanislaus, no matter whether you are German, English or simply Jew—so long as you are good. Not long-faced, miserable, narrow-minded ' good ', but cultivating that essential goodness which brings happiness, laughter, light hearts and the real joy of living."

He beamed on them all, then said, " Alice, my dear, you look tired; Julius, you were very late last night—or was it very early this morning ? Stanislaus, you have a great deal of work before you—you must rest."

" I believe," Alice said, " that you are sending us all to bed, like children, Grandpapa."

" Clever woman ! Yes, I am sending you all to bed, except Max. I want to talk to Max. Good night, and God bless you."

As the door closed, Isaac said, " *Nu*, Max. Come and sit down. Five minutes and we, too, will go to bed. Well, the story draws to its close—my story at least. It is a long time since my Uncle Stanislaus saved a little frightened boy and took him to Germany to treat him like his own son.

" It has been a story with patches which were very bright, as when I met your beloved mother. In a café she had been crying. I had to lend her my handkerchief, she had lost her own. Dear Rose. When you were children, those were bright times; the house filled with laughter, the sweet smell of good cooking and cleanliness, the sense that it was lived in by happy, hopeful people.

"Then the tramp of the jackboots came nearer, the clouds gathered, and the storm broke and it seemed that everything was shattered. Now we have been brought out of Egypt and out of the House of Bondage. All except one of us. Yes, I have heard, Max. We will not talk of it. I have mourned him—as my son. It has been a grief to me, but that was the only possible ending. Had we ever met again, we should all of us have remembered too much. I wished you to know that I knew.

"Yes, a long life and many blessings, and chief among them you, my son. Now, we shall go to bed, and on the Sabbath you and I will go together to *shule*, to say, ' Thank You, for all You have done for us.'"

He paused, and with that half-sly expression which always amused Max said, "And if there is any of that good wine—in the second bottle—left, we might finish it before we go. One last toast, eh ? "

"An admirable idea, Papa. There ! Now, what is the toast to be ? "

Isaac considered, then, still smiling, said, " Oh, quite simple, I think. Yes, we will drink to what is essentially good, all over the world."

Gardone Riviera,
  July, 1952.